# THE SPOILERS

Desmond Bagley was born in 1923 in Kendal, Westmorland, and brought up in Blackpool. He began his working life, aged 14, in the printing industry and then did a variety of jobs until going into an aircraft factory at the start of the Second World War.

When the war ended he decided to travel to southern Africa, going overland through Europe and the Sahara. He worked en route, reaching South Africa in 1951.

He became a freelance journalist in Johannesburg and wrote his first published novel, *The Golden Keel*, in 1962. In 1964 he returned to England and lived in Totnes for twelve years. He and his wife then moved to Guernsey in the Channel Islands. Here he found the ideal place for combining his writing with his other interests, which included computers, mathematics, military history, and entertaining friends from all over the world.

Desmond Bagley died in April 1983. Two previously unpublished Bagley novels have since been published: the first, *Night of Error*, was published in 1984, the second, *Juggernaut*, in 1985. Both were on the bestseller lists for many weeks.

DESMOND BAGLEY

# The Spoilers

Fontana
*An Imprint of HarperCollinsPublishers*

Fontana
An Imprint of HarperCollins*Publishers*
77–85 Fulham Palace Road,
Hammersmith, London W6 8JB

Published by Fontana 1971
39 38 37 36 35 34 33

First published in Great Britain by
Collins 1969

Copyright © L. J. Jersey 1969

ISBN 0 00 617302 0

Set in Janson

Printed in Great Britain by
HarperCollinsManufacturing Glasgow

This one is for Pat and Philip Bawcombe
and, of course, Thickabe

# 1

She lay on the bed in an abandoned attitude, oblivious of the big men crowding the room and making it appear even smaller than it was. She had been abandoned by life, and the big men were there to find out why, not out of natural curiosity but because it was their work. They were policemen.

Detective-Inspector Stephens ignored the body. He had given it a cursory glance and then turned his attention to the room, noting the cheap, rickety furniture and the threadbare carpet which was too small to hide dusty boards. There was no wardrobe and the girl's few garments were scattered, some thrown casually over a chair-back and others on the floor by the side of the bed. The girl herself was naked, an empty shell. Death is not erotic.

Stephens picked up a sweater from the chair and was surprised at its opulent softness. He looked at the maker's tab and frowned before handing it to Sergeant Ipsley. 'She could afford good stuff. Any identification yet?'

'Betts is talking to the landlady.'

Stephens knew the worth of that. The inhabitants of his manor did not talk freely to policemen. 'He won't get much. Just a name and that'll be false, most likely. Seen the syringe?'

'Couldn't miss it, sir. Do you think it's drugs?'

'Could be.' Stephens turned to an unpainted whitewood chest of drawers and pulled on a knob. The drawer opened an inch and then stuck. He smote it with the heel of his hand. 'Any sign of the police surgeon yet?'

'I'll go and find out, sir.'

'Don't worry; he'll come in his own good time.' Stephens turned his head to the bed. 'Besides, she's not in too much of a hurry.' He tugged at the drawer which stuck again. 'Damn this confounded thing!'

A uniformed constable pushed open the door and closed it behind him. 'Her name's Hellier, sir – June Hellier. She's been here a week – came last Wednesday.'

Stephens straightened. 'That's not much help, Betts. Have you seen her before on your beat?'

Betts looked towards the bed and shook his head. 'No, sir.'

'Was she previously known to the landlady?'

'No, sir; she just came in off the street and said she wanted a room. She paid in advance.'

'She wouldn't have got in otherwise,' said Ipsley. 'I know this old besom here – nothing for nothing and not much for sixpence.'

'Did she make any friends – acquaintances?' asked Stephens. 'Speak to anyone?'

'Not that I can find out, sir. From all accounts she stuck in her room most of the time.'

A short man with an incipient pot belly pushed into the room. He walked over to the bed and put down his bag. 'Sorry I'm late, Joe; this damned traffic gets worse every day.'

'That's all right, Doctor.' Stephens turned to Betts again. 'Have another prowl around and see what you can get.' He joined the doctor at the foot of the bed and looked down at the body of the girl. 'The usual thing – time of death and the reason therefor.'

Doctor Pomray glanced at him. 'Foul play suspected?'

Stephens shrugged. 'Not that I know of – yet.' He indicated the syringe and the glass which lay on the bamboo bedside table. 'Could be drugs; an overdose, maybe.'

Pomray bent down and sniffed delicately at the glass. There was a faint film of moisture at the bottom and he was just about to touch it when Stephens said, 'I'd rather you didn't, Doctor. I'd like to have it checked for dabs first.'

'It doesn't really matter,' said Pomray. 'She was an addict, of course. Look at her thighs. I just wanted to check what her particular poison was.'

Stephens had already seen the puncture marks and had drawn his own conclusions, but he said, 'Could have been a diabetic.'

Pomray shook his head decisively. 'A trace of phlebo-thrombosis together with skin sepsis – no doctor would allow that to happen to a diabetic patient.' He bent down and squeezed the skin. 'Incipient jaundice, too; that shows liver damage. I'd say it's drug addiction with the usual lack of care in the injection. But we won't really know until after the autopsy.'

'All right, I'll leave you to it.' Stephens turned to Ipsley and said casually, 'Will you open that drawer, Sergeant?'

'Another thing,' said Pomray. 'She's very much under-weight for her height. That's another sign.' He gestured towards an ashtray overflowing untidily with cigarette-stubs. 'And she was a heavy smoker.'

Stephens watched Ipsley take the knob delicately between thumb and forefinger and pull open the drawer smoothly. He switched his gaze from the smug expression on Ipsley's face, and said, 'I'm a heavy smoker too, Doctor. That doesn't mean much.'

'It fills out the clinical picture,' argued Pomray.

Stephens nodded. 'I'd like to know if she died on that bed.'

Pomray looked surprised. 'Any reason why she shouldn't have?'

Stephens smiled slightly. 'None at all; I'm just being careful.'

'I'll see what I can find,' said Pomray.

* * *

9

There was not much in the drawer. A handbag, three stockings, a pair of panties due for the wash, a bunch of keys, a lipstick, a suspender-belt and a syringe with a broken needle. Stephens uncapped the lipstick case and looked inside it; the lipstick was worn right down and there was evidence that the girl had tried to dig out the last of the wax, which was confirmed by the discovery of a spent match with a reddened end caught in a crack of the drawer. Stephens, an expert on the interpretation of such minutiae, concluded that June Hellier had been destitute.

The panties had a couple of reddish-brown stains on the front, stains which were repeated on one of the stocking tops. It looked very much like dried blood and was probably the result of inexpert injection into the thigh. The keyring contained three keys, one of which was a car ignition key. Stephens turned to Ipsley. 'Nip down and see if the girl had a car.'

Another key fitted a suitcase which he found in a corner. It was a de-luxe elaborately fitted case of the type which Stephens had considered buying as a present for his wife – the idea had been rejected on the grounds of excessive expense. It contained nothing.

He could not find anything for the third key to fit so he turned his attention to the handbag, which was of fine-grained leather. He was about to open it when Ipsley came back. 'No car, sir.'

'Indeed!' Stephens pursed his lips. He snapped open the catch of the handbag and looked inside. Papers, tissues, another lipstick worn to a nubbin, three shillings and fourpence in coins and no paper money. 'Listen carefully, Sergeant,' he said. 'Good handbag, good suitcase, car key but no car, good clothes except the stockings which are cheap, gold lipstick case in drawer, Woolworth's lipstick in bag – both worn out. What do you make of all that?'

'Come down in the world, sir.'

Stephens nodded as he pushed at the few coins with his

forefinger. He said abruptly, 'Can you tell me if she was a virgin, Doctor?'

'She wasn't,' said Pomray. 'I've checked that.'

'Maybe she was on the knock,' offered Ipsley.

'Possibly,' said Stephens. 'We can find out – if we have to.'

Pomray straightened. 'She died on this bed all right; there's the usual evidence. I've done all I can here. Is there anywhere I can wash?'

'There's a bathroom just along the hall,' said Ipsley. 'It's not what I'd call hygienic, though.'

Stephens was sorting the few papers. 'What did she die of, Doctor?'

'I'd say an overdose of a drug – but what it was will have to wait for the autopsy.'

'Accidental or deliberate?' asked Stephens.

'That will have to wait for the autopsy too,' said Pomray. 'If it was a really massive overdose then you can be pretty sure it was deliberate. An addict usually knows to a hair how much to take. If it's not too much of an overdose then it could be accidental.'

'If it's deliberate then I have a choice between suicide and murder,' said Stephens musingly.

'I think you can safely cut out murder,' said Pomray. 'Addicts don't like other people sticking needles into them.' He shrugged. 'And the suicide rate among addicts is high once they hit bottom.'

A small snorting noise came from Stephens as he made the discovery of a doctor's appointment card. The name on it rang a bell somewhere in the recesses of his mind. 'What do you know about Dr Nicholas Warren? Isn't he a drug man?'

Pomray nodded. 'So she was one of his girls, was she?' he said with interest.

'What kind of a doctor is he? Is he on the level?'

Pomray reacted with shock. 'My God! Nick Warren's

11

reputation is as pure as the driven snow. He's one of the top boys in the field. He's no quack, if that's what you mean.'

'We get all kinds,' said Stephens levelly. 'As you know very well.' He gave the card to Ipsley. 'He's not too far from here. See if you can get hold of him, Sergeant; we still haven't any positive identification of the girl.'

'Yes, sir,' said Ipsley, and made for the door.

'And, Sergeant,' called Stephens. 'Don't tell him the girl's dead.'

Ipsley grinned. 'I won't.'

'Now look here,' said Pomray. 'If you try to pressure Warren you'll get a hell of a surprise. He's a tough boy.'

'I don't like doctors who hand out drugs,' said Stephens grimly.

'You know damn-all about it,' snapped Pomray. 'And you won't fault Nick Warren on medical ethics. If you go on that tack he'll tie you up in knots.'

'We'll see. I've handled tough ones before.'

Pomray grinned suddenly. 'I think I'll stay and watch this. Warren knows as much – if not more – about drugs and drug addicts as anyone in the country. He's a bit of a fanatic about it. I don't think you'll get much change out of him. I'll be back as soon as I've cleaned up in this sewer of a bathroom.'

Stephens met Warren in the dimly lit hall outside the girl's room, wanting to preserve the psychological advantage he had gained by not informing the doctor of the girl's death. If he was surprised at the speed of Warren's arrival he did not show it, but studied the man with professional detachment as he advanced up the hall.

Warren was a tall man with a sensitive yet curiously immobile face. In all his utterances he spoke thoughtfully, sometimes pausing for quite a long time before he answered. This gave Stephens the impression that Warren

12

had not heard or was ignoring the question, but Warren always answered just as a repetition was on Stephens's tongue. This deliberateness irritated Stephens, although he tried not to show it.

'I'm glad you were able to come,' he said. 'We have a problem, Doctor. Do you know a young lady called June Hellier?'

'Yes, I do,' said Warren, economically.

Stephens waited expectantly for Warren to elaborate, but Warren merely looked at him. Swallowing annoyance, he said, 'Is she one of your patients?'

'Yes,' said Warren.

'What were you treating her for, Doctor?'

There was a long pause before Warren said, 'That is a matter of patient-doctor relationship which I don't care to go into.'

Stephens felt Pomray stir behind him. He said stiffly, 'This is a police matter, Doctor.'

Again Warren paused, holding Stephens's eye with a level stare. At last he said, 'I suggest that if Miss Hellier needs treatment we are wasting time standing here.'

'She will not be requiring treatment,' said Stephens flatly.

Again Pomray stirred. 'She's dead, Nick.'

'I see,' said Warren. He seemed indifferent.

Stephens was irritated at Pomray's interjection, but more interested in Warren's lack of reaction. 'You don't seem surprised, Doctor.'

'I'm not,' said Warren briefly.

'You were supplying her with drugs?'

'I have prescribed for her – in the past.'

'What drugs?'

'Heroin.'

'Was that necessary?'

Warren was as immobile as ever, but there was a flinty

13

look in his eye as he said, 'I don't propose to discuss the medical treatment of any of my patients with a layman.'

A surge of anger surfaced in Stephens. 'But you are not surprised at her death. Was she a dying woman? A terminal case?'

Warren looked at Stephens consideringly, and said, 'The death rate among drug addicts is about twenty-eight times that of the general population. That is why I am not surprised at her death.'

'She was a heroin addict?'

'Yes.'

'And you have supplied her with heroin?'

'I have.'

'I see,' said Stephens with finality. He glanced at Pomray, then turned back to Warren. 'I don't know that I like that.'

'I don't care whether you like it or not,' said Warren equably. 'May I see my patient – you'll be wanting a death certificate. It had better come from me.'

Of all the bloody nerve, thought Stephens. He turned abruptly and threw open the door of the bedroom. 'In there,' he said curtly.

Warren walked past him into the room, followed closely by Pomray. Stephens jerked his head at Sergeant Ipsley, indicating that he should leave, then closed the door behind him. When he strode to the bed Warren and Pomray were already in the midst of a conversation of which he understood about one word in four.

The sheet with which Pomray had draped the body was drawn back to reveal again the naked body of June Hellier. Stephens butted in. 'Dr Warren: I suggested to Dr Pomray that perhaps this girl was a diabetic, because of those puncture marks. He said there was sepsis and that no doctor would allow that to happen to his patient. This girl was your patient. How do you account for it?'

Warren looked at Pomray and there was a faint twitch

14

about his mouth that might have been a smile. 'I don't have to account for it,' he said. 'But I will. The circumstances of the injection of an anti-diabetic drug are quite different from those attendant on heroin. The social ambience is different and there is often an element of haste which can result in sepsis.'

In an aside to Pomray he said, 'I taught her how to use a needle but, as you know, they don't take much notice of the need for cleanliness.'

Stephens was affronted. 'You *taught* her how to use a needle! By God, you make a curious use of ethics!'

Warren looked at him levelly and said with the utmost deliberation, 'Inspector, any doubts you have about my ethics should be communicated to the appropriate authority, and if you don't know what it is I shall be happy to supply you with the address.'

The way he turned from Stephens was almost an insult. He said to Pomray, 'I'll sign the certificate together with the pathologist. It will be better that way.'

'Yes,' said Pomray thoughtfully. 'It might be better.'

Warren stepped to the head of the bed and stood for a moment looking down at the dead girl. Then he drew up the sheet very slowly so that it covered the body. There was something in that slow movement which puzzled Stephens; it was an act of . . . of tenderness.

He waited until Warren looked up, then said, 'Do you know anything of her family?'

'Practically nothing. Addicts resent probing – so I don't probe.'

'Nothing about her father?'

'Nothing beyond the fact that she had a father. She mentioned him a couple of times.'

'When did she come to you for drugs?'

'She came to me for treatment about a year and a half ago. For treatment, Inspector.'

'Of course,' said Stephens ironically, and produced a

15

folded sheet of paper from his pocket. 'You might like to look at this.'

Warren took the sheet and unfolded it, noting the worn creases. 'Where did you get it?'

'It was in her handbag.'

It was a letter typed in executive face on high quality paper and bore the embossed heading: REGENT FILM COMPANY, with a Wardour Street address. It was dated six months earlier, and ran:

> *Dear Miss Hellier,*
>
> *On the instructions of your father I write to tell you that he will be unable to see you on Friday next because he is leaving for America the same afternoon. He expects to be away for some time, how long exactly I am unable to say at this moment.*
>
> *He assures you that he will write to you as soon as his more pressing business is completed, and he hopes you will not regret his absence too much.*
>
> *Yours sincerely,*
>
> *D. L. Walden*

Warren said quietly, 'This explains a lot.' He looked up. 'Did he write?'

'I don't know,' said Stephens. 'There's nothing here.'

Warren tapped the letter with a finger-nail. 'I don't think he did. June wouldn't keep a secondhand letter like this and destroy the real thing.' He looked down at the shrouded body. 'The poor girl.'

'You'd better be thinking of yourself, Doctor,' said Stephens sardonically. 'Take a look at the list of directors at the head of that letter.'

Warren glanced at it and saw: Sir Robert Hellier (Chairman). With a grimace he passed it to Pomray.

'My God!' said Pomray. '*That* Hellier.'

'Yes, *that* Hellier,' said Stephens. 'I think this one is going to be a stinker. Don't you agree, Dr Warren?' There was an unconcealed satisfaction in his voice and a dislike in his eyes as he stared at Warren.

## II

Warren sat at his desk in his consulting-room. He was between patients and using the precious minutes to catch up on the mountain of paperwork imposed by the Welfare State. He disliked the bureaucratic aspect of medicine as much as any doctor and so, in an odd way, he was relieved to be interrupted by the telephone. But his relief soon evaporated when he heard his receptionist say, 'Sir Robert Hellier wishes to speak to you, Doctor.'

He sighed. This was a call he had been expecting. 'Put him through, Mary.'

There was a click and a different buzz on the line. 'Hellier here.'

'Nicholas Warren speaking.'

The tinniness of the telephone could not disguise the rasp of authority in Hellier's voice. 'I want to see you, Warren.'

'I thought you might, Sir Robert.'

'I shall be at my office at two-thirty this afternoon. Do you know where that is?'

'That will be quite impossible,' said Warren firmly. 'I'm a very busy man. I suggest I find time for an appointment with you here at my rooms.'

There was a pause tinged with incredulity, then a splutter. 'Now, look here . . .'

'I'm sorry, Sir Robert,' Warren cut in. 'I suggest you come to see me at five o'clock today. I shall be free then, I think.'

Hellier made his decision. 'Very well,' he said brusquely, and Warren winced as the telephone was slammed down at the other end. He laid down his handset gently and flicked a switch on his intercom. 'Mary, Sir Robert Hellier will be seeing me at five. You might have to rearrange things a bit. I expect it to be a long consultation, so he must be the last patient.'

'Yes, Doctor.'

'Oh, Mary: as soon as Sir Robert arrives you may leave.'

'Thank you, Doctor.'

Warren released the switch and gazed pensively across the room, but after a few moments he applied himself once more to his papers.

Sir Robert Hellier was a big man and handled himself in such a way as to appear even bigger. The Savile Row suiting did not tone down his muscular movements by its suavity, and his voice was that of a man unaccustomed to brooking opposition. As soon as he entered Warren's room he said curtly and without preamble, 'You know why I'm here.'

'Yes; you've come to see me about your daughter. Won't you sit down?'

Hellier took the chair on the other side of the desk. 'I'll come to the point. My daughter is dead. The police have given me information which I consider incredible. They tell me that she was a drug addict – that she took heroin.'

'She did.'

'Heroin which you supplied.'

'Heroin which I prescribed,' corrected Warren.

Hellier was momentarily taken aback. 'I did not expect you to admit it so easily.'

'Why not?' said Warren. 'I was your daughter's physician.'

'Of all the bare-faced effrontery!' burst out Hellier. He leaned forward and his powerful shoulders hunched under his suit. 'That a doctor should prescribe hard drugs for a young girl is disgraceful.'

'My prescription was . . .'

'I'll see you in jail,' yelled Hellier.

'. . . entirely necessary in my opinion.'

'You're nothing but a drug pedlar.'

Warren stood up and his voice cut coldly through Hellier's tirade. 'If you repeat that statement outside this room I shall sue you for slander. If you will not listen to what I have to say then I must ask you to leave, since further communication on your part is pointless. And if you want to complain about my ethics you must do so to the Disciplinary Committee of the General Medical Council.'

Hellier looked up in astonishment. 'Are you trying to tell me that the General Medical Council would condone such conduct?'

'I am,' said Warren wryly, and sat down again. 'And so would the British Government – they legislated for it.'

Hellier seemed out of his depth. 'All right,' he said uncertainly. 'I suppose I should hear what you have to say. That's why I came here.'

Warren regarded him thoughtfully. 'June came to see me about eighteen months ago. At that time she had been taking heroin for nearly two years.'

Hellier flared again. 'Impossible!'

'What's so impossible about it?'

'I would have known.'

'How would you have known?'

'Well. I'd have recognized the . . . the symptoms.'

'I see. What are the symptoms, Sir Robert?'

Hellier began to speak, then checked himself and was silent. Warren said, 'A heroin addict doesn't walk about with palsied hands, you know. The symptoms are much subtler than that – and addicts are adept at disguising them. But you might have noticed something. Tell me, did she appear to have money troubles at that time?'

Hellier looked at the back of his hands. 'I can't remember

19

the time when she didn't have money troubles,' he said broodingly. 'I was getting pretty tired of it and I put my foot down hard. I told her I hadn't raised her to be an idle spendthrift.' He looked up. 'I found her a job, installed her in her own flat and cut her allowance by half.'

'I see,' said Warren. 'How long did she keep the job?'

Hellier shook his head. 'I don't know – only that she lost it.' His hands tightened on the edge of the desk so that the knuckles showed white. 'She robbed me, you know – she stole from her own father.'

'How did that happen?' asked Warren gently.

'I have a country house in Berkshire,' said Hellier. 'She went down there and looted it – literally looted it. There was a lot of Georgian silver, among other things. She had the nerve to leave a note saying that she was responsible – she even gave me the name of the dealer she'd sold the stuff to. I got it all back, but it cost me a hell of a lot of money.'

'Did you prosecute?'

'Don't be a damned fool,' said Hellier violently. 'I have a reputation to keep up. A fine figure I'd cut in the papers if I prosecuted my own daughter for theft. I have enough trouble with the Press already.'

'It might have been better for her if you had prosecuted,' said Warren. 'Didn't you ask yourself why she stole from you?'

Hellier sighed. 'I thought she'd just gone plain bad – I thought she'd taken after her mother.' He straightened his shoulders. 'But that's another story.'

'Of course,' said Warren. 'As I say, when June came to me for treatment, or rather, for heroin, she had been addicted for nearly two years. She said so and her physical condition confirmed it.'

'What do you mean by that?' asked Hellier. 'That she came to you for heroin and not for treatment.'

'An addict regards a doctor as a source of supply,' said

20

Warren a little tiredly. 'Addicts don't want to be treated –
it scares them.'

Hellier looked at Warren blankly. 'But this is monstrous.
Did you give her heroin?'

'I did.'

'And no treatment?'

'Not immediately. You can't treat a patient who won't
be treated, and there's no law in England which allows of
forcible treatment.'

'But you pandered to her. You *gave* her the heroin.'

'Would you rather I hadn't? Would you rather I had let
her go on the streets to get her heroin from an illegal source
at an illegal price and contaminated with God knows what
filth? At least the drug I prescribed was clean and to British
Parmacopoeia Standard, which reduced the chance of
hepatitis.'

Hellier looked strangely shrunken. 'I don't understand,'
he muttered, shaking his head. 'I just don't understand.'

'You don't,' agreed Warren. 'You're wondering what has
happened to medical ehtics. We'll come to that later.' He
tented his fingers. 'After a month I managed to persuade
June to take treatment; there are clinics for cases like hers.
She was in for twenty-seven days.' He stared at Hellier
with hard eyes. 'If I had been her I doubt I could have
lasted a week. June was a brave girl, Sir Robert.'

'I don't know much about the . . . er . . . the actual
treatment.'

Warren opened his desk drawer and took out a cigarette-
box. He took out a cigarette and then pushed the open box
across the desk, apparently as an afterthought. 'I'm sorry;
do you smoke?'

'Thank you,' said Hellier, and took a cigarette. Warren
leaned across and lit it with a flick of his lighter, then lit his
own.

He studied Hellier for a while, then held up his cigarette.
'There's a drug in here, you know, but nicotine isn't

21

particularly powerful. It produces a psychological dependency. Anyone who is strong-minded enough can give it up.' He leaned forward. 'Heroin is different; it produces a physiological dependency – the *body* needs it and the mind has precious little say about it.'

He leaned back. 'If heroin is withheld from an addicted patient there are physical withdrawal symptoms of such a nature that the chances of death are about one in five – and that is something a doctor must think hard about before he begins treatment.'

Hellier whitened. 'Did she suffer?'

'She suffered,' said Warren coldly. 'I'd be only too pleased to tell you she didn't, but that would be a lie. They all suffer. They suffer so much that hardly one in a hundred will see the treatment through. June stood as much of it as she could take and then walked out. I couldn't stop her – there's no legal restraint.'

The cigarette in Hellier's fingers was trembling noticeably. Warren said, 'I didn't see her for quite a while after that, and then she came back six months ago. They usually come back. She wanted heroin but I couldn't prescribe it. There had been a change in the law – all addicts must now get their prescriptions from special clinics which have been set up by the government. I advised treatment, but she wouldn't hear of it, so I took her to the clinic. Because I knew her medical history – and because I took an interest in her – I was able to act as consultant. Heroin was prescribed – as little as possible – until she died.'

'Yet she died of an overdose.'

'No,' said Warren. 'She died of a dose of heroin dissolved in a solution of methylamphetamine – and that's a cocktail with too much of a kick, the amphetamine was not prescribed – she must have got it somewhere else.'

Hellier was shaking. 'You take this very calmly, Warren,' he said in an unsteady voice. 'Too damned calmly for my liking.'

'I have to take it calmly,' said Warren. 'A doctor who becomes emotional is no good to himself or his patients.'

'A nice, detached, professional attitude,' sneered Hellier. 'But it killed my June.' He thrust a trembling finger under Warren's nose. 'I'm going to have your hide, Warren. I'm not without influence. I'm going to break you.'

Warren looked at Hellier bleakly. 'It's not my custom to kick parents in the teeth on occasions like this,' he said tightly. 'But you're asking for it – so don't push me.'

'Push you!' Hellier grinned mirthlessly. 'Like the Russian said – I'm going to bury you!'

Warren stood up. 'All right – then tell me this: do you usually communicate with your children at second hand by means of letters from your secretary?'

'What do you mean?'

'Six months ago, just before you went to America, June wanted to see you. You fobbed her off with a form letter from your secretary, for God's sake!'

'I was very busy at the time. I had a big deal impending.'

'She wanted your help. You wouldn't give it to her, so she came to me. You promised to write from America. Did you?'

'I was busy,' said Hellier weakly. 'I had a heavy schedule – a lot of flights . . . conferences . . .'

'So you didn't write. When did you get back?'

'A fortnight ago.'

'Nearly six months away. Did you know where your daughter was? Did you try to find out? She was still alive then, you know.'

'Good Christ, I had to straighten out things over here. Things had gone to hell in my absence.'

'They had, indeed!' said Warren icily. 'You say that you found June a job and set her up in a flat. It sounds very nice when put that way, but I'd say that you threw her out. In the preceding years did you try to find out why her behaviour had changed? Why she needed more and more

23

money? In fact I'd like to know how often you saw your daughter. Did you supervise her activities? Check on the company she was keeping? Did you act like a father?'

Hellier was ashen. 'Oh, my God!'

Warren sat down and said quietly, 'Now I'm really going to hurt you, Hellier. Your daughter hated your guts. She told me so herself, although I didn't know who you were. She kept that damned patronizing secretary's letter to fuel her hatred, and she ended up in a sleazy doss-house in Notting Hill with cash resources of three shillings and fourpence. If, six months ago, you'd have granted your daughter fifteen minutes of your precious time she'd have been alive now.'

He leaned over the desk and said in a rasping voice, 'Now tell me, Hellier; who was responsible for your daughter's death?'

Hellier's face crumpled and Warren drew back and regarded him with something like pity. He felt ashamed of himself; ashamed of letting his emotions take control in such an unprofessional way. He watched Hellier grope for a handkerchief, and then got up and went to the cupboard where he tipped a couple of pills from a bottle.

He returned to the desk and said, 'Here, take these – they'll help.' Unresistingly, Hellier allowed him to administer the pills and gulped them down with the aid of a glass of water. He became calmer and presently began to speak in a low, jerky voice.

'Helen – that's my wife – June's mother – my ex-wife – we had a divorce, you know. I divorced her – June was fifteen then. Helen was no good – no good at all. There were other men – I was sick of it. Made me look a fool. June stayed with me, she said she wanted to. God knows Helen didn't want her around.'

He took a shaky breath. 'June was still at school then, of course. I had my work – my business – it was getting bigger and more involved all the time. You have no idea how big and complicated it can get. International stuff, you know. I travelled a lot.' He looked blindly into the past. 'I didn't realize . . .'

Warren said gently, 'I know.'

Hellier looked up. 'I doubt it, Doctor.' His eyes flickered under Warren's steady gaze and he dropped his head again. 'Maybe you do. I suppose I'm not the only damned fool you've come across.'

In an even voice, trying to attune himself to Hellier's mood, Warren said, 'It's hard enough to keep up with the younger generation even when they're underfoot. They seem to have a different way of thought – different ideals.'

Hellier sighed. 'But I could have *tried*.' He squeezed his hands together tightly. 'People of my class tend to think that parental neglect and juvenile delinquency are prerogatives of the lower orders. Good Christ!'

Warren said briskly, 'I'll give you something to help you sleep tonight.'

Hellier made a negative gesture. 'No, thanks, Doctor; I'll take my medicine the hard way.' He looked up. 'Do you know how it started? How did she . . . ? How could she . . . ?'

Warren shrugged. 'She didn't say much. It was hard enough coping with present difficulties. But I think her case was very much the standard form; cannabis to begin with – taken as a lark or a dare – then on to the more potent drugs, and finally heroin and the more powerful amphetamines. It all usually starts with running with the wrong crowd.'

Hellier nodded. 'Lack of parental control,' he said bitterly. 'Where do they get the filthy stuff?'

'That's the crux. There's a fair amount of warehouse looting by criminals who have a ready market, and there's smuggling, of course. Here in England, where clinics prescribe heroin under controlled conditions to Home Office registered addicts, it's not so bad compared with the

States. Over there, because it's totally illegal, there's a vast illicit market with consequent high profits and an organized attempt to push the stuff. There's an estimated forty thousand heroin addicts in New York alone, compared with about two thousand in the whole of the United Kingdom. But it's bad enough here – the number is doubling every sixteen months.'

'Can't the police do anything about illegal drugs?'

Warren said ironically, 'I suppose Inspector Stephens told you all about me.'

'He gave me a totally wrong impression,' mumbled Hellier. He stirred restlessly.

'That's all right; I'm used to that kind of thing. The police attitude largely coincides with the public attitude – but it's no use chivvying an addict once he's hooked. That only leads to bigger profits for the gangsters because the addict on the run must get his dope where he can. And it adds to crime because he's not too particular where he gets the money to pay for the dope.' Warren studied Hellier, who was becoming noticeably calmer. He decided that this was as much due to the academic discussion as to the sedation, so he carried on.

'The addicts are sick people and the police should leave them alone,' he said. 'We'll take care of them. The police should crack down on the source of illegal drugs.'

'Aren't they doing that?'

'That's not so easy. It's an international problem. Besides, there's the difficulty of getting information – this is an illegal operation and people don't talk.' He smiled. 'Addicts don't like the police and so the police get little out of them. On the other hand, I don't like addicts – they're difficult patients most doctors won't touch – but I understand them, and they tell me things. I probably know more about what's going on than the official police sources.'

'Then why don't you tell the police?' demanded Hellier.

Warren's voice went suddenly hard. 'If any of my

patients knew that I was abusing their confidence by blabbing to the police, I'd lose the lot. Trust between patient and doctor must be absolute – especially with a drug addict. You can't help them if they don't trust you enough to come to you for treatment. So I'd lose them to an illicit form of supply; either an impure heroin from the docks at an inflated price, or an aseptic heroin with no treatment from one of my more unethical colleagues. There are one or two bad apples in the medical barrel, as Inspector Stephens will be quick enough to tell you.'

Hellier hunched his big shoulders and looked broodingly down at the desk. 'So what's the answer? Can't you do anything yourself?'

'Me!' said Warren in surprise. 'What could I do? The problem of supply begins right outside England in the Middle East. I'm no story-book adventurer, Hellier; I'm a medical doctor with patients, who just makes ends meet. I can't just shoot off to Iran on a crazy adventure.'

Hellier growled deep in his throat, 'You might have fewer patients if you were as crazy as that.' He stood up. 'I'm sorry about my attitude when I first came in here, Dr Warren. You have cleared up a lot of things I didn't understand. You have told me my faults. You have told me of your ethics in this matter. You have also pointed out a possible solution which you refuse to countenance. What about *your* faults, Dr Warren, and where are your ethics now?'

He strode heavily to the door. 'Don't bother to see me out, Doctor; I'll find my own way.'

Warren, taken wrong-footed, was startled as the door closed behind Hellier. Slowly he returned to the chair behind his desk and sat down. He lit a cigarette and remained in deep thought for some minutes, then shook his head irritably as though to escape a buzzing fly.

Ridiculous! he thought. Absolutely ridiculous!

But the maggot of doubt stirred and he could not escape its irritation in his mind no matter how hard he tried.

That evening he walked through Piccadilly and into Soho, past the restaurants and strip joints and night clubs, the chosen haunt of most of his patients. He saw one or two of them and they waved to him. He waved back in an automatic action and went on, almost unaware of his surroundings, until he found himself in Wardour Street outside the offices of the Regent Film Company.

He looked up at the building. 'Ridiculous!' he said aloud.


III


Sir Robert Hellier also had a bad night.

He went back to his flat in St James's and was almost totally unaware of how he got there. His chauffeur noted the tight lips and lowering expression and took the precaution of ringing the flat from the garage before he put away the car. 'The old bastard's in a mood, Harry,' he said to Hellier's man, Hutchins. 'Better keep clear of him and walk on eggs.'

So it was that when Hellier walked into his penthouse flat Hutchins put out the whisky and made himself scarce. Hellier ignored both the presence of the whisky and the absence of Hutchins and sank his bulk into a luxurious armchair, where he brooded deep in thought.

Inside he writhed with guilt. It had been many more years than he could remember since anyone had had the guts to hold up a mirror wherein he could see himself, and the experience was harrowing. He hated himself and, perhaps, he hated Warren even more for rubbing his nose into his shortcomings. Yet he was basically honest and he recognized that his final remarks and abrupt exit from Warren's rooms had been the sudden crystallization of his

28

desire to crack Warren's armour of ethics – to find the feet of clay and to pull Warren down to his own miserable level.

And what about June? Where did she come into all this? He thought of his daughter as he had once known her – gay, light-hearted, carefree. There was nothing he had not been prepared to give her, from the best schools to good clothes by fashionable designers, parties, continental holidays and all the rest of the good life.

Everything, except myself, he thought remorsefully.

And then, unnoticed in the interstices of his busy life, a change had come. June developed an insatiable appetite for money; not, apparently, for the things money can buy, but for money itself. Hellier was a self-made man, brought up in a hard school, and he believed that the young should earn their independence. What started out to be calm discussions with June turned into a series of flaming rows and, in the end, he lost his temper and then came the break. It was true what Warren had said; he had thrown out his daughter without making an attempt to find the root cause of the change in her.

The theft of the silver from his home had only confirmed his impression that she had gone bad, and his main worry had been to keep the matter quiet and out of the press. He suddenly realized, to his shame, that the bad press he was likely to get because of the inquest had been uppermost in his mind ever since he had seen Inspector Stephens.

How had all this happened? How had he come to lose first a wife and then a daughter?

He had worked – by God, how he had worked! The clapper-clawing to the top in an industry where knives are wielded with the greatest efficiency; the wheeling and dealing with millions at stake. The American trip, for instance – he had got on top of those damned sharp Yanks – but at what cost? An ulcer, a higher blood pressure than his doctor liked and a nervous three packets of cigarettes a day as inheritance of those six months.

And a dead daughter.

He looked around the flat, at the light-as-air Renoir on the facing wall, at the blue period Picasso at the end of the room. The symbols of success. He suddenly hated them and moved to another chair where they were at his back and where he could look out over London towards the Tudor crenellations of St James's Palace.

Why had he worked so hard? At first it had been for Helen and young June and for the other children that were to come. But Helen had not wanted children and so June was the only one. Was it about then that work became a habit, or perhaps an anodyne? He had thrown himself wholeheartedly into the curious world of the film studios where it is a toss-up which is the more important, money or artistry; and not a scrap of his heart had he left for his wife.

Perhaps it was his neglect that had forced Helen to look elsewhere – at first surreptitiously and later blatantly – until he had got tired of the innuendoes and had forced the divorce.

But where, in God's name, had June come into all this? The work was there by then, and had to be done; decisions had to be taken – by him and by no one else – and each damned decision led to another and then another, filling his time and his life until there was no room for anything but the work.

He held out his hands and looked at them. Nothing but a machine, he thought despondently. A mind for making the right decisions and hands for signing the right cheques.

And somewhere in all this, June, his daughter, had been lost. He was suddenly filled with a terrible shame at the thought of the letter Warren had told him about. He remembered the occasion now. It had been a bad week; he was preparing to carry a fight to America, and everything had gone wrong so he was rushed off his feet. He remembered being waylaid by Miss Walden, his secretary, in a corridor between offices.

'I've a letter for you from Miss Hellier, Sir Robert. She would like to see you on Friday.'

He had stopped, somewhat surprised, and rubbed his chin in desperation, wanting to get on but still wanting to see June. 'Oh, damn; I have that meeting with Matchet on Friday morning – and that means lunch as well. What do I have after lunch, Miss Walden?'

She did not consult an appointment book because she was not that kind of secretary, which was why he employed her. 'Your plane leaves at three-thirty – you might have to leave your lunch early.'

'Oh! Well, do me a favour, Miss Walden. Write to my daughter explaining the situation. Tell her I'll write from the States as soon as I can.'

And he had gone on into an office and from there to another office and yet another until the day was done – the 18-hour working day. And in two more days it was Friday with the conference with Matchet and the expensive lunch that was necessary to keep Matchet sweet. Then the quick drive to Heathrow – and New York in no time at all – to be confronted by Hewling and Morrin with their offers and propositions, all booby-trapped.

The sudden necessity to fly to Los Angeles and to beat the Hollywood moguls on their own ground. Then back to New York to be inveigled by Morrin to go on that trip to Miami and the Bahamas, an unsubtle attempt at corruption by hospitality. But he had beaten them all and had returned to England with the fruits of victory and at the high point of his career, only to be confronted by the devil of a mess because no one had been strong enough to control Matchet.

In all that time he had never once thought of his daughter.

The dimming light concealed the greyness of his face as he contemplated that odious fact. He sought to find excuses and found none. And he knew that this was not the worst – he knew that he had *never* given June the opportunity of communicating with him on the simple level of one human being to another. She had been something in the background of his life, and the knowledge hurt him that she had been *something* and not *someone*.

Hellier got up and paced the room restlessly, thinking of all the things Warren had said. Warren had seemed to take drug addiction as a matter of course, a normal fact of life to be coped with somehow. Although he had not said so outright, he had implied it was his task to clear up the mess left by the negligence of people like himself.

But surely someone else was to blame. What about the profit-makers? The pushers of drugs?

Hellier paused as he felt a spark of anger flash into being, an anger which, for the first time, was not directed against himself. His was a sin of omission, although not to be minimized on that account. But the sin of commission, the deliberate act of giving drugs to the young for profit, was monstrous. He had been thoughtless, but the drug pedlars were evil.

The anger within him grew until he thought he would burst with the sheer agony of it, but he deliberately checked himself in order to think constructively. Just as he had not allowed his emotions to impede his negotiations with Matchet, Hewling and Morrin, so he brought his not inconsiderable intellect to bear unclouded on this new problem. Hellier, as an efficient machine, began to swing smoothly into action.

He first thought of Warren who, with his special knowledge, was undoubtedly the key. Hellier was accustomed to studying closely the men with whom he dealt because their points of strength and weakness showed in subtle ways. He went over in his mind everything Warren had said and the way in which he had said it, and seized upon two points. He was certain Warren *knew* something important.

But he had to make sure that his chosen key would not break in his hand. Decisively he picked up the telephone and dialled a number. A moment later he said, 'Yes, I know it's late. Do we have that firm of investigators still on our books? They helped us on the Lowrey case . . . Good! I want them to investigate Dr Nicholas Warren MD. Repeat that. It must be done discreetly. Everything there is to know about him, damn it! As fast as possible . . . a report in three days . . . oh, damn the expense! – charge it to my private account.'

Absently he picked up the decanter of whisky. 'And another thing. Get the Research Department to find out all they can about drug smuggling – the drug racket in general. Again, a report in three days . . . Yes, I'm serious . . . it might make a good film.' He paused. 'Just one thing more; the Research Department mustn't go near Dr Warren . . . Yes, they're quite likely to, but they must steer clear of him – is that understood? Good!'

He put down the telephone and looked at the decanter in some surprise. He laid it down gently and went into his bedroom. For the first time in many years he ignored his normal meticulous procedure of hanging up his clothes and left them strewn about the floor.

Once in bed the tensions left him and his body relaxed. It was only then that the physical expression of his grief came to him and he broke down. Waves of shudders racked his body and this man of fifty-five wet the pillow with his tears.

# 2

Warren was – and was not – surprised to hear from Hellier again. In the forefront of his mind he wondered what Hellier was after and was almost inclined to refuse to see him. In his experience prolonged post-mortems with the survivors did no one any good in the long run; they merely served to turn guilt into acceptance and, as a moral man, he believed that the guilty should be punished and that self-punishment was the most severe form.

But in the remote recesses of his mind still lurked the nagging doubt which had been injected by Hellier's final words and so, somewhat to his surprise, he found himself accepting Hellier's invitation to meet him in the St James's flat. This time, oddly enough, he was not averse to meeting Hellier on his own ground – that battle had already been won.

Hellier greeted him with a conventional, 'It's very good of you to come, Doctor,' and led him into a large and softly luxurious room where he was waved courteously to a chair. 'Drink?' asked Hellier. 'Or don't you?'

Warren smiled. 'I have all the normal vices. I'd like a Scotch.'

He found himself sipping a whisky so good that it was almost criminal to dilute it with water, and holding one of Hellier's monogrammed cigarettes. 'We're a picturesque lot, we film people,' said Hellier wryly. 'Self-advertisement is one of our worst faults.'

Warren looked at the intertwined R H stamped in gold on the handmade cigarette, and suspected that it was not

Hellier's normal style and that he went about it coldblood-edly in what was a conformist industry. He said nothing and waited for Hellier to toss a more reasonable conver-sational ball.

'First, I must apologize for the scene I made in your rooms,' said Hellier.

'You have already done so,' said Warren gravely. 'And in any case, no apology is necessary.'

Hellier settled in a chair facing Warren and put his glass on a low table. 'I find you are very well thought of in your profession.'

Warren twitched an eyebrow. 'Indeed!'

'I've been finding out things about the drug racket – I think I have it pretty well taped.'

'In three days?' said Warren ironically.

'In the film industry, by its very nature, there must be an enormous fund of general knowledge. My Research Department is very nearly as good as, say, a newspaper office. If you put enough staff on to a problem you can do a lot in three days.'

Warren let that go and merely nodded.

'My research staff found that in nearly one-third of their enquiries they were advised to consult you as a leading member of the profession.'

'They didn't,' said Warren succinctly.

Hellier smiled. 'No, I told them not to. As you said the other day, you're a very busy man. I didn't want to disturb you.'

'I suppose I should thank you,' said Warren with a straight face.

Hellier squared his shoulders. 'Dr Warren, let us not fence with each other. I'm putting all my cards on the table. I also had you independently investigated.'

Warren sipped whisky and kept steady eyes on Hellier over the glass. 'That's a damned liberty,' he observed mildly. 'I suppose I should ask you what you found.'

Hellier held up his hand. 'Nothing but good, Doctor. You have an enviable reputation both as a man and as a physician, besides being outstanding in the field of drug addiction.'

Warren said satirically, 'I should like to read that dossier sometime – it would be like reading one's obituary, a chance which comes to few of us.' He put down his glass. 'And to what end is all this . . . this effort on your part?'

'I wanted to be sure that you are the right man,' said Hellier seriously.

'You're talking in riddles,' said Warren impatiently. He laughed. 'Are you going to offer me a job? Technical adviser to a film, perhaps?'

'Perhaps,' said Hellier. 'Let me ask you a question. You are divorced from your wife. Why?'

Warren felt outrage, surprise and shock. He was outraged at the nature of the question; surprised that the urbane Hellier should have asked it; shocked because of the intensive nature of Hellier's investigation of him. 'That's my affair,' he said coldly.

'Undoubtedly.' Hellier studied Warren for a moment. 'I'll tell you why your wife divorced you. She didn't like your association with drug addicts.'

Warren put his hands on the arms of the chair preparatory to rising, and Hellier said sharply, 'Sit down, man; listen to what I've got to say.'

'It had better be good,' said Warren, relaxing. 'I don't take kindly to conversations of this nature.'

Hellier stubbed out his cigarette and lit another. 'That tells me more about you than it does about your wife, whom I am not interested in. It tells me that the interests of your profession come ahead of your personal relationships. Are you aware that you are considered to be a fanatic on the subject of drugs?'

'It has been brought to my attention,' said Warren stiffly.

Hellier nodded. 'As you pointed out – and as I have

36

found in my brief study – drug addicts are not the most easy patients. They're conceited, aggressive, deceitful, vicious, crafty and any other pejorative term you care to apply to them. And yet you persist against all the odds in trying to help them – even to the extent of losing your wife. That seems to me to show a great deal of dedication.'

Warren snorted. 'Dedication my foot! It's just what goes with the job. All those vices you've just mentioned are symptoms of the general drug syndrome. The addicts are like that because of the drugs, and you can't just leave them to stew because you don't like the way they behave.' He shook his head. 'Come to the point. I didn't come here to be admired – especially by you.'

Hellier flushed. 'I was making a point in my own peculiar way,' he said. 'But I'll come to the nub of it. When I came to see you, you said that the problem was in stopping the inflow of illicit drugs and you said it was an international problem. You were also damned quick to say that you weren't prepared to jump off to Iran on a crazy adventure.' He stuck out his finger. 'I think you know something, Dr Warren; and I think it's something definite.'

'My God!' said Warren. 'You jump to a fast conclusion.'

'I'm used to it,' said Hellier easily. 'I've had a lot of experience – and I'm usually right. I get paid for being right and I'm highly paid. Now, why Iran? Heroin is ultimately derived from opium, and opium comes from many places. It could come from the Far East – China or Burma – but you said the problem of illegal supply begins in the Middle East. Why the Middle East? And why pick Iran in particular? It could come from any of half a dozen countries from Afghanistan to Greece, but you took a snap judgment on Iran without a second thought.' He set down his glass with a tiny click. 'You know something definite, Dr Warren.'

Warren stirred in his chair. 'Why this sudden interest?'

'Because I've decided to do something about it,' said

Hellier. He laughed briefly at the expression on Warren's face. 'No, I haven't gone mad; neither do I have delusions of grandeur. You pointed out the problem yourself. What the devil's the good of patching up these damned idiots if they can walk out and pick up a fresh supply on the nearest corner? Cutting off the illegal supply would make your own job a lot easier.'

'For God's sake!' exploded Warren. 'There are hundreds of policemen of all nationalities working on this. What makes you think you can do any better?'

Hellier levelled a finger at him. 'Because you have information which for reasons of your own – quite ethical reasons, I am sure – you will not pass on to the police.'

'And which I will pass on to you – is that it?'

'Oh, no,' said Hellier. 'You can keep it to yourself if you wish.' He stabbed a finger towards Warren again. 'You see, *you* are going to do something about it.'

'Now I know you're crazy,' said Warren in disgust. 'Hellier, I think you've been knocked off balance; you're set on some weird kind of expiation and you're trying to drag me into it.' His lips twisted. 'It's known as shutting the stable door after the horse has gone, and I want no part of it.'

Unperturbedly, Hellier lit another cigarette, and Warren suddenly said, 'You smoke too much.'

'You're the second doctor to tell me that within a fortnight.' Hellier waved his hand. 'You see, you can't help being a doctor, even now. At our last meeting you said something else – "I'm a doctor who just makes ends meet".' He laughed. 'You're right; I know your bank balance to a penny. But suppose you had virtually unlimited funds, and suppose you coupled those funds with the information I'm certain you have and which, incidentally, you don't deny having. What then?'

Warren spoke without thinking. 'It's too big for one man.'

'Who said anything about one man? Pick your own team,' said Hellier expansively.

Warren stared at him. 'I believe you mean all this,' he said in wonder.

'I might be in the business of spinning fairy tales for other people,' said Hellier soberly. 'But I don't spin them for myself. I mean every word of it.'

Warren knew he had been right; Hellier *had* been pushed off balance by the death of his daughter. He judged that Hellier had always been a single-minded man, and now he had veered off course and had set his sights on a new objective. And he would be a hard man to stop.

'I don't think you know what's involved,' he said.

'I don't *care* what's involved,' said Hellier flatly. 'I want to hit these bastards. I want blood.'

'Whose blood – mine?' asked Warren cynically. 'You've picked the wrong man. I don't think the man exists, anyway. You need a combination of St George and James Bond. I'm a doctor, not a gang-buster.'

'You're a man with the knowledge and qualifications I need,' said Hellier intensely. He saw he was on the edge of losing Warren, and said more calmly, 'Don't make a snap decision now, Doctor; just think it over.' His voice sharpened. 'And pay a thought to ethics.' He looked at his watch. 'Now what about a bite to eat?'

II

Warren left Hellier's flat comfortable in stomach but uneasy in mind. As he walked up Jermyn Street towards Piccadilly Circus he thought of all the aspects of the odd proposition Hellier had put to him. There was no doubt that Hellier meant it, but he did not know what he was getting into –

not by half; in the vicious world of the drug trade no quarter was given – the stakes were too high.

He pushed his way through the brawling crowds of Piccadilly Circus and turned off into Soho. Presently he stopped outside a pub, looked at his watch, and then went in. It was crowded but someone companionably made room for him at a corner of the bar and he ordered a Scotch and, with the glass in his hand, looked about the room. Sitting at a table on the other side were three of his boys. He looked at them speculatively and judged they had had their shots not long before; they were at ease and conversation between them flowed freely. One of them looked up and waved and he raised his hand in greeting.

In order to get to his patients, to acquire their unwilling trust, Warren had lived with them and had, at last, become accepted. It was an uphill battle to get them to use clean needles and sterile water; too many of them had not the slightest idea of medical hygiene. He lived in their half-world on the fringes of crime where even the Soho prostitutes took a high moral tone and considered that the addicts lowered the gentility of the neighbourhood. It was enough to make a man laugh – or cry.

Warren made no moral judgments. To him it was a social and medical problem. He was not immediately concerned with the fundamental instability in a man which led him to take heroin; all he knew was that when the man was hooked he was hooked for good. At that stage there was no point in recrimination because it solved nothing. There was a sick man to be helped, and Warren helped him, fighting society at large, the police and even the addict himself.

It was in this pub, and in places like it, that he had heard the three hard facts and the thousand rumours which constituted the core of the special knowledge which Hellier was trying to get from him. To mix with addicts was to mix with criminals. At first they had been close-mouthed when he was around, but later, when they discovered that his lips were equally tight, they spoke more freely. They knew who – and what – he was, but they accepted it, although to a few he was just another 'flaming do-gooder' who ought to keep his long nose out of other people's affairs. But generally he had become accepted.

He turned back to the bar and contemplated his glass. Nick Warren – do-it-yourself Bond! he thought. Hellier is incredible! The trouble with Hellier was that he did not know the magnitude of what he had set out to do. Millionaire though he was, the prizes offered in the drug trade would make even Hellier appear poverty-stricken, and with money like that at stake men do not hesitate to kill.

A heavy hand smote him on the back and he choked over his drink. 'Hello, Doc; drowning your sorrows?'

Warren turned. 'Hello, Andy. Have a drink.'

'Most kind,' said Andrew Tozier. 'But allow me.' He pulled out a wallet and peeled a note from the fat wad.

'I wouldn't think of it,' said Warren drily. 'You're still unemployed.' He caught the eye of the barman and ordered two whiskies.

'Aye,' said Tozier, putting away his wallet. 'The world's becoming too bloody quiet for my liking.'

'You can't be reading the newspapers,' observed Warren. 'The Russians are acting up again and Vietnam was still going full blast the last I heard.'

'But those are the big boys,' said Tozier. 'There's no room for a small-scale enterprise like mine. It's the same everywhere – the big firms put the squeeze on us little chaps.' He lifted his glass. 'Cheers!'

Warren regarded him with sudden interest. Major Andrew Tozier; profession – mercenary soldier. A killer for hire. Andy would not shoot anyone indiscriminately – that would be murder. But he was quite prepared to be employed by a new government to whip into line a regiment of half-trained black soldiers and lead them into action. He was a walking symptom of a schizophrenic world.

'Cheers!' said Warren absently. His mind was racing with mad thoughts.

Tozier jerked his head towards the door. 'Your consulting-room is filling up, Doc.' Warren looked over and saw four young men just entering; three were his patients but the fourth he did not know. 'I don't know how you stand those cheap bastards,' said Tozier.

'Someone has to look after them,' said Warren. 'Who's the new boy?'

Tozier shrugged. 'Another damned soul on the way to hell,' he said macabrely. 'You'll probably meet up with him when he wants a fix.'

Warren nodded. 'So there's still no action in your line.'

'Not a glimmer.'

'Maybe your rates are too high. I suppose it's a case of supply and demand like everything else.'

'The rates are *never* too high,' said Tozier, a little bleakly. 'What price would you put on *your* skin, Doc?'

'I've just been asked that question – in an oblique way,' said Warren, thinking of Hellier. 'What is the going rate, anyway?'

'Five hundred a month plus a hell of a big bonus on completion.' Tozier smiled. 'Thinking of starting a war?'

Warren looked him in the eye. 'I just might be.'

The smile faded from Tozier's lips. He looked at Warren closely, impressed by the way he had spoken. 'By God!' he said. 'I think you're serious. Who are you thinking of tackling? The Metropolitan Police?' The smile returned and grew broader.

Warren said, 'You've never really gone in for private enterprise, have you? I mean a private war as opposed to a public war.'

Tozier shook his head. 'I've always stayed legal or, at any rate, political. Anyway, there are precious few people

42

financing private brawls. I take it you don't mean carrying a gun for some jumped-up Soho "businessman" busily engaged in carving a private empire? Or bodyguarding?'

'Nothing like that,' said Warren. He was thinking of what he knew of Andrew Tozier. The man had values of a sort. Not long before, Warren had asked why he had not taken advantage of a conflict that was going on in a South American country.

Tozier had been scathingly contemptuous. 'Good Christ! That's a power game going on between two gangs of top-class cut-throats. I have no desire to mow down the poor sons of bitches of peasants who happen to get caught in the middle.' He had looked hard at Warren. 'I choose my fights,' he said.

Warren thought that if he did pick up Hellier's ridiculous challenge then Andy Tozier would be a good man to have around. Not that there was any likelihood of it happening.

Tozier was waving to the barman, and held up two fingers. He turned to Warren, and said, 'You have something on your mind, Doctor. Is someone putting the pressure on?'

'In a way,' said Warren wryly. He thought Hellier had not really started yet; the next thing to come would be the moral blackmail.

'Give me his name,' said Tozier. 'I'll lean on him a bit. He won't trouble you any more.'

Warren smiled. 'Thanks, Andy; it's not that sort of pressure.'

Tozier looked relieved. 'That's all right, then. I thought some of your mainliners might have been ganging up on you. I'd soon sort *them* out.' He put a pound note on the counter and accepted the change. 'Here's mud in your eye.'

'Supposing *I* needed bodyguarding,' said Warren carefully. 'Would you take on the job – at your usual rates?'

Tozier laughed loudly. 'You couldn't afford me. I'd do it for free, though, if it isn't too long a job.' A frown creased his forehead. 'Something really is biting you, Doc. I think you'd better tell me what it is.'

'No,' said Warren sharply. If – and it was a damned big 'if' – he went deeper into this then he could not trust anyone, not even Andy Tozier who seemed straight enough. He said slowly, 'If it ever happens it will take, perhaps, a few months, and it will be in the Middle East. You'd get paid your five hundred a month plus bonus.'

Tozier put down his glass gently. 'And it's not political?'

'As far as I know it isn't,' said Warren thoughtfully.

'And I bodyguard *you*?' Tozier seemed bewildered.

Warren grinned. 'Perhaps there'd be a bit of fetching and carrying in a fierce sort of way.'

'Middle East and not political – maybe,' mused Tozier. He shook his head. 'I usually like to know more about what I'm getting into.' He shot Warren a piercing glance. 'But you I trust. If you want me – just shout.'

'It may never happen,' warned Warren. 'There's no firm commitment.'

'That's all right,' said Tozier. 'Let's just say you have a free option on my services.' He finished his drink with a flourish and bumped down the glass, looking at Warren expectantly. 'Your round. Anyone who can afford my rates can afford to buy me drinks.'

Warren went home and spent a long time just sitting in a chair and gazing into space. In an indefinable way he somehow felt committed, despite what he had said to Andy Tozier. The mere act of meeting the man had put ideas into his head, ideas that were crazy mad but becoming more real and solid with every tick of the clock. At one point he got up restlessly and paced the room.

'Damn Hellier!' he said aloud.

He went to his desk, drew out a sheet of paper, and began writing busily. At the end of half an hour he had, perhaps, twenty names scribbled down. Thoughtfully he scanned his list and began to eliminate and in another fifteen minutes the list was reduced to five names,

ANDREW TOZIER
JOHN FOLLET
DAN PARKER
BEN BRYAN
MICHAEL ABBOT

## III

Number 23, Acacia Road, was a neat, semi-detached house, indistinguishable from the hundreds around it. Warren pushed open the wooden gate, walked the few steps necessary to get to the front door and past the postage-stamp-sized front garden, and rang the bell. The door was opened by a trim, middle-aged woman who greeted him with pleasure.

'Why, Dr Warren; we haven't seen you for a long time.' Alarm chased across her face. 'It's not Jimmy again, is it? He hasn't been getting into any more trouble?'

Warren smiled reassuringly. 'Not that I know of, Mrs Parker.'

He almost felt her relief. 'Oh!' she said. 'Well, that's all right, then. Do you want to see Jimmy? He's not in now – he went down to the youth club.'

'I came to see Dan,' said Warren. 'Just for a friendly chat.'

'What am I thinking of,' said Mrs Parker. 'Keeping you on the doorstep like this. Come in, Doctor. Dan just got home – he's upstairs washing.'

Warren was quite aware that Dan Parker had just reached home. He had not wanted to see Parker at the garage where he worked so he had waited in his car and followed him home. Mrs Parker ushered him into the front room. 'I'll tell him you're here,' she said.

Warren looked about the small room; at the three pottery ducks on the wall, at the photographs of the children on the sideboard and the other photograph of a much younger Dan Parker in uniform. He did not have to wait long. Parker came into the room and held out his hand. 'This is a pleasure we didn't expect, Doctor.' Warren, grasping the hand, felt the hardness of callouses. 'I was only sayin' to Sally the other day that it's a pity we don't see more of you.'

'Perhaps it's just as well,' said Warren ruefully. 'I'm afraid I put the breeze up Mrs Parker just now.'

'Aye,' said Parker soberly. 'I know what you mean. But we'd still like to see you, sociable like.' The warm tones of the Lancastrian were still heard, although Parker had lived in London for many years. 'Sit down, Doctor; Sally'll be bringing in tea any minute.'

'I've come to see you on . . . a matter of business.'

'Oh, aye,' said Parker comfortably. 'We'll get down to it after tea, then, shall we? Sally has to go out, anyway; her younger sister's a bit under the weather, so Sally's doin' a bit o' baby-sitting.'

'I'm sorry to hear that,' said Warren. 'How's Jimmy these days?'

'He's all right now,' said Parker. 'You straightened him out, Doctor. You put the fear o' God into him – an' I keep it there.'

'I wouldn't be too hard on him.'

'Just hard enough,' said Parker uncompromisingly. 'He'll not get on that lark again.' He sighed. 'I don't know what kids are comin' to these days. It weren't like that when I were a lad. If I'd a' done what young Jimmy did, me father would a' laid into me that hard with his strap. He had a heavy hand, had me dad.' He shook his head. 'But it wouldn't a' entered our heads.'

46

Warren listened to this age-old plaint of the parents without a trace of a smile. 'Yes,' he agreed gravely. 'Things have changed.'

Sally Parker brought in the tea – a cut down, southern version of the traditional northern high tea. She pressed homemade cakes and scones on Warren, and insisted on refilling his cup. Warren studied Parker unobtrusively and tried to figure out how to broach the delicate subject in such a way as to ensure the greatest co-operation.

Daniel Parker was a man of forty. He had joined the Navy during the last few months of the war and had elected to make a career of it. In the peacetime Navy he had forged ahead in his stubborn way despite the inevitably slow rate of promotion. He had fought in Korean waters during that war and had come out of it a petty officer with the heady prospect of getting commissioned rank. But in 1962 a torpedo got loose and rolled on his leg, and that was the end of his naval career.

He had come out of the Navy with one leg permanently shortened, a disability pension and no job. The last did not worry him because he knew he was good with his hands. Since 1963 he had been working as a mechanic in a garage, and Warren thought his employer was damned lucky.

Mrs Parker looked at her watch and made an exclamation. 'Oh, I'll be late. You'll have to excuse me, Doctor.'

'That's all right, Mrs Parker,' said Warren, rising.

'You get off, lass,' said Parker. 'I'll see to the dishes, an' the doctor an' me will have a quiet chat.' Mrs Parker left, and Parker produced a stubby pipe which he proceeded to fill. 'You said you wanted to see me on business, Doctor.' He looked up in a puzzled way, and then smiled. 'Maybe you'll be wantin' a new car.'

'No,' said Warren. 'How are things at the garage, Dan?'

Parker shrugged. 'Same as ever. Gets a bit monotonous at times – but I'm doin' an interestin' job now on a Mini-Cooper.' He smiled slowly. 'Most o' the time I'm dealin' wi' the troubles o' maiden ladies. I had one come in the other day – said the car was usin' too much petrol. I tested it an' there was nothin' wrong, so I gave it back. But she was back in no time at all wi' the same trouble.'

He struck a match. 'I still found nothin' wrong, so I said to her, 'Miss Hampton, I want to drive around a bit with you just for a final check,' so off we went. The first thing she did was to pull out the choke an' hang her bag on it – said she thought that was what it was for.' He shook his head in mild disgust.

Warren laughed. 'You're a long way from the Navy, Dan.'

'Aye, that's a fact,' said Parker, a little morosely. 'I still miss it, you know. But what can a man do?' Absently, he stroked his bad leg. 'Still, I daresay it's better for Sally an' the kids even though she never minded me bein' away.'

'What do you miss about it, Dan?'

Parker puffed at his pipe contemplatively. 'Hard to say. I think I miss the chance o' handling fine machinery. This patching up o' production cars doesn't stretch a man – that's why I like to get something different, like this Mini-Cooper I'm workin' on now. By the time I'm finished wi' it Issigonis wouldn't recognize it.'

Warren said carefully, 'Supposing you were given the chance of handling naval equipment again. Would you take it?'

Parker took the pipe out of his mouth. 'What are you gettin' at, Doctor?'

'I want a man who knows all about torpedoes,' Warren said bluntly.

Parker blinked. 'I know as much as anyone, I reckon, but I don't see . . .' His voice tailed off and he looked at Warren in a baffled way.

'Let me put it this way. Supposing I wanted to smuggle something comparatively light and very valuable into a country that has a seaboard. Could it be done by torpedo?'

48

Parker scratched his head. 'It never occurred to me,' he said, and grinned. 'But it's a bloody good idea. What are you thinkin' o' doin' the Excise with? Swiss watches?'

'What about heroin?' asked Warren quietly.

Parker went rigid and stared at Warren as though he had suddenly sprouted horns and a tail. The pipe fell from his fingers to lie unregarded as he said, 'Are you serious? I'd a' never believed it.'

'It's all right, Dan,' said Warren. 'I'm serious, but not in the way you mean. But could it be done?'

There was a long moment before Parker groped for his pipe. 'It could be done all right,' he said. 'The old Mark XI carried a warhead of over seven hundred pounds. You could pack a hell of a lot o' heroin in there.'

'And the range?'

'Maximum five thousand, five hundred yards if you pre-heat the batteries,' said Parker promptly.

'Damn!' said Warren disappointedly. 'That's not enough. You said batteries. Is this an electric torpedo?'

'Aye. Ideal for smugglin' it is. No bubbles, you see.'

'But not nearly enough range,' said Warren despondently. 'It was a good idea while it lasted.'

'What's your problem?' asked Parker, striking a match.

'I was thinking of a ship cruising outside the territorial waters of the United States and firing a torpedo inshore. That's twelve miles – over twenty-one thousand yards.'

'That's a long way,' said Parker, puffing at his pipe. It did not ignite and he had to strike another match and it was some time before he got the pipe glowing to his satisfaction. 'But maybe it could be done.'

Warren ceased to droop and looked up alertly. 'It could?'

'The Mark XI came out in 1944 an' things have changed since then,' said Parker thoughtfully. He looked up. 'Where would you be gettin' a torpedo, anyway?'

'I haven't gone into that yet,' said Warren. 'But it

shouldn't be too difficult. There's an American in Switzerland who has enough war surplus arms to outfit the British forces. He should have torpedoes.'

'Then they'd be Mark XIs,' said Parker. 'Or the German equivalent. I doubt if anythin' more modern has got on the war surplus market yet.' He pursed his lips. 'It's an interestin' problem. You see, the Mark XI had lead-acid batteries – fifty-two of 'em. But things have changed since the war an' you can get better batteries now. What I'd do would be to rip out the lead-acid batteries an' replace with high-power mercury cells.' He stared at the ceiling dreamily. 'All the circuits would need redesignin' an' it would be bloody expensive, but I think I could do it.'

He leaned forward and tapped his pipe against the fireplace, then looked Warren firmly in the eyes. 'But not for smugglin' dope.'

'It's all right, Dan; I haven't switched tracks.' Warren rubbed his chin. 'I want you to work with me on a job. It will pay twice as much as you're getting at the garage, and there'll be a big bonus when you've finished. And if you don't want to go back to the garage there'll be a guaranteed steady job for as long as you want it.'

Parker blew a long plume of smoke. 'There's a queer smell to this one, Doctor. It sounds illegal to me.'

'It's not illegal,' said Warren quickly. 'But it could be dangerous.'

Parker pondered. 'How long would it take?'

'I don't know. Might be three months – might be six. It wouldn't be in England, either; you'd be going out to the Middle East.'

'And it could be dangerous. What sort o' danger?'

Warren decided to be honest. 'Well, if you put a foot wrong you could get yourself shot.'

Parker laid down his pipe in the hearth. 'You're askin' a bloody lot, aren't you? I have a wife an' three kids – an' here you come wi' a funny proposition that stinks to high heaven an' you tell me I could get shot. Why come to me, anyway?'

'I need a good torpedo man – and you're the only one I know.' A slight smile touched Warren's lips. 'It's not the most crowded trade in the world.'

Parker nodded his agreement. 'No, it's not. I don't want to crack meself up, but I can't think of another man who can do what you want. It 'ud be a really bobby-dazzler of a job, though – wouldn't it? Pushin' the old Mark XI out to over twenty thousand yards – just think of it.'

Warren held his breath as he watched Parker struggle against temptation, then he sighed as Parker shook his head and said, 'No, I couldn't do it. What would Sally say?'

'I know it's a dangerous job, Dan.'

'I'm not worried about that – not for meself. I could have got killed in Korea. It's just that . . . well, I've not much insurance, an' what would she do with three kids if anythin' happened to me?'

Warren said, 'I'll tell you this much, Dan, I don't think the worst will happen, but if it does I'll see that Sally gets a life pension equal to what you're getting now. No strings attached – and you can have that in writing.'

'You're pretty free wi' your money – or is it your money?' asked Parker shrewdly.

'It doesn't matter where it comes from. It's in a good cause.'

Parker sighed. 'I'd trust you that far. I know you'd never be on the wrong side. When is this lark startin'?'

'I don't know,' said Warren. 'It might not even start at all. I haven't made up my mind yet. But if we do get going it will be next month.'

Parker chewed the stem of his pipe, apparently unaware it had gone out. At last he looked up, bright-eyed. 'All right, I'll do it. Sally'll give me hell, I expect.' He grinned. 'Best not to tell her, Doctor. I'll cook up a yarn for her.' He scratched his head. 'I must see me old Navy mates an' see

51

if I can get hold of a service manual for the Mark XI – there ought to be some still knockin' around. I'll need that if I'm goin' to redesign the circuits.'

'Do that,' said Warren. 'I'd better tell you what it's all about.'

'No!' said Parker. 'I've got the general drift. If this is goin' to be dangerous then the less I know the better for you. When the time comes you tell me what to do an' I'll do it – if I can.'

Warren asked sharply, 'Any chance of failure?'

'Could be – but if I get all I ask for then I think it can be done. The Mark XI's a nice bit o' machinery – it shouldn't be too hard to make it do the impossible.' He grinned. 'What made you think o' goin' about it this way? Tired of treatin' new addicts?'

'Something like that,' said Warren.

He left Parker buzzing happily to himself about batteries and circuits and with a caution that this was not a firm commitment. But he knew that in spite of his insistence that the arrangements were purely tentative the commitment was hardening.

IV

He telephoned Andrew Tozier. 'Can I call on you for some support tonight, Andy?'

'Sure, Doc; moral or muscular?'

'Maybe a bit of both. I'll see you at the Howard Club – know where that is?'

'I know,' said Tozier. 'You could choose a better place to lose your money, Doc; it's as crooked as a dog's hind leg.'

'I'm gambling, Andy,' said Warren. 'But not with money. Stick in the background, will you? I'll call on you if I need you. I'll be there at ten o'clock.'

'I get the picture; you just want some insurance.'

'That's it,' said Warren, and rang off.

The Howard Club was in Kensington, discreetly camouflaged in one of the old Victorian terraced houses. Unlike the Soho clubs, there were no flashing neon signs proclaiming blackjack and roulette because this was no cheap operation. There were no half-crown chips to be bought in the Howard Club

Just after ten o'clock Warren strolled through the gambling rooms towards the bar. He was coolly aware of the professional interest aroused by his visit; the doorkeeper had picked up an internal telephone as he walked in and the news would be quick in reaching the higher echelons. He watched the roulette for a moment, and thought sardonically, *If I were James Bond I'd be in there making a killing*.

At the bar he ordered a Scotch and when the barman placed it before him a flat American voice said, 'That will be on the house, Dr Warren.'

Warren turned to find John Follet, the manager of the club, standing behind him. 'What are you doing so far west?' asked Follet. 'If you're looking for any of your lost sheep you won't find them here. We don't like them.'

Warren understood very well that he was being warned. It had happened before that some of his patients had tried to make a quick fortune to feed the habit. They had not succeeded, of course, and things had got out of hand, ending in a brawl. The management of the Howard Club did not like brawls – they lowered the plushy tone of the place – and word had been passed to Warren to keep his boys in line.

He smiled at Follet. 'Just sightseeing, Johnny.' He lifted the glass. 'Join me?'

Follet nodded to the barman, and said, 'Well, it's nice to see you, anyway.'

He would not feel that way for long, thought Warren. He said, 'These are patients you're talking about, Johnny; they're sick people. I don't rule them – I'm not a leader or anything like that.'

'That's as may be,' said Follet. 'But once your hopheads go on a toot they can do more damage than you'd believe possible. And if anyone can control them, it's you.'

'I've passed around the word that they're not welcome here,' said Warren. 'That's all I can do.'

Follet nodded shortly. 'I understand, Doctor. That's good enough for me.'

Warren looked about the room and saw Andrew Tozier standing at the nearest blackjack table. He said casually, 'You seem to be doing well.'

Follet snorted. 'You can't do well in this crazy country. Now we're having to play the wheel without a zero and that's goddam impossible. No club can operate without an edge.'

'I don't know,' said Warren. 'It's an equal chance for you and the customer, so that's square. And you make your profit on the club membership, the bar and the restaurant.'

'Are you crazy?' demanded Follet. 'It just doesn't work that way. In any game of equal chances a lucky rich man will beat hell out of a lucky poor man any time. Bernoulli figured that out back in 1713 – it's called the St Petersburg paradox.' He gestured towards a roulette table. 'That wheel carries a nut of fifty thousand pounds – but how much do you think the customers are worth? We're in the position of playing a game of equal chances against the public – which can be regarded as infinitely rich. In the long run we get trimmed but good.'

'I didn't know you were a mathematician,' said Warren.

'Any guy in this racket who doesn't understand mathematics goes broke fast,' said Follet. 'And it's about time your British legislators employed a few mathematicians.' He scowled. 'Another thing – take that blackjack table; at one time it was banned because it was called a game of chance. Now that games of chance are legal they still want to ban it because a good player can beat a bad player. They don't know what in hell they want.'

'Can a good player win at blackjack?' asked Warren interestedly.

Follet nodded. 'It takes a steeltrap memory and nerves of iron, but it can be done. It's lucky for the house there aren't too many of those guys around. We'll take that risk on blackjack but on the wheel we've got to have an edge.' He looked despondently into his glass. 'And I don't see much chance of getting one – not with the laws that are in the works.'

'Things are bad all round,' said Warren unfeelingly. 'Maybe you'd better go back to the States.'

'No, I'll ride it out here for a while.' Follet drained his glass.

'Don't go,' said Warren. 'I had a reason for coming here. I wanted to talk to you.'

'If it's a touch for your clinic I'm already on your books.'

Warren smiled. 'This time I want to give *you* money.'

'This I must stick around to hear,' said Follet. 'Tell me more.'

'I have a little expedition planned,' said Warren. 'The pay isn't much – say, two-fifty a month for six months. But there'll be a bonus at the end if it all works out all right.'

'Two-fifty a month!' Follet laughed. 'Look around you and figure how much I'm making right now. Pull the other one, Doctor.'

'Don't forget the bonus,' said Warren calmly.

'All right; what's the bonus?' asked Follet, smiling.

'That would be open to negotiation, but shall we say a thousand?'

'You kill me, Warren, you really do – the way you make jokes with a straight face.' He began to turn away. 'I'll be seeing you, Doctor.'

55

'Don't go, Johnny. I'm confident you'll join me. You see, I know what happened to that Argentinian a couple of months ago – and I know how it was done. It was a little over two hundred thousand pounds you rooked him of, wasn't it?'

Follet stopped dead and turned his head to speak over his shoulder. 'And how did you learn about that?'

'A good story like that soon gets around, Johnny. You and Kostas were very clever.'

Follet turned back to Warren and said seriously, 'Dr Warren: I'd be very careful about the way you talk – especially about Argentinian millionaires. Something might happen to you.'

'I dare say,' agreed Warren. 'And something might happen to you too, Johnny. For instance, if the Argentinian were to find out how he'd been had, he'd raise a stink, wouldn't he? He'd certainly go to the police. It's one thing to lose and quite another to be cheated, so he'd go to the police.' He tapped Follet on the chest. 'And the police would come to you, Johnny. The best that could happen would be that they'd deport you – ship you back to the States. Or would it be the best? I hear that the States is a good place for Johnny Follet to keep away from right now. It was something about certain people having long memories.'

'You hear too damn' much,' said Follet coldly.

'I get around,' said Warren with a modest smile.

'It seems you do. You wouldn't be trying to put the bite on me, would you?'

'You might call it that.'

Follet sighed. 'Warren, you know how it is. I have a fifteen per cent piece of this place – I'm not the boss. Whatever was done to the Argentinian was done by Kostas. Sure, I was around when it happened, but it wasn't my idea – I wasn't in on it, and I got nothing out of it. Kostas did everything.'

'I know,' said Warren. 'You're as pure as the driven snow. But it won't make much difference when they put you on a VC-10 and shoot you back to the States.' He paused and said contemplatively. 'It might even be possible to arrange for a reception committee to meet you at Kennedy Airport.'

'I don't think I like any of this,' said Follet tightly. 'Supposing I told Kostas you were shooting your mouth. What do you suppose would happen to you? I've never had a beef against you, and I don't see why you're doing this. Just watch it.'

As he turned away, Warren said, 'I'm sorry, Johnny; it seems as though you'll be back in the States before the month's out.'

'That does it,' said Follet violently. 'Kostas is a bad guy to cross. Watch out for your back, Warren.' He snapped his fingers and a man who was lounging against the wall suddenly tautened and walked over to the bar. Follet said, 'Dr Warren is just leaving.'

Warren glanced over at Andy Tozier and held up a finger. Tozier strolled over and said pleasantly, 'Evening, all.'

'Johnny Follet wants to throw me out,' said Warren.

'Does he?' said Tozier interestedly. 'And how does he propose to do that? Not that it matters very much.'

'Who the hell's this?' snapped Follet.

'Oh, I'm a friend of Dr Warren,' said Tozier. 'Nice place you've got here, Follet. It should be an interesting exercise.'

'What are you talking about? What exercise?'

'Oh, just to see how quickly it could be taken apart. I know a couple of hearty sergeant types who could go through here like a dose of salts in less than thirty minutes. The trouble about that, though, is that you'd have a hell of a job putting back the pieces.' His voice hardened. 'My advice to you is that if Dr Warren wants to talk to you, then you pin back your hairy ears and listen.'

Follet took a deep breath and blew out his cheeks. 'All right, Steve; I'll sort this out,' he said to the man next to him. 'But stick around – I might need you fast.' The man nodded and returned to his position against the wall.

'Let's all have a nice, soothing drink,' suggested Tozier.

'I don't get any of this,' protested Follet. 'Why are you pushing me, Warren? I've never done anything to you.'

'And you won't, either,' observed Warren. 'In particular you won't say anything about this to Kostas because if anything happens to me all my information goes directly to the places where it will do most good.'

Tozier said, 'I don't know what this is all about, but if anything happens to Dr Warren then a certain Johnny Follet will wish he'd never been born, whatever else happens to him.'

'What the hell are you ganging up on me for?' said Follet desperately.

'I don't know,' said Tozier. 'Why are we ganging up on him, Doc?'

'All you have to do is to take a holiday, Johnny,' said Warren. 'You come with me to the Middle East, help me out on a job, and then come back here. And everything will be as it was. Personally, I don't care how much money you loot from Argentinian millionaires. I just want to get a job done.'

'But why pick on me?' demanded Follet.

'I didn't pick on you,' said Warren wearily. 'You're all I've got, damn it! I have an idea I can use a man of your peculiar talents, so you're elected. And you don't have much say about it, either – you daren't take the chance of being pushed back to the States. You're a gambler, but not that much of a gambler.'

'Okay, so you've whipsawed me,' said Follet sourly. 'What's the deal?'

'I'm running this on the "need to know" principle. You don't have to know, you just have to do – and I'll tell you when to do it.'

58

'Now, wait a goddam minute . . .'

'That's the way it is,' said Warren flatly.

Follet shook his head in bewilderment. 'This is the screwiest thing that ever happened to me.'

'If it's any comfort, brother Jonathan, I don't know what's going on, either,' said Tozier. He eyed Warren thoughtfully. 'But Doc here is showing unmistakable signs of acting like a boss, so I suppose he is the boss.'

'Then I'll give you an order,' said Warren with a tired grin. 'For God's sake, stop calling me "Doc". It could be important in the future.'

'Okay, boss,' said Tozier with a poker face.


V


Warren did not have to go out to find Mike Abbot because Mike Abbot came to him. He was leaving his rooms after a particularly hard day when he found Abbot on his doorstep. 'Anything to tell me, Doctor?' asked Abbot.

'Not particularly,' said Warren. 'What are you looking for?'

'Just the usual – all the dirt on the drug scene.' Abbot fell into step beside Warren. 'For instance, what about Hellier's girl?'

'Whose girl?' said Warren with a blank face.

'Sir Robert Hellier, the film mogul – and don't go all po-faced. You know who I mean. The inquest was bloody uninformative – the old boy had slammed down the lid and screwed it tight. It's amazing what you can do if you have a few million quid. Was it accidental or suicide – or was she pushed?'

'Why ask me?' said Warren. 'You're the hotshot reporter.'

Abbot grinned. 'All I know is what I write for the papers

59

– but I have to get it from somewhere or someone. This time the someone is you.'

'Sorry, Mike – no comment.'

'Oh well; I tried,' said Abbot philosophically. 'Why are we passing this pub? Come in and I'll buy you a drink.'

'All right,' said Warren. 'I could do with one. I've had a hard day.'

As they pushed open the door Abbot said, 'All your days seem to be hard ones, judging by the way you've been knocking it back lately.' They reached the counter, and he said, 'What'll you have?'

'I'll have a Scotch,' said Warren. 'And what the devil do you mean by that crack?'

'No harm meant,' said Abbot, raising his hands in mock fright. 'Just one of my feebler non-laughter-making jokes. It's just that I've seen you around inhaling quite a bit of the stuff. In a pub in Soho and a couple of nights later in the Howard Club.'

'Have you been following me?' demanded Warren.

'Christ, no!' said Abbot. 'It was just coincidental.' He ordered the drinks. 'All the same, you seem to move in rum company. I ask myself – what is the connection between a doctor of medicine, a professional gambler and a mercenary soldier? And you know what? I get no answer at all.'

'One of these days that long nose of yours will get chopped off at the roots.' Warren diluted his whisky with Malvern water.

'Not as bad as losing face,' said Abbot. 'I make my reputation by asking the right questions. For instance, why should the highly respected Dr Warren have a flaming row with Johnny Follet? It was pretty obvious, you know.'

'You know how it is,' said Warren tiredly. 'Some of my patients had been cutting up ructions at the Howard Club. Johnny didn't like it.'

'And you had to take your own private army to back you up?' queried Abbot. 'Tell me another fairy tale.' The barman was looking at him expectantly so Abbot paid him, and said, 'We'll have another round.' He turned back to Warren, and said, 'It's all right, Doctor; it's on the expense account – I'm working.'

'So I see,' said Warren drily. Even now he had not made up his mind about Hellier's proposition. All the moves he had made so far had been tentative and merely to ensure that he could assemble a team if he had to. Mike Abbot was a putative member of the team – Warren's choice – but it seemed that he was dealing himself in, anyway.

'I know this is a damnfool question to ask a pressman,' he said. 'But how far can you keep a secret?'

Abbot cocked an eyebrow. 'Not very far. Not so far as to allow someone to beat me to a story. You know how cutthroat Fleet Street is.'

Warren nodded. 'But how independent are you? I mean, do you have to report on your investigations to anyone on your paper? Your editor, perhaps?'

'Usually,' said Abbot. 'After all, that's where my pay cheque comes from.' Wise in the way of interviews, he waited for Warren to make the running.

Warren refused to play the game. 'That's a pity,' he said, and fell silent.

'Oh, come now,' said Abbot. 'You can't just leave it all at that. What's on your mind?'

'I'd like you to help me – but not if it's going to be noised about the newspaper offices. You know what a rumour factory your crowd is. You'll know what the score is, but no one else must – or we'll come a cropper.'

'I can't see my editor buying that,' observed Abbot. 'It's too much like that character in the South Sea Bubble who was selling shares in a company – "but nobody to know what it is." I suppose it's something to do with drugs?'

'That's right,' said Warren. 'It will involve a trip to the Middle East.'

Abbot brightened. 'That sounds interesting.' He

drummed his fingers on the counter. 'Is there a real story in it?'

'There's a story. It might be a very big one indeed.'

'And I get an exclusive?'

'It'll be yours,' said Warren. 'Full rights.'

'How long will it take?'

'That is something I don't know.' Warren looked him in the eye. 'I don't even know if it's going to start. There's a lot of uncertainty. Say, three months.'

'A hell of a long time,' commented Abbot, and brooded for a while. Eventually he said, 'I've got a holiday coming up. Supposing I talk to my editor and tell him that I'm doing a bit of private enterprise in my own time. If I think it's good enough I'll stay on the job when my holiday is up. He might accept that.'

'Keep my name out of it,' warned Warren.

'Sure.' Abbot drained his glass. 'Yes, I think he'll fall for it. The shock of my wanting to work on my holiday ought to be enough.' He put down the glass on the counter. 'But I'll need convincing first.'

Warren ordered two more drinks. 'Let's sit at a table, and I'll tell you enough to whet your appetite.'


VI

The shop was in Dean Street and the neatly gold-lettered sign read: SOHO THERAPY CENTRE. Apart from that there was nothing to say what was done on the premises; it looked like any Dean Street shop with the difference that the windows were painted over in a pleasant shade of green so that it was impossible to see inside.

Warren opened the door, found no one in sight, and walked through into a back room which had been turned into an office. He found a dishevelled young man sitting at a desk and going through the drawers, pulling everything out and piling the papers into an untidy heap on top of the desk. As Warren walked in, he said, 'Where have you been, Nick? I've been trying to get hold of you.'

Warren surveyed the desk. 'What's the trouble, Ben?'

'You'd never believe it if I told you,' said Ben Bryan. He scrabbled about in the papers. 'I'll have to show you. Where the devil is it?'

Warren dumped a pile of books off a chair and sat down. 'Take it easy,' he advised. 'More haste, less speed.'

'Take it easy? Just wait until you see this. You won't be taking it as easy as you are now.' Bryan rummaged some more and papers scattered.

'Perhaps you'd better just tell me,' suggested Warren.

'All right . . . no, here it is. Just read that.'

Warren unfolded the single sheet of paper. What was written on it was short and brutally to the point. 'He's throwing you out?' Warren felt a rage growing within him. 'He's throwing *us* out?' He looked up. 'Can he break the lease like that?'

'He can – and he will,' said Bryan. 'There's a line of fine print our solicitor didn't catch, damn him.'

Warren was angrier than he had ever been in his life. In a choked voice he said, 'There's a telephone under all that junk – dig it out.'

'It's no good,' said Bryan. 'I've talked to him. He said he didn't realize the place would be used by drug addicts; he says his other tenants are complaining – they say it lowers the tone of the neighbourhood.'

'God Almighty!' yelled Warren. 'One's a strip joint and the other sells pornography. What the hell have they to complain of? What stinking hypocrisy!'

'We're going to lose our boys, Nick. If they don't have a place to come to, we'll lose the lot.'

Ben Bryan was a psychologist working in the field of drug addiction. Together with Warren and a couple of medical students he had set up the Soho Therapy Centre as a means of getting at the addicts. Here the addicts could talk to people who understood the problem and many had been referred to Warren's clinic. It was a place off the streets where they could relax, a hygienic place where they could take their shots using sterile water and aseptic syringes.

'They'll be out on the streets again,' said Bryan. 'They'll be taking their shots in the Piccadilly lavatories, and the cops will chase them all over the West End.'

Warren nodded. 'And the next thing will be another outbreak of hepatitis. Good God, that's the last thing we want.'

'I've been trying to find another place,' said Bryan. 'I was on the telephone all day yesterday. Nobody wants to know our troubles. The word's got around, and I think we're black-listed. It must be in this area – you know that.'

Something exploded within Warren. 'It will be,' he said with decision. 'Ben, how would you like a really good place here in Soho? Completely equipped, regardless of expense, down to hot and cold running footmen?'

'I'd settle for what we have now,' said Bryan.

Warren found an excitement rising within him. 'And, Ben – that idea you had – the one about a group therapy unit as a self-governing community on the lines of that Californian outfit. What about that?'

'Have you gone off your little rocker?' asked Bryan. 'We'd need a country house for that. Where would we get the funds?'

'We'll get the funds,' said Warren with confidence. 'Excavate that telephone.'

His decision was made and all qualms gone. He was tired of fighting the stupidity of the public, of which the queasiness of this narrow-gutted landlord was only a single example. If the only way to run his job was to turn into a synthetic James Bond, then a James Bond he'd be.

But it was going to cost Hellier an awful of money.

# 3

Warren was ushered into Hellier's office in Wardour Street after passing successfully a hierarchy of secretaries, each more svelte than the last. When he finally penetrated into the inner sanctum, Hellier said, 'I really didn't expect to see you, Doctor. I expected I'd have to chase you. Sit down.'

Warren came to the point abruptly. 'You mentioned unlimited funds, but I take that to be a figure of speech. How unlimited?'

'I'm pretty well breeched,' said Hellier with a smile. 'How much do you want?'

'We'll come to that. I'd better outline the problem so that you can get an idea of its magnitude. When you've absorbed that you might decide you can't afford it.'

'We'll see,' said Hellier. His smile broadened.

Warren laid down a folder. 'You were right when you said I had particular knowledge, but I warn you I don't have much – two names and a place – and all the rest is rumour.' He smiled sourly. 'It isn't ethics that has kept me from going to the police – it's the sheer lack of hard facts.'

'Leaving aside your three facts, what about the rumour? I've made some damned important decisions on nothing but rumour, and I've told you I get paid for making the right decisions.'

Warren shrugged. 'It's all a bit misty – just stuff I've picked up in Soho. I spend a lot of time in Soho – in the West End generally – it's where most of my patients hang out. It's convenient for the all-night chemist in Piccadilly,' he said sardonically.

'I've seen them lining up,' said Hellier.

'In 1968 a drug ring was smashed in France – a big one. You must realize that the heroin coming into Britain is just a small leakage from the more profitable American trade. This particular gang was smuggling to the States in large quantities, but when the ring was smashed we felt the effects here. The boys were running around like chickens with their heads chopped off – the illegal supply had stopped dead.'

'Wait a minute,' said Hellier. 'Are you implying that to stop the trade into Britain it would be necessary to do the same for the States?'

'That's virtually the position if you attack it at the source, which would be the best way. One automatically implies the other. I told you the problem was big.'

'The ramifications are more extensive than I thought,' admitted Hellier. He shrugged. 'Not that I'm chauvinistic about it; as you say, it's an international problem.'

Hellier still did not seem to be disturbed about the probable cost to his pocket, so Warren went on: 'I think the best way of outlining the current rumours is to look at the problem backwards, so to speak – beginning at the American end. A typical addict in New York will buy his shot from a pusher as a "sixteenth" – meaning a sixteenth of an ounce. He must buy it from a pusher because he can't get it legally, as in England. That jerks up the price, and his sixteenth will cost him somewhere between six and seven dollars. His average need will be two shots a day.'

Hellier's mind jerked into gear almost visibly. After a moment he said, 'There must be a devil of a lot of heroin going into the States.'

'Not much,' said Warren. 'Not in absolute bulk. I daresay the illegal intake is somewhere between two and three tons a year. You see, the heroin as sold to the addict is diluted with an inert soluble filler, usually lactose – milk sugar. Depending on whether he's being cheated – and he

66

usually is – the percentage of heroin will range from one-half to two per cent. I think you could take a general average of one per cent.'

Hellier was figuring again. He drew forward a sheet of paper and began to calculate. 'If there's a sixteen-hundredth of an ounce of pure heroin in a shot, and the addicts pay, say, $6.50 . . .' He stopped short. 'Hell, that's over $10,000 an ounce!'

'Very profitable,' agreed Warren. 'It's big business over there. A pound of heroin at the point of consumption is worth about $170,000. Of course, that's not all profit – the problem is to get it to the consumer. Heroin is ultimately derived from the opium poppy, *papaver somniferum*, which is not grown in the States for obvious reasons. There's a chain of production – from the growing of the poppy to raw opium; from the opium to morphine; from morphine to heroin.'

'What's the actual cost of production?' asked Hellier.

'Not much,' said Warren. 'But that's not the issue. At the point of consumption in the States a pound of heroin is worth $170,000; at the point of the wholesaler *inside* the States it's worth $50,000; at any point outside the States it's worth $20,000. And if you go right back along the chain you can buy illicit raw opium in the Middle East for $50 a pound.'

'That tells me two things,' said Hellier thoughtfully. 'There are high profits to be made at each stage – and the cost at any point is directly related to the risks involved in smuggling.'

'That's it,' said Warren. 'So far the trade has been fragmented, but rumour has it that a change is on the way. When the French gang was busted it left a vacuum and someone else is moving in – and moving in with a difference. The idea seems to be that this organization will cut out the middlemen – they'll start with the growing of the poppy and end up with the delivery *inside* the States of small lots in any given city. A guaranteed delivery on that basis should net them $50,000 a pound after expenses have been met. That last stage – getting the stuff into the States – is a high risk job.'

'Vertical integration,' said Hellier solemnly. 'These people are taking hints from big business. Complete control of the product.'

'If this comes off, and they can sew up the States, we can expect an accelerated inflow into Britain. The profits are much less, but they're still there, and the boys won't neglect the opportunity.' Warren gestured with his hand. 'But this is all rumour. I've put it together from a hundred whispers on the grapevine.'

Hellier laid his hands flat on the desk. 'So now we come to your facts,' he said intently.

'I don't know if you could dignify them by that name,' said Warren tiredly. 'Two names and a place. George Speering is a pharmaceutical chemist with a lousy reputation. He got into trouble last year in a drug case, and the Pharmaceutical Society hammered him. He was lucky to escape a jail sentence.'

'They . . . er . . . unfrocked him?'

'That's right. This crowd will need a chemist and I heard his name mentioned. He's still in England and I'm keeping an eye on him as well as I can, but I expect him to go abroad soon.'

'Why soon? And how soon?'

Warren tapped the desk calendar. 'The opium crop isn't in yet, and it won't be for a month. But morphine is best extracted from fresh opium, so as soon as this gang have enough of the stuff to work on then Speering will get busy.'

'Perhaps we should keep a closer watch on Speering.'

Warren nodded. 'He still seems to be taking it pretty easy at the moment. And he's in funds, so he's probably on a retainer. I agree he should be watched.'

'And the other name?' enquired Hellier.

'Jeanette Delorme. I've never heard of her before. She sounds as though she could be French, but that doesn't mean much in the Middle East, if that's where she hangs out. But I don't even know that. I don't know anything about her at all. It was just a name that came up in connection with Speering.'

Hellier scribbled on a piece of paper. 'Jeanette Delorme.' He looked up. 'And the place?'

'Iran,' said Warren briefly.

Hellier looked disappointed. 'Well, that's not much.'

'I never said it was,' said Warren irritatedly. 'I thought of giving it to the police but, after all, what had I to give them?'

'They could pass it on to Interpol. Maybe they could do something.'

'You've been making too many television pictures,' said Warren abrasively. 'And believing them, at that! Interpol is merely an information centre and doesn't initiate any executive work. Supposing the word was passed to the Iranian police. No police force is incorruptible, and I wouldn't take any bets at all on the cops in the Middle East – although I hear the Iranians are better than most.'

'I appreciate your point.' Hellier was silent for a moment. 'Our best bet would appear to be this man, Speering.'

'Then you're willing to go on with it on the basis of the little information I have?'

Hellier was surprised. 'Of course!'

Warren took some papers from his file. 'You might change your mind when you see these. It's going to cost you a packet. You said I could pick a team. I've been making commitments on your behalf which you'll have to honour.' He pushed two sheets across the desk. 'You'll find the details there – who the men are, what they'll cost, and some brief biographical details.'

Hellier scanned the papers rapidly and said abruptly, 'I agree to these rates of pay. I also agree to the bonus of

£5,000 paid to each man on the *successful* completion of the venture.' He looked up. 'No success – no bonus. Fair enough?'

'Fair enough – but it depends on what you mean by success.'

'I want this gang smashed,' said Hellier in a harsh voice. 'Smashed totally.'

Warren said wryly, 'If we're going to do anything at all that is implied.' He pushed another paper across the desk. 'But we haven't come to my price.'

Hellier picked it up and, after a moment, said, 'Humph! What the devil do you want with a property in Soho? They come damned expensive.'

Warren explained, with feeling, the trouble the Soho Therapy Centre had run into. Hellier chuckled. 'Yes, people are damned hypocrites. I'd have probably been the same before . . . well, never mind that.' He got up and went to the window. 'Would a place in Wardour Street do?'

'That would be fine.'

'The company has a place just across the road here. We were using it as a warehouse but that's been discontinued. It's empty now and a bit run down, but it may suit you.' He returned to his desk. 'We were going to sell it, but I'll let you have it at a peppercorn rent and reimburse the company out of my own funds.'

Warren, who had not yet finished with him, nodded briefly and pushed yet another paper across the desk. 'And that's my bonus on the *successful* completion of the job.' Ironically he emphasized the operative word in mockery of Hellier.

Hellier glanced at the wording and nearly blew up. '*A twenty-bedroomed country house*! What the devil's this?' He glared at Warren. 'Your services come high, Doctor.'

'You asked for blood,' said Warren. 'That's a commodity with a high price. When we go into this we'll come smack into opposition with a gang who'll fight because the prize could run into millions. I think there'll be blood shed somewhere along the line – either ours or theirs. You want the blood – you pay for it.'

'By making you Lord of the Manor?' asked Hellier cynically.

'Not me – a man called Ben Bryan. He wants to establish a self-governing community for addicts; to get them out of circulation to start with, and to get them to act in a responsible manner. It's an idea which has had fair results in the States.'

'I see,' said Hellier quietly. 'All right; I accept that.'

He began to read the brief biographies of the team, and Warren said casually, 'None of those people really know what they're getting into. Suppose we come into possession of, say, a hundred pounds of heroin – that would be worth a lot of money. I don't know whether I'd trust Andy Tozier with it – probably not. I certainly wouldn't trust Johnny Follet.'

Hellier turned a page and, after a while, lifted his head. 'Are you *serious* about this – about these men you've picked? Good God, half of them are villains and the other half incomprehensible.'

'What kind of men did you expect?' asked Warren. 'This can't be done by a crowd of flag-waving saints. But not one of those men is in it for the money – except Andy Tozier. They all have their own reasons.' He took a sour look at himself and thought of Follet. 'I discover I have an unexpected talent for blackmail and coercion.'

'I can understand you picking Tozier – the professional soldier,' said Hellier. 'But Follet – a gambler?'

'Johnny is a man of many parts. Apart from being a gambler he's also a successful con man. He can think up ways of pulling money from your pocket faster than you can think up ways of stopping him. It seems to me that his talents could be used on other things than money.'

'If you put it that way I suppose it seems reasonable,' said Hellier in an unconvinced voice. 'But this man, Abbot – a newspaperman, for God's sake! I won't have that.'

'Yes, you will,' said Warren flatly. 'He's on to us, anyway, and I'd rather have him working for us than against us. He was on my original list, but he dealt himself in regardless and it would be too risky to leave him out now. He's got a good nose, better than any detective, and that's something we need.'

'I suppose that seems reasonable, too,' said Hellier glumly. 'But what doesn't seem reasonable is this man, Parker. I can't see anything here that's of use to us.'

'Dan's the only really honest man among the lot of them,' said Warren. He laughed. 'Besides, he's my insurance policy.'


## II


Hellier propounded some of the philosophy of the film business. 'Most countries – especially the poorer ones – like film companies. The boys at the top like us because we're not too stingy with our bribes. The man in the street likes us because on location we pay exceptionally high rates, by local standards, for colourfully-dressed extras. We don't mind because, when all's said and done, we're paying a damned sight less than we would at home.'

He hefted a large book, foolscap size and neatly bound. 'This is a screen play we've had on the shelf for some time. About half the scenes are set in Iran. I've decided to resurrect it, and we're going to make the film. You and your team will be employed by us. You'll be an advance team sent out to Iran by us to scout out good locations – that gives you an excuse for turning up everywhere and anywhere. How does that suit you?'

'I like it,' said Warren. 'It's a good cover.'

'You'll be provided with vehicles and all the usual junk that goes with an advance team,' said Hellier. 'Give me a list of anything else you might need.' He flicked through the pages of the script. 'Who knows? We might even make the picture,' he said sardonically.

Andy Tozier approached Warren. 'You're keeping me too much in the dark,' he complained. 'I'd like to know what I'm getting into. I don't know what to prepare for.'

'Prepare for the worst,' said Warren unhelpfully.

'That's no bloody answer. Is this going to be a military thing?'

Warren said carefully, 'Let's call it paramilitary.'

'I see. A police action – with shooting.'

'But unofficial,' said Warren. 'There might be shooting.'

Tozier stroked the edge of his jaw. 'I don't like that unofficial bit. And if I'm going to be shot at I'd like to have something handy to shoot back with. How do we arrange that?'

'I don't know,' said Warren. 'I thought I'd leave that to you. You're the expert.' Tozier made a rude noise, and Warren said, 'I don't really know what we're going to get into at the other end. It's all a bit difficult.'

Tozier pondered. 'What vehicles are they giving us?'

'A couple of new Land-Rovers. They'll be flown out to Iran with us. The country out there is pretty rough.'

'And the equipment we're getting. What does it consist of?'

'It's all part of our cover. There are some still cameras with a hell of a lot of lenses. A couple of 16-millimetre movie cameras. A video-tape outfit. A hell of a lot of stuff I can't put a name to.'

'Are there tripods with the movie cameras?' Warren nodded, and Tozier said, 'Okay, I'd like to have the Land-Rovers and all the equipment delivered to me as soon as possible. I might want to make a few modifications.'

'You can have them tomorrow.'

'And I'd like some boodle from this money mine you seem to have discovered – at least a thousand quid. My modifications come expensive.'

'I'll make it two thousand,' said Warren equably. 'You can have that tomorrow, too.'

'Johnny Follet might be more useful than I thought,' said Tozier thoughtfully. 'He knows his weapons – he was in Korea.'

'Was he? Then he'll get on well with Dan Parker.'

Tozier jerked his head. 'And who is Dan Parker?'

Warren grinned. 'You'll meet him sometime,' he promised.

'I'm coming with you,' said Ben Bryan when Warren told him of what was happening.

'And why would we need a psychiatrist?' asked Warren.

Bryan grinned. 'To inject a modicum of sanity. This is the craziest thing I've ever heard.'

'If you join us you'll be as mad as we are. Still, you might come in useful.' He looked at Bryan speculatively, then said, 'I think you'd better be in the main party. Mike Abbot can go with Parker.'

'What's he going to do?'

'He's our Trojan Horse – if we can find the Delorme woman – and that's proving to be a hell of a problem. Hellier has a team in Paris going through birth certificates, pulling out all the Jeanette Delormes and running them down. They've found eight already. On the off-chance she was born in Switzerland he has another team there.'

'Supposing she was born in Martinique?' asked Bryan.

'We can only try the obvious first,' said Warren. 'Hellier's investigators are good – I know because they did a bang-up job on me. Anyway, he's spending money as though he has his own printing press. We're already into him for over

£70,000.' He grinned. 'Still, that's only a couple of years' upkeep on his yacht.'

'I've never heard of a rich man really keen to part with his money,' said Bryan. 'You must have knocked the props clean from under him. You made him take a look at himself – a good, clear-eyed look – and he didn't like what he saw. I wish I could do the same to some of my patients. Perhaps you should change your profession.'

'I have – I'm in the business of raising private armies.'

Everything seemed to happen at once.

It may have been luck or it may have been good investigative practice, but the Delorme woman was traced, not through the patient sifting of birth certificates, but from a pipeline into the French Sûreté. It seemed that Mike Abbot had a friend who had a friend who . . .

Hellier tossed a file over to Warren. 'Read that and tell me what you think.'

Warren settled back in his chair and opened the folder.

*Jeanette Véronique Delorme: Born April 12, 1937 at Chalons. Parents . . .*

He skipped the vital statistics in order to come to the meat of it.

*'. . . three months' imprisonment in 1955 for minor fraud; six months' imprisonment in 1957 for smuggling over Franco-Spanish border; left France in 1958.'*

Then followed what could only be described as a series of hypotheses.

*Believed to have been involved in smuggling from Tangier to Spain, 1958–1960; smuggling arms to Algeria, 1961–1963; smuggling drugs into Italy and Switzerland, 1963–1967. Believed to have been implicated in the murders of Henry Rowe (American) 1962; Kurt Schlesinger (German), Ahmed ben*

*Bouza (Algerian) and Jean Fouget (French) 1963; Kamer Osman (Lebanese) and Pietro Fuselli (Italian) 1966.*

*Operational Characteristics: Subject is good organizer and capable of controlling large groups; is ruthless and intolerant of errors; is careful not to become personally involved in smuggling activities, but may have been director of large-scale jewel thefts, south of France, 1967. This, however, may be considered doubtful.*

*Present Whereabouts: Beirut, Lebanon.*

*Present Status: Not wanted for crime in Metropolitan France.*

There were a couple of smudgy photographs which had not survived the copying process at all well, but which showed a blonde of indeterminate age.

Warren blew out his cheeks. 'What a hell-cat she must be.' He tapped the folder. 'I think this is the one – everything fits.'

'I think so, too,' said Hellier. 'I've stopped everything else and narrowed it down to her. A man has already flown out to Beirut to pinpoint her.'

'I hope someone has told him to be careful,' said Warren.

'He just has to find out where she lives and . . . er . . . her standing in the community. That shouldn't be too risky. Then he pulls out and you take over.'

'I'll get Dan Parker out there as soon as we know something definite. Mike Abbot will support him – I'm not sure Dan could pull it off on his own. This might need the sophisticated touch. Oh, and we have a volunteer – Ben Bryan will be joining the Iran group.'

'I'm glad to hear that Mr Bryan is going to earn his manor house,' said Hellier, a shade acidly. 'There's still nothing on your man, Speering.'

'He'll make a move soon,' said Warren with certainty. His confidence had risen because the dossier on Jeanette Delorme fitted in so tidily.

'Well, the same thing applies. There'll be an investigator

76

with him all the way – probably on the same plane if he flies. Then you'll take over.'

Speering moved two days later, and within twelve hours Warren, Tozier, Follet and Bryan were in the air in a chartered aircraft which also carried the two Land-Rovers. Parker and Abbot were already on their way to the Lebanon.

## III

It was snowing in Tehran.

Follet shivered as the sharp wind cut through his jacket. 'I thought this place was supposed to be hot.' He looked out across the airport at the sheer wall of the Elburz Mountains and then up at the cold grey sky from which scudded a minor blizzard. 'This is the Middle East?' he asked doubtfully.

'About as Middle as you can get,' said Tozier. 'Still, it's March and we're nearly five thousand feet above sea level.'

Follet turned up his collar and pulled the lapels close about his throat. 'Where the hell is Warren?'

'He's clearing the vehicles and the gear through customs.' He smiled grimly. The modifications he had made to the Land-Rovers were such that if they were discovered then all hell would break loose in the customs shed, and Warren and Bryan would find themselves tossed into jail without a quibble. But he had not told Warren what the modifications were, which was all to the good. True innocence is better than bluff when faced with the X-ray eye of the experienced customs official.

All the same he breathed more easily when Follet touched him on the shoulder and pointed. 'Here they come,' he said, and Tozier saw with relief a Land-Rover bearing down upon them. On its side it bore the neat legend: *Regent Film Company. Advance Unit.* The tension left him.

Warren poked his head through the side window. 'Ben's just behind me,' he said. 'One of you jump in.'

'Did you have any trouble?' asked Tozier.

Warren looked surprised. 'No trouble at all.'

Tozier smiled and said nothing. He walked around to the back of the vehicle and stroked one of the metal struts which held up the canopy. Follet said, 'Let me get in and out of this goddam wind. Where are we going?'

'We're booked in at the Royal Tehran Hilton. I don't know where it is but it shouldn't be too difficult to find.' He pointed to a minibus filling up with passengers, which had the name of the hotel on its side. 'We just follow that.'

Follet got in and slammed the door. He looked broodingly at the alien scene, and said abruptly, 'Just what in hell are we doing here, Warren?'

Warren glanced at the rear view mirror and saw that the other Land-Rover had arrived. 'Following a man.'

'Jeeze, you're as close-mouthed as that strongarm of yours. Or are you keeping him in the dark, too?'

'You just do as you're told, Johnny, and you'll be all right,' advised Warren.

'I'd feel a hell of a lot better if I knew what I was supposed to do,' grumbled Follet.

'Your turn will come.'

Follet laughed unexpectedly. 'You're a funny one, Warren. Let me tell you something; I like you – I really do. You had me over a barrel; you offered me a thousand when you knew I'd take peanuts. Then you raised the bonus to five thousand when you didn't have to. Why did you do that?'

Warren smiled. 'The labourer is worthy of his hire. You'll earn it.'

'Maybe I will, but I don't see how right now. Anyway, I

just wanted to say I appreciated the gesture. You can depend on me – for anything reasonable, that is,' he added hastily. 'Tozier was talking about unreasonable things – like being shot at.'

'You ought to have got used to that in Korea.'

'You know,' said Follet, 'I never did. Funny the things a man can never get used to, isn't it?'

The Royal Tehran Hilton was on the outskirts of the city, a caravanserai designed specifically for the oilmen and businessmen flocking into Iran under the impetus of the booming economy underwritten by the reforming regime of Mohammad Rezi Pahlevi, King of Kings and Light of the Aryans. It had not been an easy drive from the airport because of the propensity of the local inhabitants to regard a road as a race track. Several times Warren had been within an ace of serious trouble and when they reached the hotel he was sweating in spite of the cold.

They registered, and Warren found a message awaiting him. He waited until he was in his room before ripping open the envelope, and found but a single inscrutable line of writing: *Your room – 7.30 p.m. Lane.* He looked at his watch and decided he had just time to unpack.

At 7.29 there was a discreet knock. He opened the door and a man said, 'Mr Warren? I believe you're expecting me. My name is Lane.'

'Come in, Mr Lane,' said Warren, and held open the door wider. He studied Lane as he took off his coat; there was not much to the man – he could have been anybody – a virtue in a private detective.

Lane sat down. 'Your man is staying here at the Hilton – his reservation is for a week. He's here right now, if you want him.'

'Not alone, I trust,' said Warren.

'That's all right, Mr Warren; there are two of us on the

79

job. He's being watched.' Lane shrugged. 'But he won't move – he likes to stay close to where the bottles are.'

'He drinks a lot?'

'He may not be an alcoholic, but he's pushing it. He lives in the bar until it closes, then has a bottle sent to his room.'

Warren nodded. 'What else can you tell me about Mr Speering?'

Lane took a notebook from his pocket. 'He's been getting around. I have a list of all this stuff written up which I'll let you have, but I can tell it to you in five minutes.' He flipped open the notebook. 'He was met at the airport by one of the locals – an Iranian, I think – and brought here to the hotel. I wasn't able to nail down the Iranian; we'd just arrived and we weren't equipped,' he said apologetically.

'That's all right.'

'Anyway, we haven't seen the Iranian since. Speering went out next day to a place on Mowlavi, near the railway station. I have the address here. He came out of there with a car or, rather, an American jeep. It isn't a hire car, either – I've been trying to check on the registration, but that's a bit difficult in a strange city like this one.'

'Yes, it must be,' said Warren.

'He went from there to a firm of wholesale pharmaceutical chemists – name and address supplied – where he spent an hour and a half. Then back to the Hilton where he spent the rest of the day. That was yesterday. This morning he had a visitor – an American called John Eastman; that was up in his room. Eastman stayed all morning – three hours – then they had lunch in the Hilton dining-room.'

'Any line on Eastman?'

Lane shook his head. 'A full-time check on a man really takes four operatives – there are only two of us. We couldn't do anything about Eastman without the risk of losing Speering. Our instructions were to stick to Speering.' Lane consulted his notebook again. 'Eastman left soon after lunch today, and Speering hasn't moved since. He's down in the bar right now. That's the lot, Mr Warren.'

'I think you've done well under the circumstances,' said Warren. 'I have some friends here; I'd like to let them get a look at Speering for future reference. Can that be arranged?'

'Nothing easier,' said Lane. 'All you have to do is have a drink.' He took out an envelope which he gave to Warren. 'That's all we have on Speering; registration number of his jeep, names and addresses of the places he's been to in Tehran.' He paused. 'I understand that finishes our job – after I've pointed the man out.'

'That's right. That's all you were asked to do.'

Lane seemed relieved. 'This one's been tricky,' he confided. 'I don't have any trouble in London, and I've done jobs in Paris and Rome. But a Westerner here stands out like a sore thumb in some parts of the city and that makes following a man difficult. When do you want to see Speering?'

'Why not now?' said Warren. 'I'll collect my chaps.'

Before going into the bar Warren paused and said, 'We're here on business. Mr Lane will indicate unobtrusively the man we've come to see – and the operative word is *see*. Take a good look at him so that you'll recognize him again anywhere – but don't make it obvious. The idea is to see and not be seen. I suggest we split up.'

They crossed the foyer and went into the bar. Warren spotted Speering immediately and veered away from him. He had seen Speering on several occasions in London and, although he did not think he was known to Speering, it was best to make sure he was not observed. He turned his back on the room, leaned on the bar counter and ordered a drink.

The man next to him turned. 'Hi, there!'

Warren nodded politely. 'Good evening.'

'You with IMEG?' The man was American.

'IMEG?'

The man laughed. 'I guess not. I saw you were British and I guessed you might be with IMEG.'

'I don't even know what IMEG is,' said Warren. He looked into the mirror at the back of the bar and saw Tozier sitting at a table and ordering a drink.

'It's just about the biggest thing to hit this rathole of a country,' said the American. He was slightly drunk. 'We're reaming a forty-inch gas line right up the middle – Abadan right to the Russian border. Over six hundred million bucks' worth. Money's flowing like . . . like money.' He laughed.

'Indeed!' said Warren. He was not very interested.

'IMEG's bossing the show – that's you British. Me – I'm with Williams Brothers, who are doing the goddam work. Call that a fair division of labour?'

'It sounds like a big job,' said Warren evasively. He shifted his position and saw Follet at the other end of the bar.

'The biggest.' The American swallowed his drink. 'But the guys who are going to take the cream are the Russkis. Christ, what a set-up! They'll take Iranian gas at under two cents a therm, and they've pushed a line through to Trieste so they can sell Russian gas to the Italians at over three cents a therm. Don't tell me those Bolshevik bastards aren't good capitalists.' He nudged Warren. 'Have a drink.'

'No, thanks,' said Warren. 'I'm expecting a friend.'

'Aw, hell!' The American looked at his watch. 'I guess I've gotta eat, anyway. See you around.'

As he left, Tozier came up to the bar with his drink in his hand. 'Who's your friend?'

'A lonely drunk.'

'I've seen your man,' said Tozier. 'He looks like another drunk. What now?'

'Now we don't lose him.'

'And then?'

Warren shrugged. 'Then we find out what we find out.'

Tozier was silent for a while. He pulled out his cigarette case, lit a cigarette and blew out a long plume of smoke. 'It's not good enough, Nick. I don't like acting in the dark.'

'Sorry to hear it.'

'You'll be even sorrier when I pull out tomorrow.' Warren turned his head sharply, and Tozier said, 'I don't know what you're trying to do, but you can't run this operation by keeping everything under wraps. How the hell can I do a job if I don't know what I'm doing?'

'I'm sorry you feel that way about it, Andy. Don't you trust me?'

'Oh, I trust you. The trouble is that you don't trust me. So I'm pulling out, Nick – I'll be back in London tomorrow night. You've got something on Johnny Follet, and you might have something on Ben Bryan for all I know. But I'm clean, Nick; I'm in this for honest reasons – just for the money.'

'So stay and earn it.'

Tozier shook his head gently. 'Not without knowing what I'm getting into – and why. I told you once that I like to have something to shoot back with if someone shoots at me. I also like to know why he's shooting at me. Hell, I might approve of his reasons – I might even be on his side if I knew the score.'

Warren's hand tightened on his glass. He was being pushed into a decision. 'Andy, you do jobs for money. Would you smuggle dope for money?'

'The problem has never come up,' said Tozier reflectively. 'Nobody has ever made the proposition. Are you asking me, Nick?'

'Do I look like a dope smuggler?' said Warren in disgust.

'I don't know,' said Tozier. 'I don't know how a dope smuggler behaves. I do know that the straightest people get bent under pressure. You've been under pressure for quite some time, Nick; I've watched you struggle against it.' He drained his glass. 'Now that the question has arisen,' he said, 'the answer is no. I wouldn't smuggle dope for money. And I think you've turned into a right son of a bitch, Nick; you've tried to con me into this thing and it hasn't worked, has it?'

Warren blew out his cheeks and let the air escape in a long sigh. Internally he was cheering to the sound of trumpets. He grinned at Tozier. 'You've got the wrong end of the stick, Andy. Let me tell you about it – around the corner out of the sight of Speering.'

He took Tozier by the arm and steered him to a table and in five minutes had given him the gist of it. Tozier listened and a slightly stupefied expression appeared on his face. He said, 'And that's all you have to go on? Have you gone out of your mind?'

'It's not much,' admitted Warren. 'But it's all we have.'

Suddenly, Tozier chuckled. 'It's just mad enough to be interesting. I'm sorry if I got things wrong just now, Nick; but you were being so bloody mysterious.' He nodded ruefully. 'I can see the position you were in – you can't trust anyone in this racket. Okay, I'm with you.'

'Thanks, Andy,' said Warren quietly.

Tozier called up a waiter and ordered drinks. 'Let's get practical,' he said. 'You were right in one thing – I wouldn't let a breath of this leak out to Johnny Follet. If there's any money in it Johnny will want to cut his share, and he won't be too particular how he does it. But all the same, he's a good man to have along, and we can use him as long as you keep that stranglehold tight. What have you got on him, anyway?'

'Does it matter?'

Tozier shrugged. 'I suppose not. Now, what are your ideas on Speering?'

'He's come here to extract morphine from opium. I'm fairly sure of that,' said Warren. 'That's why he went to a

84

wholesale pharmaceutical firm yesterday. He was ordering supplies.'

'What would he need?'

'Pharmaceutical quality lime, methylene chloride, benzene, amyl alcohol and hydrochloric acid, plus a quantity of glassware.' Warren paused. 'I don't know if he intends transforming the morphine into heroin here. If he does he'll need acetic acid as well.'

Tozier frowned. 'I don't quite understand this. What's the difference between morphine and heroin?'

The drinks arrived and Warren did not reply until the waiter had gone. 'Morphine is an alkaloid extracted from opium by a relatively simple chemical process. Heroin is morphine with its molecular structure altered by an even simpler process.' He grimaced. 'That job could be done in a well-equipped kitchen.'

'But what's the difference?'

'Well, heroin is the acetylated form of morphine. It's soluble in water, which morphine is not, and since the human body mostly consists of water it gets to the spot faster. Various properties are accentuated and it's a damned sight more addictive than morphine.'

Tozier leaned back. 'So Speering is going to extract the morphine. But where? Here in Iran? And how is the morphine – or heroin – going to get to the coast? South to the Persian Gulf? Or across Iraq and Syria to the Mediterranean? We have to find out one hell of a lot of things, Nick.'

'Yes,' said Warren gloomily. 'And there's one big problem I can't see past at all. It's something I haven't even discussed with Hellier.'

'Oh! Well, you'd better spit it out.'

Warren said flatly. 'There's no opium in Iran.'

Tozier stared at him. 'I thought all these Middle East countries were rotten with the stuff.'

'They are – and so was Iran under the old Shah. But this

new boy is a reformer.' Warren leaned his elbows on the table. 'Under the old Shah things went to hell in a bucket. He was running Iran on the lines of the old Roman Empire – in order to keep in sweet with the populace he kept the price of grain down to an artificial low level. That was a self-defeating policy because the farmers found they couldn't make a living growing grain, so they planted poppies instead – a much more profitable crop. So there was less and less grain and more and more opium.' He grimaced. 'The old Shah didn't mind because he created the Opium Monopoly; there was a government tax and he got a rake-off from every pound collected.'

'A sweet story,' said Tozier.

'You haven't heard the half of it. In 1936 Iranian opium production was 1,350 metric tons. World requirements of medicinal opium were 400 tons.'

Tozier jerked. 'You mean the old bastard was smuggling the stuff.'

'He didn't need to,' said Warren. 'It wasn't illegal. He *was* the law in Iran. He just sold the stuff to anyone who had the money to pay for it. He was on to a good thing, but all good things come to an end. He pushed his luck too far and was forced to abdicate. There was a provisional government for a while, and then the present Shah took over. Now, he was a really bright boy. He wanted to drag this woebegone country into the twentieth century by the scruff of its neck, but he found that you can't have industrialism in a country where seventy-five per cent of the population are opium addicts. So he clamped down hard and fast, and I doubt if you can find an ounce of illegal opium in the country today.'

Tozier looked baffled. 'Then what is Speering doing here?'

'That's the problem,' said Warren blandly. 'But I don't propose asking him outright.'

'No,' said Tozier pensively. 'But we stick to him closer than his shirt.'

A waiter came and said enquiringly, 'Mistair Warren?'

'I'm Warren.'

'A message for you, sir.'

'Thank you,' Warren raised his eyebrows at Tozier as he tipped the waiter. A minute later he said, 'It's from Lane. Speering has given up his reservation – he's leaving tomorrow. Lane doesn't know where he's going, but his jeep has been serviced and there are water cans in the back. What do you suppose that means?'

'He's leaving Tehran,' said Tozier with conviction. 'I'd better get back to check on the trucks; I'd like to see if the radios are still in working order. We'll leave separately – give me five minutes.'

Warren waited impatiently for the time to elapse, then got up and walked out of the bar. As he passed Speering he almost stopped out of sheer surprise. Speering was sitting with Johnny Follet and they were both tossing coins.


IV


Speering headed north-west from Tehran on the road to Qazvin. 'You get ahead of him and I'll stick behind,' said Tozier to Warren. 'We'll have him like the meat in a sandwich. If he turns off the road I'll get on to you on the blower.'

They had kept an all night watch on Speering's jeep but it had been a waste of time. He had a leisurely breakfast and did not leave Tehran until ten, and with him was a sharp-featured Iranian as chauffeur. They trailed the jeep through thick traffic out of the city and once they were on the main road Warren put on a burst of speed, passed Speering, and then slowed down to keep a comfortable distance ahead. Follet, in the passenger seat, kept a sharp eye astern, using the second rear view mirror which was one of Tozier's modifications.

To the right rose the snow-capped peaks of the Elburz Mountains but all around was a featureless plain, dusty and monotonous. The road was not particularly good as far as Warren could judge, but he had been educated to more exacting standards than the Iranian driver and he reflected that by Iranian standards it was probably excellent. After all, it was the main arterial highway to Tabriz.

As soon as he became accustomed to driving the Land-Rover he said to Follet abruptly, 'You were talking to Speering last night. What about?'

'Just passing the time of day,' said Follet easily.

'Don't make a mistake, Johnny,' said Warren softly. 'You could get hurt – badly.'

'Hell, it was nothing,' protested Follet. 'It wasn't even my doing. He came over to me – what else was I expected to do besides talk to him?'

'What did you talk about?'

'This and that. Our jobs. I told him I was with Regent Films. You know – all this crap about the film we're making. He said he worked for an oil company.' He laughed. 'I took some of his money off him, too.'

'I saw you,' said Warren acidly. 'What did you use – a two-headed penny?'

Follet raised his hands in mock horror. 'As God is my judge, I didn't cheat him. You know that's not my style. I didn't have to, anyway; he was pretty near blind drunk.' His eyes flicked up to the mirror. 'Slow down a bit – we're losing him.'

From Tehran to Qazvin was nearly a hundred miles and it was almost one o'clock when they neared the outskirts of the town. As they were driving through the loudspeaker crackled into life. 'Calling Regent Two. Calling Regent Two. Over.'

Follet picked up the microphone and thumbed the switch. 'You're coming in fine, Regent One. Over.'

Tozier's voice was thin and distorted. 'Our man has stopped at a hotel. I think he's feeding his face. Over.'

'That's a damned good idea; I'm hungry myself,' said Follet, and raised an eyebrow at Warren.

'We'll pull off the road at the other side of town,' said Warren. 'Tell him that.' He carried on until he was well past the outskirts of Qazvin and then pulled up on a hard shoulder. 'There's a hamper in the back,' he said. 'I gave Ben the job of quartermaster; let's see how good he is.'

Warren felt better after chicken sandwiches and hot coffee from a flask, but Follet seemed gloomy. 'What a crummy country,' he said. 'We've travelled a hundred miles and those goddam mountains haven't changed an inch.' He pointed to a string of laden camels coming down the road. 'What's the betting we end up on the back of a thing like that?'

'We could do worse,' said Warren thoughtfully. 'I have the idea that these Land-Rovers are a shade too conspicuous for a shadowing job like this.' He picked up a map. 'I wonder where Speering is going.'

Follet looked over his shoulder. 'The next town is Zanjan – another hundred goddam miles.' He looked around. 'Christ, isn't this country horrible? Worse than Arizona.'

'You've been there?'

'Hell, I was born there. I got out by the time I was old enough to run away. I'm a city boy at heart. The bright lights for me.' He hummed a phrase of *Broadway Melody* and reached forward and took a pack of cards from the dash shelf. 'I'll be going back, too, so I'd better keep in practice.'

Warren heard the crisp flick of the cards and glanced sideways to see Follet riffle-shuffle with unbelievable dexterity, something far removed from the amateur's awkwardness. 'I thought you said you didn't cheat.'

'I don't – but I can if I have to. I'm a pretty fair card

mechanic when I want to be.' He grinned engagingly. 'It's like this; if you have a piece of a casino like I have back in London, you don't have to cheat – as long as the house has an edge. It's the edge that counts, you see. You don't suppose Monte Carlo gets by because of cheating, do you?'

'It's supposed to be an honest game.'

'It's one hundred per cent honest,' said Follet stoutly. 'As long as you have the percentages going for you then you're all right and cheating isn't necessary. I'll show you what I mean because right now I feel lucky. On this road we've been meeting about twenty cars an hour – I'll give you even money that in the next hour two of those cars will have the same last two digits in the registration number. Just a game to pass the time.'

Warren thought it out. There were a hundred possible numbers 00 to 99. If Follet restricted it to twenty cars then it seemed that the odds were on Warren's side. He said carefully, 'For the first twenty cars you're on.'

'For a hundred pounds,' said Follet calmly. 'If I win you can add it to my bonus – if and when. Okay?'

Warren breathed hard, then said, 'All right.'

The quiet hum from the loudspeaker altered as a carrier wave came on, and then Ben Bryan said, 'Calling Regent Two. Our man is getting ready to move. Over.'

Warren unhooked the microphone. 'Thanks, Regent One. We'll get moving slowly and let him catch up. The grub was pretty good, Ben; you're elected caterer for the duration. Over.'

The loudspeaker made a rude squawk and lapsed into silence. Warren grinned and pressed the self-starter. 'Keep an eye to the rear, Johnny, and tell me when Speering shows up.'

Follet produced a pen. 'You call the numbers – I'll write them down. Don't worry; I'll keep an eye on Speering.'

The game served to while away the time. It was a

monotonous drive on a montonous road and it was something for Warren to do. With Follet keeping watch to the rear there was nothing for him to do except drive and to speed up or slow down at Follet's instruction so as to keep a safe distance ahead of Speering. Besides he was tending to become sleepy and the game kept him awake.

He called out the numbers as the oncoming cars passed, and Follet scribbled them down. Although Follet's attention was, in the main, directed towards Speering, Warren noticed that once in a while he would do a spot check of a number called. He smiled – Follet would never trust anyone. When fifteen numbers had been called without duplication Warren had high hopes of winning his hundred pounds and he became more interested – this was more than a way of passing the time.

On the eighteenth number Follet suddenly said, 'That's it – number five and number eighteen are the same – thirty-nine. You lose, Warren. You've just raised my bonus by a hundred.' He put the pen back into his shirt pocket. 'That was what is known as a proposition. Another name for it is a sucket bet. You didn't have much of a chance.'

'I don't see it,' said Warren.

Follet laughed. 'That's because you're a mathematical ignoramus. You figured that because there were a hundred possibles and only twenty chances that the odds were four to one in your favour, and that I was a chump for offering evens. You were the chump because the odds were actually in my favour – no less than seven to one. It pays to understand mathematics.'

Warren thought it over. 'I still don't see it.'

'Look at it this way. If I'd bet that a *specific* number would come up twice in the first twenty then I would have been a chump. But I didn't. I said *any two numbers* in the first twenty would match.'

Warren frowned. He still did not get the point, but he had always been weak in mathematics. Follet said, 'A proposition can be defined as a bet which looks good to the sucker but which is actually in favour of the smart guy who offers it. You dig into the holes and corners of mathematics – especially probability theory – and you'll find dozens of propositions which the suckers fall for every time.'

'You won't catch me again,' said Warren.

Follet chuckled. 'Want to bet on it? It's surprising how often a sucker comes back for more. Andy Tozier fell for that one, too. He'll fall again – I'll take the whole of his bonus from him before we're through with this caper.' He glanced at the mirror. 'Slow down, will you? This road's becoming twisty.'

They drove on and on until they came to Zanjan, and Follet said, 'I see the jeep – I think he's coming through.' Two minutes later he said, 'I've lost him.'

The radio broke into life with a crackle of mid-afternoon static caused, presumably, by the stormy weather over the mountains to the west. ' . . . turned off to left . . . hotel . . . follow . . . got that? Over.'

Follet clicked a switch. 'Speering turned off to the left by the hotel and you want us to follow. Is that it, Andy? Over.'

'That's it . . . quickly . . . out.'

Warren pulled to a halt, and Follet said, 'I'll take over – you look a bit beat.'

'All right,' said Warren. They changed seats and Warren stretched his shoulders and slumped in the passenger seat. He had been driving all day and the Land-Rover was a bit harder to handle than his saloon car. They went back into Zanjan and by the hotel found a road leading off to the west; it was signposted in Arabic script which Warren could make no sense of. Follet wheeled around and Warren grabbed the maps.

The new road deteriorated rapidly and, because it was heading into the mountains, became more sinuous and tricky. Follet drove a shade faster than was absolutely safe in an effort to catch up with Tozier and Bryan, and the vehicle bumped and shuddered. At last they caught a glimpse of a dust cloud ahead. 'That should be Andy.' After a while he said, 'It's Andy, all right.' He eased the speed a little. 'I'll drop back a bit – we don't want to eat his dust from here to hell-and-gone.'

As they drove deeper into the mountains their speed dropped. The road surface was very bad, ridged in bone-jarring corrugations and washed out in places where storm-swelled freshets had swept across. The gradients became steeper and the bends tighter, so much so that Follet was forced to use the extra-low gearing that is the speciality of the Land-Rover. The day wore on to its end.

Warren had the maps on his knee attached to a clipboard and kept his eye on the compass. They were heading west-ward all the time and, after checking the map again, he said, 'We're heading into Kurdistan.' He knew that this was the traditional route for smuggling opium out of Iran into Syria and Jordan, and again he felt confident that he was right – this was more than a coincidence.

Follet turned another corner and drove down one of the few straight stretches of road. At this point the road clung to the side of a mountain with a sheer cliff on the right and an equally sheer drop on the left. 'Look at that,' he said jerkily and nodded across the valley.

The road crossed the valley and rose again to climb the side of the mountain on the other side. In the far distance a cloud of brick-red dust picked out by the sun indicated a speeding car. 'That's Speering,' said Follet. 'Andy is still in the valley bottom. If we can see Speering then he can see us. If he doesn't know we're following him then he's blind or dead drunk.'

'It can't be helped,' said Warren grimly. 'That's the way it is.'

'You can tell me something,' said Follet. 'What the hell happens at sunset? Have you thought of that?'

Warren had thought of it and it had been worrying him. He looked at his watch and estimated that there was less than an hour to go. 'We'll keep going as far as we can,' he said with no expression in his voice.

Which was not very far. Within half an hour they came upon the other Land-Rover parked by the roadside with Ben Bryan flagging them down. Just beyond him Tozier was standing, looking over the mountains. Follet halted and Warren leaned from the window. 'What's up, Ben?'

Bryan's teeth showed white against his dusty face and the mountain wind whipped his hair. 'He's beaten us, Nick. Take a look over there where Andy is.'

Warren stepped down and followed him towards Tozier who turned and said, 'You tell me which way he went.'

There were five possible exits from the rocky area on top of the plateau. 'Five roads,' said Tozier. 'You tell me which one he picked.'

'No tracks?'

'The ground is hard where it isn't naked rock.' Tozier looked about. 'This seems to be a main junction, but it isn't on the map.'

'The road we've been travelling on isn't on the map, either,' said Warren. He squatted and balanced the clipboard on his knee. 'I reckon we're about there.' He made a small cross on the map. 'About thirty miles inside Kurdistan.' He stood up and walked to the edge of the road and gazed westward to where the setting sun fitfully illuminated the storm clouds over the red mountains. 'Speering could be heading clear to the Iraqi border.'

'He won't make it tonight,' said Tozier. 'Not on these roads in these mountains. What do we do, Nick?'

'What the devil can we do?' said Warren violently. 'We've lost him right at the start of the game. It's four to one against us that we pick the right road – a sucker bet.' He suppressed his futile rage. 'We can't do much now. It's nearly dark so we'd better make camp.'

Tozier nodded. 'All right; but let's do it out of sight of any of these roads.'

'Why? What's the point?'

'No point, really.' Tozier shrugged. 'Just on general security principles. It gets to be a habit in my game.'

He walked towards the trucks leaving Warren in a depressed mood. We've blown it at this end, he thought; I hope to God that Mike and Dan have better luck. But he did not feel like betting on it – that would be another sucker bet.

# 4

'This is the life,' said Michael Abbot. He sipped from a tall frosted glass and watched with more than idle interest as a nubile girl clad in the briefest of brief bikinis stepped on to the diving-board. She flexed her knees, stood poised for a moment, and then cleft the air in a perfect swallow dive to plunge with minimum splash into the Mediterranean.

Dan Parker was unimpressed. 'We're wastin' time.'

'It can't be hurried,' said Abbot. He had talked this over with Parker before, and Dan had reluctantly agreed that this was the best way. There were two possible approaches that could be made; the approach direct, which was to introduce themselves to the Delorme woman as potential allies. The trouble with that was that if it failed then it was a complete failure with nothing to fall back upon. The approach indirect was to somehow make Delorme come to them. If it did not work within a reasonable period of time then the direct approach was indicated.

Abbot leaned forward to watch the girl who was now climbing out of the water. 'We'll get there in time.'

'So we sit around in this fancy hotel while you get pissed on those fancy drinks. Is that it?' Parker was feeling edgy. He was out of place in the Hotel Saint-Georges and he knew it.

'Take it easy, Dan,' said Abbot calmly. 'It's early days. If we can't approach her then we have to find out who her friends are – and that's what we're doing now.'

Jeanette Delorme moved in the highest Lebanese society; she lived in a de luxe villa in the mountains at Hammana, and she could afford to eat two days running at the Hotel

Saint-Georges. Getting close to her was the problem. Somehow they had to snuggle up to her and that, thought Abbot, was like snuggling up to a rattlesnake. He had read the dossier on her.

The only approach, as he saw it, was to find out who her associates were – her more disreputable associates – and then to lay out some ground bait. It was going to be very slow – much too slow for the liking of Dan Parker – but it was the only way. And so they were sitting in a discreet corner of the Hotel Saint-Georges while Delorme lunched with an unknown friend who would be checked on as soon as they parted. The previous day had been a repetition – and a bust. Her companion then had proved to be a paunchy Lebanese banker of pristine reputation and decidedly not disreputable enough for their purpose.

Abbot watched the girl step on to the diving-board again. He said suddenly, 'Do you know why this hotel is called the Saint-Georges, Dan?'

'No,' said Parker briefly in a tone which indicated that he could not care less.

Abbot waved his glass largely. 'Saint George killed the dragon right here in Beirut. So they tell me. Probably here in Saint George's Bay. But I've always thought the Christians pinched that bit from Greek mythology – Perseus and Andromeda, you know.' He gestured towards the girl on the diving-board. 'I wouldn't mind slaying a dragon myself if she were the prize.'

Parker moved restlessly in his chair, and Abbot thought he would have to do something about him. Dan would be all right once he had something to do with his hands, but this alien environment tended to unnerve him. He said, 'What's on your mind, Dan?'

'I still think this is a waste o' time.' Parker took out a handkerchief and mopped his brow. 'I wish I could have a beer. What wouldn't I give for a pint?'

'I don't see why you shouldn't have that,' said Abbot and looked about for a waiter. 'Why didn't you order one?'

'What! In this place?' Parker was surprised. He associated English beer with the Edwardian glass of a London pub or the low beams of a country inn. 'I didn't think they'd serve it in a place as posh as this.'

'They make a living by serving what people want,' said Abbot drily. 'There's a Yank behind us drinking his Budweiser, so I don't see why you shouldn't have your pint.' He caught the eye of a waiter who responded immediately. 'Have you any English beer?'

'Certainly, sair; what would you like? Bass, Worthington, Watney's . . .'

'Watney's'll do fine,' said Parker.

'And I'll have another of these.' Abbot watched the waiter depart. 'See, Dan, it's easy.'

'I'd never 'a' thought it,' said Dan in wonder.

Abbot said, 'If an English millionaire comes here and can't get his favourite tipple he raises the roof, and that's bad for business. We'll probably have to pay a millionaire's price, but it's on the old expense account.'

Dan's wonder increased even more when he was presented with a pewter tankard into which he promptly disappeared. He came up for air with froth on his upper lip. 'It's a bit o' right stuff,' he said. 'Cold but in good condition.'

'Maybe it'll lighten your day,' said Abbot. He glanced at the bar check, winced, and turned it over so Dan would not see it. That would certainly take the edge off his simple pleasure, even though Hellier was paying for it. He slid his eyes sideways at Parker and saw that the familiar taste of the beer had eased him. 'Are you sure you're right about this torpedo thing? I mean, it can be done?'

'Oh, aye; I can do it. I can make those fish do tricks.'

'We don't want it to do tricks. We just want it to go a

hell of a long way – five times further than it was designed to go.'

'Don't you worry yourself about that,' said Dan comfortably. 'I can do it. What I want to know is, can these people find a torpedo? They're not the easiest thing to come by, you know.'

That had been worrying Abbot, too, although he had not admitted it. It was one thing for Warren to come up with the nutty idea of smuggling by torpedo and another thing to implement it. If Delorme could not lay her hands on a torpedo then the whole scheme was a bust. He said, 'We'll worry about that when we come to it.'

They indulged in idle conversation, while Abbot surveyed the procession to the diving-board with the air of a caliph at the slave market. But he still kept an eye on the restaurant entrance, and after half an hour had passed, he said quietly, 'Here she is. Drink up, Dan.'

Parker knocked back his second pint with the ease of long practice. 'Same as yesterday, then?'

'That's right. We follow the man – we know where we can pick her up.' Abbot paid the check while Parker sauntered out in the wake of Jeanette Delorme and her companion. He caught up just as Parker was unlocking the car.

'Fourth car along,' said Parker. 'It should be a doddle. But I hope this isn't another bloody banker.'

'I'll drive,' said Abbot, and slid behind the wheel. He watched the big Mercedes pull away, then engaged gear and drifted into the traffic stream three cars behind. 'I don't think this one's a banker. He has no paunch, for one thing; and he certainly doesn't look Lebanese.'

'I noticed you watchin' all those naked popsies paradin' up an' down in front of the hotel,' said Parker. 'But what do you think of that one ahead of us?'

'Our Jeanette?' Abbot concentrated on piloting the car out of the Rue Minet El Hosn. 'I've never thought of her in *that* way,' he said satirically. 'Come to think of it, she's not bad-looking but I've never had the chance of giving her a real slow and loving once-over. It's a bit hard to assess a woman when you're not supposed to be looking at her.'

'Come off it,' scoffed Parker.

'Oh, all right. She's a bit long in the tooth for me.' Abbot was twenty-six. 'But trim – very trim – very beddable.' He grimaced. 'But I think it would be like getting into bed with a spider.'

'What the hell are you talkin' about?'

'Didn't you know – female spiders eat their mates after they've had their bit of fun.' He turned into the Avenue Bliss, following the Mercedes at a discreet distance. As they passed the American University he said, 'I wonder why they're going this way; there's nothing at the end of here but the sea.'

'We'll see soon enough,' said Parker stolidly.

The Avenue Bliss gave way to the Rue Manarah and still the Mercedes carried on. As they rounded a bend the sea came into view, and Parker said warningly, 'Watch it! He's pullin' in.'

Abbot went by and rigidly prevented himself from looking sideways. He turned the corner and parked on the Corniche. 'That was a hotel,' he said, and pondered. He made up his mind. 'I'm going in there. As soon as that Mercedes takes off you follow it if the man is in it. Don't wait for me.'

'All right,' said Parker.

'And, Dan; be unobtrusive.'

'That goes for you too,' said Parker. He watched Abbot turn the corner into the Rue Manarah and then swung the car round to where he could get a view of the hotel entrance and still be in a position to follow the Mercedes which was still parked outside. Presently Delorme and the man came out together with a page who packed a lot of luggage in the boot.

100

The Mercedes took off smoothly and he followed, and soon found himself going along a familiar road – past the Lebanese University and Khaldeh airport on the way to Hamınana. He was almost tempted to turn back but he went on all the way until he saw Jeanette Delorme safely home with her guest. Then he drove back to Beirut, running into heavy traffic on the way back to the hotel.

Abbot was taking it easy when Parker walked in. 'Where the devil have you been, Dan?'

'The traffic's bloody awful at this time o' day,' said Parker irascibly. 'She took him home an' you know what the road out o' town is like. She took him home – bags an' all. Stayin' with her as a house guest, like.' He grinned. 'If he disappears then you'll know she really is a bloody spider. Did you get anythin'?'

'I did,' said Abbot. 'By exerting my famous charm on a popsy in that hotel I found that he is an American, his name is John Eastman, and he flew in from Tehran yesterday. Did you hear that, Dan? *Tehran*. It's the first link.'

II

It may have been the first link but it wasn't the last because Eastman proved to be almost as inaccessible as Delorme herself. 'A snooty lot, these heroin smugglers,' observed Abbot. 'They don't mix with the common herd.'

So they applied the same technique to Eastman. It was a painfully slow task to keep him under observation and then to tag his associates and they would have given up had they not known with certainty that they were on the right track. For Abbot received a letter from Hellier who was acting as a clearing house for information.

'Good news and bad,' said Abbot after he had read it.

'Let's have the bad news first,' said Parker. 'I might need to be cheered up after hearin' it.'

'Warren has lost Speering. He disappeared into the blue in the middle of Kurdistan. It's up to us now, Dan. I bet Nick's climbing the wall,' he said reflectively.

'We're not much forrarder,' said Parker gloomily.

'Oh, but we are. That's the good news. Eastman saw Speering the day before he gave Nick the slip. That directly links Speering with Delorme. This is the first bit of concrete evidence we've had yet. Everything else was just one of Nick Warren's hunches.'

Parker brightened. 'Aye, that's so. Well, let's get on wi' it.'

So they got on with it, but it was a long time before Abbot made the decision. 'This is the man,' he said. 'This is where we cast our bread upon the waters and hope it'll come back buttered on both sides.'

'Picot?'

Picot was a long way down the line. He knew a man who knew a man who knew Eastman. He was accessible and, Abbot hoped, receptive to new ideas if they were cast his way. He was also, to a keen and observant eye, a crook, which further raised Abbot's hopes.

'How do we tackle him?' asked Parker.

'The first thing is to move into a cheaper hotel.' He looked at Parker consideringly. 'We're not rolling in cash – but we're not dead broke. We're hungry for loot, but careful. We have something to sell and we want the best price, so we're cagey. Got the picture?'

Parker smiled sombrely. 'That bit about not rollin' in cash'll come easy to me; I've never had much money. How do we broach the subject to Picot?'

'We play it by ear,' said Abbot easily.

Picot frequented a café in the old town near the Port, and when Abbot and Parker strolled in the next evening he was sitting at a table reading a newspaper. Abbot selected a table just in front and to the side of him, and they sat down. Abbot wrinkled his nose as he looked at the food-spotted menu and ordered for both of them.

Parker looked about the place and said in a low voice, 'What now?'

'Take it easy,' said Abbot softly. 'Let it come naturally.' He turned and looked at the little pile of newspapers and magazines on Picot's table, obviously there for the use of the customers. In English, he said, 'Excuse me, monsieur; do you mind?'

Picot looked up and nodded shortly. 'Okay with me.' His English was incongruously tinged with a mixed French and American accent.

Abbot took a magazine and flipped the pages idly until the waiter served them, putting down many plates, two drinks and a jug of water. Abbot poured a little water into his glass and there was a swirl of milkiness. 'Cheers, Dan.'

Hesitantly Parker did the same, drank and spluttered. He banged down the glass. 'What is this stuff? Cough mixture?'

'The local white lightning – arak.'

Parker investigated his palate with his tongue. 'I haven't tasted anything like this since I were a boy.' He looked surprised as he made the discovery. 'Aniseed balls!' He sniffed the glass. 'It's no drink for a grown man. Any chance of a Watney's in here?'

Abbot grinned. 'I doubt it. If you want beer you have a choice of Lebanese French and Lebanese German.'

'Make it the German,' said Parker, so Abbot ordered him a Henninger Byblos and turned back to find him regarding the contents of the plates with deep suspicion.

'For God's sake, stop acting like a tourist, Dan,' he said with irritation. 'What do you expect here – fish and chips?'

'I like to know what I'm eatin',' said Parker, unmoved.

'It's *mezza*,' said Abbot loudly. 'It's filling and it's cheap. If you want anything better go to the Saint-Georges – but

I'm not paying. I'm getting fed up with you. I have a good mind to call the whole thing off.'

Parker looked startled but subsided as Abbot winked. The beer arrived and Parker tasted it and put down the glass. 'It'll do, I suppose.'

Abbot said quietly, 'Do you think you could . . . er . . . get pissed?'

Parker flicked the glass with his fingernail. 'It 'ud take more than this stuff. It's like maiden's water.'

'But you could try, couldn't you? You might even become indiscreet.'

'Then buy me another,' said Parker, and drained the glass with one mighty swallow.

Abbot made a good meal but Parker picked at his food fastidiously and drank more than was apparently good for him. His voice became louder and his words tended to slur together, and he seemed to be working up to a grievance. '*You* want to call it off – how do you suppose I feel? I get this idea – a bloody good idea – an' what are you doin' about it? Nothin' but sittin' on your upper-class bottom, that's what.'

'Quiet, Dan!' urged Abbot.

'I won't be bloody quiet! I'm gettin' tired o' your snipin', too.' His voice took on an ugly mimicry. "Don't do this, Dan; don't do that, Dan; don't eat wi' your mouth open, Dan." Who the hell do you think you are?'

'Oh, for God's sake!' said Abbot.

'You said you could help me wi' what I've got – an' what ha' you done? Sweet Fanny Adams!'

'It takes time to make the contact,' said Abbot wearily.

'You said you *had* the contacts,' said Parker venomously.

'What have you got to complain about,' said Abbot in a high voice. 'You're not paying for all this, are you? If it wasn't for me you'd still be on your arse in London fiddling around with beat-up cars and dreaming of how to make a quick fortune. I've laid out nearly a thousand quid on this, Dan – doesn't that count for anything?'

'I don't care whose money it is. You're still doin' nothin' an' you're wastin' my time.' Parker gestured largely towards the open door. 'That harbour's full o' ships, an' I bet half of 'em are in the smugglin' racket. They'd go for what I have in me noggin an' they'd pay big for it, too. You talk about me sittin' on me arse; why don't you get up off yours?'

Abbot was trying – unsuccessfully – to quiet Parker. 'For God's sake, shut up! Do you want to give everything away? How do you know this place isn't full of police?'

Parker struggled to his feet drunkenly. 'Aw, hell!' He looked around blearily. 'Where is it?'

Abbot looked at him resignedly. 'Through there.' He indicated a door at the back of the café. 'And don't get talking to any strange men.' He watched Parker stagger away, shrugged, and picked up the magazine.

A voice behind him said, 'Monsieur?'

He turned and found Picot looking at him intently. 'Yes?'

'Would I be right if I said that you and your friend are looking for . . . employment?'

'No,' said Abbot shortly, and turned away. He hesitated perceptibly and turned back to face Picot. 'What makes you think that?'

'I thought maybe you were out of work. Sailors, perhaps?'

'Do I look like a sailor?' demanded Abbot.

Picot smiled. 'No, Monsieur. But your friend . . .'

'My friend's business is his.'

'And not yours, monsieur?' Picot raised his eyebrows. 'Then you are definitely not interested in employment?'

'What kind of employment?'

'Any man, particularly a sailor who has . . . ingenious ideas . . . there is always an opening for him in the right place.'

'I'm not a sailor. My friend was at one time. There'd have to be a place for me. We're great friends – inseparables, you know.'

Picot examined his finger-nails and smiled. 'I understand, monsieur. A great deal would depend on the ideas your friend has in mind. If you could enlighten me then it could be worth your while.'

'If I told you then you'd know as much as me, wouldn't you?' said Abbot cunningly. 'Nothing doing. Besides, I don't know who you are. I don't go a bundle on dealing with total strangers.'

'My name is Jules Fabre,' said Picot with a straight face.

Abbot shook his head. 'Means nothing to me. You *could* be a big-timer for all I know – and then again, you could be a cheap crook.'

'That's not very nice, monsieur,' said Picot reproachfully.

'I didn't intend it to be,' said Abbot.

'You are making things difficult,' said Picot. 'You can hardly expect me to buy something unknown. That is not good business. You would have to tell me sooner or later.'

'I'm not too worried about that. What Dan – my friend – has can only be made to work by him. He's the expert.'

'And you?'

Abbot grinned cheekily. 'You can say I'm his manager. Besides, I've put up the money so far.' He looked Picot up and down insultingly. 'And talking about money – what we've got would cost a hell of a lot, and I don't think a cheap chiseller like you has it, so stop wasting my time.' He turned away.

'Wait,' said Picot. 'This secret you have – how much do you expect to sell it for?'

Abbot swung around and stared at Picot. 'Half a million American dollars. Have you got that much?' he asked ironically.

Picot's lips twitched and he lowered his voice. 'And this is for smuggling?'

'What the hell do you think we've been talking about all this time?' demanded Abbot.

Picot became animated. 'You want to get in touch with someone at the top? I can help you, monsieur; but it will cost money.' He rubbed his finger and thumb together meaningfully and shrugged. 'My expenses, monsieur.'

Abbot hesitated, then shook his head. 'No. What we have is so good that the man at the top will pay you for finding us. Why should I grease your palm?'

'Because if you don't, the man at the top will never hear of you. I'm just trying to make a living, monsieur.'

Parker came back and sat down heavily. He picked up an empty bottle and banged it down. 'I want another beer.'

Abbot half-turned in his seat. 'Well, buy one,' he said irritably.

'Got no money,' said Parker. 'Besides,' he added belligerently, 'you're Mr Moneybags around here.'

'Oh, for Christ's sake!' Abbot took out his wallet, peeled off a note from the thin wad, and threw it on the table. 'Buy yourself a bucketful and swill in it. You can drown in the stuff for all I care.' He turned to Picot. 'All right – how much, you bloody twister?'

'A thousand pounds – Lebanese.'

'Half now and the other half when contact has been made.' He counted out notes and dropped them in front of Picot. 'All right?'

Picot put out his hand and delicately took the money. 'It will do, monsieur. What is your name and where can I find you?'

'My name doesn't matter and I'll be in here most evenings,' said Abbot. 'That's good enough.'

Picot nodded. 'You had better not be wasting time,' he warned. 'The man at the top has no use for fools.'

'He'll be happy with what we have,' said Abbot confidently.

'I hope so.' Picot looked at Parker who had his nose deep in a glass. 'Your friend drinks too much – and talks too loudly. That is not good.'

'He's all right. He's just become edgy because of the waiting, that's all. Anyway, I can control him.'

'I understand your position – exactly,' said Picot drily. He stood up. 'I will be seeing you soon.'

Abbot watched him leave, then said, 'You were great, Dan. The stage lost a great actor somewhere along the line.'

Parker put down his glass and looked at it without enthusiasm. 'I was pretty good at amateur theatricals at one time,' he said complacently. 'You paid him something. How much?'

'He gets a thousand pounds; I paid half.' Abbot laughed. 'Keep your hair on, Dan; they're Lebanese pounds – worth about half-a-crown each.'

Parker grunted and swirled the beer in his glass. 'It's still too much. This stuff is full of piss and wind. Let's go somewhere we can get a real drink, and you can tell me all about it.'

## III

Nothing happened next day. They went to the café at the same time in the evening but Picot was not there, so they had a meal, chatted desultorily and went away. Despite his confident attitude Abbot was wondering whether Picot was genuine or whether he had paid over £60 to a smooth grafter he would never see again.

They were just about to leave for the café the next evening when there was a knock at the door. Abbot raised his eyebrows at Parker and went to open it. 'Who's there?'

'Fabre.'

He opened up. 'How did you know we were here?'

'That does not matter, Monsieur Abbot. You wish to speak to someone – he is here.' He jerked his eyes sideways. 'That will be five hundred pounds.'

Abbot glanced to where a tall man stood in the shadowed corridor. 'Don't try to con me, Fabre. How do I know it's the man I want? It could be one of your put-up jobs. I'll talk to him first, then you'll get your money.'

'All right,' said Picot. 'I'll be in the usual place tomorrow.'

He walked away down the corridor and Abbot waited at the door. The tall man moved forward and, as his face came out of shadow, Abbot knew he had hit the jackpot. It was Eastman. He stepped on one side to let him enter, and Eastman said in a flat mid-western accent, 'Was Picot trying to shake you down?'

Abbot closed the door. 'Who?' he said blankly. 'He said his name was Fabre.'

'His name is Picot and he's a chiselling nogoodnik,' said Eastman without rancour.

'Talking about names,' said Abbot. 'This is Dan Parker and I'm Mike Abbot. And you are . . . ?' He let the question hang in the air.

'The name is Eastman.'

Abbot smiled. 'Sit down, Mr Eastman. Dan, pull up a chair and join the congregation.'

Eastman sat down rigidly on the chair offered. 'I'm told you have something to sell me. Start selling.'

'I'll start off, Dan,' said Abbot. 'You can chip in when things become technical.' He looked at Eastman. 'I'm told there's a fair amount of smuggling goes on around here. Dan and I have got an idea – a good idea. The trouble is we don't have the capital to pull it off ourselves, so we're open to offers – on a participation basis, of course.'

'You don't get offered a cent until I know what you're talking about.'

'This is where the conversation gets tricky,' said Abbot. 'However, Dan tells me it doesn't matter very much if you know the secret. He thinks he's the only one around who can make it work. Of course, it wouldn't work with too much weight or bulk. What are you interested in smuggling?'

Eastman hesitated. 'Let's say gold.'

'Let's say gold,' agreed Abbot. 'Dan, how much could you carry – in weight?'

'Up to five hundred pounds.'

'Interested?' asked Abbot.

'Maybe. What's the gimmick?'

'This works when coming in from the sea. You shoot it in by torpedo.' Abbot looked at Eastman as though expecting a round of applause.

Eastman sighed and put his hands on the table as though to lever himself up. 'You're wasting my time,' he said. 'Sorry.'

'Wait a minute,' said Abbot. 'Why are we wasting your time?'

Eastman stared at him and shook his head sadly. 'It's been tried before and it doesn't work very well. You're out of luck, boys.'

'Perhaps you were using the wrong torpedoes.'

'Perhaps.' Eastman looked at Abbot with renewed interest. 'What have you got?'

'You tell me what you want, then maybe we can get together.'

Eastman smiled thinly. 'Okay, I'll play ball; I've got ten minutes spare. A torpedo has only worked well once. That was on the Austrian-Italian border; a few smart-alick amateurs got hold of a torpedo and started smuggling across one of the little lakes up there. Booze one way and tobacco the other. They had the customs cops going nuts trying to

110

figure out how it worked. Then some jerk shot off at the mouth and that was the end of it.'

'So?' said Abbot. 'It worked, didn't it?'

'Oh, it worked – but only across a half-assed pond. A torpedo doesn't have the range for what I want.'

'Can you get hold of a torpedo?'

'Sure – but for what? Those we can get hold of don't have the range, and those we could use are on the secret lists. Boy, if I could get hold of one of the modern underwater guided missile babies I'd be made.'

Parker broke in. 'What kind of torpedo can you get?'

Eastman shrugged. 'Those on the international arms market – models of the 'forties and 'fifties. Nothing really up to date.'

'What about the British Mark XI?'

'Those are available, sure. With a maximum range of three miles – and what the hell's the good of that?'

'Fifty-five hundred yards wi' batteries brought up to heat,' corrected Parker.

Abbot grinned. 'I think you'd better tell him, Dan.'

Parker said deliberately, 'I can get fifteen miles out o' a Mark XI.'

Eastman sat up straight. 'Are you on the level?'

'He is,' said Abbot. 'Danny boy can make a Mark XI sit up and do tricks. Meet Mr Parker, the best petty officer and torpedo mechanic the Royal Navy ever had.'

'You interest me,' said Eastman. 'Are you sure about that fifteen miles?'

Parker smiled slowly. 'I can pep up a Mark XI so you can stay safely outside the legal twelve mile limit an' shoot her ashore at thirty knots. No bubbles, either.'

'And carrying five hundred pounds' weight?'

'That's right.'

Eastman pondered. 'What about accuracy?'

'That depends on the fish you give me – some o' the guidance gear is a bit rough sometimes. But I can doctor it

111

up if you let me have sea trials.' Parker scratched his jaw. 'I reckon I could give an accuracy o' three inches in a hundred yards – that's less than seventy yards out either way at fifteen miles.'

'Jesus!' said Eastman. 'That's not too bad.'

'You should be able to find a quiet beach that big,' said Abbot. 'You'll have to find one that slopes pretty shallowly, but that shouldn't be too difficult.'

'Wait a minute,' said Parker. 'That's the accuracy o' the fish I'm talkin' about. Currents are somethin' else. You shoot across a current an' the fish is goin' to be carried sideways, an' don't forget it'll be in the water for half an hour. If you have a cross-current of as little as half a knot then the fish will get knocked five hundred yards off course. Still, if you can plot the current you can compensate, an' you might avoid the problem altogether if you shoot at slack water.'

'Yeah, that can be gotten around.' Eastman nibbled at a joint of his thumb thoughtfully. 'You seem pretty certain about this.'

'I am,' said Parker. 'But it's goin' to cost you a hell of a lot. There's a torpedo in the first place an' a tube to go wi' it; there's high-power mercury cells to be bought an' they don't come cheap, an' there's . . .'

'. . . the cost of our services,' said Abbot smoothly. 'And we don't come cheap, either.'

'If you can pull it off you'll get taken care of,' said Eastman. 'If you don't you'll get taken care of another way.' His eyes were chilling.

Parker was unperturbed. 'I'll show you that it can be done first. You'll have sea trials.'

'Right,' said Eastman. 'I'll have to see the boss about this first.'

'The boss!' said Abbot in surprise. 'I thought you were the boss.'

'There are a lot of things you don't know,' said Eastman.

112

'Stick around and stay available.' He stood up. 'Where are you guys from?'

'London,' said Abbot.

Eastman nodded. 'Okay – I'll be seeing you soon.'

'I don't want to seem too pushing,' said Abbot, 'but what about a retainer? Or shall we say you've just taken an option on our services which has to be paid for?'

'You've got a nerve.' Eastman pulled out his wallet. 'How much did Picot stick you for?'

'A thousand Lebanese pounds. Half down, half later.'

'Okay – here's two-five; that gives you two thousand clear profit so far – and you haven't done anything yet. If Picot asks you for the other five hundred tell him to see me.' He smiled thinly. 'He won't, though.' He turned abruptly and walked out of the room.

Abbot sat down slowly and turned to Parker. 'I hope to God you can handle your end. We've hooked them at last, but they've also hooked us. If we can't deliver we'll be in trouble.'

Parker filled his pipe with steady hands. 'They'll get what they want – an' maybe a bit more.' He paused. 'Do you think he'll check back to London?'

'He's sure to. You're all right, Dan; there's nothing in your background to worry him.' Abbot stretched. 'As for me – I had a flaming row with my editor just before I left, specially laid on. I'll bet the echoes are still reverberating down Fleet Street. He grinned. 'I was fired, Dan – out on my can for unprofessional conduct unbefitting a journalist and a gentleman. I only hope it'll satisfy Eastman and company.'

# IV

Eastman did not keep them waiting long. Three days later he rang up and said, 'Hello, Abbot; put on your best bib and tucker – you're going on the town tonight.'

'Where to?'

'Le Paon Rouge. If you don't have decent clothes, buy some out of the dough I gave you.'

'Who's paying for the night out?' asked Abbot in his character as a man on the make.

'It'll be paid for,' said Eastman. 'You're meeting the boss. Be on your best behaviour. I'll send a car for you at nine-thirty.'

Abbot put the phone on the hook slowly and turned to find Parker regarding him with interest. 'Have you got a dinner-jacket, Dan?'

Parker nodded. 'I packed it on the off-chance I'd need it.'

'You'll need it tonight. We've been invited to the Paon Rouge.'

'That'll be the third time I've worn it, then,' said Parker. He put his hand on his belly. 'Might be a bit tight. What's the Paon Rouge?'

'A night-club in the Hotel Phoenicia. We're meeting the boss, and if it's who I think it is, we've got it made. We've just been told tactfully to shave and brush our teeth nicely.'

'The Hotel Phoenicia – isn't that the big place near the Saint-Georges?'

'That's it. Do you know what a five-star hotel is, Dan?'

Parker blinked. 'The Saint-Georges?' he hazarded.

'Right! Well, there aren't enough stars in the book to classify the Phoenicia. Dope-smuggling must be profitable.'

* * *

114

They were picked up by the black Mercedes and driven to the Phoenicia by an uncommunicative Lebanese. Parker was unhappy because his doubts about his evening wear had been confirmed; his dress shirt had taken a determined grip on his throat and was slowly throttling him, and his trousers pinched cruelly at waist and crotch. He made a mental note to start a course of exercises to conquer his middle-age spread.

The name of Eastman dropped to an impressively-dressed major-domo brought them to Eastman's table with remarkable alacrity. The Paon Rouge was fashionably dark in the night-club manner, but not so dark that Abbot could not spot his quarry; Eastman was sitting with Jeanette Delorme and rose at their approach. 'Glad you could make it,' he said conventionally.

'Delighted, Mr Eastman,' said Abbot. He looked down at the woman. 'Is *this* the boss?'

Eastman smiled. 'If you cross her you'll find out.' He turned to her. 'This is Abbot, the other is Parker. Gentlemen – Miss Delorme.'

Abbot inclined his head and studied her. She was dressed in a simple sheath which barely covered her upperworks and she appeared to be, at the most, twenty-five years old. He knew for a fact that she was thirty-two, but it was wonderful what money could do. A very expensive proposition was Miss Delorme.

She crooked a finger at him. 'You – sit here.' There was a minor flurry as flunkies rearranged chairs and Abbot found himself sitting next to her and facing Parker, with a glass of champagne in his fingers. She studied Parker for a moment, then said, 'If what Jack tells me is true, I may be willing to employ you. But I need proof.' Her English was excellent and almost unaccented.

'You'll get your proof,' said Abbot. 'Dan will give you that.'

Parker said, 'There's plenty of sea out there. You can have trials.'

'Which torpedo would be most suitable?'

'Doesn't really matter,' said Parker. 'As long as it's an electric job.'

She twirled her glass slowly in her fingers. 'I have a friend,' she said. 'He was a U-boat captain during the war. His opinion of the British torpedo was very low. He said that on half the firings the British torpedo went wild.' Her voice became sharp. 'That would not be permissible.'

'Christ, no!' said Eastman. 'We can't lose a torpedo – not with what it will be carrying. It would be too goddam expensive.'

'Ah, you're talking about the early British torpedoes,' said Parker. 'The Mark XI was different. Your U-boat skipper was dead right – the early British fish were bloody awful. But the Mark XI was a Chinese copy o' the German fish an' it was very good when it came into service in '44. We pinched it from the Jerries, an' the Yanks pinched it from us. Any o' those torpedoes would be good enough but I'd rather have the old Mark XI – it's more familiar, like. But they're all pretty much the same an' just differ a bit in detail.'

'On what basis will you get the extra performance?'

'Look,' said Parker, leaning forward earnestly. 'The Mark XI came out in '44 an' it had lead-acid batteries – that was all they had in them days. Twenty-five years have gone by since then, an' things have changed. The new kalium cells – that's mercury oxide-zinc – pack a hell o' a lot more power, an' you can use that power in two ways. You can either increase the range or the speed. I've designed circuits for both jobs.'

'We're interested in increasing range,' said Eastman.

Parker nodded. 'I know. It's goin' to cost you a packet,' he warned. 'Mercury cells ain't cheap.'

'How much?' asked Delorme.

Parker scratched his head. 'Every time you shoot a fish it'll cost you over a thousand quid just for the power.'

She looked at Eastman, who interpreted, 'A thousand pounds sterling.'

Abbot sipped his champagne. 'The cost of everything is going up,' he observed coolly.

'That's a fact,' said Parker with a grin. 'Back in '44 the whole bloody torpedo only cost six hundred quid. I dunno what they cost now, though.'

'Fifteen hundred pounds,' said Eastman. 'That's the going rate on the surplus market.'

'There you are,' said Parker. 'Another thousand for a trial an' another for the real job, plus, say, five hundred for conversion. That's four thousand basic. Then there's our share on top o' that.'

'And what is your share?' asked Jeanette Delorme.

'A percentage of the profits,' said Abbot.

She turned to him. 'Indeed! And where do you come in on this? It seems that Parker is doing all the work.'

Abbot smiled easily. 'Let's say I'm his manager.'

'There are no passengers in the organization,' she said flatly.

Parker broke in. 'Me an' Mike are mates – I go where he goes, an' vicey-versey. Besides, I'll see he works hard – I can't do it all meself.'

'It's a package deal, you see,' said Abbot. 'And you talk business to me.'

'The profits on smuggling gold are not very big,' she said doubtfully.

'Oh, come off it,' said Abbot in disgust. 'You're not smuggling gold – you're running dope.'

She looked at Eastman and then back at Abbot. 'And how do you know that?' she asked softly.

'Just putting two and two together. There was a whisper in London – that's why we came out here.'

'That was one whisper too many,' she snapped.

Abbot smiled. 'I wouldn't worry too much about it. I was a professional in the whisper-listening business. It was just a matter of chance, and coming out here was a hell of a long shot.' He shrugged. 'But it's paid off.'

'Not yet,' she said pointedly. 'How much do you want?'

'Twenty per cent of the take,' said Abbot promptly.

She laughed. 'Oh, what a stupid man we have here. Don't you think so, Jack?' Eastman grinned, and she said seriously, 'You will get one per cent and that will make you very rich, Monsieur Michael Abbot.'

'I may be stupid,' said Abbot, 'but I'm not crazy enough to take one per cent.'

Eastman said, 'I think you are crazy if you expect to get any kind of a percentage. We're not going to work that way.'

'That's right,' said Delorme. 'We'll give you a flat rate for the work. What would you say to a hundred thousand American dollars?'

Abbot raised his eyebrows. 'Each?'

She hesitated fractionally. 'Of course.'

'I'd say it's not on,' said Abbot, shaking his head. 'We'd want at least double that. Do you think I don't know what the profits are in this racket?'

Eastman chuckled raspingly. 'You're both stupid and crazy. Hell, you've given us the idea anyway. What's to prevent us going ahead without you?'

'Now who's being stupid?' asked Abbot. He pointed to Parker. 'Torpedo mechanics aren't easy to come by, and those who can do a conversion like this are even rarer. But a mechanic who can and is willing to run dope is as rare as a hen's tooth. You can't do it without us – and you know it.'

'So you figure you've got us over a barrel,' said Eastman ironically. 'Look, buster; a week ago we didn't even know you existed. We don't *need* you, you know.'

118

'But it's still a good idea, Jack,' said Delorme thoughtfully. 'Maybe Abbot will meet us half way.' She turned to him. 'This is final – take it or leave it. Three hundred thousand dollars for the two of you. One hundred thousand deposited in a bank here on the successful completion of trials – the rest when the job is done.'

Abbot said, 'What do you think, Dan?'

Parker's mouth was open. He closed it, and said, 'You have the business head; I'll leave it to you, Mike.' He swallowed convulsively.

Abbot pondered for a long time. 'All right; we'll take it.'

'Good!' said Delorme, and smiled radiantly. 'Order some more champagne, Jack.'

Abbot winked at Parker. 'Satisfied, Dan?'

'I'm happy,' said Parker faintly.

'I think payment by result is the best way,' said Abbot, and looked sideways at Eastman. 'If we'd have stuck to a percentage, Jack here would have cheated the pants off us. He wouldn't have shown us the books, that's for certain.'

Eastman grinned. 'What books?' He held up a finger and the sommelier came running.

Delorme said, 'I'd like to dance.' She looked at Abbot who began to rise, and said, 'I think I'll dance with . . . Mr Parker.'

Abbot subsided and watched her allow the bemused Parker to take her on to the floor. His lips quirked into a smile. 'So that's the boss. Something I hadn't expected.'

'If you're thinking what I think you're thinking – forget it,' advised Eastman. 'Jeanette isn't a girl to be monkeyed around with. I'd just as soon fight a buzz-saw with my bare hands.' He nodded towards the dance floor. 'Is Parker as good as he says he is?'

'He'll do the job. What's the cargo?'

Eastman hesitated briefly, then said, 'You'll get to know, I guess. It's heroin.'

'A full cargo – the whole five hundred pounds?'

'Yeah.'

Abbot whistled and calculated briefly. He laughed. 'That's worth about twenty-five million dollars, at least. I topped Jeanette's one per cent, anyway.'

'You're in the big time now,' said Eastman. 'But don't forget – you're still only a hired hand.' He lit a cigarette. 'That whisper you heard in London. Who did it come from?'

Abbot shrugged. 'You know how it is – a piece comes from here and another from there. You put them all together and get some sort of picture. I've had experience at it – I was a reporter.'

'I know,' said Eastman calmly. 'You've been checked out. We've got nothing on Parker yet, though.' He stared at Abbot with hard eyes. 'You'd better not still be a reporter, Abbot.'

'I couldn't get a job on the *Tolpuddle Gazette*,' said Abbot bitterly. 'Not with the reputation I've got now. If you've been checking on me you know I was given the bum's rush. That's why I decided to come on this lark and make some real money.'

'Just a penny ante blackmailer,' agreed Eastman.

'They couldn't prove anything,' said Abbot defensively.

'Just keep your nose clean while you're with us,' said Eastman. 'Now, what can you tell us about Parker? The boss wants him checked out, too. She's very security-minded.'

Abbot obligingly gave him a run-down on Parker, sticking entirely to the known facts. There was no harm in that because the truth was exactly what would serve best. He had just finished when Jeanette and Parker returned to the table, Parker pink in the face.

Jeanette said, 'I don't think Dan is accustomed to modern dancing. What about you, Mike Abbot?'

Abbot stood up. 'Would you like to test me on a trial run?'

In reply she opened her arms as the opening bars of

120

music started and he stepped forward. It was a slow and rather old-fashioned number so he took her in his arms and said, as they stepped on to the floor, 'What's a nice girl like you doing in a business like this?'

'I like the money,' she said. 'Just as you do.'

'You must be making quite a lot,' he said thoughtfully. 'It's not everyone who can lay hands on a hundred thousand dollars' loose cash – that's the boodle for the successful trial, in case you've forgotten. I take it this isn't a one-shot venture?'

'What do you care?'

'I like to stick where the money is. It would be nice if this built up into a regular income.'

She moved closer to him. 'There is no reason why not. All that is required is that you do your work and keep your mouth shut. Both are essential to your general health.'

'Would that be a threat?' asked Abbot lightly.

She snuggled up to him, pressing her body against his. 'It would. Nobody plays tricks with me, Monsieur Abbot.'

'No tricks intended,' said Abbot, chilled at the disparity between her words and her present actions. He had seen her dossier and it chimed in exactly with Eastman's description. A buzz-saw, he had said. Anyone laying a hand on Delorme or any of her dubious enterprises would draw back a bloody stump at best. And there was a list of six names of varied nationality to demonstrate the worst. He danced with five-foot-six of warm womanhood pressed vibrantly against him and thought that perhaps she was a spider, after all.

She breathed into his ear, 'You dance very well, Mike.' He winced as her teeth nipped his earlobe.

'Thanks, but there's no need to be so enthusiastic,' he said drily.

She giggled. 'Dan was shocked. He kept talking about his wife and children. Does he really have a wife and children?'

'Of course. Three kids, I think.'

'He is a peasant type,' she said. 'His brains are in his hands. You are different.'

Abbot chuckled internally at the outrage Parker would show at being described as a peasant. 'How am I different?'

'You know very well,' she said. 'Welcome to the organization, Mike. We'll try to keep you very happy.'

He grinned in the semi-darkness. 'Does that include Jack Eastman?'

'Never mind Jack Eastman,' she said, her voice suddenly sharp. 'Jack will do what I tell him. He doesn't . . .' She stopped speaking and made a sinuous movement so that her breasts nuzzled his chest. '*I'll* keep you very happy,' she whispered.

The music stopped and she stepped away from him after a lingering moment. He escorted her back to the table and thought he saw a satirical gleam in Eastman's eye.

'I'm not tired yet,' she said. 'It's nice having three escorts. Come on, Jack.'

Eastman took her on to the floor again and Abbot dropped into the chair next to Parker. He found he was sweating slightly. Must be the heat, he thought, and picked up his newly refilled champagne glass.

Parker looked at the throng on the dance floor. 'That woman scares me,' he said gloomily.

'What did she do – try to rape you on the floor?'

'Bloody near.' Parker's brow turned pink again. 'By God, if my missus could have seen me there'd be a divorce tomorrow.' He tugged at his collar. 'She's a man-eater, all right.'

'It seems as though our jobs are neatly allocated,' said Abbot. 'You look after the torpedo and I look after Jeanette.' He sipped his champagne. 'Or she looks after me, if I understood her correctly.'

He found he was smiling.

\* \* \*

122

They stayed for quite a while at the Paon Rouge, dining and watching the cabaret. They left at about two in the morning to find the Mercedes waiting outside. Eastman got in the front next to the driver and Abbot found himself rubbing shoulders and legs with Jeanette who wore a shimmering silver cape.

The car moved away, and after a while he looked out of the window at the sea and said, 'It would be helpful if I knew where we were going.'

'You'll find out,' she said, and opened her cigarette case. 'Give me a light.'

He flicked his lighter and saw Parker sitting on the other side of Jeanette, easing his tight collar. 'You're the boss.'

The car proceeded smoothly on the road out of Beirut towards Tripoli and he wondered where it was taking them – and why. He did not wonder long because presently it swung off the road and drew up in front of a large wooden gate which was swung open by an Arab. The car rolled into a large yard and stopped.

They got out and Abbot looked around. As far as he could see in the darkness it seemed to be some sort of factory. A large shed loomed against the night sky, and beyond the moon sparkled on the sea. 'This way,' said Eastman, and Abbot followed him into an office.

The first thing he saw when the lights snapped on was his own suitcase against the wall. 'What the hell . . . ?'

'You'll be staying here,' said Eastman. 'There are two beds in the next room. No bathroom, I'm afraid – but there's a wash-basin.' He glanced at Jeanette and then his gaze came back to Abbot. 'You should be quite comfortable,' he said sardonically. 'Ali will do your cooking.'

Jeanette said, 'You'll stay here until after the trials of the torpedo. How long you stay depends on yourselves.' She smiled and said lightly, 'But I'll come to see you – often.' She turned to Parker and said abruptly, 'How long to make the conversion?'

Parker shrugged. 'Two weeks – with the right equipment. A hell of a long time, or never, without it. But I'll have to have a torpedo first.'

She nodded. 'Come with me.' They followed her from the office and across the yard to the big shed. Ali, the Arab, produced a big key and unlocked the door, then stood back to allow them to enter. The shed was on two levels and they came out on a platform overlooking the main workshop. A flight of wooden stairs led down to ground level.

Abbot looked over the rail, and said, 'Well, I'm damned! You were pretty sure of us, weren't you?'

Illumined under harsh lighting was a sleek and deadly-looking torpedo set up on trestles, gleaming because of the thin film of protective oil which covered it. To Abbot it looked enormous, and the first thought that came into his head was: How in hell did this bitch lay her hands on a torpedo at three days' notice?

## 5

Warren checked the maps again, and his pen traced out the record of their journeys. The two weeks they had spent in Kurdistan had been wasted, but he did not see how they could have done differently. There had been a chance, admittedly a slim one, of running across Speering, and they could not have passed it by. But it had been a futile two weeks.

So they had returned to Tehran in the hope of finding something, what he did not know. All he knew was that he had failed, and failed dismally. Every time he had to write to Hellier confessing failure he cursed and fretted. The only bright spot was that Abbot and Parker seemed to be making good in the Lebanon – it seemed that his 'insurance policy' might pay off in the end. But now they had dropped out of sight and he did not know what to make of it.

Johnny Follet took it all phlegmatically. He did not know what Warren was looking for so assiduously, nor did he care so long as he was paid. He had long ago written off his resentment against Warren and was quite enjoying himself in Tehran, and took it as a pleasant and exotic holiday. He wandered the streets and saw the sights, and presently found himself some congenial companions.

Ben Bryan was also uneasy, if not as much as Warren, but that may have been because he did not have Warren's overall responsibility. He and Waren pored over the maps of north-west Iran trying to figure out where Speering could have gone to ground. 'It's no use,' said Ben. 'If these maps were up to the standard of British Ordnance Survey we might have a hope, but half the damned roads up there aren't even shown here.'

'So what do we do?' asked Warren.

Ben did not know, and they all idled in low gear.

Andy Tozier had a problem – a minor problem, true – but still a problem, and it puzzled him mightily. He was losing money steadily to Johnny Follet and he could not see how the trick was worked. The money he lost was not much when considered against the number of games played, but the steady trickle annoyed him.

He spoke to Warren about it. 'On the face of it, it's a fair game – I can't see how he does it.'

'I wouldn't trust Johnny to play a fair game,' said Warren. 'What is it this time?'

'It goes like this. We each have a coin, and we match coins. We don't toss them, so the element of chance is eliminated as far as that goes – we each have control as to whether we show a head or a tail. Got that?'

'It seems all right so far,' said Warren cautiously.

'Yes,' said Tozier. 'Now, if I show heads and he shows tails he pays me thirty pounds. If I show tails and he shows heads he pays me ten pounds.'

Warren thought about it. 'Those are two of the four possible occurrences.'

'Right!' said Tozier. 'The other two occurrences are both heads or both tails. If either of those happen I pay him twenty pounds.'

'Wait a minute,' said Warren, and scribbled on a piece of paper. 'There are four possible cases of which you can win two and he can win two. Taking all four cases as equal – which they are – if they all happen you will win forty pounds – and so will he. It seems a fair game to me.' It also seemed a childish game but that he did not say.

'Then why the hell is he winning?' demanded Tozier. 'I'm nearly a hundred pounds down already.'

'You mean to say that you never win?'

126

'Oh, no. I win games and so does he – but he wins more often. It's a sort of see-saw, but he seems to have more weight than I have and my money tends to roll towards him. The thing that makes me wild is that I can't figure the gimmick.'

'Perhaps you'd better stop playing.'

'Not until I find out how he does it,' said Tozier determinedly. 'The thing that gets me is that it isn't as though he could ring in a double-headed penny – that wouldn't help him. Hell, it would make it worse for him because then I'd *know* what he was calling and I'd act accordingly.' He grinned. 'I'm willing to go another hundred just to find the secret. It's a profitable game – I could use it myself if I knew how.'

'It seems as though you'll have plenty of time to play,' said Warren acidly. 'We're getting nowhere here.'

'I've been thinking about that,' said Tozier. 'I've had an idea. What about that pharmaceutical place where Speering ordered his supplies? They'd deliver the stuff, wouldn't they? So they must have an address somewhere in their records. All we have to do is to extract it somehow.'

Warren looked at him wearily. 'Are you suggesting a burglary?'

'Something like that.'

'I've thought of it, too,' admitted Warren. 'But just tell me one thing. How the devil are we going to recognize what we want even if we see it? These people keep records in Persian, which is a foreign language to begin with, and in Arabic script which none of us can read. Could you sort it out, Andy?'

'Hell, I hadn't thought of that,' said Tozier. 'My colloquial Arabic isn't bad but I can't read the stuff.' He looked up. 'Do you mind if I talk to Johnny about this?'

Warren hesitated. 'Not as long as you stick to generalities. I don't want him knowing too much.'

'I won't tell him more than he ought to know. But it's

127

about time he was put to work. He's a good con man and if we can't get the information in any other way then perhaps we can get it by Johnny's fast talk.'

So Tozier talked to Johnny Follet and Johnny listened. 'Okay,' he said. 'Give me a couple of days and I'll see what I can come up with.' He disappeared into the streets of Tehran and they did not see him for four days. When he came back he reported to Tozier, 'It can be done. It'll take a bit of fooling around, but it can be done. You can have the information in less than a week.'

## II

Follet's plan was so diabolical that it raised the hairs on the back of Warren's head. He said, 'You've got an evil mind, Johnny.'

'I guess so,' said Follet insouciantly. 'There's a part for everyone – the more the merrier. But for Christ's sake take it seriously; it's got to look good and real.'

'Tell me more about this man.'

'He's assistant to the Chief Clerk in the Stores Department of the company. That means he issues goods against indents and keeps the books on quantities. He's just the guy to have the information you need – or to be in a position to get it. There's no money involved because he never handles it; all that is done by the main office. That's a pity in a way because we lose a chance of really hooking him.'

'Why don't we just bribe him?' asked Tozier.

'Because the guy's honest, that's why – or a reasonable facsimile. Suppose we tried to bribe him and it didn't take? He'd report to his bosses and the information would be whisked out of that office so fast that we wouldn't get another chance at it. And they might tell the police and then we'd be in trouble.'

'They might not tell the police,' said Warren. 'We don't know how much this firm is involved with Speering, but it's my guess that it's in on the whole thing. It must be. Any firm issuing certain chemicals and equipment has a damned good idea of what they'll be used for. It's my guess that this crowd is in it up to its collective neck.'

'What thing?' asked Follet alertly.

'Never mind, Johnny; carry on with what you were saying.'

Follet shrugged. 'This guy – Javid Raqi – is a bright boy. He speaks English well, he's had a good education and he's ambitious. I guess that chief clerk won't last long with friend Javid on his heels. He has only one flaw – he's a gambler.'

Tozier smiled. 'Your flaw, Johnny?'

'Not mine,' said Follet promptly. 'He's a sucker gambler. Now, that doesn't mean he's a fool. He's learned to play poker – the guys working on the gas line taught him – and he's a good player. I know because he's gotten some of my dough right now and I didn't have to let him win it, either – he gouged it out of me like a pro. But it means he can be got at – he can be had; and once he's been got at then we squeeze him goddam hard.'

Warren wrinkled his nose distastefully. 'I wish there were some other way of doing this.'

'Never give a sucker an even break,' said Follet, and turned to Tozier. 'The whole scheme hinges on that videotape gadget. How well does it work?'

'I have it set up in my room; it works very well.'

'That I have to see for myself,' said Follet. 'Let's all go up there.'

They all went up to Tozier's room and Tozier switched on the TV and pointed to the videotape machine. 'There it is. It's already connected to the TV set.'

The machine looked very much like an ordinary tape recorder, although bulkier than most. The tape, however, was an inch wide and the reels were oversized. Follet bent down and examined it interestedly. 'I'd like to get this just right; this gadget will take in everything – sight and sound both?'

'That's it,' said Tozier.

'How's the quality?'

'If you use the video-camera there's a bit of blurring, particularly on movement, but if you take a taping of a TV programme then the reproduction is indistinguishable from the original.' He looked at the TV screen. 'I'll show you now.'

A man was speaking and his voice was heard as Tozier turned up the volume. Warren did not know the language but it seemed to be a news broadcast because the man disappeared and a street scene replaced him, although his voice continued. Tozier bent down and flicked a switch and the reels began to run, much faster than a normal recording machine. 'We're recording now.'

'That tape's fairly whipping through,' commented Follet. 'How long can you record?'

'An hour.'

'Hell, that's plenty.' He regarded the television screen for a while, then said, 'Okay, let's have a repeat.'

Tozier ran the tape back and switched the television set to a previously selected unused channel. He stopped the recorder and set it to playback, then snapped the starting switch. On the television screen appeared the street scene they had just witnessed, together with the voice of the announcer.

Follet bent forward with a critical eye on the screen. 'Hey, this quality's fine. It's just about as good as the original, like you said. This is going to work.'

He straightened. 'Now, look, the action starts on Saturday and you've got to get it right. Not only have you got to get every word right, but the way you say the word. No false notes.' He looked at them appraisingly. 'You're amateurs at this game, so we'll have some rehearsals. Imagine we're putting on a play and I'm the producer. You only have to play to an audience of one.'

'I can't act,' said Bryan. 'I never could.'

'That's okay – you can work this television gadget. As for the rest of us – I'll play the easy guy, Andy does the hard-nosed stuff, and Warren can be the boss.' Follet grinned as he saw the expression on Warren's face. 'You don't say much and you say it quietly. The way I figure it the less acting you do the better. An ordinary conversational tone can sound real menacing in some situations.'

He looked about the room. 'Now, where do we put Ben and the video-tape?'

Tozier went to the window, opened it and looked out. 'I think I can run a line into your room, Johnny. We can settle Ben in there.'

'Good enough,' said Follet. He slapped his hands together. 'Okay, first rehearsal – beginners, please.'


### III


At twelve-thirty on Saturday they waited in a lounge just off the foyer of the hotel, not exactly in hiding but certainly concealed from casual inspection. Follet nudged Warren. 'There he is – I told him to wait for me in the bar. You go in first; Andy will give you time to settle, and I'll be in right after. Get going.'

As Warren left, he said a little worriedly to Tozier, 'I hope Ben doesn't ball up his bit with the television.'

Warren crossed the foyer and entered the bar where he ordered a drink. Javid Raqi was seated at a table and appeared to be somewhat nervous, although probably not

131

as nervous as Warren as he steeled himself to play his part in the charade. Raqi was a young man of about twenty-five, smartly dressed in European fashion from top to toe. He was darkly handsome if you like Valentino looks, and probably had a great future. Warren felt sorry for him.

Tozier appeared at the door, his jacket draped carelessly over his arm. He walked forward, past Raqi, and something apparently dropped from a pocket to plop right at Raqi's feet. It was a fat wallet of brown leather. Raqi looked down and stooped, then straightened with the wallet in his hand. He looked towards Tozier who had walked on without missing a pace, then followed him to the bar.

Warren heard the murmur of voices and then the louder tones of Tozier. 'Well, thank you. That was very careless of me. Allow me to buy you a drink.'

Johnny Follet was now in the room, on Raqi's heels. 'Hi, Javid; I didn't know you two knew each other.' There was surprise in his voice.

'We don't, Mr Follet,' said Raqi.

'Oh!' said Tozier. 'So this is who you were talking about, Johnny. Mr Raqi – that's the name, isn't it? – just rescued my wallet.' He opened it to display a thick wad of notes. 'He could have taken the lot without winning it.'

Follet chuckled. 'He'll probably take it anyway. He's a right sharp poker-player.' He looked around. 'There's Nick. It'll be a foursome, Javid; does that suit you?'

Raqi said a little shyly, 'That's all right, Mr Follet.'

'The hell with Mr Follet. We're all friends here. I'm Johnny and this is Andy Tozier – and coming over is Nick Warren. Gentlemen, Javid Raqi, the best poker-player I've come across in Tehran – and I'm not kidding.'

Warren smiled stiffly at Raqi and murmured something conventional. Follet said, 'Don't buy a drink, Andy; let's go where the action is. I have everything laid on – booze and food both.'

They all went up to Tozier's room, where the television

132

set had been moved over to the window. Follet had laid on quite a spread; there was cold chicken, sausages of various sorts and salads, together with some unopened bottles of whisky. Everything was set for a long session. Unobtrusively, Warren looked at his watch – it read just after twelve – exactly half an hour slow. He wondered how Follet would doctor the expensive-looking watch he saw on Raqi's slim brown wrist without Raqi knowing it had been done.

Follet opened a drawer and tossed a sealed pack of cards on to the table. 'There you are, Javid; you have first deal. Stranger's privilege – but you won't be a stranger long. Go easy on the water in mine, Nick.'

Warren poured four drinks and brought them to the table. Raqi was shuffling the cards. He seemed to do it expertly enough, although Warren was no judge of that. He was not as good as Follet, of that he was sure.

Follet looked about the table. 'We'll be confining ourselves to draw poker, gentlemen – there'll be none of your fancy wild hands here; this is a serious game for serious gamblers. Let's play poker.'

Raqi dealt the cards, five to each, and said in a quiet voice, 'Jacks or better open.'

Warren looked at his cards. He was not a good poker-player, although he knew the rules. 'That doesn't matter,' Follet had said. 'You don't want to win, anyway.' But he had schooled Warren in a couple of intensive lessons all the same.

At the end of the first hour he was losing – about four thousand rials to the bad – say twenty-two pounds. Tozier had lost a little, too, but not nearly as much. Follet had won a little and Raqi was on top, winning about five thousand rials.

Follet riffled the cards. 'What did I tell you? This boy can play poker,' he said jovially. 'Say, that's a nice watch you have there, Javid. Mind if I have a look at it?'

Raqi was flushed with success and was not nearly as shy

and nervous as he had been at first. 'Of course,' he said easily, and slipped it from his wrist.

As Follet took it, Warren said, 'You speak very good English, Javid. Where did you learn it?'

'I studied at school, Nick; then I went to night classes.' He smiled. 'This is where I practise it – at the poker table.'

'You're doing very well.'

Tozier counted his money. 'Play poker,' he said. 'I'm losing.'

Follet grinned. 'I warned you Javid would take your wad.' He held out the watch on his forefinger, but somehow it seemed to slip and it dropped to the floor. Follet pushed back his chair and there was a crunch. 'Oh, hell!' he exclaimed in disgust, and picked up the watch. 'I've bust the dial.' He held it to his ear. 'It's still going, though.'

Raqi held out his hand, 'It does not matter, Johnny.'

'It matters to me,' said Follet. 'I'll have it fixed for you.' He dropped it into his shirt pocket. 'No, I insist,' he said over Raqi's expostulations. 'I did the damage – I'll pay for the fixing. Whose deal is it?' Raqi subsided.

They continued to play and Raqi continued to win. As far as Warren could judge he was a good natural poker-player and he did not think Follet was discreetly assisting him, although he did not have the special knowledge to know if this was correct. He did know that he himself was losing steadily, although he played as best he could. Tozier recouped his earlier losses and stood about even, but Follet was on the losing side.

The haze of cigarette smoke in the room grew thicker and Warren began to get a slight headache. This was not his idea of a pleasant Saturday afternoon's entertainment. He glanced at his watch and saw that it read half-past-two. Ben Bryan, in the next room, ought to be busy taping the television programme.

At quarter to three Tozier threw in his hand with an

expression of disgust. 'Hey!' he said in alarm. 'You'd better make that call.'

Follet looked at his watch. 'Christ, I nearly forgot. It's quarter to three already.' He stood up and walked over to the telephone.

'I thought it would be later than that,' said Raqi in mild surprise.

Warren uncovered his watch with the dial turned towards Raqi. 'No – that's all it is. It might be a bit late for us, though.'

Follet had his hand on the telephone when Tozier said curtly, 'Not that one, Johnny. Make the call from the lobby.' He jerked his head at Raqi meaningly.

'Javid's all right,' said Follet easily.

'I said make it from the lobby.'

'Don't be so hard-nosed, Andy. Here you have a guy who was honest enough to give you back your wallet when he didn't know who the hell you were. Why cut him out?'

Warren said quietly, 'You always were a hard case, Andy.'

Raqi was looking from face to face, not understanding what was going on. Tozier shrugged with ill-grace. 'No skin off my nose – but I thought you wanted to keep it quiet.'

'It doesn't matter,' said Warren indifferently. 'Javid's all right – we know that. Make the call, Johnny; it's getting late. If we argue over it any more we'll miss post time.'

'Okay,' said Follet and began to dial. His body screened the telephone from view. There was a pause. 'Is that you, Jamshid? . . . Yeah, I know; things are bad all round . . . this time I'm going to win, I promise you . . . I'm still in time for the three o'clock race – make it twenty thousand rials on Al Fahkri.' He turned and grinned at Raqi. 'Yeah, on the nose . . . and, say, put on another two thousand for a friend of mine.'

He put down the telephone. 'The bet's on, boys; the

odds are eight to one. And there's two thousand on for you, Javid.'

'But, Johnny, I don't bet the horses,' protested Raqi. 'Two thousand rials is a lot of money.'

'Have it on the house,' said Follet generously. 'Andy's putting up the stake as a penance. Aren't you, Andy?'

'Go to hell,' said Tozier morosely.

'Quit worrying, Javid,' said Follet. 'I'll stake you.' He turned to Warren. 'The kid can stay and watch. None of us can speak the lingo, so he can tell us which horse wins – as if we didn't know.'

'Why don't you keep your big mouth shut?' said Tozier in exasperation.

'It's all right, Andy,' said Warren. 'Johnny's right; you're a mean, ungrateful bastard. How much did you have in your wallet when you dropped it?'

'About a hundred thousand rials,' said Tozier reluctantly.

Follet was outraged. 'And you're being hard-nosed about giving the kid a reward,' he cried. 'Hell, you don't even have to pay it yourself. Jamshid will do the paying.' He turned to Raqi. 'You know Jamshid, kid?'

Raqi gave a small smile. He was embarrassed because he was unaccountably the centre of an argument. 'Who doesn't in Tehran? Anyone who bets the horses goes to Jamshid.'

'Yeah, he's got quite a reputation,' agreed Follet. 'He pays out fast when you win, but God help you if you don't pay him equally fast when you lose. A real tough baby.'

'What about watching us win our money?' suggested Warren. He nodded towards the television set. 'The race should be coming on soon.'

'Yeah,' said Follet and stepped over to the set. Warren crossed his fingers, hoping that Ben had done his job. He had already got the name of the winner of the three o'clock race and transmitted it to Follet during the fake telephone call to Jamshid, but if he had fumbled the recording then the whole scheme was a dead loss.

A voice swelled in volume, speaking Persian, and then the screen filled with a view of a racecourse crowd. Follet looked at the screen appraisingly, and said, 'About five minutes to go.' Warren let out his pent-up breath silently.

'What's he saying?' asked Tozier.

'Just talking about the horses,' said Raqi. He listened for a while. 'That's Al Fahkri – your horse – number five.'

'Our horse, Javid,' said Follet jovially. 'You're in on this.' He got up and went to the impromptu bar at the sideboard. 'I'll pour the drinks for the celebration now. This race will be fast.'

'You seem certain you'll win,' said Raqi.

Follet turned and winked largely. 'Certain isn't the word for it. This one's blue chip – a gilt-edged security.' He took his time pouring the drinks.

Tozier said, 'They're coming up to the post, Johnny.'

'Okay, okay; it doesn't really matter, does it?'

The commentator's voice rose as the race started, and Warren thought that it did not matter whether you understood the language or not, you could never mistake a horse race for anything else. Raqi was tense as Al Fahkri forged ahead of the pack on the heels of the leading horse. 'He stands a chance.'

'More than that,' said Follet unemotionally. 'He's going to win.'

Al Fahkri swept ahead to win by two lengths.

Warren got up and switched off the set. 'That's it,' he said calmly.

'Here, kid; have a drink on Jamshid,' said Follet, thrusting a glass into Raqui's hand. 'The honest bookie who never welshes. You're a bit richer than you were this morning.'

Raqi looked at the three of them in turn. Warren had produced a notebook and was methodically jotting down figures; Tozier was gathering up the cards scattered on the table; Follet was beaming in high good humour. He said, hesitantly, 'The race was . . . arranged?'

'Fixed is the word, kid. We've bought a couple of good jockeys. I told you it was a gilt-edged investment.'

Guilt-edged would be more like it, thought Warren.

Follet took a wallet from his jacket which was draped over the back of a chair and counted out notes. 'You don't have to wait to collect from Jamshid,' he said. 'I'll do that when I collect ours.' He tossed a roll of currency on the table before Raqi. 'It was eight to one – there's your sixteen thousand.' He grinned. 'You don't get your stake back because it wasn't yours. Okay, kid?'

Raqi took the money in his hands and gazed at it in wonder. 'Go ahead,' said Follet. 'Take it – it's yours.'

'Thanks,' said Raqi, and put the money away quickly.

Tozier said briefly, 'Let's play poker.'

'That's an idea,' said Follet. 'Maybe we can win that sixteen thousand from Javid.' He sat down as Warren put away the notebook. 'What's the score so far, Nick?'

'Just under two million,' said Warren. 'I think we ought to give it a rest for a while.'

'When we're hitting the big time? You must be crazy.'

'Jamshid will be getting worried,' said Warren. 'I know we've played it clever – he doesn't know the three of us are a syndicate – but he'll tumble to it if we don't watch it. Knowing Jamshid, I wouldn't like that to happen. I'd like to stay in one piece for a while longer.'

'Okay,' said Follet resignedly. 'Next Saturday is the last – for a while. But why not make it a really big hit this time?'

'No!' said Tozier abruptly.

'Why not? Supposing we put on a hundred thousand at ten to one. That's another quick million.' Follet spread his hands. 'Makes the arithmetic easier, too – a million each.'

'It's too risky,' Warren insisted.

'Say, I have an idea,' said Follet excitedly. 'Jamshid

doesn't know Javid here. Why can't Javid lay the bet for us? It's good for us and it's good for him. He can add his own dough and make a killing for himself. How about that, Javid?'

'Well, I don't know,' said Raqi uncertainly.

Tozier looked interested. 'It *could* work,' he said thoughtfully.

'You could be a rich man, Javid,' said Follet. 'You take that sixteen thousand you just won and you could turn it into a hundred and sixty thousand – that's as much as the three of us made today. And you can't miss – that's the beauty of it.'

Raqi took the lure as a trout takes a fly. 'All right,' he said suddenly. 'I'll do it.'

'Very well,' said Warren, capitulating. 'But this is the last time this year. Is that understood?'

Follet nodded, and Tozier said, 'Let's play poker.'

'Until six o'clock,' said Warren. 'I have a date tonight. Win or lose we stop at six.'

He won back most of his losses during the rest of the afternoon. Some of it was made by a big pot won on an outrageous bluff, but he seemed to have much better hands. At six o'clock he was down a mere thousand rials. He had unobtrusively put his watch right, too.

'That's it,' said Follet. 'See you next week, Javid.' He winked. 'You'll be in the big time then.'

When Raqi had gone Warren got up and stretched. 'What a way to pass a day,' he said.

'Our boy's very happy,' said Follet. 'He's broken into the big time and it hasn't cost him a cent. Let's figure out how much he's into us for. What did you lose, Warren?'

'A thousand as near as damn it.'

'Andy?'

'Close on three thousand. He can play poker.'

'That he can,' said Follet. 'I had to cut into him after the race – I didn't want him to think he can make more playing poker than playing the horses.' He looked up at Warren. 'You're no poker player. Now, let's see – I'm out a thousand, so he's taken a total of twenty-one thousand, including that dough I gave him for the race. He'll be back next week.'

'Greedy for more,' said Tozier. 'I thought you said he was honest.'

'There's a bit of larceny in all of us,' said Follet. 'Cheating a bookie is considered respectable by a lot of upright citizens – like smuggling a bottle of whisky through customs.' He picked up the pack of cards and riffled them. 'There's an old saying among con men – you can't cheat an honest man. If Javid was really honest this thing wouldn't work. But he's as honest as most.'

'Can you really take money off him at poker?' asked Warren. 'A lot depends on that.'

'I was doing it this afternoon, wasn't I?' demanded Follet. 'You ought to know that better than anyone. You don't think you started winning by your own good play.' He extended the pack to Warren. 'Take the top card.'

Warren took it. It was the nine of diamonds.

Follet was still holding the pack. 'Put it back. Now I'm going to deal that top card on to the table. Watch me carefully.' He picked up the top card and spun it smoothly on to the table in front of Warren. 'Now turn it over.'

Warren turned over the ace of clubs.

Follet laughed. 'I'm a pretty good second dealer. I dealt the second card, not the top card, but you didn't spot it.' He held up his hand. 'If you see any guy holding a pack of cards like this, don't play with him. That's the mechanic's grip, and he'll second deal you, bottom deal you, and strip your pockets. I'll take Javid Raqi all right.'

# IV

It was a long week. Warren understood the necessity for inaction but it still irked him. Tozier and Follet played their coin-matching game interminably and Tozier steadily lost, much to his annoyance. 'I'll figure this out if it's the last thing I do,' he said, and Follet chuckled comfortably.

Warren could not see the fascination the game held for Tozier. It seemed to be a childish game although there *was* the problem of why Follet won so consistently in what seemed to be an even game in which there was no possibility of cheating.

Bryan was as restless as Warren. 'I feel out of it,' he said. 'Like a spare wheel. I feel as though I'm doing nothing and going nowhere.'

'You're not the only one who feels that way,' said Warren irritably.

'Yes, but I was stuck playing with that bloody video recorder while you three were having all the fun.'

'That's the most important part, Ben.'

'Maybe – but it's over now. You won't need the recorder this time. So what do I do – twiddle my thumbs?'

Follet looked up. 'Wait a minute.' He eyed Ben speculatively. 'Maybe we're passing up a chance here. I think we can use you, Ben, but it'll need a bit of rehearsal with me and Andy. It'll be important, too. Are you game for it?'

'Of course,' said Bryan eagerly.

So the three of them went to Follet's room with Follet saying, 'Nothing to trouble you with, Nick; it's best you don't know what's going to happen. You're a lousy actor, anyway, and I want this to come as a real surprise.'

\* \* \*

Came Saturday and Javid Raqi arrived early. Follet had telephoned him and suggested a lengthened session starting in the morning, and Raqi had eagerly agreed. 'We've got to have time to strip the little bastard,' said Follet cynically.

They started to play poker at ten-thirty and, to begin with, Raqi won as he had the previous week. But then things seemed to go against him. His three kings were beaten by Warren's three aces; his full house was beaten by Tozier's four threes; his ace-high flush was beaten by Follet's full house. Not that this seemed to happen often but when it did the pots were big and Raqi lost heavily. His steady trickle of winning hands was more than offset by his few occasional heavy losses.

By midday he had exhausted the contents of his wallet and hesitantly drew out an envelope. Impatiently he ripped it open and spilled a pile of money on to the table.

'Are you sure you want to do that?' asked Follet gently.

'I still have money – plenty money,' said Raqi tensely.

'No offence,' said Follet as he gathered the cards. 'I guess you know what you're doing. You're a big boy now.' He dealt cards. Javid Raqi lost again.

By two in the afternoon Raqi was almost cleaned out. He had been holding his own for about half an hour and the money in front of him – about a thousand rials – ebbed and flowed across the table but, in the main, stayed steady. Warren guessed that Follet was organizing that and he felt a little sick. He did not like this cat and mouse game.

At last Tozier looked at his watch. 'We'd better switch to the horses,' he said. 'There's not much time.'

'Sure,' said Follet. 'Put up the stake, Nick; you're the banker. Javid, you know what to do?'

Raqi looked a little pale. 'Just make the phone call,' he said listlessly as Warren counted out large denomination notes on to the table.

'Hell, no!' said Follet. 'Jamshid doesn't accept credit bets over twenty-five thousand, and we three are putting up a hundred thousand. You have to stake it at Jamshid's place – cash on the barrel head. How much are you putting in, Javid?'

Raqi swallowed. 'I don't know.' He made a feeble gesture at the table. 'I've . . . I've lost it,' he said plaintively.

'Too bad,' said Tozier evenly. 'Better luck next time.'

Warren patted the notes together. 'A hundred thousand,' he said, and pushed the stack across the table.

'You'll still put this on for us, won't you?' said Follet, pushing the money across to Raqi. 'You said you would.'

Raqi nodded. He hesitated, then said, 'Could . . . could you . . . er . . . could you lend me some – until it's over?'

Follet looked at him pityingly. 'Hey, kid; you're in the big time now. You play with your own dough. You might swap nickels and dimes in a penny-ante school but not here.'

Tozier's snort of disgust seemed to unnerve Raqi and he flinched as though someone had hit him. 'But . . . but . . .' he stammered.

Warren shook his head. 'Sorry, Javid; but I thought you understood. Everybody here stands his own racket.' He paused. 'I suppose you could say it's not good form – not good etiquette – to borrow.'

Raqi was sweating. He looked at the backs of his hands which were trembling, and thrust them into his pockets. He swallowed. 'When do I have to go to Jamshid's?'

'Any time before the nags go to the post,' said Follet. 'But we'd like to get the dough in fairly early. We don't want to miss out on this – it's the big one.'

'Do you mind if I go out for a few minutes?' asked Raqi.

'Not so long as you're back in time,' said Follet. 'This is the big one, like I told you.'

Raqi got up. 'I'll be back soon,' he said in a husky voice. 'Not more than half an hour.' He went out and seemed to stumble at the door.

Follet listened for the click of the latch, then said softly, 'He's hooked.'

'But *will* he come back?' asked Warren.

'He'll be back. When you put a sucker on the send he *always* comes back,' said Follet with cynical certitude.

'How much did we take him for?' asked Tozier.

Follet counted money and did a calculation. 'I make it just over forty-eight thousand. He must have drawn out his savings for the big kill, but we got to it first. He'll be sweating blood right now, wondering where to raise the wind.'

'Where will he get it?' asked Warren.

'Who cares? But he'll get it – that's a certainty. He *knows* he's on to a good thing and he won't pass up the chance now. He won't be able to resist cheating Jamshid, so he'll find the dough somehow.'

Tozier and Follet matched coins while they waited for Raqi to come back – a sheep to the slaughter – and Follet came out the worse for a change. He shrugged. 'It doesn't matter – the percentages are still on my side.'

'I wish I knew how,' said Tozier venomously. 'I'll get to the bottom of this one yet. I think I can see a way.'

There was a soft knock at the door. 'That's our boy,' said Follet.

Javid Raqi came into the room quietly when Follet opened the door. He came up to the table and looked at the hundred thousand rials, but he made no move to touch the money. Warren said, 'All right, Javid?'

Slowly Raqi put out his hands and took the wad of notes. 'Yes,' he said. 'I'm ready.' He turned suddenly to Follet. 'This horse *will* be all right – it *will* win?' he asked urgently.

'Christ!' said Follet. 'You're holding a hundred thousand of our money and you ask that? Of course it will win. It's all set up.'

'Then I'm ready to go,' said Raqi, and swiftly put away the money.

'I'll go with you,' said Follet. He grinned. 'It's not that we don't trust you, but I'd hate some smart guy to knock you off when you're carrying our dough. Consider me a bodyguard.' He put on his jacket. 'We'll be back to watch the race,' he said as he left, shepherding Raqi before him.

Warren sighed. 'I feel sorry for that boy.'

'So do I,' said Tozier. 'But it's as Johnny said – if he were honest this would never be happening to him.'

'I suppose so,' said Warren, and fell silent. Presently he stirred and said, 'Supposing the horse wins?'

'It won't,' said Tozier positively. 'Johnny and I picked the sorriest screw we could find. It *might* win,' he conceded, 'if every other horse in the race breaks a leg.'

With what might have been a chuckle Warren said, 'But what if it does win? Someone must have faith in it.'

'Then we'll have won a hell of a lot of money – and so will Raqi, depending on how much of a stake he's been able to raise. We'll have to go through the whole business of breaking him again. But it won't happen.'

He began to match coins with himself and Warren paced up and down restlessly. Follet and Raqi were away for quite a long time and arrived back just as Warren switched on the set to get the race. Raqi sat at his place at the table; a slight, self-contained figure. Follet was jovial. 'Javid has the jitters. I keep telling him it'll be okay, but he can't stop worrying. He's been plunging, too – I reckon this is a bit too rich for his blood.'

'How much did you back the nag for?' asked Tozier curiously.

Raqi did not answer, but Follet gave a booming laugh. 'Fifty thousand,' he said. 'And the odds are fifteen to one. Our boy stands to make three-quarters of a million rials. I keep telling him it's okay, but he doesn't seem to believe me.'

Tozier whistled. Three-quarters of a million rials was about £4,000 – a fortune for a young Iranian clerk. Even his fifty thousand stake was a bit rich – about £260 – approximating to a sizeable bite of Raqi's annual income. He said, 'Where did you get that much? Did you go home and break open your piggy bank?'

Warren said sharply, 'Shut up! The race is about to start.'

'I'll pour the drinks for the celebration,' said Follet, and went over to the sideboard. 'You guys can cheer for me – the nag's name is Nuss el-leil.'

'I don't get the lingo,' said Tozier. 'What's that mean, Javid?'

Raqi opened bloodless lips. He did not take his eyes off the screen as he answered, 'Midnight.'

'A good name for a black horse,' commented Tozier. 'There they go.'

Warren glanced sideways at Raqi who was sitting tensely on the edge of his chair, the bluish gleam of the television screen reflected in his eyes. His hands were clasped together in a knuckle-whitening grip.

Tozier jerked irritably. 'Where the blazes is that horse? Can you see it, Javid?'

'It's lying fourth,' said Raqi. A moment later he said, 'It's dropped back to fifth – no, sixth.' A tremor developed in his hands.

'What's that bloody jockey up to?' demanded Tozier. 'He's throwing it away, damn him!'

Fifteen seconds later the race ended. Nuss el-leil was not even placed.

Follet stood transfixed at the sideboard. 'The little bastard double-crossed us,' he breathed. In a moment of savagery he hurled a full glass of whisky at the wall where it smashed explosively. 'I'll fix his goddam wagon come tomorrow,' he yelled.

Warren switched off the set. 'Calm down, Johnny. I told you it couldn't last forever.'

'Yeah, but I didn't reckon it would end this way,' said

Follet bellicosely. 'I thought Jamshid would cotton on to us. I didn't think I'd be gypped by that little monkey on the horse. Wait until I get my hands around his scrawny neck.'

'You'll leave him alone,' said Warren sharply. In a more placatory tone he said, 'So we've lost a hundred thousand – that's only five per cent of our winnings up to now. We're all right.' He sat at the table and gathered the cards. 'Who's for a game?'

'I reckon Johnny's right,' said Tozier in a hard voice. 'We can't let this pass. No jock is going to get the better of me, I tell you that. When I buy a jockey, he bloody well stays bought.'

'Forget it,' said Warren curtly. 'That particular game is over – we move on to something else. I told you this was the last time, didn't I?' He looked over his shoulder. 'For God's sake, come over here and sit down, Johnny. The world hasn't come to an end. Besides, it's your deal.'

Follet sighed as he took his seat. 'Okay – but it goes against the grain – it really does. Still, you're the boss.' He riffle-shuffled the pack and pushed it across the table. 'Your cut.'

Javid Raqi sat frozen and did not move.

'Hey!' said Follet. 'What's the matter, kid? You look as though you've seen a ghost.'

Two big tears squeezed from Raqi's eyes and rolled down his cheeks.

'For God's sake!' said Tozier in disgust. 'We've got a cry-baby on our hands.'

'Shut up, Andy!' said Warren savagely.

'What's the matter, Javid?' asked Follet. 'Couldn't you stand the racket? Couldn't you afford the fifty thousand?'

Raqi seemed to be staring at an inward scene of horror. His olive complexion had turned a dirty green and he was trembling uncontrollably. He moistened his lips, and whispered, 'It wasn't mine.'

'Oh, that's bad,' said Follet commiseratingly. 'But remember what I told you – you should always play with your own money. I did tell you that, you know – and so did Nick.'

'I'll lose my job,' said Raqi. His voice was filled with desperation. 'What will my wife say? What will she say?' His voice rose and cracked. Suddenly he was babbling in Persian and none of them could understand what he was saying.

Follet's hand came out sharply and cracked Raqi across the cheek, shocking him into silence. 'Sorry about that, Javid; but you were becoming hysterical. Now, calm down and talk sense. Where did you get the dough?'

'From the place I work,' said Raqi, swallowing hard. 'The chief clerk has a safe – and I have a key. He keeps money for out-of-hand expenses. I went back to the office and . . . and . . .'

'Stole the money,' said Tozier flatly.

Raqi nodded dejectedly. 'He'll know as soon as he opens the safe on Monday. He'll know it's . . .'

'Take it easy, kid,' said Follet. 'You're not in jail yet.'

That was an aspect that had not hit Raqi, and he stared at Follet with renewed horror. Follet said, 'Maybe we can help you.'

'Count me out,' said Tozier uncompromisingly. 'I'm not going to subsidize a freeloading kid who's still wet behind the ears. If he can't stand the heat, let him get out of the kitchen. He should never have come into this game, anyway. I told you that in the first place.'

Warren looked at Follet who just shrugged, and said, 'I guess that's so. You've gotta learn by your mistakes, kid. If we bail you out now, you'll do it again some time else.'

'Oh, no; I promise – I promise.' Raqi spread his arms wide on the table, grovelling before Follet. 'Help me – please help me – I promise . . .'

'Oh, for Christ's sake, stand up and be a man!' barked

148

Tozier. He stood up. 'I can't stand scenes like this. I'm getting out.'

'Wait a minute,' said Follet. 'I think I've got something.' He pointed his finger at Tozier. 'Weren't you telling me about a guy who wanted to get something from the company this kid works for? Something about some chemicals?'

Tozier thought for a moment, then nodded. 'What about it?'

'How much would he pay?'

'How the hell do I know?' said Tozier in a pained voice. 'This chap was working an angle in which I wasn't interested.'

'You could always ask him. There's a telephone there.'

'Why should I? There's nothing in it for me.'

'For Pete's sake, can't you be human for once in your goddam life?' asket Folled in an exasperated voice.

Warren's voice was quiet but it cut through the room with authority. 'Use the phone, Andy.'

'Oh, all right.' Tozier picked up his jacket. 'I think I have the number here somewhere.'

Follet patted Raqi on the shoulder. 'Bear up, Javid; we'll get you out of this jam somehow.' He sat next to him and began to talk to him quietly.

Tozier mumbled to someone on the telephone. At last he put it down and crossed the room with a paper in his hand. 'This man wants to know who's been ordering these chemicals – especially in quantity. He wants to know where they were despatched to. He also wants to know of any transactions concerning a man called . . .' He peered at the paper. '. . . Speering. That's it.' He rubbed the side of his jaw. 'I screwed him up to forty thousand but he wouldn't go higher for the information.'

'Why does he want it?' asked Warren.

'I reckon he's in industrial espionage.'

Follet took the sheet of paper. 'Who cares why he wants

it so long as Javid can deliver?' He gave the paper to Raqi. 'Can you get that stuff?'

Raqi wiped his eyes and looked carefully. He nodded, and whispered, 'I think so. All this is in the stock ledgers.'

'But the guy will only go to forty thousand, damn him,' said Follet. 'For crying out loud, I'm game to help make up the difference.'

'Count me out on that,' said Tozier grimly. 'I've done my bit.'

'Nick?'

'All right, Johnny; we'll split it between us.' Warren sorted out five thousand rials from the money on the table and passed it to Follet.

'There, you see, Javid; we've got ten thousand here. All you have to do to get the other forty thousand is to go back to the office. You have the key?'

Raqi nodded, and allowed Follet to help him to his feet. 'It will take time,' he said.

'Half an hour. That's all it took to loot the safe this afternoon,' said Tozier brutally.

Follet saw Raqi to the door and closed it gently. He turned, and said, 'We're nearly there. There's just one thing more to be done.'

Warren sighed. 'It can't be any dirtier than what we've done already. What is it?'

'You're not concerned in it, so rest easy,' said Follet. 'Now, all we have to do is wait. I'm going to see Ben – I'll be back in ten minutes.'

It seemed, to Warren, an eternity before Raqi returned. The minutes ticked by and he contemplated the sort of man he was becoming under the stress of this crazy adventure. Not only was he guilty of blackmailing Follet, but he had assisted in the corruption of a young man who had hitherto been blameless. It was all right for Follet to preach that you can't cheat an honest man; the men who offer the thirty pieces of silver are just as guilty as he who accepts them.

Again there was the expected knock at the door and Follet went to open it. Raqi had pulled himself together a little and did not seem so woebegone; there was more colour in his cheeks and he did not droop as he had when he left.

Follet said, 'Well, kid; did you get it?'

Raqi nodded. 'I took it from the ledgers in English – I thought that would help.'

'It surely would,' said Follet, who had forgotten that problem. 'Let me have it.'

Raqi gave him three sheets of paper which he passed to Tozier. 'You'll see it gets to the right place, Andy.' Tozier nodded, and Follet gave Raqi a bundle of money. 'There's your fifty thousand, Javid. You'd better put it back in the safe real fast.'

Raqi was just putting the money into his pocket when the door burst open. A man stood there, his face concealed by a scarf, and holding an automatic pistol. 'Stay still, everyone,' he said indistinctly. 'And you won't get hurt.'

Warren looked on unbelievingly as the man took a step forward. He wondered who the devil this was and what he thought he was doing. The stranger wagged the gun sideways. 'Over there,' he said, and Raqi and Follet moved under the threat to join Warren at the other side of the room.

'Not you,' said the man, as Tozier began to obey. 'You stay there.' He stepped up to Tozier and plucked the papers from his hand. 'That's all I want.'

'Like hell!' said Tozier and lunged for him. There was a sharp crack and Tozier stopped as though he had hit a brick wall. A stupid expression appeared on his face and his knees buckled. Slowly, like a falling tree, he toppled, and as he dropped to the ground a gush of blood spurted from his mouth.

151

There was a bang as the door closed behind the visitor, and a faint reek of gunsmoke permeated the atmosphere.

Follet was the first to move. He darted over to Tozier and knelt down beside him. Then he looked up in wonder. 'Good Christ – he's dead!'

Warren crossed the room in two strides, his professional instincts aroused, but Follet straight-armed him. 'Don't touch him, Nick; don't get any blood on you.' There was something odd in Follet's tone that made him stop.

Raqi was shaking like an aspen in a hurricane. A moaning sound came from his lips – not words, but the mere repetition of his vocalized gasps – as he stared in horror at the blood spattered on the cuff of his jacket. Follet took him by the arm and shook him. 'Javid! Javid, stop that! Do you hear me?'

Raqi became more coherent. 'I'm . . . I'm all . . . right.'

'Listen carefully, then. There's no need for you to be mixed up in this. I don't know what the hell it's all about, but you can get clear if you're quick about it.'

'How do you mean?' Raqi's rapid breathing was slowing.

Follet looked down at Tozier's body. 'Nick and I will get rid of him. Poor guy; he was a bastard if ever there was one, but I wouldn't have wished this on him. That information his friend wanted must have been really something.' He turned to Raqi. 'If you know what's good for you you'll get out of here and keep your mouth shut. Go to the office, put the dough back in the safe, go home and say nothing. Do you understand?'

Raqi nodded.

'Then get going,' said Follet. 'And walk – don't run. Take it easy.'

With a choked cry Raqi bolted from the room and the door slammed behind him.

Follet sighed and rubbed the back of his neck. 'Poor Andy,' he said. 'The chivalrous son-of-a-bitch. Okay, you can get up now. Arise, Lazarus.'

Tozier opened his eyes and winked, then leaned up on one elbow. 'How did it look?'

'Perfect. I thought Ben had really plugged you.'

Warren stepped over to Follet. 'Was that play-acting really necessary?' he asked coldly.

'It was really necessary,' said Follet flatly. 'Let's suppose we hadn't blown him off that way. Some time in the next few days he'd start to think and put things together, and it wouldn't take an egghead to figure he'd been conned. That boy's not stupid, you know; it's just that we rushed him – we didn't give him time to think straight.'

'So?'

'So now he'll *never* be able to think straight about what happened. The fact of sudden death does that to people. As long as he lives he'll never be able to figure out what really happened; he'll never know who shot and killed Andy – or why. Because it doesn't tie in with anything else. So he'll keep his mouth shut in case he's implicated in murder. That's why we had to blow him off with the cackle bladder.'

'With the *what*?'

'The cackle bladder.' Follet gestured. 'Show him, Andy.'

Tozier spat something from his mouth into his hand. 'I nearly swallowed the damn' thing.'

He held out his hand to disclose a reddened piece of limp rubber. Follet said, 'It's just a little rubber bag filled with chicken blood – a cackle bladder. It's used quite often to dispose of the chumps when they're no longer needed around.' He sniggered. 'It's the only other good use for a contraceptive.'

Ben Bryan came in, grinning. 'How did I do, Johnny?'

'You did fine, Ben. Where are those papers?' He took them from Bryan and slapped them into Warren's limp hand. 'Those are what you wanted.'

'Yes,' said Warren bitterly. 'These are what I wanted.'

'You wanted them – you've got them,' said Follet tensely. 'So use them. But don't come the big moral act with me, Warren. You're no better than anyone else.'

He turned away abruptly and walked out of the room.

# 6

They drove again among the ochre-red mountains of Kurdistan along the winding and precipitous roads. Warren was thankful to be in the lead; somewhere behind and hidden in the cloud of dust were Tozier and Follet in the second Land-Rover and he did not envy them. Bryan was driving and Warren navigating, trying to find his way to a spot pin-pointed on the map. This was more difficult than had at first appeared; at times Warren felt as though he were in Alice's Looking Glass Land because the roads, unmarked on the map, twisted and turned sinuously and often it seemed that the best way to approach a given point was to drive in the opposite direction.

And again, it was only by a considerable stretch of the imagination that these scratch marks in the mountains could be called roads. Ungraded, stony, washed-out and often on the living rock, these tracks had been worn by the pads of thousands of generations of camels over hundreds, possibly thousands of years. Alexander had marched through those mountains, riding among his *hetaeroi* to the conquest of Persia and the penetration of India, and Warren judged that the roads had not been repaired since.

Several times they passed groups of the nomadic Kurds who were presumably in search of greener pastures, although where those pastures could possibly be Warren did not know. The whole land was a wilderness of rock and eroded bare earth with minimal hardy vegetation which sprouted in crevices in the bare hillsides, sparse and spindly but with the clinging tenacity of life. And it was all brown and burnt and there was no green at all.

He checked the map again, then lifted it to reveal the three sheets of paper which Javid Raqi had abstracted from his office at so much expense of the spirit. The information had been a constant worry to Warren ever since he had seen it. He had been prepared for a reasonable amount of chemicals – enough to extract, at most, a hundred pounds of morphine from the raw opium. But this was most unreasonable.

The quantities involved were fantastic – enough methylene chloride, benzene, amyl alcohol, hydrochloric acid and pharmaceutical lime to extract no less than two tons of morphine. *Two tons!* He felt chilled at the implications. It would provide enough heroin to saturate the United States illicit market for a year with plenty left over. If this amount got loose then the pushers would be very busy and there would be an explosion of new addicts.

He said, 'I've checked the figures again, Ben – and they still don't make sense.'

Bryan slowed as he approached a difficult corner. 'They are startling,' he admitted.

'Startling!' echoed Warren. 'They're damned nearly impossible. Look, Ben; it calls for twenty tons of raw opium – twenty tons, for God's sake! That amount of opium would cost nearly a million pounds on the illegal market. Do you think the Delorme woman has that much capital to play with?'

Bryan laughed. 'If I had that much money I'd retire.' He twisted the wheel. 'I've just had a thought, though. Perhaps Raqi fudged the figures in his excitement. He was translating from an oriental script into western notation, remember. Perhaps he made the identical mistake throughout, and uprated by a constant factor.'

Warren chewed his lip. 'But what factor? Let's say he made an error of a factor of ten – that brings us to about four hundred pounds of morphine. That's still a hell of a lot, but it's much more reasonable.'

'How much would that be worth to Delorme?' asked Bryan.

'About twenty million dollars, landed in the States.'

'Yes,' said Bryan judiciously. 'I think I'd call that reasonable.' He slammed into low gear as they breasted a rise. 'How much longer before we get to whosit's place – what's his name?'

'Sheikh Fahrwaz.' Warren checked the map. 'If everything goes well – which it won't on past form – we should be there in an hour.'

The Land-Rover roared up to the top of the mountain pass, and Bryan slowed as they reached the crest. Warren, looking through the dusty windscreen, suddenly tensed. 'Reverse, Ben,' he said sharply. 'Quickly, now – get off the skyline.'

Bryan crashed the gears, infected by the excitement transmitted by Warren, and the Land-Rover lurched backwards in a series of jerks and came to a halt. 'Run back down the road,' said Warren. 'Run as far as you can and flag Andy to stop. Ask him to join me on foot. And don't slam that door when you get out.'

He opened the door and jumped to the ground, and as he ran up to the crest of the pass he veered to one side and headed for a clump of rocks which would give cover. When he arrived at the top he was panting, but more with excitement than exertion. He crouched behind the rocks and then slowly raised his head to get a view of the valley below.

Against a background of the usual arid hills on the other side of the valley there was a smear of green, cultivated land, chequer-boarded into fields, and in the middle was a cluster of buildings, low and flat-topped – either a small village or a biggish farm. This was the settlement of Sheikh Fahrwaz, the man who had ordered vast quantities of non-agricultural chemicals, and it was where Warren hoped to find Speering.

He heard a stone clatter behind him and turned his head to see Tozier approaching with Follet close behind. He waved them down and they came up more cautiously and joined him in looking down upon the valley. 'So this is it,' said Tozier after a while. 'What now?'

Follet said suddenly, 'Those people have been in big trouble.'

Warren looked down. 'How do you make that out?'

'Haven't you got eyes?' asked Follet. 'Look at those bomb craters. There's a line of them right across the valley – one bomb just missed that big building. Someone's had a crack at these boys from the air.'

It appeared that Follet was right. The line of craters stretched across the valley, starting from just below them and arrowing straight towards the settlement and beyond. Tozier reached behind for his binoculars. 'Who would want to bomb them unless it was the Iranian Air Force?' He juggled with the focusing. 'It was a poor attempt, though. That building hasn't been touched; there's no sign of repair work on the wall near the crater.'

'Are you sure they're bomb craters?' asked Warren. Something niggled at the back of his mind.

'I've seen plenty of them in Korea,' said Follet.

'Yes, they're bomb craters,' confirmed Tozier. 'Not very big bombs.'

This was a new element in the situation and something else for Warren to worry about. He put it to one side, and said, 'So what do we do?'

Bryan joined them. 'We just go down there,' he said, and jerked his head back at the vehicles. 'Our cover's good enough to carry it off. Even these people will have heard of motion pictures.'

Tozier nodded. 'Half of us go down,' he corrected. 'One vehicle. The other stays up here out of sight and keeps a listening watch on the radio.'

'What's the general procedure?' asked Warren. He had

no illusions about himself, and he knew that Tozier, the professional, knew more than he about an operation of this sort. He was quite prepared to take orders.

Tozier squinted at the valley. 'I've searched many an innocent-looking village in my time, looking for arms caches mostly. But then we went in as an open operation – bristling with guns. We can't do that here. If the people down there are innocent, they'll be hospitable; if they're guilty, they'll *seem* to be hospitable. We've got to get a look into every building, and every one we're barred from is a black mark against them. After that we play it as it comes. Let's go.'

'So it'll be you and me,' said Warren. 'While Ben and Johnny stay up here.'

The road wound down to the fertile oasis of the valley where the green vegetation looked incredibly refreshing. Some of the fields were bare and had the shallow lines of primitive ploughing, but most of them were under crops. Tozier, who was driving, said, 'Would you recognize an opium poppy if you saw one? You might find them here.'

'There's none that I can see,' said Warren. 'Wait a minute – can you go across there?' he pointed.

'I don't see why not.' Tozier twisted the wheel and the Land-Rover left the road and bumped across open country. It did not make any appreciable difference to the bounce and jolt – the road was purely symbolic. 'Where are we going?'

'I want to have a look at those craters,' said Warren. 'The idea of bombing worries me – it doesn't make sense.'

Tozier drove to the nearest crater and left the engine idling. They got out and looked across the valley floor towards the settlement. The line of craters stretched out towards the buildings, equally spaced at fifty-yard intervals. Tozier looked at the nearest and said, 'If that's not a bomb crater then I'm a duck-billed platypus. You can see how the earth has been thrown up around the edge.'

'Let's have a closer look,' said Warren, and started walking. He climbed over the soft earth at the crater's edge, looked inside and started laughing. 'You're a duck-billed platypus, Andy. Look here.'

'Well, I'm damned!' said Tozier. 'It's just a hole.' He stepped inside the crater, took a pebble and dropped it into the hole. There was a long pause and then a very faint splash. He straightened up and looked along the line of craters – of holes – with a puzzled expression. 'This is even crazier. Who'd want to dig a hell of a lot of deep wells at fifty-yard intervals and in a dead straight line?'

Warren snapped his fingers. 'I've got it! I nearly had it when Follet pointed them out, but I couldn't pin it down. This is a *qanat*.'

'A who-what?'

'A *qanat* – an underground canal.' He turned and looked back at the hills. 'It taps an aquifer in the slopes over there, and leads water to the village. I was studying Iran before we came out here and I read about them. Iran is pretty well honeycombed with the things – there's a total of nearly two hundred thousand miles of *qanats* in the country.'

Tozier scratched his head. 'Why can't they build their canals on the surface like other people?'

'It's for water supply,' said Warren. 'They lose less by evaporation if the channel is underground. It's a very old system – the Persians have been building these things for the last three thousand years.' He grinned with relief. 'These aren't bomb craters – they're ventilation shafts; they have to have them so the workmen aren't asphyxiated when they're doing repairs.'

'Problem solved,' said Tozier. 'Let's go.'

They set off again and drove back to the road and then towards the settlement. The buildings were of the common sort they had seen elsewhere – walls made of rammed earth, flat roofs, and all of them single storey which would conveniently make a search easier. As they got nearer they saw goats grazing under the watchful eye of a small boy who waved as they passed, and there were scrawny chickens which scattered as they approached the courtyard of the largest building.

Tozier drew up inside. 'If you want to tell me anything let it wait until we're alone. These people might have more English then they'll admit to. But I must say everything looks peaceful.'

It did not seem so to Warren because a crowd of small boys rushed forward towards the unexpected visitors and were capering about in the dust, their shrill voices raised high. The women who had been about were vanishing like wraiths, drawing their shawls about their faces and hurrying out of sight through a dozen doors. He said, 'There are a hell of a lot of rooms to look into; and if Fahrwaz has a harem that will make things difficult.'

They descended to the ground and the small boys engulfed them. Tozier raised his voice. 'Better lock up or we'll be missing a lot of gear.'

Another voice was raised in harsh command and the boys scattered, running across the courtyard as though the devil were at their heels. A tall man stepped forward, richly dressed and straight-backed, though elderly. The haft of the curved knife in his sash glinted with jewels, a stone shone in his turban and others from the rings on his fingers. His face was thin and austere, and his beard was grey.

He turned and spoke in a low voice to his companion, who said – astonishingly in English – 'Sheikh Fahrwaz welcomes you. His house is yours.' He paused, then added sardonically, 'I wouldn't take that too literally – it's just a figure of speech.'

Warren recovered enough to say, 'Thank you. My name is Nicholas Warren and this is Andrew Tozier. We're looking for locations to make a film.' He indicated the inscription on the side of the Land-Rover. 'We work for Regent Films of London.'

'You're off the beaten track. I'm Ahmed – this is my father.' He spoke to the old man and the Sheikh nodded his head gravely and muttered a reply. Ahmed said, 'You're still welcome, although my father cannot really approve. He is a good Moslem and the making of images is against the Law.' He smiled slightly. 'For myself, I couldn't give a damn. You need not lock your truck – nothing will be stolen.'

Warren smiled. 'It's . . . er . . . unexpected to find English spoken in this remote place.'

Ahmed smiled a little mockingly. 'Do you think I should have a big sign put up there on the Djebel Ramadi – "English Spoken Here"?' He gestured. 'My father wishes you to enter his house.'

'Thank you,' said Warren. 'Thank you very much.' He glanced at Tozier. 'Come on, Andy.'

The room into which they were led was large. Sheepskin rugs were scattered on the floor and the walls were hidden behind tapestries. Several low settees surrounded a central open space which was covered by a fine Persian carpet, and coffee was already being brought in on brass trays.

'Be seated,' said Ahmed, and sank gracefully on to one of the settees. Warren tactfully waited until Sheikh Fahrwaz had settled himself and then sat down, doing his best to imitate the apparently awkward posture of Ahmed, which Ahmed did not seem to find awkward at all. Tozier followed suit and Warren could hear his joints crack.

'We have had European visits before,' said Ahmed. 'My father is one of the old school, and I usually instruct visitors in our customs. It pleases my father when they do what is right in his eyes, and does no harm to anyone.' He smiled engagingly. 'Afterwards we will go to my quarters and drink a lot of whisky.'

'That's very kind of you,' said Warren. 'Isn't it, Andy?'

'I could do with a stiff drink,' admitted Tozier.

Ahmed spoke to his father, then said, 'We will now have coffee. It is a little ceremonious, but it will not take long. My father wishes to know how long you have been in Kurdistan.'

'Not very long,' said Warren. 'We came in from Gilan two days ago.'

Ahmed translated this to his father, then said, 'You take the brass coffee cup in your right hand. The coffee is very hot and already sweetened – perhaps too sweet for your palate. Is this your first time in Kurdistan?'

Warren thought it better to tell the truth; unnecessary lies could be dangerous. He picked up the cup and cradled it in the palm of his hand. 'We were here a few weeks ago,' he said. 'We didn't find just what we wanted so we went back to Tehran to rest for a while.'

'No,' said Ahmed. 'Kurdistan is not a restful place.' He turned to Sheikh Fahrwaz and ripped off a couple of sentences very fast, then he said, 'You drink the coffee all at once, then you put the cup on the tray – upturned. It will make a sticky mess, but that doesn't matter. What is this film you are going to make, Mr Warren?'

'I'm not going to make the film,' said Warren. 'I'm just an advance man scouting locations as called for by the script.' He drank the coffee; it was hot and sickly sweet, and the cup was half full of grounds which he pushed back with his tongue. He brought the cup down and turned it over on the tray. Old Sheikh Fahrwaz smiled benevolently.

'I see,' said Ahmed. 'Just the other two cups and then we are finished. You make my father very happy when you understand our Kurdish hospitality.' He drank his coffee apparently with enjoyment. 'Are you the . . . er . . . the man in charge, Mr Warren?'

'Yes.' Warren followed Ahmed's example and picked up the second cup. 'Andy – Mr Tozier, here – is more of a technician. He concerns himself with camera angles and things like that.' Warren did not know how a unit like this was supposed to operate, and he hoped he was not dropping too many clangers.

'And there are just the two of you?'

'Oh, no,' said Warren blandly. 'Four of us in two vehicles. The others had a puncture and stopped to change the wheel.'

'Ah, then we must extend our hospitality to your friends. Night is falling.'

Warren shook his head. 'It is not necessary. They are fully equipped for camping.'

'As you say,' said Ahmed, and turned to his father.

They got through the third and last cup of the coffee ceremony and Sheikh Fahrwaz arose and uttered a sonorous and lengthy speech. Ahmed said briefly, 'My father extends to you the use of his house for the night.'

Warren gave Tozier a sideways glance and Tozier nodded almost imperceptibly. 'We'll be delighted. I'd just like to get some things from the Land-Rover – shaving kit and so forth.'

'I'll get it,' said Tozier promptly.

'Why, Mr Tozier,' said Ahmed chidingly, 'I was beginning to think the cat had got your tongue.' He brought out the English idiom triumphantly.

Tozier grinned. 'I leave the talking to the boss.'

'Of course you may leave,' said Ahmed. 'But *after* my father – that is the custom.'

Sheikh Fahrwaz bowed and disappeared through a doorway at the back of the room, and Tozier went out into the courtyard. He reached into the cab, unhooked the microphone and tossed it carelessly into the back. Luckily it had a long lead. He climbed into the back and, as he was unstrapping his case, he pressed the switch, and said in a low voice, 'Calling Regent Two; calling Regent Two. Come in – come in. Over.'

Follet's voice from the speaker in front was a bit too loud for comfort. 'Johnny here. Are you okay? Over.'

'We'll be all right if you speak more softly. We're staying the night. Keep listening in case anything happens. Over.'

'I can't keep the set alive all night without moving,' said Follet more quietly. 'It'll run the batteries flat. Over.'

'Then keep a listening watch every hour on the hour for ten minutes. Got that? Over.'

'Got it. Good luck. Out.'

Tozier unpacked everything he and Warren would need and then stowed the microphone away out of sight. When he went back into the house he found Warren and Ahmed chatting. 'Ahmed has just been telling me how he came by his English,' said Warren. 'He lived in England for seventeen years.'

'Oh,' said Tozier. 'That's interesting. How come?'

Ahmed waved gracefully. 'Let us talk about it over a drink. Come, my friends.' He led them from the room, across the courtyard and into what were unmistakably his own quarters, which were furnished completely in European style. He opened a cabinet. 'Whisky?'

'Thank you,' said Warren civilly. 'It's very kind of you.'

Ahmed poured the drinks and Warren noted he drank Chivas Regal. 'My father does not approve, but I do as I wish in my own rooms.' He handed a glass to Warren. 'The Prophet is against alcohol, but would God allow us to make it if we weren't to use it?' He held up the bottle and said jocularly, 'And if I sin, at least my sins are of the finest quality. Mr Tozier, your drink.'

'Thank you.'

Ahmed poured himself a healthy slug. 'Besides, the very word alcohol is Arabic. I must say I acquired a taste for Scotch whisky in England. But sit down, gentlemen; I think you will find those seats more comfortable than those of my father.'

'How did you get to England?' asked Warren curiously.

'Ah, what a long story,' said Ahmed. 'Do you know much of our Kurdish politics?'

'Nothing at all. What about you, Andy?'

'I've heard of the Kurdish problem, but I've never known what it is,' said Tozier.

Ahmed laughed. 'We Kurds prefer to call it the Iranian problem, or the Iraqi problem, or the Turkish problem; we don't look upon ourselves as a problem, but that is quite natural.' He sipped his whisky. 'During the war Iran was occupied, as you know, by you British in the south and by the Russians in the north. When the occupying forces left the Russians played one of their favourite tricks by leaving a Fifth Column behind. For this purpose they tried to use the Kurds. The Mehabad Kurdish Republic was set up, backed by the Russians, but it was short-lived and collapsed as soon as the new Iranian government moved an army to the north.'

He waved his glass. 'That was in 1946 when I was five years old. My father was involved, and with Mullah Mustapha Barzani, he took refuge in Russia.' He tapped his chest. 'But me he sent to England where I lived until 1963. My father is a wise man; he did not want all his family in Russia. You English have a saying about too many eggs in one basket – so I was sent to England, and my elder brother to France. That explains it, does it not?'

'This Mullah what's-his-name – who is he?' asked Tozier.

'Mullah Mustapha Barzani? He is one of our Kurdish leaders. He is still alive.' Ahmed chuckled gleefully. 'He is in Iraq with an army of twenty thousand men. He causes the Iraqis a lot of trouble. Me, I am also a Barzani; that is, a member of the Barzani tribe of which the Mullah is the leader. And so, of course, is my father.'

'How did your father get back into Iran?' asked Warren.

'Oh, there was a sort of amnesty,' said Ahmed, 'and he was allowed to return. Of course he is watched; but all Kurds are watched, more or less. My father is now old and no longer inclined to politics. As for me – I never was. Life in England conditions one to be . . . gentle!'

Warren looked at the knife in Ahmed's sash and wondered if it was entirely ceremonial. Tozier said, 'Where do the Iraqis and Turks come into all this?'

'Ah, the Kurdish problem. That is best explained with a map – I think I have one somewhere.' Ahmed went to a bookcase and pulled out what was obviously an old school atlas. He flicked the pages, and said, 'Here we are – the Middle East. In the north – Turkey; in the east – Iran; to the west – Iraq.' His finger swept in a line from the mountains of eastern Turkey south along the Iraqi-Iranian border.

'This is the homeland of the Kurds. We are a divided people spread over three countries, and in each country we are a minority – an oppressed minority, if you like. We are divided and ruled by the Persians, the Iraqis and the Turks. You must admit this could lead to trouble.'

'Yes, I can see that,' said Tozier. 'And it's happening in Iraq, you say.'

'Barzani is fighting for Kurdish autonomy in Iraq,' said Ahmed. 'He is a clever man and a good soldier; he has fought the Iraqis to a standstill. With all their war planes, tanks and heavy artillery the Iraqis have not been able to subdue him – so now President Bakr is reduced to negotiation.' He smiled. 'A triumph for Barzani.'

He closed the atlas. 'But enough of politics. Have more whisky and tell me of England.'


II


Warren and Tozier left rather late the next morning. Ahmed was prodigal in his hospitality, but they did not see Sheikh Fahrwaz again. Ahmed kept them up late at night talking about his life in England and quizzing them about current English affairs. In the morning, after breakfast, he said, 'Would you like to see the farm? It's typically Kurdish, you know.' He smiled charmingly. 'Perhaps I will yet see my father's farm on the screen.'

The tour of the farm was exhaustive – and Ahmed was exhausting. He showed them everything and kept up a running commentary all the time. It was after eleven when they were ready to leave. 'And where do you go now?' he asked.

Tozier looked at his watch. 'Johnny hasn't turned up yet; maybe he's in trouble. I think we ought to go back and find him. What do you say, Nick?'

'It might be as well,' said Warren. 'But I bet he's gone back to have another look at that encampment he was so enthusiastic about. I think we'd better chase him up.' He smiled at Ahmed. 'Thank you for your hospitality – it's been most kind.'

'Typically Kurdish,' said Ahmed cheerfully.

They exchanged a few more polite formalities and then departed with a wave from Ahmed and his 'God speed you,' in their ears. As they bumped back along the road to the pass Warren said, 'What did you think of that?'

Tozier snorted. 'Too bloody good to be true, if you ask me. He was altogether too accommodating.'

'He certainly took a lot of trouble over us,' said Warren. '"Typical Kurdish hospitality",' he quoted.

'Hospitality, my backside,' said Tozier violently. 'Did you notice he took us into every building – into every room? It was as though he was deliberately demonstrating he had nothing to hide. How did you sleep?'

'Like the dead,' said Warren. 'He was very liberal with his Chivas Regal. I felt woozy when I turned in.'

'So was I,' said Tozier. 'I usually have a better head for Scotch than that.' He paused. 'Maybe we were doped with some of that morphine we're looking for. Is that possible?'

'It's possible,' said Warren. 'I must admit I felt a bit dreary when I woke up this morning.'

'I have a vague idea there was quite a bit of movement during the night,' said Tozier. 'I seem to remember a lot of coming and going with camels. The trouble is I don't know if it really happened or if it was a dream.'

They came to the top of the pass and Warren looked back. The settlement looked peaceful and innocent – a pleasant pastoral scene. Typically Kurdish, he thought sardonically. And yet Sheikh Fahrwaz was the consignee for those damned chemicals. He said, 'We saw everything there was to be seen down there, therefore there was nothing to hide. Unless . . .'

'Unless?'

'Unless it's so well hidden that Ahmed knew we wouldn't spot it.'

'How much room would Speering need for his laboratory, or whatever it is?'

Warren considered the ridiculous amount of chemicals that Javid Raqi had come up with. 'Anything from two hundred square feet to two thousand.'

'Then it's not there,' said Tozier flatly. 'We'd have seen it.'

'Would we?' said Warren thoughtfully. 'You said you've searched villages for arms caches. Where did you usually find them?'

'Oh, for God's sake!' said Tozier, thumping the wheel violently. 'Underground, of course. But just in bits and pieces – a few here and there. There was never any big-scale construction like you'd need here.'

'It wouldn't be too difficult. The ground in the valley bottom isn't rocky – it's soil over red clay; quite soft, really.'

'So you think we ought to go back and have a look. That's going to be difficult, as well as being dicey.'

'We'll talk about it with the others. There's Ben now.'

Bryan waved them off the road into a little side valley

169

which was hardly more than a ravine, and jumped on to the running-board as they passed. After two hundred yards the ravine bent at right-angles and they saw the other vehicle parked, with Follet sitting on the ground in front of it. He looked up as they stopped. 'Any trouble?'

'Not yet,' said Tozier briefly. He joined Follet. 'What's that you've got there?'

'A photograph of the valley. I took a dozen with the Polaroid camera.'

'Those could be useful. We have to go in there again – discreetly. Let's have a look at them, Johnny – all of them.'

Follet spread the photographs on the bonnet of the Land-Rover. After a while Tozier said, 'There's not much joy here. Anyone coming down the pass can be spotted in daylight, and you can lay odds that a watch is kept. It's four miles from the bottom of the pass to the settlement – eight miles there and back – that's a long way at night on foot. And when we get there we have to stumble around in the dark looking for something that might not be there. I can't see it.'

'What are you looking for?' asked Follet.

'A secret underground room,' said Warren.

Follet pulled a face. 'How in hell do you expect to find that?'

'I don't know how we're going to find it,' said Warren a little wearily.

Bryan leaned over and picked up a photograph. 'Andy seems more concerned about getting to the settlement unseen,' he said. 'There's more than one way of skinning a cat.' His finger traced the lane of 'craters'. 'Tell me more about this underground channel.'

'The *qanat*? It's just a means of tapping water from the mountains and leading it to the valley.'

'How big is it? Big enough for a man to walk through?'

Warren nodded. 'It must be.' He tried to remember what

he had read about them. 'They send men down to keep them in repair.'

'There you are,' said Bryan. 'You don't have to go stumbling around. That's an arterial highway pointing straight at the settlement. You can pop down a hole here and pop up another there just like a rabbit.'

Tozier stared at him for a moment. 'You make it sound so easy,' he said with heavy irony. 'What's the slope in these things, Nick?'

'Not much. Just enough to keep the water moving.'

'How deep is the water?'

'I don't think that's very much, either. Maybe a foot.' Warren felt a sense of desperation. 'Look, Andy; I don't know much about this. All I know is what I've read.'

Tozier ignored that. 'What's the footing like? Is it flat?'

Warren closed his eyes, trying to visualize the illustrations he had seen. At last he said, 'Flat, I think.'

Tozier looked at the photographs. 'We go down the pass on foot just after dark. We drop down a shaft into the *qanat*. If the footing is reasonable we ought to make two miles an hour – that's two hours to the settlement. We come up as close as possible and we can search until just before daybreak. Then we pop back down our hole and come back underground and unseen. We take our chances coming up the pass in daylight – there's a reasonable amount of cover. It's becoming practicable.'

Follet snorted. 'Practicable! I think it's crazy. Burrowing underground, for Christ's sake!'

'Supposing the *qanat* route is practicable,' said Warren. 'I doubt it, but let's suppose we can do it. How are we going to search the settlement without being nabbed?'

'You never know your luck unless you try,' said Tozier. 'In any case, can you suggest anything else?'

'No,' said Warren. 'I can't, damn it!'

# III

Tozier supervised the preparations. He hauled more rope out of the Land-Rovers than Warren had thought they carried – light nylon rope with a high breaking strain. From a toolbox he took crampons. 'Dropping down a shaft will be easy,' he said. 'We can do that on the end of a rope. Getting up another might be difficult. We'll need these.'

He produced high-powered electric torches and knives to go in their belts, but Warren was surprised when he began to take apart one of the photographic tripods. 'What are you doing?'

Tozier paused. 'Supposing you find this laboratory – what do you intend to do?'

'Destroy it,' said Warren tightly.

'How?'

'I thought of burning it, or something like that.'

'That might not work underground,' said Tozier, and continued to strip the tripod. He took off the tubular aluminium legs and from them shook several brown cylinders. 'This will do it, though. You don't need much gelignite to make a thorough mess of a relatively small installation.'

Warren gaped as he watched Tozier wrap the gelignite into a neat bundle with strips of insulating tape. Tozier grinned. 'You left the fighting preparations to me – remember?'

'I remember,' said Warren.

Then Tozier did something even more surprising. Using a screwdriver he removed the clock from the dashboard. 'This is already gimmicked,' he said. 'See that spike on the back? That's a detonator. All we do is to ram that into one of those sticks of gelignite and we can set the clock to

172

explode it at any time up to twelve hours in advance.' He laughed. 'The art of preparation is the art of war.'

'Got any more surprises?' asked Warren drily.

Tozier looked at him seriously and jerked his thumb in the direction of the settlement. 'Those boys are gangsters and they'll use gangster's weapons – knives and pistols. In these parts maybe rifles, too. But I'm a soldier and I like soldier's tools.' He patted the side of the Land-Rover. 'These aren't the same vehicles that left the factory. The Rover company wouldn't recognize some of the parts I put in, but then, neither would a customs officer.'

'So?'

'So what does a gun look like?'

Warren shook his head in a baffled way. 'It has a barrel, a trigger, a stock.'

'Yes,' said Tozier. He went to the back of the Land-Rover and began to take out one of the struts which held up the canopy. He hauled it out and the canopy sagged slightly but not much. 'There's your barrel,' he said, thrusting it into Warren's hands. 'Now we want the breech mechanism.'

He began to strip the vehicle of odd bits of metal – the cigarette lighter from the dashboard was resolved into its component parts, an ashtray which was apparently a metal pressing turned out to be a finely machined slide, springs were picked out of the toolbox and within ten minutes Tozier had assembled the gun.

'Now for the stock,' he said, and unstrapped the spade from the side of the Land-Rover. With a twist of his wrist it came neatly in half and the handle part was slotted into the gun to form a shoulder rest. 'There you are,' he said. 'An automatic machine-pistol. There's so much metal in a truck that no one recognizes small components for what they are – and the big bits you disguise as something else.' He held out the gun. 'We couldn't just walk into the country with a thing like this in our hands, could we?'

'No,' said Warren, fascinated. 'How many of those have you got?'

'Two of these little chaps and a rather decent air-cooled machine-gun which fits on one of the tripods. Ammunition is the difficulty – it's hard to disguise that as anything else, so we haven't got much.' He jerked his thumb. 'Every one of those sealed cans of unexposed film carries its share.'

'Very ingenious.'

'And then there's the mortar,' said Tozier casually. 'You never know when a bit of light artillery will come in useful.'

'No!' said Warren abruptly. 'Now, that's impossible.'

'Be my guest,' said Tozier, waving at the Land-Rover. 'If you find it you can have my bonus – or as much of it as Johnny Follet leaves me with.'

He went away, leaving Warren to look at the Land-Rover with renewed interest. A mortar was a big piece of equipment, and search as he would he could not find anything remotely resembling one, nor could he find any mortar bombs – sizeable objects in themselves. He rather thought Tozier was pulling his leg.

They made the final preparations and drove up to the top of the pass and parked the Land-Rovers off the road behind some boulders. At sunset they began to descend the pass. Going down into the valley was not too difficult; it was not yet so dark that they could not see a few yards in front of them, but dark enough to make it improbable that they should be seen from a distance. From the top of the pass to the first ventilation shaft of the *qanat* was just over a mile, and when they got there it would have been quite dark but for the light of the newly risen moon.

Tozier looked up at the sky. 'I'd forgotten that,' he said. 'It could make it dicey at the other end. We're damned lucky to have this underground passage – if it works.' He began to uncoil a rope.

'Hold on,' said Warren. 'Not this shaft.' He had just

remembered something. 'This will be the head well – the water's likely to be deep at the bottom. Try the next shaft.'

They walked about fifty yards along the line of the *qanat* until they came to the next shaft, and Tozier unslung the rope. 'How deep are these things, Nick?'

'I haven't a clue.'

Tozier picked up a pebble and dropped it down the hole, timing its fall by the ticking of his watch. 'Less than a hundred feet. That's not too bad. We might have to come up this one in a hurry.' He gave one end of the rope to Bryan.

'Here, Ben; belay that around something – and make sure it's something that won't shift.'

Bryan scouted around and found a rock deeply embedded in the earth around which he looped the rope, tying it off securely. Tozier hauled on it to test it, then fed the other end into the shaft. He handed his machine-pistol to Warren. 'I'll go first. I'll flash a light three times if it's okay to come down.' He sat on the edge of the shaft, his legs dangling, then turned over on to his belly and began to lower himself. 'See you at the bottom,' he whispered, the sound of his voice coming eerily from the black hole.

He went down hand over hand using his knees to brace against the wall of the shaft which was about three feet in diameter. One by one he came to the bits of cloth he had tied to the rope at ten-foot intervals and by which he could judge his distance and, at just past the ninety-foot mark, his boots struck something solid and he felt the swirl of water over his ankles.

He looked up and saw the paler blackness of the sky. It flickered a little and he guessed someone was looking down the shaft. He groped for his torch, flashed it three times upwards, then he shone it around and down the *qanat*. It stretched away, three feet wide and six feet high, into the distance, far beyond the range of his light. The bare earthen walls were damp and the water flowed about nine inches deep.

He felt the rope quiver as someone else started down the shaft and a scattering of earth fell on his head. He stepped out of the way downstream and presently Warren joined him, gasping for breath. Tozier took the gun and said, 'This is it, Nick.' He played the light on the earthen roof. 'God help us if that caves in.'

'I don't think it will,' said Warren. 'If there's a danger of that they put in big pottery hoops to retain it. Don't forget that people are working down here pretty regularly to keep the waterway unrestricted. They don't want to get killed, either.' He forebore to tell Tozier that the men who worked in the *qanats* had an aptly descriptive name for them – they called them 'the murderers'.

'How old do you think this is?' asked Tozier.

'I don't know. Could be ten years – could be a thousand, or even more. Does it matter?'

'I don't suppose so.'

Bryan joined them and was soon followed by Follet. Tozier said, 'The shaft we want to go up is the thirty-fifth from here . . .'

'The thirty-fourth,' said Warren quietly.

'Oh yes; I forgot we skipped the first one. We'll all keep a count just in case. If there's an argument the majority vote wins. And we go quietly because I don't know how sounds carry up the shafts. I go first with a gun, Nick next, then Ben and lastly Johnny with the other gun as rearguard. Let's go.'

It was ridiculously easy and they made far better time than Warren had expected – at least three miles an hour. As Bryan had said, it was a main highway pointing at the farm. The footing was firm and not even muddy or slippery so that it was even easier than walking in the middle of an English stream. The water was not so deep as to impede them unduly and Tozier's powerful torch gave plenty of light.

Only once did they run into a minor difficulty. The water deepened suddenly to two feet and then to three. Tozier halted them and went ahead to kick down a dam of soft earth where there had been a small roof fall. The pent-up water was released and gurgled away rapidly until it fell to the normal nine inches or so.

But still, it was a hard slog and Warren was relieved when Tozier held up his hand for them to stop. He turned and said softly, 'This shaft is thirty-three – are we agreed on that?' They were. He said, 'Now we go canny. Remember that the settlement is just above us. Gently does it.'

They carried on into the darkness with Tozier meticulously checking his paces. Suddenly he stopped so that Warren almost collided with him. 'Do you hear anything?' he asked in a low voice.

Warren listened and heard nothing but the gentle chuckle of the water. 'No,' he said, and even as he said it he heard a throb which rapidly died away. They kept quiet, but heard nothing more.

At last Tozier said, 'Come on – it's only another twenty yards.' He pushed on and stopped under the shaft. Abruptly he turned and whispered, 'There's a light up there. Have a look and tell me what you think it is.'

Warren squeezed past him and looked up the shaft. Far above he saw the pale circle of the sky but there was another and brighter light shining on the wall of the shaft not so far up, which seemed to be emanating from the side of the shaft itself. He estimated that it was about fifty feet up.

He drew back and said quietly, 'We were looking for something underground, weren't we? I think this is it. The place would have to be ventilated somehow so they're using the *qanat* shaft. And this shaft is the nearest to the farm.'

Tozier's voice was filled with incredulity. 'You think we've stumbled across it first crack out of the box?'

Follet said out of the darkness, 'Everybody's lucky sometime. Why not us?'

There was a sound. The distant but distinct noise of someone coughing. 'Someone's awake,' breathed Tozier. 'We can't do anything yet.' He peered up the shaft. 'If they ever sleep they'll put the light out. I'll keep watch – the rest of you go back, say, a hundred yards. And keep quiet.'

Thus began one of the most uncomfortable periods of Warren's life. It was nearly three hours before Tozier flashed for them and he knew what his feet would look like when he took off his boots; they would be as white as a fish's belly and as wrinkled as a washerwoman's hands. He made a mental note to issue surgical spirits when – and if – they got back, otherwise everyone could become crippled with blisters.

So he was very glad when Tozier gave the signal and he was able to move up and to stretch his cramped limbs. 'Everything all right?'

'The light has been off for nearly an hour. I thought I heard someone snoring a while back, so let's hope he's still asleep. I think I'll nip up and have a look. You'll have to give me a boost up to the shaft.'

'Take it easy.'

'I will,' said Tozier with grim humour. 'I was studying the light before it went out. I reckon that's the main entrance to their cubby-hole. Well, here goes – I'll drop a rope for you.'

Warren, Bryan and Follet braced themselves, forming a human stepladder up which Tozier could climb. He hoisted himself up, felt the sides of the shaft with his hands, and then brought up one leg so that the crampons on his boot bit into the clay. He pushed, straightening his leg, and dug in with the other boot. It was not too difficult – he had made worse climbs, but never in such darkness. Slowly he went up, his back braced against the wall and his feet climbing the opposite wall in the chimney technique he had once learned at mountain school.

Halfway he stopped, and rested for a couple of minutes and then started again, feeling it easier as he got the rhythm so that the second half of the climb was done much more quickly than the first. And so he came to the ledge, broad enough to stand on, that had been cut into the side of the shaft. He risked a flash of his light and saw a support post, so he uncoiled his rope, tied one end securely to the post, and dropped the rest down the shaft.

Warren came up next with his gun which Tozier took and cocked with a metallic click. Then Bryan came, and Follet soon after, and all four of them were crammed on the narrow ledge. Tozier flashed his light and they saw a door. He pushed it gently and it swung open without a sound, so he passed inside – gun first.

Follet went next because he too had a gun, and Warren and Bryan were close behind. Tozier switched on his light and the beam roved about, striking bright reflections from the glassware set up on benches. The light moved on and settled on a bed where a man lay sleeping. He moved restlessly under the glare, and Tozier whispered, 'Take him, Johnny.'

Follet moved forward into the light. He crossed the room in three strides, his hand came up holding something black, and when it game down there was a dull thump and a muffled gasp.

Tozier searched the room with his light, looking for other sleepers, but he found none. 'Close the door, Ben,' he said. 'Johnny, light that Coleman lamp.'

The bright light from the lamp was enough to show Warren that they had found the right place. There was only the one room, carved out of the alluvial clay, the roof supported by rough timber. It reminded him very much of the dug-outs of the trenches of the First World War which he had seen depicted on the screen. The room was cramped because nearly half of it was filled with boxes, and the rest with benches full of equipment.

Tozier said, 'Take a look, Nick. Is this what you're looking for?'

Warren cast a professional eye on the bench set-up. 'By God, it is!' He sniffed at some of the open bottles, then found some white powder and cautiously put the tip of his tongue to a couple of granules held on his fingertip. He grimaced. 'This is it, all right.'

Bryan straightened up from the bed. 'He's out cold. What did you hit him with, Johnny?'

Follet grinned and held up a stubby, leather-covered cosh.

'It's Speering, all right,' said Bryan. 'He's been growing a beard, but I recognize him.'

'He can't have been working on his own,' said Tozier.

Warren was probing among the benches. 'He'd need a few assistants, but once he'd made this set-up he could get by with unskilled labour as long as he did the supervision. Some of our hospitable Kurds upstairs, I suppose.' He looked about the room, at the coffee-pot and the dirty plates and the empty whisky bottles. 'Ahmed doesn't give him Chivas Regal, I see. He's been living down here all the time, I think. They couldn't let him give the game away by allowing him to walk around the settlement.'

His gaze settled on the boxes and he investigated one that had been opened. 'Christ Almighty!'

Tozier looked over his shoulder at the cylindrical objects. 'What are they – cheeses?'

'That's opium,' said Warren. 'And it's Turkish opium, by God! Not Iranian at all.'

'How do you know it's Turkish?'

'The shape – only the Turks pack it that way.' He stepped back and looked at the stack of boxes. 'If these are all full there must be ten tons of the stuff here.'

180

Tozier tested the weight of a couple of boxes at random. 'They're full, all right.'

Warren began to think that the figures supplied by Raqi were correct, after all. He found a corner of the room used for chemical storage and started to check the remaining chemicals against Raqi's list. After a while he said, 'As near as I can get to it he's used about half – but where's the morphine?'

Follet made a muffled exclamation which was covered by Tozier's voice as he held up a rectangular block. 'What's this?'

Warren took it and scratched the surface with his finger-nail. 'More opium – wrapped in poppy leaves. From Afghanistan, I'd say. It looks as though they've been getting the stuff from all over the Middle East.' He tossed it on to the bench. 'But I'm not interested in that – I want the morphine.'

'What would it look like?'

'A fine white powder – like table salt or castor sugar. And there ought to be a hell of a lot of it.'

They searched the room carefully and eventually Follet said excitedly, 'What's this?' He hefted a large glass carboy half full of white powder.

Warren sampled it gingerly. 'This is it. This is morphine.'

'Cut or uncut?' asked Follet.

'It's pure – or as pure as you can make the stuff in a slum like this.'

Follet whistled. 'So this is what you were after. You played it close to your chest, didn't you, Warren?' He tested the weight of the carboy. 'Jesus! There must be twenty pounds here. This lot should be worth half a million bucks.'

'Don't get any ideas, Johnny,' said Tozier.

Warren whirled around. 'Twenty pounds! I'm looking for a hundred times that amount.'

181

Follet stared at him. 'You serious? You must be joking, Doc.'

'This isn't a thing to joke about,' said Warren savagely. He flung out his arm and pointed to the boxes of opium stacked against the wall. 'There's enough opium there to extract a ton of morphine. Speering had used half his chemicals so we can say his job was half done – he's been here long enough to have extracted a ton of morphine with help – and the scale of this laboratory set-up is just about right, too. So where the hell is it?' His voice rose.

'Not so loud,' said Tozier warningly. He nodded to where Speering lay breathing stertorously on the bed. 'We could ask him?'

'Yeah,' said Follet. 'But he might make a noise while we're doing it.'

'Then we'll take him with us,' said Tozier. 'Some of the way.' He turned back to Warren. 'What do you want done with this place?'

'I want it wrecked,' said Warren coldly. 'I want it totally destroyed.'

'Half a million bucks,' said Follet, and tapped the carboy with his foot. 'An expensive bang.'

'Would you have any other ideas?' asked Tozier softly.

'Hell, no,' said Follet. 'It's not my line. I stay on the legal side – although I must say I've been stretching it a bit on this trip.'

'All right; then stick Speering down the shaft. Nick, you can give me a hand with the explosives.'

Follet ripped a sheet into strips and began to truss up Speering, ending by making a gag and stuffing it into his mouth. 'That's in case he comes to half-way down the shaft. Give me a hand with him, Ben.'

They lashed the rope around Speering's slack body, dragged him through the doorway and began to lower him down the shaft. When the strain eased off the rope they knew he had touched bottom, and Follet prepared to follow. He went over to Tozier and said, 'Ben and I are going down now.'

'Okay. Wait for Nick and me at the bottom.' Tozier looked at his watch. 'I'm setting the time of the bang at three hours from now. That should give us time to get out with a bit to spare.'

Follet left and Tozier completed setting the charges. The last thing he did was to set the clock carefully and, very delicately, to push over a small lever. 'She's cocked,' he said. 'An alarm clock to wake up Ahmed. Come on, Nick, let's get the hell out of here. Armed charges always make me nervous.'

Warren launched himself into the darkness of the shaft and went down the rope hand over hand until his feet splashed in water. 'Over here,' whispered Bryan, and Warren splashed up-stream.

Follet said, 'Our friend is coming round.' He flashed his light on Speering who rolled his eyes wildly while choked sounds came from behind the gag. A long knife came into view and highlights slithered along the blade held before Speering's eyes. 'You make a noise and you'll end up with a cut throat.'

Speering became abruptly silent.

There was a muffled thump and a splash from the direction of the shaft. 'All right,' said Tozier. 'Let's move fast. Can Speering walk?'

'He'd better,' said Follet. 'I'll be right behind him with this pig-sticker.' He flashed his light on Speering's feet and cut away the bonds. 'Get on your feet, you son-of-a-bitch; get on your feet and move.'

Despite the encumbrance of Speering they travelled rapidly up the *qanat*. Tozier went first with Speering right behind urged on by the fear of Follet and his knife, while Bryan and Warren brought up the rear. Because Speering's hands were bound he found it difficult to keep his balance

– he plunged about from side to side of the *qanat*, ricocheting from one wall to the other, and sometimes fell to his knees, while Follet pricked him mercilessly with the knife and kicked him to his feet.

After three-quarters of an hour of punishing progress Tozier called a halt. 'It's time to have a breather,' he said. 'Besides, we want to talk to Speering, don't we? It should be safe enough here.' He flashed his light upwards. 'We're well between shafts. Take out the gag, Johnny.'

Follet brought up the knife close to Speering's face. 'You keep quiet – you understand?' Speering nodded, and Follet inserted the knife under the cloth that held the gag in place and ripped it free. 'Spit it out, buster.'

Speering coughed and choked as he ejaculated the wad of sheeting that filled his mouth. Blood ran down his cheek and matted his beard from the gash where Follet had cut him in hacking away the gag. He swallowed violently, and whispered, 'Who are you?'

'You don't ask questions,' said Tozier. 'You answer them. Carry on, Nick.'

'How much morphine did you extract, Speering? And where is it now?'

Speering had not yet recovered his breath. His chest heaved as he shook his head. 'Oh boy!' said Follet. 'We're talking to a dead man.'

Tozier moved suddenly and viciously. His hand came up fast and he rocked Speering with a hard double slap. 'My friend is right,' he said softly. 'Answer the questions – or you're dead.'

'How much morphine did you extract, Speering?' asked Warren quietly.

'They'll kill me,' gasped Speering. 'You don't know them.'

'Who?' asked Tozier.

'Fahrwaz and Ahmed.' Speering was terrified. 'You don't know how bad they are.'

184

'You don't know how bad *we* are,' said Follet reasonably. 'Take your choice – die now or die later.' He pricked Speering's throat with the knife. 'Answer the question – how much morphine?'

Speering arched away in an attempt to get away from the knife. 'A thou . . . thousand kilograms.'

Tozier glanced at Warren. 'You just about hit it. That's twenty-two hundred pounds. All right, Speering; where is it?'

Speering shook his head violently. 'I don't know. I swear I don't know.'

'When did it leave?'

'Last night – they took it away in the middle of the night.'

'That must have been while we were there,' said Tozier thoughtfully. 'They lifted the stuff right out from under our noses. Where did they take it?'

'I don't know.'

'But you can guess,' said Follet, putting a fraction more pressure on the knife. A trickle of blood ran down Speering's neck. 'I bet you can guess real good.'

'Iraq,' Speering burst out. 'They said it was going to Iraq.'

'We're about thirty miles from the Iraqi border,' said Tozier. 'It begins to add up. I'd swear I heard camels last night. Did they take the stuff out on camel back?'

Speering tried to nod but ran his throat on to the knife-point. 'Yes,' he said weakly.

'Why didn't you acetylate the morphine here?' asked Warren. 'Where are they going to turn it into heroin?'

'I was going to do it here,' said Speering, 'but they changed their minds. They took it away last night. I don't know anything more than that.'

Tozier looked at Warren. 'Wouldn't they need Speering for that?'

'Maybe not. It's not too difficult a job. It looks as though we threw a scare into Ahmed. He got the stuff out of the way prematurely as a safety precaution, I'd say.'

'As a safety precaution it worked,' said Tozier grumpily. 'If he hadn't done it we'd have copped the lot. As it is, we've lost it. The stuff will be in Iraq by now.' He turned to Speering. 'Are you sure you don't know where it was going to in Iraq? You'd better tell the truth.'

Speering twitched his eyes back and forth. 'Come on, baby,' said Follet encouragingly. 'It's the last question.'

Speering gave in. 'I don't know exactly – but it's somewhere near Sulaymaniyeh.'

Tozier checked the time. 'Gag him again, Johnny. The road to Iraq goes past Fahrwaz's settlement. We have to be on time when the balloon goes up.'

'What can we do with Speering?' asked Warren.

'What can we do with him? We leave him here. With his hands tied and a gag in his mouth he can't do much. Hurry it along, Johnny.'

Three minutes later they were on their way again without Speering. As they left Warren turned round and flashed his light down the *qanat*. Speering was slumped against the wall in the position they had left him, but then he turned and stumbled away in the opposite direction. Warren met the eyes of Ben Bryan. 'Come on, Ben; let's go.'

Bryan hesitated fractionally, then fell in behind Warren who was making good time to catch up with the others who had already drawn well ahead.

Warren's mind was busy with the implications of what he had learned. The mountains of Kurdistan formed part of an age-old smuggler's route – Fahrwaz and Ahmed would know them well and he had no doubt that the morphine could be smuggled into Iraq with little difficulty. The writ of the law did not run strongly in any part of Kurdistan and had broken down completely in Iraqi Kurdistan where the government forces were held at arm's length.

He plugged along mechanically behind Follet and wondered what the devil they were going to do now. It was evident that Tozier had no doubts. 'The road to Iraq goes past Fahrwaz's settlement,' he had said, and had taken it for granted that they were going to Iraq. Warren envied him his stubborn tenacity.

His train of thought was broken by Bryan thumping him on the back. 'Stop,' said Ben. 'Tell Tozier.'

Warren passed the word on and Tozier stopped. 'What is it?'

'Speering is going to die,' said Bryan. 'The last I saw of him he was heading in the other direction. If he doesn't get killed in the explosion the roof of the *qanat* will cave in and he'll be trapped. So he'll die.'

'He can climb a shaft,' said Follet.

'With his hands tied behind his back?'

'He's going to die,' said Tozier flatly. 'So?'

'But to die like that!' said Bryan desperately. 'Tied up and stumbling around in the dark.'

'Don't you think he deserves it?'

'I wouldn't want anyone to die like that. I'm going back.'

'For Christ's sake!' said Tozier. 'We haven't time. We have to get back to the vehicles and be on our way before the big bang. That settlement is going to swarm like an ant heap when that underground room goes off pop, and I want to be on the other side when it happens.'

'You go ahead,' said Bryan. 'I'll catch you up.'

'Hold it, Ben,' said Warren. 'What are you going to do?'

'Untie his hands and turn him round,' said Bryan. 'It gives him a chance.'

'It gives him a chance to raise a goddam squawk,' said Follet sourly.

'To hell with it, I'm going back,' said Bryan, and broke away suddenly. Warren flicked on his light and saw him retreating rapidly into the darkness of the *qanat*.

'The damned fool,' said Tozier in a gravelly voice.

Warren hesitated uncertainly. 'What do we do?'

'I'm getting out of here,' said Follet. 'I'm not risking my life for a guy like Speering.'

'Johnny's right,' said Tozier. 'There's no point in waiting here. We'll bring the trucks down the pass and stand by to pick up Ben. Let's move.'

It seemed the best thing to do. After an initial pause Warren followed, splashing on the heels of Follet. Tozier imposed a back-breaking pace, secure in the knowledge of free passage ahead and spurred by the imminence of the impending explosion behind. They passed shaft after shaft with monotonous regularity and Warren checked each one off in his mind.

Tozier finally stopped. 'This is it.'

'Can't be,' gasped Warren. 'I only make it thirty-one.'

'You're wrong,' said Tozier with certainty. 'I have hold of the rope. The sooner we're all on the surface, the better I'll be pleased.'

He went up the shaft and was followed by Warren, who collapsed gasping for breath on the raised rim. Tozier helped Follet up, then said, 'Johnny and I will go for the trucks. You stay here and give us a flash when you hear the engines.' He and Follet disappeared into the darkness and there was just the rattle of loose stones to indicate their passage.

Warren looked up at the sky. The moon was setting behind the mountains but still shed a bright and even light over the rocky landscape so that he could see the roofs of the settlement in the distance. He waited for a while in the profound silence then leaned over the shaft and called, 'Ben – Ben, where are you?'

His voice echoed hollowly in the shaft, but there was no reply. He bit his lip. Undoubtedly Ben had acted stupidly – but was he wrong? Warren felt a turmoil within himself, an unaccustomed battle between idealism and self-interest which was something he had not felt before. Hesitantly he grasped the rope and prepared to let himself down the shaft, and then he paused, wondering if this was the right thing to do, after all. What about the others? Would he not be endangering the lives of them all if he went down after Bryan?

He dropped the rope and disconsolately sat on the edge of the shaft, fighting it out within himself. Presently he heard a low rumble of an engine and cautiously flashed his light in that direction, being careful to shield it with his hand so that no glimmer could be seen from the settlement in the distance. A Land-Rover loomed up suddenly and stopped, its engine dropping to the thrum of idling speed. Tozier got out and walked over. 'Any sign of him?'

'Nothing,' said Warren despondently.

'Bloody idealists!' said Tozier. 'They get on my wick.'

'He's in the profession of life-saving,' said Warren. 'It's hard to change suddenly. So what do we do now?'

Tozier peered at the illuminated fingers of his watch which he carried face inward on his wrist. 'She'll blow in thirty minutes. I was hoping to be on the other side of the settlement by then.' He sighed in exasperation. 'That bloody young idiot has cocked everything up.'

'You push off,' said Warren. 'I'll wait for Ben.'

'No,' said Tozier. 'I'll wait. You and Johnny head for the settlement. When the bang goes off make a break for it – you should be able to get through in the excitement. Wait for me on the other side. If you hear any shooting be prepared to come back in and bail us out.'

'I don't know if that's a . . .' began Warren.

'For Christ's sake, move,' said Tozier forcefully. 'I know what I'm doing and I've had more experience. Get going.'

Warren ran for the second Land-Rover and told Follet what was happening. Follet said, 'You'd better drive then.' He lifted his machine-pistol. 'It'll leave me free to shoot.'

Warren got in and drove off, trying to make as little noise as possible. They bumped across the valley floor towards the settlement, making a speed of less then ten miles an hour, while Follet kept glancing at his watch with a worried eye. At last Warren braked gently; ahead he could see the first low, flat-roofed buildings but there was no movement in the moonlight. The only sound was the gentle throb as the engine ticked over.

'Less than a minute to go,' whispered Follet.

Even as he spoke there was a deep thump as though a giant had coughed explosively, and the ground quivered under them. A plume of dust shot into the air from the shaft of the *qanat* nearest the settlement – the shaft which had formed the secret entrance to the underground laboratory. It rose higher and higher in the form of a ring, coiling and glittering in the moonlight as though the giant had blown a smoke ring. There was a brief change in the skyline of roofs, but it was so imperceptible that Warren could not pin it down.

Follet smote him on the shoulder. 'Go, man – go! Lights!'

The Land-Rover bucked ahead under fierce acceleration, its headlamps glaring at the settlement, and the engine roared and roared again as he slammed through the gears. He felt the wheels spin as he accelerated too fast and then they were off in a jolting ride he would never forget.

All was speed and motion and suddenly-seen vignettes caught in the brightness of the lights – a flutter of hens in the road rudely awakened and alarmed by the explosion, a brown face at a window, eyes squinting as they were dazzled, a man flattened against a wall with arms outspread where he sheltered from their mad rush.

Suddenly Follet yelled, 'Watch it!' and Warren slammed on the brakes. Ahead of them a crack in a wall widened slowly and the wall toppled into the road in what appeared to Warren's heightened senses to be slow motion. There was a crash and a billowing cloud of dust into which the Land-Rover lurched and crunched to a halt. The dust swirled into the cab and Warren coughed convulsively as his mouth was filled.

'Goddam jerry-built houses,' grumbled Follet.

Warren rammed the gear lever into reverse and backed out fast. As the dust settled he saw that the road ahead was completely blocked. Somewhere there was the flat report of a gun being fired. 'Better get out of here,' said Follet. 'See if we can find a way around.'

Warren kept going in reverse because there was no room to turn. At the first clear space he swung around and looked for an exit roughly in the direction he wanted to go. More shots were fired but no bullets seemed to come close. Follet pointed. 'Try down there. Move it, for Christ's sake!'

As Warren headed the Land-Rover at the narrow street something thumped against the side. Follet swung his machine-pistol out of the side window and pressed the trigger. There was a sound as of cloth ripping as he emptied half a magazine. 'Just to keep their heads down,' he shouted.

The Land-Rover plunged down the street which seemed to become even narrower and there was a clang as it scraped a wall. Ahead a man ran out and stood pointing a gun at them. Warren ducked involuntarily and stamped harder with his foot. The Land-Rover bucked and drove ahead; there was a soft thump and a last vision of two hands thrown up despairingly and a rifle thrown into the darkness.

Then they were out of the street and on the other side of the settlement with blackness in front of them as far as they could see. Follet tugged at Warren's arm. 'Switch off the lights so they'll lose us.' He looked back. 'I wonder how Andy's doing?'

Tozier was looking towards the settlement when the explosion happened. He saw the dust cloud climb into the air and presently the ground shivered beneath his feet under

191

the transmitted shock and he heard the sound. A sudden breeze drove upward from the mouth of the shaft against his face and then was gone and there was a noise which he could not interpret.

He bent down and shouted, 'Ben!' There was no answer.

He hesitated, biting his lip, and then seized the rope and lowered himself into the shaft. At the bottom he flashed his light around. Everything appeared to be normal so he shouted again. A piece of earth broke from the roof and splashed into the water.

He pointed his lamp downwards and frowned as he estimated the depth of water. Surely it had not been as deep as that before. He pulled out his knife and stuck it into the *qanat* wall just above the water level and his frown deepened as he saw the water level slowly rise to cover the haft of the knife.

His light, pointing down the *qanat*, showed nothing as he went forward. By the time he had gone a hundred yards and passed two shafts the water was swirling about his thighs, and then he saw the roof fall that blocked the *qanat* completely. This primitive tunnel with an unsupported roof had not been able to withstand the hammer blow of the explosion even at this distance, and he wondered how much of the *qanat* had collapsed.

There was nothing he could do, so he turned away and by the time he reached the rope the water was chest high, fed from the underground spring upstream in the mountains. When he reached the surface he was soaked and shivering in the cold night air, but he ran without a backward glance at the deadly trap that had entombed Bryan and Speering. In his profession death was a commonplace to be accepted. Nothing he could do would now help Bryan and he would be hard put to it to save his own skin.

He drove to the edge of the settlement carefully and stopped, switching off the engine so he could hear better. There was much to hear – shouting and a babble of voices

– and there were lights now as Ahmed and his men tried to find the extent of the damage. Tozier grinned coldly as he heard the centre of activity move over to the left towards the *qanat*.

He removed the shoulder-rest from the machine-pistol, cocked it and laid it on the seat next to him, ready to hand. Then he restarted the engine and crept forward in the darkness without switching on his lights – this was a time for cunning, not bravado; Ahmed's men were now roused and he could not tear through the settlement as he had advised Warren to do.

He moved forward steadily past the first buildings, and as he came into an open space he was spotted. There was a shout and somebody fired a gun, and there was a faint response of other and fainter shouts from further away. Even as he manipulated the gear lever there was another shot; he saw the muzzle discharge as a flicker in the darkness ahead so he switched on his lights to see what he was up against.

The Land-Rover gained momentum and he saw three men ahead of him, their hands upflung to shade their eyes against the sudden dazzle. He groped for the gun on the seat and was just in time to raise it as one of the men jumped on to the running-board, wrenching the door open and reaching for him. He lifted the gun and fired twice and there was a choked cry. When he had time to take his eyes from the road he risked a glance sideways and saw that the man was gone.

He looked up to the rear view mirror and saw the flicker of rifle fire in the darkness behind him which disappeared with shocking suddenness as a bullet whipped past his head to shiver the mirror to fragments. He swung the wheel to turn a corner and pawed at his brow to wipe a sticky wetness from his eyes where the blood dripped from a deep cut.

Then he skidded to a halt as he faced the same fallen wall

193

that had confronted Follet and Warren. He cursed as he put the Land-Rover into reverse and ducked as a bullet hit the side of the body. The quick, sharp report of several rifles shooting simultaneously made him grab his machine-pistol, thumb it on to rapid fire and squirt a magazine full of bullets in a deadly spray towards the indistinct figures behind him.

Follet had been listening intently to the rising crescendo of gunfire in the settlement. When he heard the rip of the machine-pistol he said, 'They've cornered Andy. Let's go get him out.'

Warren, who had already turned the vehicle around in preparation for this moment, moved into action, and they started on their way back. Follet said, 'I think they've trapped him in the same place where they nearly got us. You know where to go.'

Warren drove down the narrow street and past the crumpled body of the man he had run down. At the corner, sheltering from the threat of Tozier's gun, was a crowd of Kurds who were taken by surprise by this newly-launched attack in their rear. Follet leaned from the window and pressed the trigger and they ran for cover. One did not make it – he lurched as though he had tripped over something invisible and went head over heels and lay still.

'Straight on,' yelled Follet. 'Then turn round.'

The tyres squealed as Warren pulled the Land-Rover in a too tight turn at too high a speed. His lights illuminated the other vehicle, and Follet leaned out and yelled, 'Come on, Andy, what the hell are you waiting for?'

Tozier's Land-Rover jerked backwards into the clear space and shot up the narrow street with Warren close behind, while Follet squeezed off regular bursts to the rear to discourage pursuit. They broke from the settlement with Warren close on Tozier's tail, and drove a full three miles before pulling to a halt at the top of the high ground above the valley.

Follet looked down at the lights in the valley, but none was moving. 'They're not following us,' he said. 'They wouldn't chase us in the dark without lights.'

Warren felt squeezed and empty. It was the first time anyone had shot at him with intent to kill. He lifted trembling hands, then looked towards the other vehicle. 'I didn't see Ben,' he said.

There was the crunch of boots on gravel and Tozier appeared at his side window, his face blood-smeared. 'Ben won't be coming,' he said quietly. 'He bought it.'

'It was his own goddam fault,' said Follet in a high voice.

'Yes,' agreed Warren sadly. 'It was his own fault. You're sure, Andy?'

'I'm sure,' said Tozier with finality. He looked back at the valley. 'We'd better go. I want to be over the Iraqi border before Ahmed wakes up to what's really happened.'

He walked away and Warren heard a door slam. The two vehicles moved off slowly.

# 7

Dan Parker ran his hand lovingly along the smooth flank of the torpedo. It came away sticky with thin oil. 'The old Mark XI,' he said. 'I never really expected to see one o' these again.'

'You'd better make it work,' said Eastman. 'These things cost a lot of dough.'

'It'll cost a lot more before I'm finished,' said Parker equably. 'I'll be needin' some equipment.' He looked around the bare shed. 'There's room enough here.'

'What will you need?' asked Jeanette Delorme.

'Some machine tools to start with; a lathe, a small milling machine – universal type for preference – an' a drill press. An' a hell of a lot o' small tools, spanners an' suchlike – I'll make a list o' those.'

'Get it from him now, Jack,' she said. 'Give him everything he wants. I'm going home.'

'What about me?' asked Eastman.

'Take a taxi,' she said, and walked out.

Abbot smiled at Eastman. 'She's the boss all right. I can see that straight away.'

'I can do without any cracks from you,' said Eastman unsmilingly. He turned to Parker. 'Anything else?'

'Oh yes,' said Parker, who was studying the business end of the torpedo. 'This is a warhead; I hope there's nothin' in it.'

'It was ordered empty.'

'That's a relief. Old TNT is bloody unreliable stuff. But this is no good anyway.'

'What the hell . . . ?'

'Take it easy,' said Parker. 'No harm done. But if you want a practice run to prove the thing out I'll need a practice head as well as this one. If you shot off this fish now it would sink at the end of the run, an' you wouldn't want that. A practice head has a flotation chamber to keep the torpedo from sinkin' an' a Holmes light so you can find it. You'll be able to get a practice head from the same place you got this.' He slapped the side of the torpedo. 'Wherever that is.'

'Okay, you'll get your practice head. Anything else?'

'The batteries, o' course. They're pretty important, aren't they? I'll put those on the list, too – types an' quantities. They'll set you back a packet.' He studied the torpedo. 'I'll be wantin' to run her in here, so we'd better have some way o' clampin' her down. Two concrete pillars wi' proper clamps.' He looked up. 'These things develop a hell of a torque an' we don't want her jumpin' all over the bloody shed.' He slapped the side of his game leg. 'That's what busted me out o' the Navy.'

Abbot paced out the length of the torpedo. 'It's bigger than I thought. I didn't realize they were as big as this.'

'Twenty-one-inch diameter,' said Parker. 'Twenty-two-feet, five-an'-four-fifths inches long. Weight in war trim – thirty-six-hundred an' thirty-one pounds.' He slapped the warhead. 'An' she packs a hell of a punch – seven hundred an' eighteen pounds o' TNT in here.'

'We can pack over seven hundred pounds in there?' asked Eastman alertly.

Parker shook his head. 'Five hundred I said an' five hundred I meant. I'm goin' to put some batteries in the head. Have you thought how you're goin' to launch her?'

'You're the expert,' said Eastman. 'You tell me.'

'There are three ways. From a tube underwater, like from a submarine; from a tube above water, like from a destroyer; from an aeroplane. I wouldn't recommend the last – not if you're carrying valuables. It's apt to bugger the guidance system.'

'Okay,' said Eastman. 'Airplanes are out. What about the other ways?'

'I don't suppose you can lay your hands on a destroyer,' said Parker meditatively. 'An' torpedo tubes look a bit out o' place anywhere else, if you get my meanin'. I think your best bet is underwater launchin'; it's nice an' inconspicuous. But that means a ship wi' a bit o' draught to it.'

Eastman nodded. 'I like your thinking – it makes sense.'

'You should be able to get a submarine-type tube from the same place you got this fish. I can jury-rig air bottles for the launchin'.'

'You'll get your tube,' promised Eastman.

Parker yawned. 'I'm tired,' he said. 'I'll make out your list tomorrow.'

'The boss said now,' Eastman pointed out.

'She'll have to bloody well wait,' snapped Parker. 'I'm too tired to think straight. This is not goin' to be a quick job an' another eight hours isn't goin' to make any difference.'

'I'll tell her that,' said Eastman ironically.

'You do that, mate,' said Parker. 'Let's start as we mean to go on, shall we?' He looked Eastman in the eye. 'If you want a rush job you can have it – but I won't guarantee the result. If I can do it my way you get my guarantee.' He grinned. 'You wouldn't want to lose the fish when it's carryin' a full load of dope, would you?'

'No, goddam it!' Eastman flinched involuntarily at the thought.

'There you are, then,' said Parker with a wave of his hand. 'You push off an' come back in the morning at about ten o'clock an' I'll have your list all ready. We know where to bed down.'

'Okay,' said Eastman. 'I'll be back tomorrow.' He walked away across the shed and up the wooden staircase. At the top he turned. 'Just one thing: you don't leave here – either of you. Ali is here to see you don't. He's a bad bastard when he's aroused, so watch it.'

Abbot said, 'We'll watch him.'

Eastman grinned genially. 'That's not what I said, but you've got the idea.' He opened the door and they heard him speak in a low voice. When he went out the Arab, Ali, came in. He did not descend the stairs but just stood leaning on the rail watching them.

Abbot glanced at Parker. 'You were pushing him a bit, weren't you?'

'Just gettin' meself a bit of elbow room,' said Parker. He grinned. 'I was a petty officer an' I've met that type before. You meet plenty o' snotty officers in the service who try to run you ragged. But a good craftsman has always got 'em by the balls an' the trick is to squeeze just hard enough to let 'em know it. They get the message in no time at all.'

'I hope you can make it stick,' said Abbot. He looked at the torpedo. 'They got hold of this thing in jig time – I wonder how they were able to lay their hands on it so fast. It strikes me that this is an efficient mob. I think we'll have to watch how we go very carefully.' He looked up at the Arab speculatively.

'I wasn't kiddin' when I said I was tired,' said Parker. 'An' I want to get out o' this bloody monkey suit – it's killin' me. Let's go to bed, for God's sake!'


II


Once provided with his list Eastman moved fast. Within two days most of the equipment needed was installed, and while this was being done the torpedo was removed so that no workman would see it. All that was being done, as far

199

as they were concerned, was the establishment of a small machine-shop.

Then the work began on the torpedo itself. Abbot was astonished at the complexity of it and his respect for Parker increased. Any man who could master such a complicated instrument and treat it with the casual insouciance that Parker did was worthy of a great deal of respect.

They took out the lead-acid batteries – fifty-two of them – and piled them in a corner of the shed. 'I'll be needin' those to test the motor later,' said Parker. 'There's no point in usin' the expensive ones. But then they'd better be taken out to sea an' dumped. Any naval man who caught sight o' those would know what they are, an' that might give the game away.'

Eastman made a note of it and Abbot privately thought that Parker was entering into the spirit of things a little too wholeheartedly. He said as much when they were alone and Parker grinned. 'We have to make it look good, don't we? Every little helps. Eastman is gettin' quite matey an' that could be useful.' Abbot had to agree.

Parker took out the motor for cleaning. 'It's in good nick,' he said, and stroked it almost lovingly. 'A beautiful job. Ninety-eight horsepower an' only that big. A really lovely bit of work an' designed to be blown to hell.' He shook his head. 'It's a bloody funny world we live in.'

He stripped the torpedo meticulously while Abbot did the fetching and carrying and the cleaning of the less important pieces. He demanded – and got – special oils and greases to pack the glands, and expensive wiring for his redesigned circuits, while his new mercury batteries cost a small fortune in themselves. He preached like an evangelist, and the word he preached was 'perfection.' 'Nothing is too good,' he proclaimed flatly. 'This is goin' to be the best torpedo that ever took water.'

And it was very likely so. No service torpedo ever had such undivided and loving attention, and Abbot came to the conclusion that only a prototype fussed over by nervous boffins prior to service tests could be compared with this lone torpedo.

Eastman got the point very early in the game under Parker's needling attitude. He saw that Parker was really putting up a magnificent effort and he co-operated whole-heartedly to give him everything he needed. And that was not really to be wondered at, thought Abbot, when you considered that riding in the warhead would be dope worth $25,000,000.

Parker spent most time on the guidance system, clucking over it like a mother hen over an errant chick. If this thing packs in you've lost the lot,' he said to Eastman.

'It had better not,' said Eastman grimly.

'It won't,' said Parker in a steady voice.

'What does it do?'

'It keeps her running straight – come what may,' said Parker. 'When I quoted you a figure for accuracy o' three inches in a hundred yards I was allowin' meself a bit o' leeway. In the hands of a good mechanic a Mark XI is damned near as accurate as a rifle bullet – say, an inch in a hundred yards. O' course, the ordinary Mark XI has a short range, so even at maximum the point o' strike wouldn't be more than six feet out if she ran well. But this beauty has to run a hell of a long way so I'm aimin' to beat the record. I'm tryin' for a half-inch error in a hundred yards. It's damn' near impossible but I'm tryin' for it.'

Eastman went away very happy.

'You're putting in a lot of time and sweat on something that's going to be sabotaged,' observed Abbot.

Parker shrugged. 'Every torpedoman gets that feelin' from time to time. You take a lovely bit o' mechanism like this an' you work on it to get a performance that even the designer didn't dream of. Then you slam it against the side of a ship an' blow it to smithereens. That's sabotage of a kind, isn't it?'

'I suppose it is if you look at it that way. But it's what torpedoes are for.'

Parker nodded. 'I know this one is goin' to be sabotaged in the end but we still have sea trials to come an' she's got to work.' He looked at Abbot and said seriously, 'You know, I haven't been so bloody happy for a long time. I came out o' the Navy an' got a job tinkerin' wi' other folk's cars an' all the time I missed somethin', an' I didn't know what it was.' He waved at the stripped-down torpedo. 'Now I know – I missed these beauties.'

'Don't get too carried away,' advised Abbot. 'Remember that when it comes to the final push this thing must fail.'

'It'll fail,' said Parker glumly. His face tightened. 'But it's goin' to have one bloody good run first.' He tapped Abbot on the chest. 'If you think this thing is easy, Mike, you're dead wrong. I'm working on the edge o' the impossible all the time. A Mark XI was never designed to go fifteen miles an' to get it to travel the distance is goin' to be tricky. But I'll do it an' I'll enjoy doin' it because this is the last chance I'll ever have of handlin' a torpedo. Now, let's get down to it.'

Every two bits of metal that could be separated were taken apart, scrutinized carefully and put back together with meticulous care. Piece by piece the whole torpedo was reassembled until the time came when it was clamped down for a bench test and Abbot saw the reason for the clamps. Even running at a quarter power it was evident that it would have run wild in the shed had it not been secured.

Parker professed satisfaction and said to Eastman, 'What about the tube? I've done all I can wi' the fish.'

'Okay,' said Eastman. 'Come with me.'

He took them a little way up the coast to a small shipyard, and pointed to a worn-out coaster of about 3,000 tons. 'That's the ship – the *Orestes*; Greek-owned and registered in Panama.'

Parker looked at her dubiously. 'Are you goin' to cross the Atlantic in that?'

'I am – and so are you,' said Eastman. 'She's done it before and she can do it again; she only has to do it once more and then she'll be lost at sea.' He smiled. 'She's under-insured and we're not even going to press too hard for that – we don't want anybody getting too nosy about what happened to her. If you're going to install an underwater tube you'll have to cut a hole in the hull. How are you going to do that?'

'Let's have a closer look,' said Parker, so they went aboard. He spent a lot of time below, up in the bows, then he made a sketch. 'We'll make a coffer dam. Get that made up and have it welded to the outside of the hull as marked, then I can cut a hole from the inside an' install the tube. Once that's done the thing can be ripped off. You'll have to find a diver who can keep his mouth shut – it isn't a normal shipyard job.'

Eastman grinned. 'We own the shipyard,' he said softly.

So Parker installed the launching-tube which took another week. He spent a great deal of time measuring and aligned the tube exactly fore and aft. 'All you have to do is to point the ship accurately,' he said. 'That's it – we're ready for trials.'

III

Jeanette Delorme had not been around for some time, and it worried Abbot because he wanted to have her under his eye. As it was, he and Parker were virtually prisoners and cut off from the rest of the organization. He did not know what Warren was doing, nor could he contact Hellier to tell him what was happening. With such a breakdown of communications things could go very wrong.

He said to Eastman, 'Your boss doesn't seem to be taking much interest. I haven't seen her around since that first night.'

'She doesn't mix with the working slobs,' said Eastman. 'I do the overseeing.' He fixed Abbot with a sardonic eye. 'Remember what I told you about her. I'd steer clear if I were you.'

Abbot shrugged. 'I'm thinking of the money. We're ready for the trial and I don't think you are authorized to sign cheques.'

'Don't worry about the dough,' said Eastman with a grin. 'Worry about the trial. It's set for tomorrow and she'll be there – and God help you if it doesn't work out.' As an afterthought he said, 'She's been over to the States, arranging things at that end.'

The black Mercedes called early next morning to pick up Abbot, who was wary when he found he was to be separated from Parker. 'Where will Dan be?'

'On the *Orestes*,' said Eastman.

'And me?'

'Why don't you go along and find out?' said Eastman. He seemed disgruntled.

So Abbot went with reluctance in the Mercedes to wherever it was going to take him – which proved to be the heart of Beirut. As the car passed the office of the *Daily Star*, the English-language newspaper, he fingered the envelope in his pocket and wondered how he could get in there without undue attention. He and Hellier had arranged an emergency information service, but it seemed as though he was not going to get the chance to use it.

The car took him to the yacht harbour where he was met by a trimly dressed sailor. 'Mr Abbot?' Abbot nodded, and the sailor said, 'This way, sir,' and led him to a fast-looking launch which was moored at the steps.

204

As the launch took off smoothly, Abbot said, 'Where are we going?'

'The yacht – the *Stella del Mare*.' The sailor pointed. 'There.'

Abbot studied the yacht as they approached. She was a rich man's toy of the type typically to be found in the Mediterranean. Of about two hundred tons, she would be fully equipped with every conceivable comfort and aid to navigation and would be quite capable of circumnavigating the world. But, also typically, that she would not do – these boats were usually to be found tied up for weeks at a time at Nice, Cannes, Beirut and all the other haunts of the jet-set – the floating mansions of the wealthy. It looked more and more as though heroin smuggling was profitable.

He was met at the top of the companionway by another floating flunkey dressed in a sailor suit and escorted to the sun deck. As he climbed a ladder he heard the clank of the anchor chain and the vibration of engines. It appeared that the *Stella del Mare* had been waiting for him.

On the sun deck he found Jeanette Delorme. She was stretched supine, adding to her tan, and was so dressed that the maximum amount of skin got the benefit; her bikini was the most exiguous he had ever seen – a small triangle at the loins and two nipple covers. He hadn't seen anything like it outside a Soho strip joint, and he doubted if the whole lot weighed more than an eighth of an ounce; certainly less than the dark glasses through which she regarded him.

She waved her hand lazily. 'Hello, Mike; this is Youssif Fuad.'

Abbot reluctantly looked away from her and towards the man sitting near by. The bald head, the brown lizard skin and the reptilian eyes certainly made a change for the worse. He nodded in acknowledgment. 'Morning, Mr Fuad.' He had seen Fuad before. This was the Lebanese banker with whom Delorme had had lunch, and whom he had written off as being too respectable. It just went to show how wrong you could be. Fuad was certainly not taking a sea voyage on the day of the torpedo trial for his health.

Fuad gave a quick and birdlike jerk of his head. He said petulantly, 'What is he doing here?'

'Because I want him here,' said Jeanette. 'Take a seat, Mike.'

'I thought I said I was not to be brought into . . .' Fuad stopped and shook his head again. 'I don't like it.'

Abbot, who was in a half-crouch preparatory to sitting down, straightened again. 'I know when I'm not wanted. If you whistle up that launch again, I'll be going.'

'Sit down, Mike,' said Jeanette with a whip-crack in her voice that automatically bent Abbot's knees. 'Youssif is always nervous. He's afraid of losing his respectability.' There was mockery in her voice.

'We had an agreement,' said Fuad angrily.

'So I've broken it,' said Jeanette. 'What are you going to do about it?' She smiled. 'Don't be so worried, Youssif; I'll look after you.'

There was something going on between them that Abbot did not like. Apparently he was not supposed to know about Fuad, and Fuad did not like to have his cover broken. Which made it dicey for Mike Abbot if Fuad decided to bring things back to normal. From the look of him he would not bat a lizardlike eye at murder. He looked back towards Delorme – a much more rewarding sight – and had to remind himself that she would not either.

Jeanette smiled at him. 'What have you been doing with yourself, Mike?'

'You know bloody well what I've been doing,' said Abbot baldly. 'Or else Eastman's been wasting his time.'

'Jack has told me as much as he knows,' she agreed. 'Which isn't much – he's no technician.' Her voice sharpened. 'Will this torpedo work?'

'I'm no technician, either,' said Abbot. 'But Dan Parker

seems confident.' He rubbed the side of his jaw. 'I think you'll owe us a hundred thousand dollars before the day's out.'

'Youssif has the cheque ready. I hope he'll give it to you – for your sake.'

This clear warning of the penalty for an unsuccessful trial made the sweat break out on Abbot's forehead. He thought of what Parker had said about working on the edge of the impossible, took a deep breath and forced himself to say lightly, 'Where are we going? What's the drill?' He turned his head and looked towards the receding land, more to avoid Jeanette's hidden gaze than out of interest. In a comparison of these two it was obvious that the female of the species was more deadly than the male.

She sat up suddenly, and adjusted the minimal bra which had sagged dangerously under the stress of her movement. 'We are going to join the *Orestes*. She is out there – away from the shipping routes. We have some fast boats too, to make sure we are not disturbed. This is like a naval exercise.'

'How long will we take to get out there?'

'Maybe two hours – maybe longer.'

'Say three hours each way,' said Abbot. 'And God knows how long for the trial. This is going to take all day. I'm beginning to feel seasick already. I never have liked ships.'

The tip of her tongue played along her top lip. 'I have a certain cure for seasickness,' she said. 'Infallible, I assure you. I don't think you will have time to be seasick, Mike Abbot.'

She put her hands behind her head and pushed her breasts at him, and he believed her. He glanced at Fuad who was also watching her with his lizard stare, but there was no hint of lust in those dead, ophidian eyes.

Not far over the horizon the *Orestes* lumbered through the calm morning sea on her way to the rendezvous. Parker climbed the ladder to the bridge and made the thumbs-up sign. 'Everything's under control. I'm bringin' the batteries up to heat now.'

Eastman nodded, then jerked his head towards the officer with the mildewed braid on his battered cap. 'The skipper's not too happy. He says the ship's cranky in her steering.'

'What would he expect with a bloody big hole cut off-centre in the bows?' demanded Parker. 'He'll get used to it.'

'I guess so,' Eastman was thoughtful. 'Would it help to cut another hole on the other side?'

'It might,' said Parker cautiously. 'It would equalize things a bit.'

'What's this about warming up the batteries? I didn't know you did that.'

'A warm battery delivers power quicker an' easier than a cold one. A difference o' thirty degrees Fahrenheit can increase the range by a third – an' we want all the range we can get.' Parker took out his pipe. 'I've set her to run at twelve feet. Any less than that an' she's likely to porpoise – jump in an' out o' the water. An instability like that could throw her right off course. At the end of her run she'll bob up nice an' easy like a cork, an' her Holmes light will go off so you can see her.'

'You'll be there to find the torpedo.'

'I thought you wanted me here to check the firing.'

'You can do both,' said Eastman. 'There'll be a boat waiting to take you to the other end of the course.'

Parker struck a match. 'You'll need a hell of a fast boat to outrun a torpedo.'

'We've got one. Is forty-five knots fast enough?'

'That's fast enough,' admitted Parker, and blew out a wreath of blue smoke.

Eastman sniffed distastefully and moved up wind. 'What's that you're smoking? Old socks?'

Parker grinned cheerfully. 'Feelin' queasy already?' He drew on the pipe again. 'Where did Mike go this mornin'?'

Eastman stared at the horizon. 'The boss wanted to see him,' he said morosely.

'What for?' asked Parker in surprise.

'I'll give you three guesses,' said Eastman sarcastically. 'The little bitch has hot pants.'

Parker clucked deprecatingly. 'That's no way to talk of your employer,' he observed. 'You think . . . er . . . that she an' Mike are . . . er . . . ?'

'I'll bet they're both in the sack now,' said Eastman savagely, and thumped the rail.

'Why, Jack! I do believe you're jealous.' Parker chuckled delightedly.

'The hell with that,' said Eastman in a hard voice. 'I'm immune to anything that chick does with her flaunty little ass – but she shouldn't mix pleasure with business. It could get us all into trouble. She shouldn't have . . .'

He broke off, and Parker said innocently, 'She shouldn't have what?'

'Nothing,' said Eastman brusquely, and walked away across the bridge where he talked in a low voice to the skipper.


Abbot buttoned his shirt and leaned across the tousled bed to look through the port. The things I do in the line of duty, he thought, and checked his watch. They had been at sea for just over two hours. From the compartment next to the cabin he heard the brisk splash of water as Jeanette showered, and presently she appeared, naked and dripping. She tossed him a towel. 'Dry me,' she commanded.

As he rubbed her down vigorously he was irresistibly reminded of his boyhood when he had haunted his grandfather's stables and had been taught the horseman's lore by old Benson, the chief groom. Automatically he hissed through his teeth as Benson had done when currying a horse, and wondered what the old man would have thought of this filly.

'You haven't been around much,' he said. 'I expected to see more of you.'

'You couldn't see much more of me.'

'What were you doing in the States?'

She stiffened slightly under his hands. 'How do you know I was in the States?'

'Eastman told me.'

'Jack talks too much.' After a while, she said, 'I was doing what you would expect – setting things up.'

'A successful trip?'

'Very.' She twisted free from him. 'I'm going to make a lot of money.'

Abbot grinned. 'I know. I've been trying to figure out how to carve myself a bigger share.' He studied her as she walked across the cabin. Her long-flanked body was evenly tanned and there were no betraying white patches. Evidently the minimal bikini she had worn that morning had been a concession to someone's modesty – but whose he could not imagine. Fuad's? That was a laugh.

She turned and smiled. 'It is a possibility – if the trial is a success.' As she stepped into a pair of brief panties, she said, 'What do you think of Jack Eastman?'

'He strikes me as being a tough boy,' said Abbot consideringly. 'He's no cream-puff.'

'Could you get on with him?'

'I might – if he could get along with me.'

She nodded. 'Something might be arranged.' She fastened the bra strap. 'Even if you didn't get along together something might be arranged – if you are prepared to help with the arrangements.'

Christ, what a hellcat! he thought. It was quite clear what was being tentatively offered. He could supplant Eastman by getting rid of him, and he had no illusions about what that implied. Probably by enlisting his aid in

210

rubbing out her partner she would make even more money. But then he would be in Eastman's seat – the hot seat – a target for the next gun-happy sucker to enter her sexy little life. He thought of the list of murdered men in her dossier and wondered how many of them had been her lovers. The female spider – the eater of males.

He smiled engagingly. 'It's a thought. Where does friend Fuad fit into all this?'

'Now *you* are talking too much,' she said reprovingly as she buttoned her blouse. 'He has nothing to do with you.'

'Oh yes he does. He holds the moneybags, doesn't he?'

She sat at the dressing-table and began to make up her face. 'You jump to a quick conclusion,' she said. 'But you are right.' Her eyes watched him through the mirror. 'You are very clever, Mike; much cleverer than Jack. I don't think you'd have any trouble with him at all.'

'Thanks for the vote of confidence.'

'Since you are so clever, perhaps you can tell me something. What do you know about Regent Films?'

Abbot was aware that she was watching him even though her back was turned, and hoped his expression had not changed. 'It's an English – British – film company. Quite a big one.'

'Who is at the top?'

'A man called Hellier – Sir Robert Hellier.'

She turned to him. 'So tell me – why should an English nobleman – a milord – interfere with me?'

Abbot chuckled – he could not help it. 'I suppose you could call old Hellier a nobleman. *Is* he interfering with you?'

'His company is – very much so. It has cost me a lot of money.'

Abbot kept a straight face even though he wanted to cheer. So Warren and the Iranian team had stabbed her right in the wallet she substituted for a heart. He shrugged. 'I don't know much about Hellier. He wasn't on my beat –

I didn't do films or the gossip stuff. For my money it's a respectable outfit he runs. Regent makes pretty good pictures – I've seen some of them.'

She threw down a comb with a clatter. 'These Regent people have cost me more money than you've even heard of. They're . . .' The telephone rang and interrupted her. She picked it up. 'Yes? All right.'

Abbot looked through the port and saw the *Orestes* not very far away. Jeanette said, 'Come on, Mike; we're wanted on deck. We're transferring to the other ship.'

When they arrived on deck Abbot saw a group of seamen busily engaged in lowering a boat. The *Stella del Mare* had stopped and was rolling uneasily in the slight swell, and the *Orestes* was abeam of them about two hundred yards away.

Fuad was not on deck, but Abbot caught sight of him lurking in the saloon. It seemed that Youssif Fuad was intent on concealing his association with these nefarious activities, which was why he had objected when Abbot had come on board. Jeanette, on the other hand, seemed to want Fuad more deeply involved, and Abbot wondered if he could use the issue as a point of attack.

He followed Jeanette down the companionway and stepped into the launch, and it pulled away in a lazy circle and headed for the *Orestes*. When Jeanette climbed up on to the deck of the battered coaster she was suddenly businesslike. 'All right, Jack; let's get on our way. Are you ready, Parker?'

Parker grinned easily. 'As ready as I'll ever be.'

She offered him a small, tight smile. 'You'd better make it good – but Jack's been telling me you do good work.'

The telegraph clanged, the deck vibrated as the engines increased speed, and the *Orestes* began to move. 'What's the drill?' asked Abbot.

'We go another fifteen miles,' said Eastman. 'Then turn and shoot. We have a couple of boats along the course in

212

case the torpedo comes up too soon, but we'll be pacing it anyway. It should surface somewhere near the yacht – if we get the range we need.'

Abbot laughed, and said to Parker, 'You'd better not be *too* good, Dan; it would be a hell of a joke if you slammed the torpedo into the *Stella del Mare*.'

Parker grunted. 'It wouldn't do too much damage without a warhead. But the fish would be a write-off an' I wouldn't like that.'

'Neither would I,' said Eastman. He gave Abbot an unfriendly stare and said coldly, 'I don't like your sense of humour.'

'Neither do I,' said Abbot, still smiling. 'Dan and I have a hundred thousand dollars riding with this torpedo.'

The *Orestes* ploughed on westward. Jeanette took Eastman by the elbow and they walked to the other side of the deck, deep in conversation. Abbot said, 'He's not as friendly as he was.'

Parker shook with laughter. 'Maybe he's jealous. Has he any cause to be, Mike?'

'You mean me and Delorme?' Abbot pulled a sour face. 'I don't know about jealousy, but he ought to be running scared. The bitch wants me to knock him off at an opportune moment. We had a nice friendly chat.'

'I'll bet you didn't stop at talkin',' said Parker pointedly. 'Do you mean to tell me that she asked you to kill Eastman?'

'Not in so many words, but the subject came up. Another thing – Warren's been hitting her hard over in Iran. She's really steamed up about it. She wanted to know about Regent Films.'

'That's good to know,' said Parker. 'What did you tell her?'

'I acted dumb and stuck to generalities. Maybe Warren can pull off the whole trick and let us off the hook here.'

'He can't,' said Parker. 'We're on the hook an' we're

wrigglin'. We'll have to get out o' this ourselves. I'm goin' below – I want to check the fish.'

Abbot frowned; he thought he detected a shade of nervousness in Parker – something that now showed itself for the first time. He did not like to think of what might happen if the trial proved a bust, but Parker was worried about something else – the problem of what was going to happen if the trial was a success. It was something to think about.

Very likely he and Parker would be expected to go with the *Orestes* on the final job, clear across the Atlantic to fire the torpedo ashore on some secluded beach. The snag about that was that it would never get there – Parker would see to that. And what Jeanette would do in that case was not at all problematical, although the details were hazy. Probably he and Parker would share the same concrete coffin at the bottom of the Caribbean. It was a nasty thought.

The correct course of action would be to wait until the warhead was filled with heroin and then dump the lot somehow in such circumstances that he and Parker could get away. The trouble with that line of thought was that everything depended on what Delorme did – he had no initiative at all. They would just have to wait and see what happened.

He leaned on the rail and looked gloomily at the sea, and his thoughts were long and deep. Presently he sighed and turned to watch Jeanette and Eastman who had their heads together. She would be telling him of the arrangements she had made in the States, and he would have given a lot to be able to eavesdrop. If he knew where the heroin was going then the gang in the States could be rounded up – a quick closing in on the beach with the capture of the torpedo – and he and Parker would be in the clear.

His train of thought was broken by the clang of the telegraph bell and the sudden easing of vibration. Parker came up from below and looked over the side. 'We've arrived,' he said. 'Look at that thing down there.'

Abbot saw a fast-looking boat riding easily in the water. Eastman came over, and said, 'That's to take us back to the yacht. How are you going to work this, Parker?'

'Can we talk to this ship from that boat?'

'Sure – there's radio communication.'

'Then have a word with the skipper. There's a switch near the binnacle; he presses the tit when the compass points due north magnetic. I'd like to be in that boat to watch the fish when she leaves. All the skipper has to do is to watch the compass and flick the switch. He'd better be on the wheel himself.'

'I'll tell him,' said Eastman, and went up on to the bridge.

The instructions were given and they went down to the boat which had come alongside, Jeanette and Eastman first, then Abbot and Parker. The engines opened up with a muted growl which spoke of reserve power and they moved away from *Orestes* which turned in a wide sweep on a reciprocal course. Parker watched her. 'Give me the glasses an' tell the skipper he can fire when ready. We move off when I give the word – a little over thirty knots – course due north magnetic. Everyone keep an eye astern.'

Eastman spoke into the microphone, then said, 'He'll fire when he gets his bearing – any time now.'

Parker had the glasses at his eyes and was gazing at the bows of *Orestes*. There was a pause, then Eastman said, 'He's fired,' and simultaneously Parker yelled, 'She's on her way – get goin'.' He had seen the burst of air bubbles break from the bow of *Orestes* to be swept away in the wake.

The low growl of the engines burst into an ear-shattering roar as the throttles were opened and Abbot was momentarily pinned back in his seat by the sudden acceleration. Parker was staring at the water. 'She didn't porpoise,' he yelled. 'I was a bit worried about that. She should be runnin' true.'

'What do you mean?' shouted Eastman.

'The tube's only six feet underwater an' the fish is set to run at twelve – I thought she might duck down an' then come up again sharply to break surface. But she didn't – the beauty.' Parker leaned forward. 'Tell your helmsman to keep as near to thirty-one knots as he can an' steer a straight course.'

It was a wild ride and seemed to go on for ever as far as Abbot was concerned. Even though the sea was calm there was a minor swell and the boat would ride a crest and seem to fly for a split second before coming down with a jolting crash. He touched Parker on the arm. 'How long does this go on?'

'Half an hour or so. The torpedo is makin' thirty knots so we should be a bit ahead of her. Keep your eyes peeled aft – wi' a bit o' luck you won't see a bloody thing for a while.'

Abbot stared back at the sea and at the rushing wake unreeling itself from the boat at what seemed to be a fantastic speed. After a while he found it hypnotized him and tended to make him feel sick, so he turned his head and looked at the others, blinking as the wind caught his eyes.

Jeanette was sitting as calmly as she had sat in the Paon Rouge, with one hand braced on a chrome rail. The wind streamed her blonde hair and pressed her blouse against her body. Eastman had his teeth bared in a stiff grin. Occasionally he spoke into the microphone he held, but to whom he was talking Abbot did not know. Probably he was telling the *Stella del Mare* that they were on their way. Parker was riding easily and staring aft, a light of excitement in his eyes and a big grin on his face. This was his day.

The boat rushed through the water interminably. After ten minutes they swept past a fair-sized motor launch which was making lazy circles, and Eastman stood up and waved. This was one of the boats which guarded the course. Eastman sat down abruptly as their own boat bounced violently over the wake which crossed their path – and then again. The circling boat receded into the distance behind them as they pressed on.

Abbot thought of the torpedo somewhere below and behind them if Parker was right. Although he had seen it stripped down, it was hard to realize that it was down there driving through the water undeviatingly at this speed. He looked forward at the broad shoulders of the man at the wheel and saw the muscles of his arms and back writhe as he fought to keep the boat on a straight course and that gave him some inkling of Parker's achievement – one half inch error in a hundred yards for mile after mile after mile.

They passed another circling boat and again bounced over its wake to leave it behind. Eastman looked at his watch. 'Another ten minutes,' he shouted and grinned at Parker. 'We've come ten miles – five to go.'

Parker nodded vigorously. 'Ease a knot off the speed if you can – we don't want to overrun her too much.'

Eastman turned and spoke into the helmsman's ear and the roar of the engines altered the slightest fraction. To Abbot it did not seem to make any difference to the speed; the wake streamed away behind them just as quickly in a line so straight it seemed to be ruled on the blue water. He was beginning to feel sicker; the noise was deafening and the motion upset his stomach, and he knew that if they did not stop soon he would vomit over the side. If this was water-sport it was not for him.

Presently Jeanette spoke for the first time. She stood up and pointed. '*Stella del Mare*.'

Abbot felt relieved – his ordeal was almost at an end. Parker twisted round and looked at the yacht, then beckoned to Eastman. 'Don't stop here. Run straight past on the same course. We want the torpedo, not the bloody yacht.'

Eastman nodded and spoke to the helmsman again, and they tore past the *Stella del Mare* and there was nothing ahead but the bouncing horizon. Parker shouted, 'Everyone look astern – you'll see her with her nose in the air like a bloody great pole stickin' out o' the sea, an' there'll be a light an' a bit o' smoke.'

Everyone looked but there was nothing but the *Stella del Mare* receding into the distance, and Abbot felt depressed as the minutes ticked by. He looked at his watch and noted that it had been thirty-three minutes since they had begun this mad dash across the Mediterranean. He did a mental calculation and figured they had come at least sixteen miles and possibly more. What could have gone wrong?

He remembered what Parker had said about setting the torpedo to run at a depth of twelve feet from a launch of six feet. Parker had been worried about porpoising, but what if the torpedo had just carried on down into the depths of the sea? From what Parker had previously told him, if the torpedo got much below sixty feet the pressure would damage it beyond repair and it would never be seen again.

He looked at Jeanette whose expression had never changed. What would she do about it? He could guess the answer would be violent. Parker was staring aft with a tense look on his face. His grin was gone and the crowsfeet around his eyes were etched deeper.

Thirty-four minutes – and nothing. Thirty-five minutes – and nothing. Abbot tried to catch Parker's eye, but Parker had attention only for the sea. It's a bust, decided Abbot in desperation.

Suddenly Parker was convulsed into movement. 'Thar she blows!' he yelled excitedly. 'On the starboard quarter. Cut these bloody engines.'

Abbot looked over the sea and was thankful to hear the engines die. Away in the distance bobbed the torpedo, just as Parker had described it, and a smoky yellow flame burned dimly in the strong sunlight. The boat turned and headed towards it while Parker literally danced a jig. 'Where's a boat-hook?' he demanded. 'We have to secure her.'

'What's that flame?' asked Eastman.

'The Holmes light,' said Parker. 'It's powered by sodium – the wetter it gets the hotter it burns.'

'A neat trick,' commented Eastman.

Parker turned to him and said solemnly, 'That torpedo bein' there at all is an even neater trick. I reckon she did eighteen miles an' that's not just a trick – it's a bloody miracle. Are you satisfied wi' it?'

Eastman grinned and looked at Jeanette. 'I guess we are.'

'We'll be expecting your cheque,' said Abbot to Jeanette.

She smiled at him brilliantly. 'I'll get it from Youssif as soon as we get back to the yacht.'


IV


They went back to Beirut in the *Stella del Mare*, leaving the *Orestes* to pick up the torpedo from the launch to which it was secured, with Parker vowing eternal vengeance on anyone who was so ham-fisted as to damage it in the process. In the luxurious saloon Eastman broke open the cocktail cabinet. 'I guess we all need a drink.'

Abbot dropped limply into a chair. For once Eastman had expressed exactly his own feelings. In the last hour he had gone through enough emotions to last a man a lifetime and a stiff drink would go down well. It turned into a convivial party – Eastman was jovial, Parker was drunk on success and needed no liquor to buoy him up, Jeanette was gay and sparkling, and even Youssif Fuad unbent enough to allow a fugitive smile to chase quickly across his face. Abbot was merely thankful.

Jeanette clicked her fingers at Fuad who took a folded

piece of paper from his pocket and gave it to her. She passed it to Abbot. 'The first instalment, Mike. There'll be more to come.'

He unfolded the cheque and saw that it was drawn on Fuad's own bank for $100,000 American, and wondered what would happen if he attempted to draw it before the final run of the torpedo off the American coast. But he did not comment on it – he was not supposed to know Fuad was a banker. 'I wish us many more,' he said.

Eastman raised his glass. 'To the best goddam mechanic it's been my fortune to meet.'

They drank to Parker, who actually blushed. 'It's too bad they don't have torpedo races,' said Eastman. 'You'd never be out of a job, Dan. I've not seen anything so exciting since I was at Hialeah.' He smiled at Jeanette. 'But I guess there's a lot more riding on this than I ever had on a horse race.'

Parker said, 'That's just the first bit – now we run into more problems.'

Jeanette leaned forward. 'What problems?' she asked sharply.

Parker swished his drink around in his glass. 'Normally a Mark XI torpedo has a short range – a bit over three miles. Anythin' you shoot at you can see, an' any damn' fool can see a ship three miles away. But you're different – you want to shoot at somethin' that's clear over the horizon. You saw the distance we just travelled.'

'That shouldn't be much trouble,' said Eastman. 'Not if you have a good navigator who knows where he is.'

'The best navigator in the world can't tell his position to a quarter-mile in the open sea,' said Parker flatly. 'Not without an inertial guidance system which you couldn't afford even if the Navy would sell you one. You can't buy *those* on the war surplus market.'

'So what's the answer?' asked Jeanette.

'That big derrick on the *Orestes* is about fifty feet above

220

the water,' said Parker. 'If you put a man up there in a sort o' crow's nest he could see a shade over eight miles to the horizon. What you've got to do is to put up a light on shore about the same height or higher, an' if it's bright enough it'll be seen sixteen miles or more out at sea by the chap in the crow's nest. But it needs to be done at night.'

'It's going to be a night job, anyway,' said Eastman.

Parker nodded. 'It needs polishin' up a bit, but that's the general idea.' He paused. 'There might be a few lights along the coast so you'll need to have some way of identifying the right one. You could have a special colour or, better still, put a switch in the circuit an' flash a code. The man in the crow's nest on the *Orestes* should have a telescope – one o' those things target shooters use would do, an' it should be rigidly fixed like a sort o' telescopic sight. As soon as he sees the light through it he presses the tit an' away goes the torpedo. An' it might help if he's on intercom wi' the helmsman.'

'Ideas come thick and fast from you, don't they?' said Eastman admiringly.

'I just try to earn me money,' said Parker modestly. 'I have a stake in this, you know.'

'Yeah,' said Eastman. 'Another two hundred thousand bucks. You're earning it.'

'There might be even more in it for you, Parker,' said Jeanette and smiled sweetly at Fuad. 'Youssif is neither poor nor ungenerous.'

Fuad's face set tight and firm and he hooded his eyes. To Abbot he looked as generous as someone who had just successfully robbed the church poor-box.

Jeanette's car was still awaiting them when they arrived back in the yacht harbour. 'I have something to show you,' she said to Abbot and Parker. 'Get in the car.' To Eastman she said, 'You stay with Youssif and check over with him

221

what I've told you. See if either of you can find any holes in it.'

She got into the car and sat next to Abbot and the car pulled away. Abbot wanted a chance of a private word with Parker who, intoxicated by success, had been shooting his mouth off a little too much. He would have to talk to him about that. He turned to Jeanette. 'Where are we going?'

'Back to where you came from this morning.'

'There are no surprises there,' he said. 'I've seen everything.'

She just smiled at him and said nothing, and the car drifted opulently out of Beirut along the Tripoli road back to the torpedo shed. It turned into the yard, and she said, 'Take a look inside, then come back and we'll talk about it.'

He and Parker got out and walked towards the shed. Just before they opened the door, Abbot said, 'Wait a minute, Dan; I want to talk to you. I don't think you should give them too much – as you were doing on the way back today. If that hellcat gets the idea she doesn't need us we might be in trouble.'

Parker grinned. 'They need us,' he said positively. 'Who is goin' to put new batteries into that torpedo? Eastman wouldn't have a clue, for one. We'll be all right until the end, Mike.' His face sobered. 'But what the hell is goin' to happen then I don't know. Now let's go in an' see what the big surprise is.'

They went into the shed. Parker switched on the lights and stood transfixed at the top of the stairs. 'Bloody hell!' he burst out. 'They need us an' no mistake.'

Lying on trestles below them were *three* torpedoes.

Abbot's mouth was suddenly dry. 'Three more! That's a hell of a lot of heroin.' He was filled with the terrible necessity of getting the information out to where it would do some good. But how the hell could he? Every step he took, every move he made, was under observation.

222

'If they think I'm goin' to start a bloody one-man production line they can think again,' Parker grumbled.

'Quiet, Dan, for God's sake!' said Abbot. 'I'm trying to think.' After a while he said, 'I'm going to try to pull a fast one on that bitch outside. You back me up. Just remember that you've had a hard day and all you want to do is to go to bed.'

He left the shed and crossed the yard to where the car was waiting. He bent down, and said, 'Quite a surprise. Are all those going to be loaded and shot off at once?'

Jeanette said, 'It's what Jack calls the jackpot. There's more money in it for you, of course.'

'Yes,' said Abbot. 'We'll have to discuss that – but why do it here? Why don't you and me and Dan take the night off to celebrate – say at the Paon Rouge.' He grinned. 'It's on me – I can afford it now.'

Parker said from behind him. 'Count me out, I'm too tired. All I want is me bed.'

'Well, that doesn't really matter, does it? You'll trust me to fix the finance with Jeanette?'

'O' course. You do what's right.' Parker passed his hand over his face. 'I'm goin' to turn in. Good night.'

He walked away, and Abbot said, 'What about it, Jeanette? I'm tired of being cooped up in this place. I want to stretch my wings and crow a bit.' He gestured towards the shed. 'There's a lot of work in there – I'd like to have a break before we start.'

Jeanette indicated her clothing. 'But I can't go to the Paon Rouge dressed like this.'

'That's all right,' said Abbot. 'Give me two ticks while I change, then I'll come with you to wherever you live. You change, and we go on the town. Simple.'

She smiled thoughtfully. 'Yes, that might be a good idea. How are you as a lady's maid? I gave my girl the day off.'

'That's fine,' said Abbot heartily. 'I'll be as quick as I can.'

* * *

223

Five hours later he swished brandy around his glass, and said, 'You drive a hard bargain, Jeannie, my girl, but it's a deal. You're getting us cheap, I hope you know that.'

'Mike, don't you care about anything except money?' She sounded hurt.

'Not much,' he said, and drank some brandy. 'We're two of a kind, you and me.' He signalled to a waiter.

'Yes, I think we are alike. I feel much closer to you than I do to poor Jack.'

Abbot quirked an eyebrow. 'Why *poor* Jack?'

She sat back in her chair. 'He was annoyed that you were on *Stella* today. I think he's becoming jealous. If you stay with us – with me – that will have to be settled, and settled for good.' She smiled. 'Poor Jack.'

'He's living with you, isn't he?' said Abbot. 'I think those were his clothes I saw in the wardrobe.'

'Why, I believe you are jealous, too,' she cried delightedly.

He felt a cold shiver at the nape of his neck as he pictured Jeanette and Eastman lying in bed together while she discussed the possibility of one John Eastman knocking off one Michael Abbot. This she-devil was quite capable of playing both ends against the middle. She believed in the survival of the fittest, and the survivor would get first prize – her lithe and insatiable body. It wasn't a bad prize – if you could stand the competition. The trouble was that if you played by her rules the competition would be never-ending.

He forced a smile. 'I like you and money in roughly equal proportions. As for Jack Eastman, I suggest we leave that problem for a while. He still has his uses.'

'Of course,' she said. 'But don't leave it too long.'

He pushed back his chair. 'If you'll excuse me, I have to see a man about a dog. I'll be back in a moment.'

He walked quickly into the foyer and into one of the few rooms in the Phoenicia where he could get away from

224

Delorme. He locked himself in a cubicle, took an envelope from his pocket and checked the wording on the single sheet of paper inside. Then he reinserted the sheet, sealed the envelope and addressed it carefully.

He found an attendant who obligingly brushed his jacket with subservient attention, and said, 'I'd like to have this letter delivered to the *Daily Star* office at once.'

The attendant looked dubious but brightened immediately as he heard the crisp rustle of folding money. 'Yes, sair; I'll 'ave it delivered.'

'It's important,' said Abbot. 'It must get there tonight.' He added another banknote. 'That's to make sure it arrives within the hour.'

Then he straightened his shoulders and went back to where the she-spider was waiting.

## V

Sir Robert Hellier sat behind his desk and looked at the newspaper. It was the Beirut English language paper, *Daily Star*, which he had flown to London regularly. He ignored the news pages but turned to the classified advertisements and ran his fingers down the columns. This he had done every morning for many weeks.

Suddenly he grunted and his finger checked its movement. He took a pen and slashed a ring round an advertisement. It read:

> *Mixed farm for sale near Zahleh. 2,000 acres good land; large vineyard, good farmhouse, stock, implements. Box 192.*

He heaved a sigh of relief. He had lost contact with Abbot and Parker many weeks previously and had been worried about it, but now he knew they were still around

225

he felt better. He re-read the advertisement and a frown creased his forehead as he groped for the pen.

Five minutes later he found he was sweating. Surely he had made a mistake in his calculations. Got a few too many noughts mixed in somewhere or other. The 2,000 acres mentioned in the advertisement meant that the Delorme woman intended to smuggle 2,000 pounds of heroin – that was the jumping-off point. He began right again from the start and worked it out very carefully. The end result was incredible.

He looked at the final figure again and it still shattered him. $340,000,000.

That was what 2,000 pounds of heroin would be worth to the final consumers, the drug addicts who would pay their $7.00 and $8.00 a shot. He wrote down another figure.

$100,000,000.

That was what Delorme would be paid if the dope could be safely delivered inside the States. He expected the whole thing would be worked out on a credit basis – not even the Syndicate could be expected to raise that much capital at one time. The stuff would be cached and doled out a few pounds at a time at $50,000 a pound, and Delorme would be creaming the lot. She had organized the whole business right from the Middle Eastern poppy fields, had taken all the risks and would take all the profits, which were enormous.

With shaking fingers he picked up the telephone. 'Miss Walden: cancel all my appointments for an indefinite period. Get me a plane reservation for Beirut as soon as possible, and a hotel reservation accordingly – the Saint-Georges or the Phoenicia. All that as soon as possible, please.'

He sat and looked at the advertisement, hoping to God that whoever had set it in type had made a misprint and that he was embarking on a wild goose chase.

He also hoped he could hear from Warren because Warren and the three men with him had also gone missing.

# 8

Entry into Iraq was not too difficult. They had visas for all countries in the Middle East into which it had been thought the chase might lead them, and Hellier had provided them with documents and letters of introduction which apparently carried a lot of weight. But the Iraqi officer at the border post expressed surprise that they should enter via Kurdistan and so far north, and showed an undesirable curiosity.

Tozier made an impassioned speech in throat-rasping Arabic and this, together with their credentials, got them through, although at one time Warren had visions of a jail in Iraqi Kurdistan – not the sort of place from which it would be easy to ring one's lawyer.

They filled up with petrol and water at the border post and left quickly before the officer could change his mind, Tozier in the lead and Follet riding with Warren. At noon Tozier pulled off the road and waited for the other vehicle to come up. He pulled out a pressure stove and said, 'Time for a bite to eat.'

As Follet opened cans, he said, 'This isn't much different from Iran. I don't reckon I'm very hungry – I'm full of dust.'

Tozier grinned and looked at the barren landscape. The roads were just as dusty here, and the mountains as bleak as on the other side of the border. 'It's not far to Sulaymaniyeh, but I don't know what we'll do when we get there. Take it as it comes, I suppose.'

Warren pumped up the pressure stove and put the water to boil. He looked across at Tozier, and said, 'We haven't

227

had the chance of talking much. What happened back there?'

'In the *qanat*?'

'Yes,' said Warren quietly.

'It collapsed, Nick. I couldn't get through.'

'No hope for Ben?'

Tozier shook his head. 'It would have been quick.'

Warren's face was drawn. He had been right when he told Hellier that blood would be shed, but he had not expected this. Tozier said, 'Don't blame yourself, Nick. It was his own choice that he went back. He knew the risk. It was a damn-fool thing to do anyway; it nearly did for us all.'

'Yes,' said Warren. 'It was very foolish.' He bent his head so that the others could not see his face. It was as though someone had stabbed a cold knife into his guts. He and Ben were both medical men, both lifesavers. But who had been the better – Ben Bryan, for all his foolishness and idealism, or Nicholas Warren who had brought him to the desert and his death? Warren did not relish that ugly question.

They were half-way through lunch when Tozier said casually, 'We've got visitors. I'd advise against sudden moves.'

Despite himself Warren hastily looked around. Follet went on pouring coffee with a steady hand. 'Where are they?' he asked.

'There are a couple on the hill above us,' said Tozier. 'And three or four more circling around the other side. We're being surrounded.'

'Any chance of making a break?'

'I don't think so, Johnny. The guns are too hard to get at right now. If these boys – whoever they are – are serious they'll have blocked off the road ahead and behind. And we couldn't get far on foot. We'll just have to wait until we find out the score.' He accepted the cup of coffee from Follet. 'Pass the sugar, Nick.'

'What!'

'Pass the sugar,' said Tozier patiently. 'There's no point in getting into an uproar about it. They might be just curious Kurds.'

'They might just be too goddam curious,' said Follet. 'That guy Ahmed is a Kurd, remember.' He stood up slowly and stretched. 'There's a deputation coming down the road now.'

'Anyone we know?'

'Can't tell. They're all wearing nightgowns.'

Warren heard a stone clatter behind him, and Tozier said, 'Easy does it. Just get up and look pleasant.' He stood up and turned, and the first man he saw come into view was Ahmed, the son of Sheikh Fahrwaz. 'Bingo!' said Tozier.

Ahmed stepped forward. 'Well, Mr Warren – Mr Tozier; how nice to see you again. Won't you introduce your companion?' He was smiling but Warren could detect little humour in his face.

Playing along, he said, 'Mr Follet – a member of my team.'

'Pleased to make your acquaintance,' said Ahmed brightly. 'But wasn't there another man? Don't tell me you've lost him?' He surveyed them. 'Nothing to say? I'm sure you're aware that this is no fortuitous encounter. I've been looking for you.'

'Now why should you do that?' asked Tozier in wonder.

'Need you ask? My father has doubts about your safety.' He waved his hand. 'You would not believe what dreadful people roam these hills. He has sent me to escort you to somewhere safe. Your escort, as I am sure you are aware, is all around to . . . er . . . protect you.'

'To protect us from ourselves,' said Warren ironically.

229

'Aren't you off your beat, Ahmed? Does the Iraqi government know you are in the country?'

'What the Iraqi government does not know would take far too long to detail,' said Ahmed. 'But I suggest we go. My men will put your picnic kit back in your vehicles. My men will also drive your vehicles – to save you from needless fatigue. All part of the service.'

Warren was uncomfortably aware of the rifles held by Ahmed's men and of the wide circle drawn about them. He glanced at Tozier who shrugged, and said, 'Why not?'

'Very good,' said Ahmed approvingly. 'Mr Tozier is a man of few words but much sense.' He snapped his fingers and his men moved forward. 'Let us not waste time. My father is positively aching to . . . interrogate you.'

Warren did not like the sound of that at all.


## II


The three of them were crammed into the back of one of the Land-Rovers. In the front seats were a driver and a man who sat half-turned to them, holding a pistol steadily. Sometimes, as the vehicle bounced, Warren wondered if the safety-catch was on because the man kept his finger loosely curved around the trigger, and it would not have taken much movement to complete the final pressure. Any shot fired into the back would have been certain to hit one of the bodies uncomfortably huddled among the photographic equipment.

As near as he could tell their route curved back to the east, almost as far as the Iranian border, and then straightened out in a northerly direction, heading deeper into the mountains. That meant they had circled Sulaymaniyeh, which was now left behind them. They followed a truck, a big tough brute which looked as though it had been designed for army service, and when he was able to look back he saw the other Land-Rover from time to time through the inevitable dust-cloud.

The man with the gun did not seem to object to their talking but Warren was cautious. The fluent Oxbridge accent that had come so strangely from Ahmed had warned him that no matter how villainous and foreign the man appeared it did not automatically follow that he had no English. He said, 'Is everyone all right?'

'I'll be fine as soon as whoever it is takes his elbow out of my gut,' said Follet. 'So that was Ahmed! A right pleasant-spoken guy.'

'I don't think we should talk too much business,' said Warren carefully. 'Those little pitchers might have long ears.'

Follet looked at the pistoleer. 'Long and goddam hairy,' he said distastefully. 'Needing a wash, too. Ever heard of water, bud?'

The man looked back at him expressionlessly, and Tozier said, 'Cut it out, Johnny, Nick's right.'

'I was just trying to find out something,' said Follet.

'You might just find out the hard way. Never make fun of a man with a gun – his sense of humour might be lethal.'

It was a long ride.

When night fell the headlights were switched on and the speed dropped but still they jolted deeper into the mountains where, according to Warren's hazy memory of the map, there were no roads at all. From the way the vehicle rolled and swayed this was very likely true.

At midnight the sound of the engine reverberated from the sides of a rocky gorge, and Warren eased himself up on one elbow to look ahead. The lights showed a rocky wall straight ahead and the driver hauled the Land-Rover into a ninety-degree turn and then did it again and again as the gorge twisted and narrowed. Suddenly they debouched

231

into an open place where there were lights dotted about on a hillside and they stopped.

The rear doors opened and, under the urged commands of the man with the gun, they crawled out. Dark figures crowded about them and there was a murmur of voices. Warren stretched thankfully, easing his cramped limbs, and looked about at the sheer encroaching hills. The sky above was bright with the full moon which showed how circumscribed by cliffs this little valley was.

Tozier rubbed his thigh, looked up at the lights in the cliff side, and said sardonically, 'Welcome to Shangri-la.'

'Very well put,' said Ahmed's voice from the darkness. 'And just as inaccessible, I assure you. This way, if you please.'

And if I don't please? thought Warren sourly, but made no attempt to put it to the test. They were hustled across the valley floor right to the bottom of a cliff where their feet found a narrow and precipitous path which wound its way up the cliff face. It was not very wide – just wide enough to be dangerous in the darkness, but probably able to take two men abreast in full daylight. It emerged on to a wider ledge half-way up the cliff, and he was able to see that the lights came from caves dotted along the cliff face.

As they were marched along the ledge he peered into the caves, which were pretty well populated. At a rough estimate he thought that there could not be very much less than two hundred men in this community. He saw no women.

They were brought to a halt in front of one of the larger caves. It was well illuminated and, as Ahmed went inside, Warren saw the tall figure of Sheikh Fahrwaz arise from a couch. Tozier gave a muffled exclamation and nudged him. 'What is it?' he whispered.

Tozier was staring into the cave, and then Warren saw what had attracted his attention. Standing near Fahrwaz was a short, wiry, muscular man in European clothing. He lifted his hand in greeting at Ahmed's approach and then stood by quietly as Ahmed talked to Fahrwaz. 'I know that man,' whispered Tozier.

'Who is he?'

'I'll tell you later – if I can. Ahmed's coming back.'

As Ahmed came out of the cave he made a sign and they were pushed further along the ledge and out of sight of Fahrwaz. They went about twenty yards and were stopped in front of a door let into the rock face. Someone opened it with much key-jangling, and Ahmed said, 'I trust you won't find the accommodation too uncomfortable. Food will be sent; we try not to starve our guests . . . unnecessarily.'

Hands forced Warren through the doorway and he stumbled and fell, and then someone else fell on top of him. When they had sorted themselves out in the darkness the door had slammed and the key turned in the lock.

Follet said breathily, 'Pushy bastards, aren't they?'

Warren drew up his trouser-leg and felt his shin, encountering the stickiness of blood. A cigarette-lighter clicked and sparked a couple of times and then flared into light, casting grotesque shadows as Tozier held it up. The cave stretched back into the darkness and all was gloom in its furthest recesses. Warren saw some boxes and sacks stacked against one side but not much more because the light danced about and so did the shadows as Tozier moved about exploratively.

'Ah!' said Tozier with satisfaction. 'This is what we want.' The flame grew and brightened as he applied it to a stump of candle.

Follet looked around. 'This must be the lock-up,' he said. 'Store room too, by the look of it, but first a lock-up. Every military unit needs a lock-up – it's a law of nature.'

'Military!' said Warren.

'Yes,' said Tozier. 'It's a military set-up. A bit rough and

233

ready – guerrilla, I'd say – but definitely an army of sorts. Didn't you see the guns?' He set down the candle on a box.

'This is something I didn't expect,' said Warren. 'It doesn't fit in with drugs.'

'Neither does Metcalfe,' said Tozier. 'That's the man who was with Fahrwaz. Now I really am puzzled. Metcalfe and guns I can understand – they go together like bacon and eggs. But Metcalfe and dope is bloody impossible.'

'Why? Who is this man?'

'Metcalfe is . . . well, he's just Metcalfe. He's as bent as they come, but there's one thing he's known for – he won't have anything to do with drugs. He's had plenty of opportunity, mark you, because he's a smart boy, but he's always turned down the chance – sometimes violently. It's a sort of phobia with him.'

Warren sat down on a box. 'Tell me more.'

Tozier prodded a paper sack and looked at the inscription on the side. It contained fertilizer. He pulled it up and sat on it. 'He's been in my game – that's how I met him . . .'

'As a mercenary?'

Tozier nodded. 'In the Congo. But he doesn't stick to one trade; he's game for anything – the crazier the better. I believe he was kicked out of South Africa because of a crooked deal in diamonds, and I know he was smuggling out of Tangier when it was an open port before the Moroccans took over.'

'What was he smuggling?'

Tozier shrugged. 'Cigarettes to Spain; antibiotics – there was a shortage in those days; and I also heard he was smuggling guns to the Algerian rebels.'

'Was he?' said Warren with interest. 'So was Jeanette Delorme.'

'I heard a garbled story that he was mixed up in smuggling a hell of a lot of gold out of Italy, but nothing seemed to come of that. It didn't make him much richer, anyway. I'm telling you all this to show what kind of a man

234

he is. Anything goes, excepting one thing – drugs. And don't ask me why because I don't know.'

'So why is he here?'

'Because it's military. He's one of the best guerrilla leaders I know. He never was any great shakes in a formal military unit – he didn't go in for the Blanco, bullshit and square-bashing – but with guerrillas he's deadly. That's my guess for what it's worth. We know the Kurds are having a bash at the Iraqis – Ahmed told us. They've imported Metcalfe to help them out.'

'And what about the drugs which he's not supposed to like?'

Tozier was silent for a while. 'Maybe he doesn't know about them.'

Warren ruminated over that, wondering how it could be turned to advantage. He was just about to speak when the key clattered in the lock and the door swung open. A Kurd came in with a pistol ready in his hand and stationed himself with his back to the rock face. Ahmed followed. 'I said we don't starve our guests. Here is food. It may not be congenial to your European palates, but it is good food, none the less.'

Two big brass trays were brought in, each covered by a cloth. Ahmed said, 'Ah, Mr Tozier: I believe we have a friend in common. I see no reason why you and Mr Metcalfe should not have a chat later – after you have eaten.'

'I'd be pleased to see Tom Metcalfe again,' said Tozier.

'I thought you would.' Ahmed turned away, and then paused. 'Oh, gentlemen, there is just one other thing. My father needs certain information. Now, who can give it to him?' He studied Warren with a half smile on his lips. 'I don't think Mr Warren could be persuaded very easily – and Mr Tozier even less so. I regarded you carefully last time we met.'

His gaze switched to Follet. 'Now, you are an American, Mr Follet.'

'Yeah,' said Follet. 'Next time you see the American consul tell him I'd like to see him.'

'A commendable spirit,' observed Ahmed, and sighed. 'I fear you may be as obstinate as your friends. My father wishes to . . . er . . . talk to you himself, but he is an old man and in need of sleep at this late hour. So you are fortunate in that you have a few more hours.' With that he went, followed by his bodyguard, and the door slammed.

Tozier indicated the paraffin lamp on one of the trays. 'He was kind enough to leave that.'

Follet lifted a cloth. 'It's hot food.'

Tozier took the cloth from the other tray. 'I suppose we might as well eat. It's not too bad – cous-cous and chicken with coffee afterwards.'

Follet gnawed on a leg of chicken, then looked at it in disgust. 'This one must have been an athlete.'

Warren picked up a plate. 'Where do you reckon we are?'

'Somewhere up near the Turkish border,' said Follet. 'As near as I can reckon. Not far from the Iranian border, either.'

'In the Kurdish heartland,' commented Tozier. 'That might mean something – or nothing.' He frowned. 'Do you remember what Ahmed was blowing off about back in Iran, Nick? About the Kurdish political situation? What was that name he mentioned? It was someone who had the Iraqi army tied up in knots.'

'Barzani,' said Warren. 'Mullah Mustapha Barzani.'

'That's the man. Ahmed said he had an army. I wonder if this crowd is part of it.'

'It could be. I don't see how it helps us.'

'God helps those who help themselves,' said Follet practically. Still holding the chicken leg, he got up, took the candle, and began to explore the further reaches of the cave. His voice came hollowly. 'Not much here.'

'What do you expect in a jail?' asked Tozier. 'All the same, it's a good idea to see what resources we have. What's in that box you're sitting on, Nick?'

'It's empty.'

'And I'm sitting on fertilizer,' said Tozier in disgust. 'Anything else, Johnny?'

'Not much. More empty boxes; some automotive spare parts – all rusty; half a can of diesel oil; a hell of a lot of nuts and bolts; a couple of sacks of straw – that's about all.'

Tozier sighed. Follet came back, put down the candle, then picked up the lamp and shook it close to his ear. 'There's some kerosene in here and there's that straw over there – maybe we can do something with that.'

'You can't burn a cave to the ground, Johnny. We'd just asphyxiate ourselves.' Tozier went to the door. 'This is going to take some shifting – it must be four inches thick.' He cocked his head on one side. 'There's someone coming. Watch it.' He retreated from the door and sat down.

It opened and the man called Metcalfe came in. He was brushing himself down and turned his head as the door thudded behind him. Then he looked at Tozier and said without smiling, 'Hello, Andy; long time no see.'

'Hello, Tom.'

Metcalfe came forward and held out his hand, and Tozier grasped it. 'What in hell are you doing here?'

'That's a long story,' said Tozier. 'This is Nick Warren – Johnny Follet.'

'If I said, "Pleased to meet you," I'd be wrong,' said Metcalfe wryly. He looked Warren up and down with a keen eye, then glanced at Tozier. 'Here on business, Andy?'

'Sort of. We didn't come willingly.'

'I saw the boys hustling you in – I couldn't believe my eyes. It's not like you to be nabbed as easily as that.'

'Take the weight off your feet, Tom,' said Tozier. 'Which will you have – the fertilizer or the box?'

'Yeah, stay and visit with us for a while,' said Follet.

'I'll have the box,' said Metcalfe delicately. 'You're a Yank, aren't you?'

Follet burlesqued a southern accent. 'Them's fightin' words where ah comes from. Ah may have bin bawn in Arizony but ma pappy's from Jawjah.'

Metcalfe looked at him thoughtfully for a long time. 'I'm glad to see high spirits – you're going to need them. You look as though you've seen service.'

'A long time ago,' said Follet. 'Korea.'

'Ah,' said Metcalfe. He grinned and his teeth gleamed white against his sunburnt face. 'A legitimate type. And you, Warren?'

'I'm a doctor.'

'So! And what's a doctor doing wandering about Kurdistan with a bad type like Andy Tozier?'

Tozier pulled at his ear. 'Are you in employment at the moment, Tom?'

'Just wrapping something up,' said Metcalfe.

'In command?'

Metcalfe looked blank. 'In command!' His brow cleared and he laughed. 'You mean – am I training these boys? Andy, this crowd could teach us a thing or two – they've been fighting for the last thirty-five years. I've just brought a consignment in, that's all. I'm leaving in a couple of days.'

'A consignment of what?'

'What the blazes do you think? Arms, of course. What else would this lot need?' He smiled. 'I'm supposed to be asking the questions, not you. That's what old Fahrwaz sent me in here for. Ahmed didn't like it – he wanted to carve you up immediately, but the old boy thought I might solve his problem without him going to extreme lengths.' His face was serious. 'You're in a really bad spot this time, Andy.'

'What does he want to know?' asked Warren.

Metcalfe looked up. 'Everything there is to know. You

seem to have upset him somehow, but he didn't go into that with me. He thought that since I know Andy here, I might get your confidence.' He shook his head. 'You've come down in the world if you're working for a film company, Andy. So I think it's a cover – and so does Fahrwaz.'

'And what does Barzani think?' asked Tozier.

'Barzani!' said Metcalfe in surprise. 'How in hell do I know what Barzani thinks?' Suddenly he slapped his knee. 'Did you really think that Fahrwaz was one of Barzani's men? That's really funny.'

'I'm laughing my goddam head off,' said Follet sourly.

'It's time for a lesson in Kurdish politics,' said Metcalfe didactically. 'Fahrwaz used to be with Barzani – they were together when the Russkies tried to set up the Mehabad Kurdish Republic in Iran back in 1946. They even went into exile together when it collapsed. They were great chums. Then Barzani came here to Iraq, built up a following, and has been knocking hell out of the Iraqis ever since.'

'And Fahrwaz?'

'Ah, he's one of the *Pej Merga*,' said Metcalfe as though that was a full explanation.

'The self-sacrificing,' translated Tozier thoughtfully. 'So?'

'The *Pej Merga* was the hard core that Barzani could always rely on, but not any more – not since he started to dicker with President Bakr on the basis of an autonomous Kurdish province in Iran. Fahrwaz is a hawk and he thinks the Iraqis will renege on the deal, and he may be right. More importantly, he and most of the *Pej Merga* want none of a Kurdish Republic *in Iran*. They don't want Kurdistan to be split between Iraq, Iran and Turkey – they want a unified Kurdish nation and no half measures.'

'Something like the Irish problem,' observed Tozier. 'With Fahrwaz and the *Pej Merga* doing the IRA bit.'

'You've got the picture. Fahrwaz regards Barzani as a

traitor to the Kurdish nation for even listening to Bakr, but Barzani commands respect – he was fighting the Iraqis for years when Fahrwaz was sitting on his rump in Iran. If Barzani makes a deal with the Iraqis then Fahrwaz is out on a limb. That's why he's stockpiling arms as fast as he can.'

'And you're supplying them,' said Warren. 'What do you believe in?'

Metcalfe shrugged. 'The Kurds have been given a rough deal for centuries,' he said. 'If Barzani does a deal with the Iraqis and it goes sour, then the Kurds will need some insurance. I'm supplying it. Bakr came to power by a coup d'état and his regime isn't all sweetness and light. I can see Fahrwaz's point of view.' He rubbed his jaw. 'Not that I like him – he's a bit too fanatical for my taste.'

'Where is he getting his support – his money?'

'I don't know.' Metcalfe grinned. 'As long as I'm paid I don't care where the money comes from.'

'I think you might,' said Tozier softly. 'How did you bring in the arms?'

'You know better than to ask a question like that. A trade secret, old boy.'

'What are you taking out of here?'

'Nothing,' said Metcalfe in surprise. 'I get paid through a Beirut bank. You don't think I wander through the Middle East with my pockets full of gold. I'm not that stupid.'

'I think you'd better tell him all about it, Nick,' said Tozier. 'It's all falling into place, isn't it?'

'I'd like to know something first,' said Warren. 'Who contacted you originally on this arms deal? Who suggested it would be a good idea to take a load of guns to Fahrwaz? Who supplied them?'

Metcalfe smiled and glanced at Tozier. 'Your friend is too nosy for his own good. That also comes under the heading of trade secrets.'

'It wouldn't be Jeanette Delorme?' suggested Warren.

Metcalfe's eyebrows crawled up his forehead. 'You seem to know quite a lot. No wonder Fahrwaz is getting worried.'

'*You* ought to be getting worried,' said Tozier. 'When I asked you if you were taking anything out I had dope in mind.'

Metcalfe went very still. 'And what gave you that idea?' he said in a tight voice.

'Because there's a ton of pure morphine around here somewhere,' said Warren. 'Because Fahrwaz is running drugs to pay for his revolution. Because the Delorme woman is supplying the arms to pay for the drugs, and she's sitting in Beirut right now waiting to ship a consignment of heroin to the States.'

There were harsh lines on Metcalfe's face. 'I don't know that I believe this.'

'Oh, grow up, Tom,' said Tozier. 'We cleaned up Fahrwaz's place in Iran. I personally destroyed ten tons of opium – blew it to hell. He's in it up to his scrawny old neck.'

Metcalfe stood up slowly. 'I have your word on this, Andy?'

'For what it's worth,' said Tozier. 'You know me, Tom.'

'I don't like being used,' said Metcalfe in a choked voice. 'Jeanette knows I don't like drugs. If she's implicated me in this I'll kill the bitch – I swear it.' He swung on Warren. 'How much morphine did you say?'

'About a ton. My guess is that they'll convert it to heroin before shipment. If that amount of heroin gets on the illegal market in one lump I don't like to think of the consequences.'

'A ton,' whispered Metcalfe incredulously.

'It could have been double that,' said Tozier. 'But we wrecked the laboratory. Your lady-friend has been busy getting everything sewn up. This is one of the biggest smuggling operations of all time.'

Metcalfe thought about it. 'I don't think the stuff's here,' he said slowly. 'Just after I arrived a string of camels came in. There was a hell of a lot of palaver about them – all very mysterious. Everyone was kept away while the load was transferred into a truck. It left this morning.'

'So what are you going to do, Tom?' asked Tozier casually.

'A good question.' Metcalfe took a deep breath. 'The first thing is to get you out of here – and that's going to take a miracle.' He smiled wryly. 'No wonder Fahrwaz is all steamed up.'

'Can you get any weapons in to us? I'd feel better with a gun in my hand.'

Metcalfe shook his head. 'They don't trust me that much. I was searched when I came in here. There are a couple of guards outside all the time.'

Tozier stuck out his finger. 'We've got to get through that door – guards or no guards.' He stood up with a quick movement and the sack of fertilizer fell over against his leg. Impatiently he booted it away, and then stopped and gazed at it. Abstractedly he said, 'Could you find us a few bits of coal, Tom?'

'Coal in Kurdistan!' said Metcalfe derisively. He followed the line of Tozier's gaze, then bent down to read the inscription on the sack. 'Oh, I see – the Mwanza trick.' He straightened up. 'Would charcoal do?'

'I don't see why not – we don't need much. How much oil is there in that can you found, Johnny?'

'About a quart. Why?'

'We're going to blow that door off its hinges. We'll need a detonator, Tom. If you nip down to the Land-Rovers you'll find that one has a clock and the other hasn't. Unscrew the clock and bring it with you with the charcoal.'

'How do you expect me to smuggle a clock in here?'

'You'll find a way. Get going, Tom.'

Metcalfe knocked on the door and was let out. As it closed behind him Warren said, 'Do you think he's . . . safe?'

'For us – yes,' said Tozier. 'For Fahrwaz, no. I know Tom Metcalfe very well. He goes off pop if he even hears people talk about drugs. If we get out of this I'll feel bloody sorry for the Delorme woman – he'll crucify her.' He bent down and started to open the sack of fertilizer.

Follet said flatly, 'You're going to blow that door open with fertilizer. You did say that – or am I going nuts?'

'I said it,' said Tozier. 'Tom and I were in the Congo. We were just outside a place called Mwanza and the opposition had blown down a cliff so it blocked the road and we couldn't get our trucks through. We were low on ammunition and had no blasting explosives, but we had a secret weapon – a South African called van Niekerk who used to be a miner on the Witwatersrand.'

He put his hand in the sack and lifted out a handful of the white powder. 'This is agricultural fertilizer – ammonium nitrate – good for putting nitrogen into the soil. But van Niekerk knew a bit more. If you take a hundred pounds of this, six pints of fuel oil, two pounds of coal dust, and mix it all together then you get the equivalent of forty per cent blasting gelignite. I've never forgotten that. Van Niekerk scared the pants off me – he brewed the stuff in a concrete mixer.'

'Is this on the level?' said Follet unbelievingly.

'We won't need as much,' said Tozier. 'And I don't know if our substitute ingredients will work. But we'll give it a bang.' He grinned. 'And that's a hell of a bad pun. Van Niekerk said they do a lot of blasting this way in the South African gold mines. They've discovered it's safer – and cheaper – to mix up the stuff at the work face than to store gelignite in magazines.'

'But we need the charcoal,' said Warren.

'And a detonator. We might as well relax until Tom comes back.'

If he comes back, thought Warren. He sat on the box and looked glumly at the sack of fertilizer. He had said to Hellier back in London that they were going into what was virtually a war – but what a devil of a way to fight it!

### III

Metcalfe was back within the hour. He came in smoking a cigar and limping a little. As soon as the door closed he nipped the glowing end and handed it to Tozier. 'A stick of charcoal,' he said. 'I did a bit of sleight of hand with a cigar when they searched me. I have a lot more stuffed in my shoes.'

'The detonator?' asked Tozier urgently.

Metcalfe unfastened his belt and rummaged around in his trousers. From somewhere mysterious he produced the clock and handed it over, the spike of the detonator sticking out at right-angles to the back. Follet said, 'How come they didn't find that when they searched you?' His voice had an edge of suspicion.

Metcalfe grimaced. 'I rammed the detonator up my arse and walked tight. I bet it's started piles.'

'It's all for the cause,' said Tozier with a grin. 'Did you have any trouble, Tom?'

'Not a bit. I spun Fahrwaz a yarn pretty close to the truth, but left a couple of gaps in it. He sent me back to fill them in. We'd better get our plans agreed now. They won't be coming for you for a while; the old boy said he was tired and going to bed.' He looked at his watch. 'Dawn will be in three hours.'

'A night escape might be better,' said Tozier.

Metcalfe shook his head decisively. 'You wouldn't have a

chance at night. By the time you found the exit you'd be caught. The best time to make a break is at first light so you can see what you're doing – and it'll give me three hours to set up a few diversions I have in mind. How accurately can you set that clock?'

'To the nearest minute.'

'Good enough. Make it five-thirty. You'll hear a lot of action just at that time.' Metcalfe squatted on his haunches and began to draw on the sandy floor of the cave. 'Your Land-Rovers are here with the ignition keys still in place – I checked that. The exit is here. When you blow off the door you'll either kill the guards or give them a hell of a fright; in either case you needn't worry about them if you move fast. When you leave the cave turn left – *not* the way you were brought. There's a devil of a steep path down to the valley floor about ten yards along the ledge outside.'

'How steep?'

'You'll make it,' assured Metcalfe. 'Now, there's only one way in – or out – of this valley, and that's through the gorge. You make your break for your trucks, drive into the gorge and stop at the first sharp turn. I'll be right behind you in one of Fahrwaz's vehicles which I'll abandon in an immovable condition. If we can block up the gorge behind us we stand a fair chance of getting away. But wait for me, for God's sake!'

'I've got it, Tom.'

Metcalfe took off his shoes and shook a pile of black dust from them and pulled some charcoal sticks from his socks. 'I hope this stuff works,' he said doubtfully. 'If it doesn't we'll all be up the spout.'

'It's all we've got,' said Tozier. 'No use binding about it.' He looked at Metcalfe and said quietly, 'Thanks for everything, Tom.'

'Anything for an old pal,' said Metcalfe lightly. 'I'd better be going now. Remember – five-thirty.'

The guard let him out, and Warren said pensively,

'Andy, supposing there weren't any drugs involved – would Metcalfe help you out on the basis of the Old Pals' Act?'

'I'm glad I don't have to put it to the test,' said Tozier drily. 'A mercenary is like a politician – a good one is one who stays bought. I've fought on the same side as Tom Metcalfe, and I've fought in opposition. For all I know we might have shot at each other some time. I think that if it weren't for the drugs we'd have had to take our own chances. We're damned lucky he considers he's been double-crossed.'

'And that he believed us,' said Follet.

'There's that, too,' admitted Tozier. 'But Tom and I have swapped drinks and lies for a long time. We've never crossed each other up, so there's no reason why he shouldn't believe me. Come on; let's get busy.'

He set Follet and Warren to grinding the fertilizer down into an even finer powder, using plates as mortars and the backs of spoons as pestles. 'I want all those lumps out of it.'

'Is this safe?' asked Follet nervously.

'It's just fertilizer,' assured Tozier. 'Even when it's mixed it will need the detonator to explode it.' He began to figure out quantities and weights, and then began to grind down the charcoal. After a while he went to the back of the cave and rooted about in the box which contained engine spares, and came back with a pipe closed at one end with a plug. 'Just the thing we need – everything for the do-it-yourself anarchist. Ever made bombs before, Nick?'

'It's hardly likely, is it?'

'I don't suppose it is much in your line. But this isn't the first time I've had to make do. When you're on the losing side the money tends to run out and you have to do a lot of patching. I once assembled quite a serviceable tank out of six wrecks.' He smiled. 'But this lot is a little too much the Moses lark for my taste – making bricks without straw.'

He cleaned out the coffee-pot and dried it carefully, then

poured in the ground-down fertilizer and added the pow-dered charcoal a little at a time, keeping the mixture well stirred. When he thought he had the right proportions he gave it to Follet. 'Keep stirring – it'll help pass the time.'

He picked up the can of oil and looked at it dubiously. 'The recipe calls for fuel oil – I don't know if this will be suitable. Still, we won't know if we don't try, so let's do the final mix.' He poured a little of the oil into the out-held coffee pot. 'Keep on stirring, Johnny. It shouldn't get wet enough to form a paste; just damp enough to hold together when you squeeze it in your hand.'

'You can do the squeezing,' said Follet. 'The only thing I squeeze is a dame.'

Tozier laughed. 'They're just as explosive if not handled right. Give it to me.' He tried the squeeze test and added a little more oil. This proved to be too much and the mixture was rebalanced by the addition of fertilizer and charcoal. It was quite a time before he pronounced himself satisfied, but at last he said, 'That's it; now we make the bomb.'

He took the tube, checked that the plug was screwed home firmly, and began to stuff the explosive mixture into the other end, using a long bolt to ram it down. Follet watched him for a while, then said tensely, 'Andy – stop right there.'

Tozier froze. 'What's on your mind?'

'That's a steel tube, isn't it?' asked Follet.

'So?'

'And you're using a steel bolt as a ramrod. *For Christ's sake, don't strike a spark!*'

Tozier eased out his breath. 'I'll try not to,' he said, and used the bolt much more carefully. He crammed the tube full of the mixture, well packed down, took the clock and set it, then pressed the detonator spike into the end. 'There's a few bits of sheet metal back there, and the box Warren is sitting on is screwed together. That's how we fasten it to the door.'

247

It took a long time because they had to work quietly, fearing to attract the attention of the guards outside. Tozier's small penknife, which they used as a makeshift screwdriver, had all its blades broken by the time they were finished. He regarded the bomb critically, then looked at his watch. 'It took longer than I expected; it's nearly five now – just over half an hour to go.'

'I don't want to appear difficult,' said Follet. 'But we're now locked in a cave with a bomb that's about to explode. Have you thought of that little thing?'

'We should be safe enough lying at the back behind those boxes.'

'I'm glad we have a doctor along,' said Follet. 'You might come in useful, Nick, if that firecracker really works. I'm going to pick me a good safe place right now.'

Warren and Tozier followed him to the back of the cave where they built a rough barricade of boxes, then they lay down using the sacks of straw as improvised mattresses. The next half hour crawled by and Warren was mightily astonished to find himself nodding off to sleep. If anyone had told him this could – or would – happen in such a critical circumstance he would have laughed; yet it was not surprising considering that this was his second night without sleep.

Tozier's elbow jerked him into wakefulness. 'Five minutes – get ready.'

Warren found his mind full of questions. Would Tozier's ridiculous bomb work? If it did, would it work well enough? Or too well? Follet had already expressed his apprehensions on that score.

'Four minutes,' said Tozier, his eyes on his watch. 'Johnny, you go first, then Nick. I'll bring up the rear.'

The seconds ticked by and Warren found himself becoming very tense. His mouth was dry and he had an odd feeling in his stomach as though he was very hungry. In a detached manner one part of his mind checked off the symptoms and he thought – *So this is what it's like to be frightened.*

Tozier said, 'Three minutes,' and as he said it there was a sound from the door. 'Hell's teeth!' he exclaimed. 'Someone's coming in.'

Follet grunted. 'A hell of a time to pick.'

Tozier raised his head cautiously as the door creaked open, and saw men silhouetted against the grey light of dawn. The mocking voice of Ahmed echoed from the stone walls. 'What – all asleep? No guilty consciences here?'

Tozier pushed himself up on one elbow and stretched as though just aroused from sleep. 'What the hell do you want now?' he said in a grumbling voice.

'I want somebody to talk,' said Ahmed. 'Who shall it be? Who do you think we should take first, Mr Tozier?'

Tozier played for time. He looked at his watch and said, 'You start too early for my liking. Come back in an hour. Better still, don't come back at all.' *One and a half minutes to go.*

Ahmed spread his hands. 'I regret I cannot oblige you. My father sleeps lightly – he is an old man – and he is now awake and impatient.'

'All right,' said Tozier. 'Wake up, you two. I'll give you one minute to be on your feet. *One minute*, do you hear?'

Warren heard the emphasis and pressed himself to the floor of the cave. He said, 'What is it, Andy? I'm tired.'

'Ah, Mr Warren,' said Ahmed. 'I trust you slept well.' His voice sharpened. 'Up with you, all of you; or do I have to have you dragged out? My father is waiting to entertain you with some of our typical Kurdish hospitality.' He laughed.

Tozier took one glance at him before throwing himself flat. Ahmed was still laughing when the bomb exploded. It blew the door off its hinges and hurled it bodily at the laughing man and swept him aside to smear him bloodily against the rock wall. Dust billowed and far away someone screamed.

'Move!' yelled Tozier.

Follet was first out of the door as planned. He skidded to the left and stumbled over a body on the ledge and nearly went over the edge of the cliff. Warren, right behind him, shot out his arm and grabbed him before he toppled.

Follet recovered and plunged forward along the ledge. At the top of the path there was a guard, his mouth opened in surprise and desperately trying to unsling his rifle. Follet was on him before he could get the rifle free, and hit him in the face with his closed fist. The fist was wrapped around a big steel bolt and Warren distinctly heard the crunch as the man's jawbone was smashed. The guard gave a choked wail and fell aside and the way down the narrow path was open.

Follet ran down it at a dangerous speed, slipping and sliding, with his boots starting miniature avalanches of dust and pebbles. Warren stumbled over a loose stone and pitched forward and for one blind moment thought he was going to fall, but Tozier's big hand grabbed him by the belt and hauled him back. That was all the trouble they had going down to the valley floor.

Across the valley things were happening. A fusillade of small-arms fire popped off, interspersed with the deeper note of exploding grenades. One of the further caves erupted with an earth-shattering explosion and a part of the ledge on the cliff slid abruptly into the valley. Metcalfe's 'diversion' was taking on all the aspects of a small war.

In the dim light of dawn they ran towards the Land-Rovers. A man lay writhing with a broken back just below the cave in which they had been imprisoned, and Warren surmised he had been blown off the upper ledge by the force of Tozier's bomb. He jumped over the feebly moving body and hurried to catch up with Follet. Behind him he heard the regular thudding of Tozier's boots.

A small herd of camels tethered close by were much alarmed by the sudden noise and some of them plunged wildly and, tearing up their stakes, went careering up the valley ahead of them, adding to the confusion. A bee buzzed past Warren's head and there was the sharp *spaaang* and a whine as a bullet ricocheted from rock, and he realized that someone had recovered enough from the general alarm to shoot at them. But he had no time to worry about that – all his attention was directed to getting to the Land-Rovers in the shortest time possible.

There was a hundred yards to go and the breath rasped in his throat as his lungs pumped hard and his legs pumped even harder. Ahead, in front of the vehicles, three Kurds had materialized from nowhere and one was already on one knee with rifle poised to shoot at point-blank range. It seemed he could not miss but as he fired a camel cut across between them and received the bullet. Follet swerved to the right, using the staggering camel as cover, and the second of the Kurds was bowled over by another maddened beast.

Follet jumped him and put the toe of his boot into his throat with great force. He scooped up the fallen rifle and fired as he ran, rapidly but with no great accuracy. But the unexpected spray of bullets was enough to make the two opposing men duck and run for cover, and the way was clear.

Behind them all was turmoil as the frantic camels plunged and bucked and more of them tugged free of their tethers to run down the valley. Warren thought afterwards that this was the one thing that saved them; none of the Kurds near them could get a clear shot in the confusion and their bullets went wild. He reached the nearest Land-Rover, snatched open the door, and hurled himself inside.

As he twisted the ignition key he saw the other Land-Rover take off with spinning wheels with Tozier still running next to it. Tozier jumped as Follet pushed open the door and bullets sent dust spurting in fountains around where his ankles had been. But he was in the passenger seat, and Warren ground gears as he followed, hoping to God that Follet remembered the direction of the gorge.

He glanced in the wing mirror and saw a big truck wheel in line behind. That would be Metcalfe doing his best to bottle up the gorge. The movable windscreen of the truck was wide open and he saw the tanned blur of Metcalfe's face and the glint of white teeth – the man was actually laughing. In that brief glimpse he also saw that there was something wrong with the truck; it trailed a thick cloud of billowing black smoke which coiled in greasy clouds and drifted across the valley behind. Then there were a couple of quick thumps somewhere at the back of the Land-Rover and abruptly the wing-mirror shivered into fragments.

Warren revved the engine fiercely and plunged after Follet as he entered the gorge. He hazily remembered that there was a sharp bend about a hundred yards along, but it came sooner than he expected and he had to slam on anchors in a hurry to prevent himself running into Follet.

From behind there came a rending crash and he turned his head and looked back. Metcalfe had swerved and driven the truck into the wall of the gorge, jamming the entrance completely. Already he was climbing out through the open windscreen while the oily black smoke coming from the truck eddied in thick clouds. It occurred to Warren that this was deliberate – that Metcalfe had provided a smoke-screen to cover their sudden dash to the gorge.

Metcalfe ran up brandishing a sub-machine-gun. He waved to Follet in the front vehicle, and shouted, 'Get going!' Then he jumped in alongside Warren, and said breathlessly, 'There's going to be a hell of a bang any moment now – that truck's full of mortar bombs and it's burning merrily.'

Follet moved off and Warren followed, and even as they turned the corner the first explosion came from the burning truck, accompanied by what sounded like an infantry regiment doing a rapid-fire exercise. 'I burst open a few cases of small arms ammunition and scattered those in, too,' said Metcalfe. 'Getting past that truck will be bloody dangerous for the next half hour.'

Warren found his hands trembling uncontrollably on the wheel and he tried desperately to steady them as he drove along the twisting gorge. He said, 'Are we likely to meet any opposition along here?'

'Too bloody right,' said Metcalfe, and cocked the sub-machine-gun. He saw the microphone and picked it up. 'Does this thing work? Is it on net?'

'It'll work if it's switched on. I don't know if Andy will be listening, though.

'He will,' said Metcalfe with confidence, and snapped switches. 'He's too old a hand at this game to neglect his communications.' He lifted the microphone to his lips. 'Hello, Andy; can you hear me? Over.'

'I hear you, Tom,' said Tozier metallically. 'You timed everything very well. Over.'

'All part of the service,' said Metcalfe. 'There may be some opposition. Fahrwaz has an outpost at the other end of the gorge. Not more'n a dozen men, but they've got a machine-gun. Any suggestions? Over.'

There was a muffled exclamation from the loudspeaker and Tozier said, 'How long have we got? Over.'

'About twenty minutes. Half an hour at most. Over.'

The loudspeaker hummed and there was a faint crackle. 'Pull us up short and out of sight,' said Tozier. 'I think we can handle it. Out.'

Metcalfe replaced the microphone on its bracket. 'Andy's a good man,' he said dispassionately. 'He'd better be bloody good this time, though.' He twisted the satchel he was wearing to where he could unfasten it, then jerked his thumb to the rear. 'I'm going back there; I won't be long.'

He climbed into the back of the Land-Rover and Warren,

flipping an eye up to the interior mirror, saw his arm move in a rhythmic movement as though throwing something repeatedly. As he came back into the seat he tossed the empty satchel from the window.

'What were you throwing out back there?' asked Warren curiously.

'Caltrops – tyre-busters,' said Metcalfe with a grin. 'Whichever way they land there's always one sharp point sticking up. The Kurds use a lot of them when they're being chased by the Iraqi armoured car patrols. I see no reason why they shouldn't be on the receiving end for once.'

Warren's hands were steadier. This calm, matter-of-fact man was a soothing influence. He slowed for another sharp bend, and said, 'How did you cause all that racket back in the valley?'

'Started a fire in an ammunition dump,' said Metcalfe cheerily. 'And laid a time-fuse in the mortar bomb store. I also tied strings to a hell of a lot of grenades and tied the other end to the truck – when I moved off it pulled out the firing pins and they started popping off. Old Fahrwaz may still have the guns I brought, but he won't have much left to shoot out of them.'

More explosions sounded distantly behind them, the noise deadened by the rock walls of the gorge, and Metcalfe grinned contentedly. Warren said, 'How much further to go?'

'We're about half way.' He picked up the microphone and rested it on his lap. Presently he raised it to his lips and said, 'We're just about there, Andy. Stop round the next corner. Over.'

'Okay, Tom. Out.'

Warren eased to a halt as Follet slowed. Metcalfe jumped out and joined Tozier, who asked, 'What's the situation?'

Metcalfe nodded up the road. 'The gorge ends just round that corner. There's a small rocky hill – what we'd call a *kopje* in South Africa – which commands the entrance. Our boys are on top of there.'

'How far from this spot?'

Metcalfe cocked his head on one side. 'About four hundred yards.' He pointed upwards. 'If you climb up there you'll be able to see it.'

Tozier looked up, then nodded abruptly and turned to Warren. 'Nick, you'll be helping Johnny. The first thing you do is to get out the spare wheel. And do it quietly – no metallic clinks.'

Warren frowned. 'The spare wheel . . .' But Tozier had already walked away and was talking to Follet. Warren shrugged and got out the wheel brace to unfasten the nuts which held the spare wheel in place.

Metcalfe and Tozier began to climb the side of the gorge, and Follet came across to help Warren. The spare wheel came loose and Follet rolled it along the ground as though he was looking for a special place to put it. He laid it down carefully, then went back to Warren. 'Get out the jack,' he said, and surprised Warren by diving under the Land-Rover with a spanner clutched in his hand.

Warren found the jack and laid it on the ground. Follet said in a muffled voice, 'Give me a hand with this,' so Warren dropped to his knees and saw Follet busily engaged in removing the exhaust silencer. When he took hold of it he found it surprisingly heavy and only slightly warm to the touch. They dragged it clear and Follet unfastened a couple of nuts and slid out the baffles which formed an integrated unit. He nodded towards the wheel. 'Take it over there,' he said, and picked up the jack and a toolbox.

Warren dumped the silencer next to the wheel. 'What are we supposed to be doing?'

'This will be a mortar when we've assembled it,' said Follet. 'A mortar needs a base plate – that's the wheel. There's a flange on it so it makes firm contact with the ground. The silencer is the barrel – you didn't think Rover silencers are machined like that, did you?' He began to work rapidly. 'Those lugs fit here, on the wheel. Help me.'

The lugs slid home sweetly into the slots in the wheel and Follet pushed a pin through the aligned holes. 'This screw jack is the elevating mechanism,' he said. 'It fits in here like this. You fit the wheel brace and turn, and the whole barrel goes up and down. Just fasten those nuts, will you?'

He ran back to the vehicles leaving Warren a little numb with astonishment but not so much as to neglect the urgency of the occasion. Follet came back and tossed down an ordinary transparent plastic protractor. 'That screws on to the jack – it already has holes drilled.' Warren screwed the protractor in place and found that he had just installed a simple range scale.

Above his head Metcalfe and Tozier looked across at the small rocky hill. As Metcalfe had said it was about four hundred yards away and he could see quite clearly the half-dozen men standing on top. 'Has Fahrwaz got a telephone laid on – or anything like it?'

Metcalfe held his head on one side as he heard a distant thud. 'He won't need it in the circumstances,' he said. 'Those boys can hear what's going on. They're getting worried – look at them.'

The men on the hill were gazing at the entrance to the gorge and there was some gesticulating going on. Tozier produced a small prismatic compass and sighted it carefully on the hill. 'We have a mortar,' he said. 'Johnny Follet is assembling it now. We also have a light machine-gun. If we get the machine-gun up here you can hose the top of that hill and draw their fire.' He turned and took another sight on the mortar. 'As soon as we know where their machine-gun is, then we knock it out with the mortar.'

'Andy, you're a tricky bastard,' said Metcalfe affectionately. 'I always said so and, by God, I'm right.'

'Our machine-gun has no belt or drum – just a hopper

into which you dump loose rounds. You should be able to handle it.'

'It sounds like the Japanese Nambu. I can handle it.'

'You'll also be artillery spotter,' said Tozier. 'We'll be firing blind from down there. Do you remember the signals we used in the Congo?'

'I remember,' said Metcalfe. 'Let's get that machine-gun up here. I wouldn't be surprised if those boys come down the gorge to see what's happening back there.'

They climbed down and found Warren tightening the last nut on the mortar. Metcalfe looked at it unbelievingly. 'What a crazy lash-up. Does it really work?'

'It works,' said Tozier briefly. 'See how Johnny's getting on with the machine-gun. Time is getting low.'

He dropped on one knee, checked the assembly of the mortar, then began to line it up in conformity with the angles he had taken using the compass. 'We'll set it at four hundred yards,' he said. 'And hope for the best.'

'I didn't believe you when you said we had a mortar,' said Warren. 'What about shells?'

'Bombs,' said Tozier. 'We've got precious few of those. You might have noticed that we're liberally equipped with fire extinguishers. There's one under the bonnet in the engine space, one under the dash and another in the back. Six for the two trucks – and that's all the bombs we have. Help me yank 'em out.'

Metcalfe climbed up to his perch on top of the gorge again, trailing a rope behind him. Once settled he hauled up the machine-gun, filled up the hopper with rounds of ammunition, and pushed it before him so that it rested firmly on its bipod. He sighted in carefully at the little group on the hill then turned his head and waved.

Tozier held up his hand and jerked his head at Follet. 'Take that burp-gun which Tom brought along, and go back along the gorge to the first corner. If anything moves, shoot it.'

Follet indicated the mortar. 'What about this?'

'Nick and I can handle it. We're not out for rapid fire – not with only six rounds. Get going. I like to feel that my back's protected.'

Follet nodded, collected the sub-machine-gun and departed at a trot. Tozier waited two minutes and then waved to Metcalfe. Metcalfe moved his shoulders to loosen them, set his cheek against the butt and looked through the sights. There were five men clearly in view. Gently he squeezed the trigger and death streaked towards the hill at 2,500 feet per second. At that range he could not miss. Delicately he traversed the gun and a scythe of bullets chopped across the top of the hill and suddenly there was no one to be seen.

He stopped firing and waited for something to happen. Moving very slowly he brought his hand forward and dropped a handful of bullets into the hopper. That first long burst had been ruinously expensive of ammunition. He studied the hill carefully but detected nothing that moved.

A rifle cracked twice but no bullet came near him. It was just random shooting. The outpost's machine-gun was mounted so as to sweep the open ground in front of the entrance to the gorge. Apparently no one had taken into account an attack on the outpost from the rear, so it would take some little time for them to reorganize. He smiled grimly as he thought of the frantic effort that must be going on behind the hill. There would be quite a bit of consternation, too.

The rifle fired again, twice in quick succession – two of them, he judged. He was there to draw fire so he decided to tickle them up and squeezed the trigger again in a quick and economical burst of five rounds. This time he was answered in like manner by the sustained chatter of a machine-gun, and a hail of bullets swept the rocks thirty yards to his left and ten yards below.

258

He could not see where the gun was firing from so he squirted another short burst and was answered again. This time he spotted it – they had brought the machine-gun around the curve of the hill and about half way up, sheltered in a tumbled heap of boulders. He signalled to Tozier who bent down to adjust the mortar.

Tozier tugged the lanyard and the mortar barked. Warren saw the thin streak against the sky as the bomb arched in its trajectory and disappeared from sight, but Tozier was already looking at Metcalfe to find the result of the first ranging shot.

He grunted as Metcalfe waved his hand complicatedly. 'Thirty yards short – twenty to the left.' He adjusted the elevation and traversed the mortar slightly, then reloaded. 'This one ought to be better.' The mortar barked again.

The second bomb exploded dead in line with the machine-gun position but behind it. A man broke from cover and Metcalfe coolly cut him down with a short burst, then signalled to Tozier to reduce the range. The consternation must be just about complete, he thought, but changed his mind as the machine-gun rattled again and the earth just below his position fountained magically and rock splinters whined above his head. He ducked and slipped back into cover as the leaden hail beat the ground where he had been, sending his gun flying under the impact of the bullets.

But by that time the third bomb was in the air. He heard it explode and the machine-gun fire was cut off. He eased himself up and risked a look at the hill. A faint drift of smoke on the still morning air marked where it had fallen – square on the machine-gun position. A flat report sounded from behind him as the mortar fired again, and another bomb dropped in almost the same place.

He turned and yelled, 'Enough – they've had it.' He began to scramble down, slipped, and fell most of the way but landed on his feet like a cat. He ran over to the mortar and said breathlessly, 'Let's get on our way while they're still shaken. That natty little gun of yours is buggered, Andy.'

'It served its turn,' said Tozier, and put two fingers in his mouth and whistled shrilly like an urchin. 'That ought to bring Johnny.'

Warren ran for the Land-Rover and started the engine, and Metcalfe tumbled in beside him. 'Andy's a bloody wonder,' he said conversationally. 'That was a lovely bit of shooting.' His head snapped back as Warren took off with tyre-punishing acceleration. 'Take it easy – you'll do me an injury.'

The two Land-Rovers roared out of the gorge and past the hill which was still faintly wreathed in smoke. Follet in the first vehicle was hanging out of the back, his gun at the ready, but for that there was no need. Nobody shot at them, nor did they see anyone move. All Warren saw were three bundles of rags on the rocky hillside.

Metcalfe unhooked the microphone. 'Andy, let us get in front – I know the way. And we'd better move fast before young Ahmed pulls out the plug back there. Over.'

'He won't do that,' said Tozier. 'He's dead. He bumped into a door. Over.'

'Dear me,' said Metcalfe. 'He was the old man's favourite son. All the more reason for speed – Fahrwaz will be looking for us with blood in his eyes. The sooner we clear out of the country the better. That means Mosul and the international airport. Move over – I'm coming through. Out.'

He replaced the microphone, and said, 'Doctor, if you want to get back to curing people instead of killing them you'd better hope that this jalopy doesn't break down this side of Sulaymaniyeh. Now move it, Doctor – move it fast.'

# 9

Two days later they landed at Khaldeh International Airport in the Lebanon and drove into Beirut by taxi. The Land-Rovers had been left in Mosul in the care of one of Metcalfe's disreputable friends; they had outlived their usefulness and were no longer needed. 'Beirut's the place,' Tozier had said. 'It's our last chance.'

They registered at a hotel, and Warren said, 'I'm going to ring London; Hellier should be able to bring us up to date with what's been going on here. He'll know where to find Mike and Dan. Then we can figure out the next step.'

'The next step is that I get my hands around Jeanette's beautiful neck,' said Metcalfe savagely.

Warren looked at Tozier and raised his eyebrows. Tozier said softly, 'Are you still with us, Tom?'

'I'm with you. I told you I don't like being used. I can be bought – like you – but on my terms; and my terms have always meant no dope.'

'Then I suggest you leave Delorme strictly alone,' said Tozier. 'She's not important now – it's the heroin we want. Once that is destroyed, then you can have her.'

'It'll be a pleasure,' said Metcalfe.

'All right,' said Tozier. 'Johnny, hire a car – no, better make it two cars; we must be mobile. After Nick has talked to Hellier then we get down to it.'

But when Warren telephoned London he was told by Miss Walden that Hellier was in Beirut. All it took was a quick call to the Saint-Georges and half an hour later they were all sitting in Hellier's suite and he was introducing Metcalfe. 'He joined us at just the right time.'

Hellier looked around. 'Where's Bryan?'

'I'll tell you later – if you really want to know,' said Warren. He was beginning to resent Hellier. Hellier had said he wanted blood but so far he had not risked his valuable skin to get it, and things looked a lot different in the Middle East than they had in London.

Hellier pulled papers from a briefcase. 'Abbot doesn't make sense. He got word to me that the Delorme woman is smuggling two thousand pounds of heroin. I think it's ridiculous, but I can't find Abbot to confirm it or otherwise.'

'I confirm it,' said Warren. 'If it weren't for Andy and Johnny it would have been two tons instead of one.'

'You'd better tell me about that,' said Hellier.

Warren did so, not leaving anything out. When he came to what had happened to Ben Bryan he said bitterly, 'It was a damn' silly thing to do. I blame myself; I should never have let him go back.'

'Nuts!' said Follet. 'It was his own choice.'

Warren completed the tale of their adventures and when he stopped Hellier was pale. 'That's about the lot,' said Warren dispiritedly. 'We missed all along the line.'

Hellier drummed his fingers on the table. 'I don't think we can go any further with this. It's a police matter from now on – let them handle it. We have more than enough evidence for them now.'

Tozier's voice was hard. 'You can't bring the police into this – not the way the evidence was collected.' He swung around on Warren. 'How many men have you killed, Nick?'

'None that I'm aware of,' said Warren, but he knew what Tozier meant.

'No? What about coming through Fahrwaz's place in Iran, the night we blew hell out of the laboratory? Johnny is pretty certain you ran down a man.'

Follet said, 'The way we hit him he wouldn't have a

chance. Anyway, I saw him lying in the road when we went back in.'

'The man was shooting at us,' said Warren angrily.

'Tell that to the Iranian police,' said Tozier scornfully. 'As for me, I'm not pussyfooting around the truth. I've killed men on this jaunt. Ahmed was killed with my bomb, which Warren helped to make; we mortared hell out of another group – I think that between us we killed a dozen, all in all.' He leaned forward. 'Normally I'm covered – I'm employed by a government which gives me a killing licence. But this time I'm not and I can hang as high as Haman under the civil law, and so can the rest of us.' He jabbed a stiff finger towards Hellier. 'Including you. You're just as guilty – an accomplice before the act, so think of that before shouting copper.'

Hellier snorted. 'Do you really think we'd be prosecuted because of the death of scum?' he said contemptuously.

'You don't understand, do you?' said Tozier. 'Tell the silly bastard, Tom.'

Metcalfe grinned. 'It's like this. People round here are touchy about their national pride. Take the Iraqis, for instance; I don't suppose President Bakr is going to shed any tears over a few dead Kurds – he's been trying to polish off the lot himself – but no government is going to stand for a crowd of foreigners bursting into their country and shooting the place up, no matter how high the motives. Andy's dead right – you shout copper now and you'll start a diplomatic incident so big that there's no knowing where it will end. Before you know it the Russkies would be accusing Johnny of being a CIA agent and casting you as the secret head of British Intelligence. And, by God, it would take a hell of a lot of explaining away.'

Follet said, 'No cops.' His voice was final.

Hellier was silent for a while, digesting this and finding it hard going. He said at last, 'I see what you mean. Do you honestly think that your activities in Kurdistan could be construed as interfering in the internal affairs of another country?'

'By Christ, I do!' said Tozier forcefully. 'What the hell would you call it?'

'I must admit you've convinced me,' said Hellier regretfully. 'Although I still think we could plead justification.' He stared at Metcalfe. 'Some of us, that is. Smuggling arms is quite another thing.'

'Your opinion of me doesn't matter a fart in a thunderstorm,' said Metcalfe calmly. 'Anything I do I carry the can for myself. And if I'm going to stay with this crowd, you'd better keep your fat-headed opinions to your fat self.'

Hellier flushed. 'I don't know that I like your attitude.'

'I don't give a stuff if you like it or not.' Metcalfe turned to Tozier. 'Is this chap real or has someone invented him?'

Warren said sharply. 'That's enough. Shut up, Hellier; you don't know enough about it to criticize. If Metcalfe wanted to take arms to the Kurds that's his business.'

Metcalfe shrugged. 'So I picked the wrong bunch of Kurds – that was a mistake which doesn't alter the principle. Those boys have been having a rough time at the hands of the Iraqis and someone has to help them out.'

'While making money at it,' Hellier sneered.

'The labourer is worthy of his hire,' said Metcalfe. 'I risk my skin doing it.'

Tozier stood up and looked at Hellier with dislike. 'I don't think we can do much more here, Tom – not with this bag of wind around.'

'Yeah,' said Follet, pushing back his chair. 'It's a bit stuffy in here.'

Warren's voice was cutting. 'Sit down, everybody.' He looked at Hellier. 'I think an apology is in order, Sir Robert.'

Hellier subsided and mumbled, 'No offence meant. I'm sorry, Mr Metcalfe.'

Metcalfe merely nodded, and Tozier sat down. Warren

said, 'Let's stick to the real issue. How do you suppose we should go about finding Abbot and Parker, Andy?'

'Find Delorme and she'll lead you there,' said Tozier promptly.

'I've been thinking a lot about this woman,' said Warren. 'You know more about her than anyone, Tom. What can you tell us that we don't know?'

'I've been wondering a bit myself,' admitted Metcalfe. 'There are some things about this lark that don't add up. Jeanette is pretty good, but she's never been a smash success. Everything she's pulled off has made money, but the overheads are crippling, and I doubt if she has accumulated a lot of capital. All the time I've known her she's been a big spender.'

'What's the point?' asked Hellier.

'How much opium did Fahrwaz collect in Iran?'

'Twenty tons or more,' said Warren.

'There you are,' said Metcalfe. 'That's worth a hell of a lot of boodle. Where would she get it?'

'She wouldn't need it,' said Tozier. 'Not the way she's been working the deal. It was a straight swap for arms. She didn't have to put up the money for the opium – Fahrwaz would – and it wouldn't cost him a lot on his home ground and with his connections.'

'I agree it was a barter transaction,' said Metcalfe exasperatedly. 'But I delivered half a million quids' worth to Fahrwaz. That wasn't the first consignment I'd pushed into Kurdistan. Where would Jeanette get half a million?'

'Wait a minute,' said Hellier, and scrabbled in his briefcase. 'One of Abbot's early reports said something about a banker.' He flipped pages. 'Here it is. She had lunch with a man called Fuad who was traced back to the Inter-East Bank.' He picked up the telephone. 'I could bear to know something more about him. I have good financial connections here.'

'Don't make it too obvious,' warned Warren.

Hellier favoured him with a superior smile. 'Give me the credit for knowing my own job. This is a perfectly normal financial enquiry – it's done all the time.'

He spoke briefly into the telephone and listened for a long time. Then he said, 'Yes, I'd like that; anything to do with him would be welcome. Directorships and so on especially. Thank you very much. Yes, I think I'll be coming in later this week – we're making a film here. I'll ring you as soon as I'm settled and we must have lunch. You'll send the dossier on Fuad immediately? Good.'

He put down the telephone and smiled broadly. 'I thought Fuad might be the manager of Inter-East, but he's not – he owns it. That makes this interesting.'

'How?' asked Warren.

Hellier smiled jovially. 'You bank with the Midland, don't you? When did you last take the Chairman of the Midland Bank to lunch?'

Warren grimaced. 'I never have. I doubt if he knows I exist. I don't swing the financial weight to create interest in such rarefied circles.'

'And neither does Delorme, according to Metcalfe – and yet she lunches with Fuad who *owns* Inter-East.' Hellier tented his fingers. 'Banking in the Lebanon is conducted along lines which would cause grey hairs in the City of London. Ever since the spectacular fall of Intrabank the Lebanese government has been trying to clean up its financial image, but this man, Fuad, has been playing fast and loose with the proposed Code of Conduct. The rules by which he works are considered normal in the relaxed atmosphere of the Middle East, but it means that anyone who shakes hands with him had better count his fingers afterwards. My friend on the other end of that telephone keeps a permanent dossier on Fuad's doings – just for his own safety. He's sending it up to us.'

'So you think he's financing the whole deal,' said Warren.

'I think it's likely,' said Hellier. We'll know better when

I study the dossier. It's surprising what a list of director-ships tell about a man.'

'That's one angle to be worked on,' said Tozier. 'But there's another. The morphine has still to be converted into heroin. What are your views on that, Nick?'

'They have to do it somewhere. It's my bet they'll do it here in Beirut.'

'Without Speering?'

'There are other chemists, and it's not too difficult – not nearly as difficult as the extraction of morphine from opium. You acetylate the morphine and convert the base to hydro-chloride. All you need are a lot of plastic buckets, and it requires as much chemical knowledge as you get in a sixth-form stinks class.'

They discussed it for a while and came up with no positive solution. Heroin could be made practically any-where, and it was impossible to search the whole of Beirut or, possibly, the entire Lebanon.

Warren brought up the disappearance of Abbot and Parker. 'If Delorme fell for the torpedo scheme, then Parker will be busy. I think that's why they're not in plain sight.'

'Getting torpedoes would be no trouble to Jeanette,' observed Metcalfe. 'She's been running arms all over the Mediterranean for quite a few years. But that brings up something else – she'll need a ship. That cuts down the search area to the coast and the ports.'

'Not much help,' said Follet. 'There are a lot of ships.'

The telephone rang and Hellier picked it up. 'Send him up,' he said. Presently there was a discreet knock at the door which Hellier answered, and he returned with a fat envelope. 'The Fuad dossier,' he said. 'Let's see what we can find.'

He pulled out the sheaf of typescript and studied it. After a while he said in disgust, 'This man has the ethics of a Byzantine bazaar trader – he's making a lot of money. He even runs a yacht – the *Stella del Mare*.' He flipped the pages. 'According to this list of directorships he has a finger in a lot of pies – hotels, restaurants, vineyards, a couple of farms, a shipyard . . .' He looked up. 'That might bear investigation in view of what we've been discussing.'

He made a note and continued. 'A condiment and pickle factory, a garage, a general engineering works, housing developments . . .'

Warren broke in. 'Say that again.'

'Housing developments?'

'No – something about a pickle factory.'

Hellier checked back. 'Yes, sauces and pickles. He bought it quite recently. What about it?'

'I'll tell you,' said Warren deliberately. 'The acetylation of morphine makes a hell of a stink, and it's exactly the same stink you find in a pickle factory. It's the acetic acid; it smells just like vinegar.'

'Now we're getting somewhere,' said Tozier with satisfaction. 'I suggest we split this lot up. Nick investigates the pickle factory – he's the expert there. Johnny keeps tabs on Delorme, and I'll help him with that if necessary. Tom takes the shipyard angle.' He turned to Metcalfe. 'You'd better steer clear of the woman. Fahrwaz will have been screaming blue murder and she must know about it by now, and of your implication.'

'All right,' said Metcalfe. 'But I'll want her later.'

'You'll get her,' said Tozier grimly. 'Sir Robert can keep digging into Fuad because that's already paying dividends and might pay more. He's also HQ staff – he stays here and we telephone in; he correlates the operation.'

## II

Parker hummed happily as he prepared to tackle the last torpedo. He had been working long hours, eating bad food, and had been confined to the shed and its immediate vicinity for a long time, but he was supremely happy because he was doing the work he liked best of all. He was sorry the job was coming to an end for two reasons – the pleasurable part would be over and the really dangerous part beginning. But right now he was not thinking of what would happen on the other side of the Atlantic, but concentrating on opening the warhead.

Abbot was becoming increasingly edgy. He had not been able to get out of Jeanette anything concerning the operation on the American side. He badly wanted to know the place and the time, but that valuable information she kept to herself. He did not think that Eastman knew, either. Delorme played her cards very close to her beautiful chest.

Ever since the night he had taken her to the Paon Rouge he had been confined, like Parker, to the shed. He had seen a copy of the newspaper and knew that his advertisement trick had worked, but what good it would do he did not know. He frowned irritably and turned his head to see the Arab, Ali, leaning on the rail at the top of the stairs and watching him with unblinking brown eyes. That was another thing – this sense of being continually watched.

He became conscious of a sudden stillness in the workshop and looked at Parker who had his head down and was looking at the warhead. 'What's the matter?'

'Step over here,' said Parker quietly.

He joined Parker and looked down at the warhead, and at Parker's hands which trembled a little. Parker put down the tool he was holding. 'Don't make a scene,' he said,

269

'Don't do anything that'll attract the attention of that bloody Arab – but this thing is full.'

'Full of what?' asked Abbot stupidly.

'TNT, you bloody fool. What do you suppose a warhead would be full of? There's enough in here to blow this whole place a mile high.'

Abbot gulped. 'But Eastman said they'd be delivered empty.'

'Then this one got through by mistake,' said Parker. 'What's more – it has a detonator in it which I'm hopin' isn't armed. It shouldn't be armed, but then, it shouldn't be there at all – an' neither should the TNT. You'd better do your walkin' around here very quietly until I take it out.'

Abbot looked at the warhead as though hypnotized, and Parker did the necessary operation very carefully. He laid the detonator on a bench. 'That's a bit better – but not much. I don't know why this hasn't blown before. To leave a detonator in a warhead is criminal, that's what it is.'

'Yes,' said Abbot, and found himself sweating. 'What do you mean – it's not much better?'

'TNT is right funny stuff,' said Parker. 'It goes sour with age. It's not so stable any more. It becomes that sensitive it can explode on its own.' He looked sideways at Abbot. 'It's best you don't go near it, Mike.'

'Don't worry; I won't.' Automatically Abbot took a cigarette packet from his pocket, and then changed his mind at the unspoken look in Parker's eyes. 'No smoking, either, I suppose. What do we do about it?'

'We get it out. In the service they'd steam it out an' flush it away, but I want to hold on to this little lot – it could come in useful. I don't want Ali to know about it, either.'

'It's hardly likely that he'd know,' said Abbot. 'He's not a technical type. But Eastman might if he came in and saw what we were doing. What do you want the stuff for, Dan?'

'It's in my mind that a torpedo ought to explode,' said

Parker. 'That's what it's made for, an' it don't seem right it shouldn't. When these fish are launched, I want them to go off wi' a bang. That this one is full o' TNT is an act o' providence to my way o' thinkin'.'

Abbot thought of four torpedoes, each loaded with heroin worth $25,000,000 and each exploding on the American shore before the unbelieving eyes of the waiting reception committee. It would be a good ploy. 'What about your weights? You've bitched about the difficulties often enough.'

Parker winked. 'Never tell the whole truth. I've been keepin' somethin' in reserve.'

'You have only one detonator.'

'A good artificer can always make do,' pronounced Parker. 'But like as not I'll probably blow us both to hell gettin' the stuff out, so let's leave that problem until later. It may never come up.' He studied the warhead. 'I'll need some brass tools; I'll start makin' those up now.'

He went away, and Abbot, after looking at the warhead for some time, also left – walking very quietly.


Four days later Eastman surveyed the torpedoes with satisfaction. 'So you reckon we're ready to go, Dan.'

'All ready,' said Parker. 'Bar loadin' the warheads. Then you can stick the fish in the tubes an' shoot.'

'Putting that other tube in the *Orestes* improved her handling,' said Eastman. 'The skipper says she's not as cranky.'

Parker smiled. 'It equalized the turbulence. I'm ready to begin loadin' if you've got the stuff.'

'The boss is a bit worried about that,' said Eastman. 'She wants to do it herself – just to make sure.'

'Well, she can't – an' that's flat,' said Parker abruptly. 'It's a tricky job. I have to see that the centre o' gravity comes in the right place because if it doesn't I can't guarantee how the fish will behave. They have to be balanced just right.'

To have someone prying into the warheads was the last thing he wanted. 'She can stand over me an' watch while I do it,' he said at last. 'I don't mind that.'

Abbot said, 'Dan was telling me that if the balance isn't right the torpedo might dive to the bottom.'

'It would affect the steering, too,' said Parker. 'They'd be bloody erratic.'

'Okay, okay,' said Eastman, holding up his hands. 'You've convinced me – as usual. Jeanette will be here pretty soon with the load for one fish. See if you can convince her.'

Jeanette took a lot of convincing but at last she agreed, bowing to the superior weight of technical know-how which Parker dazzlingly deployed. 'As long as I'm here when you do it and the warhead is sealed,' she said.

Abbot grinned. 'You don't trust us very much.'

'Correct,' she said coolly. 'Help Jack to get the stuff in here.'

Abbot helped Eastman to haul a big cardboard box into the shed and down the stairs, and then they went back for another. Jeanette delicately tapped the box with a neatly shod foot. 'Open it.'

Parker took a knife and ripped open the top of the box. It was full of polyethylene bags, all holding a white powder. 'Those bags hold half a kilogram each,' she said. 'There are five hundred of them – one torpedo load.'

Parker straightened. 'That's not on. I said five hundred pounds – not two hundred and fifty kilos. I don't know if I can do it – it's fifty pounds over the odds.'

'Just put it in,' she said.

'You don't understand,' he said exasperatedly. 'I've balanced these torpedoes for a five hundred pound load. If you stick an extra ten per cent right at the nose it's goin' to alter the leverage arm – alter the centre o' balance.' He rubbed the side of his nose. 'It's possible, I suppose,' he said doubtfully.

'For another hundred thousand dollars?' she asked. 'Just for you. I won't tell Abbot.'

'All right,' he said. 'I'll give it a go.' He did not want to leave any heroin behind if he could help it, and it did not really matter a damn about the balance as far as he was concerned. He would make a song and dance about it and go through the motions, baffling her with science, just to avoid suspicion. 'For another hundred thou', you're on.'

'I thought you could do it,' she said, and smiled.

He thought she was getting it cheaply. A further two hundred pounds of heroin worth $10,000,000 for a mere $100,000 – if he was ever paid at all. God, the profits to be made in this business!

Eastman and Abbot came back bearing another load, and Parker began to stow the packets into the warhead very carefully. 'It's a matter o' density, too,' he said. 'This stuff isn't as solid as TNT. It takes up more room, especially in these plastic packets.'

'You're sure the warhead is waterproof?' demanded Jeanette.

'You needn't worry about that,' he assured her. 'It's as tight as a duck's arse.'

She looked mystified and Eastman chuckled. He began to poke about on the bench which was littered with tools and bits of metal. He picked up something and began to examine it, and Abbot froze as he saw it was one of the detonators Parker had been making up. 'What's this?'

Parker looked at it, and said casually, 'Contact breaker for the "B" circuit. That one wasn't working very well, so I made up another.'

Eastman tossed it in the air, caught it, and replaced it on the bench. 'You're pretty good with your hands, Dan. I think I could find you a good job over in the States.'

'I wouldn't mind that,' said Parker. 'Not if it pays as well

273

as this one.' He worked in silence for a long time with Jeanette hovering over him and peering over his shoulder. At last he said, 'That's the last packet. I'm surprised – I really am. I didn't think we'd get 'em all in. I'll screw it down tight an' you can put your seal on if you want to.'

He checked the heavily greased gasket and clamped the small hatch down, then said, 'Get the block an' tackle ready, Mike. We'll couple it to the torpedo body an' then it'll be ready to go to the *Orestes*.'

The warhead was swayed up on the block and tackle and run across to the body where Parker bolted it down firmly. 'There, miss,' he said. 'Are you happy wi' that? I feel I ought to ask for a receipt, but I doubt I'd get it.'

'I'm satisfied,' she said. 'Have it taken to the *Orestes* tonight, Jack. There'll be another load tomorrow, Parker. The *Orestes* sails the morning after.' She smiled at Abbot. 'A nice sea cruise for all of us.'


## III

Warren felt dispirited when they met in Hellier's suite to compare notes. He had had an unproductive day. 'The pickle factory is closed up tight as a drum. There's a sign outside saying it's closed for alterations.'

'How do you know that's what it said?' asked Metcalfe. 'Wasn't the sign in Arabic script?'

'I found someone to translate it into French,' said Warren tiredly. 'There was a bit of a vinegary smell, but not much. I didn't see anyone go in or come out. It was a wasted day.'

'I saw somebody go in,' said Follet unexpectedly. 'I followed the Delorme dame and she went in the back way. There was a guy with her – an American, I think – they spent about an hour there.'

'It's all linking up nicely,' said Hellier, regarding Follet with approval. 'This definitely ties up Delorme with Fuad. What about the shipyard?'

'It's not very big,' said Metcalfe. 'Impossible to get into, if you want to be unobtrusive about it. I didn't see Jeanette at all. I hired a boat and had a look at the yard from the sea. Fuad's yacht is anchored there, and there's a scrubby old coaster flying the Panamanian flag – the *Orestes*, she's called. That's all. The yard itself looks run down; not many working types about, but plenty of toughs at the main gate.'

'Perhaps it's closed for alterations, too,' said Tozier ironically. 'If they're ferrying millions of dollars' worth of heroin about Beirut they're going to be damned sure there'll be no prying eyes at the staging points. It's quite possible the *Orestes* is the ship we're looking for. Could she make the Atlantic crossing?'

'I don't see why not,' said Metcalfe. 'She's about three thousand tons. But there's more. This afternoon a truck pitched up hauling a very long trailer. I couldn't see what the trailer carried because it was covered with a tarpaulin, but it could very well have been a torpedo.'

'I'm not so sure of this torpedo bit,' said Warren. 'Parker told me a torpedo can only carry about five hundred pounds, and we know there's a ton to be smuggled.' He frowned. 'Even if Abbot and Parker scupper the first consignment that still leaves another three-quarters of a ton of heroin around. If the torpedo is sabotaged Delorme and her gang will go to ground and we'll be worse off than we are now.'

'If Jeanette can get one torpedo – which she can – then she can get four,' said Metcalfe. 'I know Jeanette – she's a go-for-broke type, and if she's convinced that a torpedo will do the trick she'll go for it wholeheartedly.'

'That's all very well,' said Warren. 'But we don't even know if Parker sold her on the idea.'

'Ah, but I have more,' said Metcalfe. 'When the truck

and trailer came out of the shipyard I followed it. It went to another place on the coast which was also locked up tight and the very devil to observe. But I paid a lot of money for the use of an attic from which I could see about a quarter of what's on the other side of the wall. There was an Arab who is apparently some kind of caretaker; there's a shortish man with broad shoulders – very muscular – and who walks with a slight limp . . .'

'Parker!' said Warren.

' . . . and there's a tall young chap with fair hair. Would that be Abbot?'

Warren nodded. 'It matches him.'

'A car came in once, stayed a few minutes and drove away again. It brought a tall man with a beaky nose and hair receding at the temples.'

'That sounds like the guy who was with the Delorme dame,' said Follet. 'Was it a black Mercedes?'

Metcalfe nodded, and Hellier said, 'I think it's quite clear we're all moving in the right direction. The point is – what do we do now?'

'I think Parker and Abbot are in a very dangerous position,' said Warren.

'And that's an understatement.' Metcalfe snorted. 'Suppose the ship sails and the torpedoes don't work because Parker has sabotaged them. Jeanette is going to be as mad as a hornet. Nobody loses that much money and stays civilized, and she's a touchy girl at the best of times. Parker and Abbot will get the chop – they'll go over the side of the *Orestes* and no one will ever hear of them again.' He brooded. 'Come to that, they might get the chop even if the torpedoes are successful. Jeanette has a passion for covering up her tracks.'

Tozier said, 'Nick, I'm very much afraid you've boobed. This torpedo trick is all right as far as it goes, but you didn't think it through. It's all very well being in a position to dump the heroin, but what about Abbot and Parker?'

276

'I think the point at issue here is very simple,' said Hellier. 'Do we attack the pickle factory or the ship?'

'Not the pickle factory,' said Warren instantly. 'Supposing they've moved some of the heroin out already? Even if we attack the factory there'll still be some of the stuff on the loose. I favour the ship where we'll have a chance of scooping the pool and getting the lot.'

'And of rescuing Parker and Abbot,' pointed out Hellier.

'That means attacking just before she sails,' said Tozier meditatively. 'And we don't know when that will be.'

'Or whether she'll be carrying the whole consignment,' said Metcalfe. 'We still don't know enough.'

'If only I could talk to Abbot for just five minutes,' said Warren.

Metcalfe snapped his fingers. 'You say Parker was in the Navy. Is there any chance he'd understand Morse?'

'It's possible,' said Warren. 'It may even be probable.'

'That attic I was in faces the setting sun,' said Metcalfe. 'I had the devil of a job because the sun got in my eyes. But it opens up possibilities and all I need is a mirror. I could heliograph.'

Warren's lips tightened. 'Unobtrusively, I hope.'

'I'll watch it,' said Metcalfe seriously.

The conference broke up. Warren was to back up Metcalfe, and Tozier and Follet were to concentrate on the shipyard, looking for a weak spot. Hellier stayed behind to co-ordinate.

Warren discussed the plan with Metcalfe, then said, 'I'd like to ask you a personal question.'

'That's all right, as long as you don't expect an honest answer.'

'You puzzle me, Metcalfe. You don't believe much in law and order, do you? And yet you're dead against dope. Why?'

Metcalfe stopped smiling. 'That's none of your business,' he said stiffly.

'Under the present circumstances I think it is,' said Warren carefully.

'Maybe you have a point,' conceded Metcalfe. 'You're afraid I might run off with the loot and diddle you all.' He smiled faintly. 'I would, too, if it wasn't dope; there's a hell of a lot of money involved. Let's just say that I once had a younger brother and leave it at that, shall we?'

'I see,' said Warren slowly.

'Maybe you do – you're in the business yourself, so Andy tells me. As for law and order, I believe in it as much as the next man, but if the poor bloody Kurds want to fight for the right to live like men then I'm prepared to transport their guns.'

'You seem to have the same point of view as Andy Tozier.'

'Andy and I get along with each other very well,' said Metcalfe. 'But let me give you a bit of advice, Nick; don't go about asking people personal questions – not anywhere east of Marseilles. It's an easy way to get seriously – and permanently – damaged.'


IV


Dan Parker sat on the stool by the bench and contemplated the one remaining torpedo. The late afternoon sun flooded the shed and his work was nearly done. Two torpedoes had been filled and taken away that morning, and this last one was to leave in a very few hours. He felt tired and a little depressed and he was acutely worried about the next stage of the adventure.

Back in London he had left his wife and his sons and he wondered if he would ever see them again. He had no illusions about what would happen on the other side of the Atlantic when four torpedoes exploded on a quiet shore and a major fortune went to destruction. He would, quite simply, be killed and he could see no way of avoiding it. His life had been at risk before, but in the random way of war; never in the cold-blooded manner which he now faced.

He blinked as a stray beam of light flickered across the bench, and pondered on possible ways out of the gruesome situation he and Abbot found themselves in. They could not attempt to escape in Beirut bcause that would be an immediate tip-off that there was something wrong with the torpedoes and the whole dangerous operation would have gone for nothing. Delorme would cut her losses and revert to whatever plans she had originally conceived. So there was nothing for it but to board the *Orestes* next day and hope for the best.

Something niggled at the back of his mind, something which was striving to express itself – something to do with himself, with his own . . . name? He frowned and tried to pin it down. What was it? What was it about the name of Parker that should be so important? He tensed as the light flickered again across the bench because he was suddenly aware that it was spelling his name out – over and over again.

He got up casually and walked over to Ali who was squatting at the bottom of the stairs. 'Hey, Ali, you bloody scoundrel, go to the office an' get me some cigarettes. Got that? Cigarettes.' He mimed the action of lighting a cigarette and pointed up the stairs.

Abbot said, 'I've got some here, Dan.'

Without turning, Parker said briefly, 'They're not my brand. Get crackin', you damned heathen!'

Ali nodded and went up the stairs. As soon as he had left the shed Parker whirled around. 'Get up there an' stop him comin' back – I don't care how you do it but keep him out o' this shed. Have an attack o' bellyache in the yard – anythin'!' Abbot nodded and ran up the stairs, prodded

279

into unquestioning action by the authoritative rasp in Parker's voice. He did not know why Parker wanted this but the tone of urgency was unmistakable. Parker returned to the bench where the light still flickered and studied it for a moment. Then he traced an imaginary line to the window through which it struck. He bent down and the light struck him full in the face and steadied so that he was blinded. He brought up his hand before his face in the thumbs-up sign and then stepped aside.

The light remained steady on the bench for a moment and then began to flicker again and to spell out words in Morse rather slowly. *Warren here . . . questions coming . . . flash light one for yes . . . two for no . . . got that . . .*

Parker took the trouble-shooting lamp which was on a long lead and set it up facing the window. He flashed it once. The reflected light from outside steadied momentarily on the bench and began again . . . *is torpedo working . . .*

Parker paused. He took that to mean: Is the method of smuggling to be by torpedo? He flashed once.

. . . *how many . . . one . . .*

Two flashes.

. . . *four . . .*

One flash.

. . . *by Orestes . . .*

One flash.

. . . *when . . . next week . . .*

Two flashes.

. . . *tomorrow . . .*

One flash.

Metcalfe, up in the attic, checked his prepared question list into which he had put a great deal of thought. He had used Warren's name because he himself was unknown to Parker, and he had to get the maximum information in the minimum time for Parker's safety. It was rather like playing the game of Twenty Questions. He flashed the next question which was all important.

*. . . is all dope going . . . repeat . . . all . . .*

One flash.

*. . . are you and Abbot going . . .*

One flash.

*. . . do you want rescue . . .*

The faint light in the shed flickered wildly and Metcalfe guessed that Parker was trying to send Morse. It was unreadable because the light was so faint and the sun in his eyes so strong. He let his light remain steady until Parker stopped, then hesitated as he saw the Arab come into view from the office. He was relieved to see Abbot step forward and waylay the Arab. Abbot pointed away from the shed and the two men went back into the office.

Metcalfe steadied the mirror again . . . *check where I am . . . can you flash Morse up here at night . . .*

One flash.

*. . . will be here all night . . . good luck . . .*

The light steadied on the bench once more and then abruptly vanished. Parker took his hand from the switch and sighed. He walked to the window and looked up at the faraway building from which the signals had come; the setting gun gleamed redly on a single pane of glass set in the roof. His depression was gone – he and Abbot were no longer alone.

He climbed the stairs and went to the door of the shed. 'Where are those bloody cigarettes?' he roared.

# V

Hellier had chartered a fast cruiser which lay in the yacht harbour and they gathered there early in the morning for a conference. Follet helped Metcalfe lift aboard the heavy suitcase he carried, then they all sat around the table in the saloon. Tozier said, 'Are you sure the *Orestes* is due to sail at nine, Tom?'

'That's what Parker signalled. We had quite a long chat.'

'What are his views?' asked Tozier.

'He doesn't want to be rescued from the shed. He and Abbot could get out themselves if they wanted to – just knock that Arab on the head and blow. But that would give the game away.'

Tozier consulted his watch. 'It's seven now. We don't have much time to make up our minds. Do we hit her before she sails – in the shipyard – or when she's at sea?'

'It must be before she sails,' said Metcalfe positively. 'We'd never get aboard her at sea. The skipper isn't going to heave to and roll out a red carpet for us – not with Eastman looking on.'

'Let me get this straight,' said Hellier. 'Eastman is sailing in the *Orestes* with Parker and Abbot. The Delorme woman is staying in Beirut.'

'Not for long,' said Warren. 'Parker says that she and Fuad are following in the yacht – going for a cruise in the Caribbean, that's the story. He reckons they'll scuttle the *Orestes* after getting rid of the torpedoes – those torpedo tubes are evidence and they daren't let the *Orestes* put into port where she'll be given a going over by Customs officers. The *Stella del Mare* will be standing by to take off the crew.'

'Maybe,' said Metcalfe cynically. 'Some of the crew, perhaps. I told you that Jeanette likes to cover up her tracks.'

'So it's the shipyard,' said Tozier. 'I suggest we hit them just before the *Orestes* is due to sail. We take over the ship and get her out to sea where we can dump the torpedoes. After that we beach her somewhere and split up.'

'We ought to surprise them,' said Metcalfe. 'We'll be coming in from the sea. They're typical landlubbers and their guards are on the landward side at the gates. But it's got to be slick and fast.' He gestured to Follet. 'Open the case, Johnny.'

Follet opened the suitcase and began to lay the contents on the table. 'I contacted some of my pals,' said Metcalfe, as the guns were laid out one by one. 'I thought we'd need these. Jeanette isn't the only one with access to weapons.' He grinned at Hellier. 'You'll get the bills later.'

Tozier picked up a sub-machine-gun. 'This is for me. What's the ammo situation?'

'There'll be enough if you don't pop off into the air, but it'll be best if we don't have to use them at all. Guns are noisy, and we don't want the port police chasing us.' He waved at the table. 'What's your fancy, Nick?'

Warren stared at the collection of pistols. 'I don't think so,' he said slowly. 'I've never used a gun. I don't think I could hit anything.'

Follet picked up a pistol and worked the action. 'You'd better have one, even if it's just to point; otherwise you might find your ass in a sling.'

Hellier reached over. 'I think I'll have this one. Not that I've had much practice. I was in the Artillery and that was too long ago.'

Metcalfe raised his eyebrows. 'Are you coming?'

'Of course,' said Hellier calmly. 'Is there any reason why not?'

Metcalfe shrugged. 'None at all. But I thought you'd be one of the back-room boys.'

Hellier glanced at Warren. 'It's partly my fault that Abbot and Parker are where they are. A long time ago I told Warren I wanted blood; I'm quite prepared to pay for it myself.'

Warren looked at the single pistol on the table. 'I'll show you how to handle it, Nick,' said Follet. 'We'll have time enough for a run-down.'

Slowly Warren stretched out his hand and picked up the pistol, feeling the unaccustomed weight of the blued metal. 'All right, Johnny,' he said. 'Show me how.'

# 10

The making and writing of reports reached a minor crescendo in countries stretching right across the Middle East. In Tehran, Colonel Mirza Davar studied one of these reports. There had been a considerable explosion quite close to the Iraqi border in the province of Kurdistan. Loud bangs were undesirable anywhere in Iran and especially so in that sensitive area. Besides, Fahrwaz seemed to be involved and the colonel did not particularly like the implications of that. Colonel Mirza Davar was Chief Intelligence Officer for the North-West Provinces.

A tap at the door introduced his secretary. 'Captain Muktarri to see you.'

'Show him in immediately.'

Captain Muktarri, by his travel-stained appearance, had evidently travelled hard and fast and in rough country. The colonel looked him up and down, and said, 'Well, Captain: what did you find?'

'There was an explosion, sir – a big one. A *qanat* was thoroughly wrecked.'

The Colonel relaxed in his chair. 'A squabble over water rights,' he said. A minor problem and not in his province; a matter for the civil police.

'That's what I thought, sir,' said Muktarri. 'Until I found this.' He put down a small square block on the desk.

The colonel picked it up, scratched it with his finger-nail and then sniffed at it delicately. 'Opium.' Although still not a matter for his own attention this was much more serious. 'And this was found on Fahrwaz's farm?'

'Yes, sir; among the debris left by the explosion. Fahrwaz

284

was not there – nor was his son. The villagers denied knowledge of it.'

'They would,' said the colonel, unimpressed. 'This is a matter for the narcotics people.' He drew the telephone towards him.

In Baghdad another Intelligence colonel was studying another report. Something odd had been going on up near the Turkish border. There had been a battle of sorts, but as he had found by intensive checking, no Iraqi troops had been involved. Which was very interesting. It seemed very much as though the Kurds had begun to fight among themselves.

He reached for the microphone and began to dictate the last of his comments on to tape. 'It is well known that the rebel leader, Al Fahrwaz, who is commonly resident across the border in Iran, has a stronghold in this area. My tentative conclusion is that Mustapha Barzani has attempted to solve the Fahrwaz problem before continuing negotiations with the Iraqi government. According to an unconfirmed report Ahmed ben Fahrwaz was killed in the fighting. Further reports will follow.'

He did not know how wrong he was.

Not two hundred yards along the same street in Baghdad a senior police officer was checking yet another report against a map. Ismail Al-Khalil had been in the Narcotics Department for many years and knew his job very well. The report told of an explosion in Iran which had wrecked an underground laboratory. Broken glassware had been found, and an immense quantity of opium together with a large amount of chemicals, the details of which were listed. He knew exactly what that meant.

His finger traced a line from Iran into northern Iraq and from thence into Syria. He returned to his desk and said to his companion, 'The Iranians are certain it crossed the

285

border.' He shrugged. 'There's nothing we can do about it – not with the political situation being what it is in Kurdistan right now. I'd better make a report – copies to go to Syria, Jordan and the Lebanon.'

Al-Khalil sat down and prepared to dictate his report, and said in parenthesis, 'The Iranians think there's as much as five hundred kilos of morphine or heroin loose. Somebody has been very lax over there.' He shook his head in regret.

The reports proliferated and one dropped on the desk of Jamil Hassan of the Narcotics Bureau in Beirut. He read it and took action, and life became very difficult for the Lebanese underworld. One of those picked up for questioning was a small-time crook named André Picot, suspected of being involved in narcotics smuggling. He was questioned for many hours but nothing could be got from him.

This was for two reasons; he knew very little anyway, and his interrogators did not know enough themselves to ask him the right questions. So, after an all-night session in front of the bright lights which gave him eyestrain but nothing else, he was released a little before nine in the morning – which was a great pity.


II


At ten minutes to nine the cruiser rocked gently on the blue water of the Mediterranean, one engine ticking over gently so that the boat barely had steerage way. Hellier was sitting in the open cockpit apparently interested in nothing else but the fishing-rod he held, but Tozier was in the saloon and keeping careful watch on the *Orestes* through binoculars. A curl of smoke from the single funnel stained the sky to show that her boilers were fired and she was preparing to move.

Warren sat in the saloon close to the door and watched Metcalfe at the wheel. He thought Metcalfe handled the boat very well and said so. Metcalfe grinned. 'I learned in a hard school. A few years ago I was running cigarettes out of Tangier into Spain with a Yank called Krupke; we had a biggish boat – a war-surplus Fairmile – which I had re-engined so she could outrun the Spanish excise cutters. If you can't learn to handle a boat doing that sort of thing you'll never learn.'

He leaned down and looked into the saloon. 'Any change, Andy?'

'No change,' said Tozier, without taking his eyes from the binoculars. 'We go in ten minutes.'

Metcalfe straightened and said over his shoulder, 'We're going to abandon this tub, Sir Robert. The charterers won't like it – you'll have a lawsuit on your hands.'

Hellier grunted in amusement. 'I can afford it.'

Warren felt the hard metal of the pistol which was thrust into the waistband of his trousers. It felt uncomfortable and he shifted it slightly. Metcalfe looked down at him, and said, 'Take it easy, Nick, and you'll be all right. Just follow up the rope and take your cue from me.'

It made Warren uncomfortable that Metcalfe should have seen his nervousness. He said curtly, 'I'll be all right when we start.'

'Of course you will,' said Metcalfe. 'We all get butterflies at this stage.' He sighed. 'I've talked myself into things like this all my life. I must be a damned fool.'

There was a metallic click from behind Warren and he turned his head to see Follet slamming a full magazine into the butt of his pistol. Metcalfe said, 'It takes us different ways. Johnny there is nervous, too; that's why he keeps checking his gun. He can never convince himself that it's

287

ready to shoot – just like the old lady who goes on holiday and is never sure she turned off the gas before she left.'

Warren shifted the gun again, and said quietly, 'We're going on board that ship with guns in our hands, ready to shoot. The crew may be quite innocent.'

'Not a chance,' scoffed Metcalfe. 'You can't fit torpedo tubes aboard a scow that size without the crew knowing it. They're all in on the act. And there'll be no shooting, either – not unless they start first.' He looked across at the *Orestes*. 'It's quite likely she'll have a skeleton crew, so that'll make it easier for us. Jeanette won't let one more person in on this than she has to.'

Tozier said, 'I don't see why we can't go in now. She's as ready as she ever will be, and so are we. We can't wait until she begins to haul anchor.'

'All right,' said Metcalfe, and swung the wheel gently. Over his shoulder he said, 'Make like a fisherman, Sir Robert.' He opened the throttle a fraction and the boat moved more purposefully through the water. With a wink at Warren, he said, 'The whole idea is to be gentle. We don't roar up with engines going full blast – we just edge in nice and easy so that even if they see us coming they won't know what the hell to make of it. By the time they do, it'll be too late, I hope.'

Tozier put down the glasses and got busy. He slung the sub-machine-gun over his shoulder and checked a coil of rope for unwanted kinks. At one end of the rope was attached a three-pronged grapnel, well padded for quietness, and he tested that it was secure. He tapped Warren on the shoulder. 'Stand back and let the dog see the rabbit,' he said, and Warren made way for him.

To an onlooker from the shore it might have seemed that the boat was drifting dangerously close to the *Orestes* which, after all, showed all the signs of getting under way. If the boat were to be caught when the screw began to turn then there could be a nasty accident. It was a thoroughly bad piece of seamanship which could not be excused even if the big, fat Englishman had caught a fish and the helmsman was diverted in his excitement.

Hellier hauled the fish out of the sea. He had bought it that morning in the fish market near the Suq des Orfèvres and a very fine specimen it was. It was a last-minute bit of camouflage devised by Follet, the master of the con game, and Hellier dexterously made it twitch on the line as though still alive. With a bit of luck this by-play would allow them to get ten yards nearer to the *Orestes* without being challenged.

The boat edged in still nearer, and Metcalfe nodded to Tozier. 'Now!' he said sharply, as he opened the throttle and spun the wheel, turning them towards the stern of the *Orestes*, but still keeping the bulk of the ship as a screen between the boat and the quay.

Tozier leaped up into the cockpit and whirled the grapnel twice about his head before casting it upwards to the stern rail. As the grapnel caught, Hellier dropped his fish smartly and grabbed the rope, hauling it taut and swinging the boat in to the side of the ship while Metcalfe put the gears into neutral. Even as he did so Tozier was climbing hand over hand, and Warren heard the light thump of his feet as he landed on deck.

Metcalfe abandoned the wheel and went next, and Warren felt apprehensive as he looked over the side of the boat towards the underhang of *Orestes*'s stern. The screw was only two-thirds submerged, the ship being in ballast, and if the skipper gave the order to move the turbulence would inevitably smash the little boat.

Follet pushed him from behind. 'Get going!' he hissed, and Warren grasped the rope and began to climb. He had not climbed a rope since his schooldays when he had been driven up ropes in the gymnasium by an athletic games master wielding a cricket stump. Warren had never been athletically-minded. But he got to the top and a hand grasped him by the scruff of the neck and hauled him over the rail.

There was no time to rest and, breathlessly, he found himself following Metcalfe. Tozier was nowhere to be seen but when Warren turned his head he found Hellier padding behind and looking ridiculous in the bright floral shirt and the shorts he had chosen as his fisherman's get-up. But there was nothing at all funny about the gun held in Hellier's meaty fist.

The deck vibrated underfoot and Metcalfe held up his hand in warning. As Warren came up, he said in a low voice, 'We just got here in time. She's under way.' He pointed. 'There's the bridge ladder – let's go.'

He ran forward lightly and climbed up on to the bridge. Even as Warren followed he thought it incredible that they should not yet have been seen; but now it came to the crunch – you don't invade a ship's bridge without the skipper having objections.

Metcalfe arrived on the bridge first and, as though by a preconceived plan, Tozier appeared simultaneously from the other side. There were four men on the bridge; the skipper, two officers and the helmsman. The skipper looked incredulously at the sub-machine-gun cradled by Tozier and whirled around only to be confronted by Metcalfe. As he opened his mouth Metcalfe snapped, '*Arrêtez!*' and then, for good measure, added in Arabic, '*Ukaf!*'

The gesture he made with the gun was good in all languages and the skipper shut his mouth. A sweeping motion from Tozier's sub-machine-gun herded the officers aside, while Metcalfe motioned the helmsman to stay where he was. Warren stood at the top of the bridge ladder and held his pistol loosely in his hand. He looked down at Hellier who stood guard at the bottom of the ladder; presumably Follet was doing the same on the other side.

The ship was still moving slowly and he could see now the widening gap of water between the *Orestes* and the quay. Metcalfe grasped the brass handle of the engine-room telegraph and rang for half speed, and the telegraph clanged again as the engineer obeyed the order. With the gun in his back the helmsman looked at Metcalfe's pointing finger and nodded vigorously. He spun the spokes of the wheel and the quay receded faster.

Suddenly there was an interruption. Eastman stepped from the bridge house and froze as he saw what was happening. His hand dipped beneath his coat and was magically full of gun. Warren brought up his own pistol to the ready and for the minutest fraction of a second the tableau was held. Then Eastman cried out under the impact of a steel bar which struck his arm from behind. His gun went off and there was a ringing clang and a whine as the bullet ricocheted from metal and away over the sea. But he still held on to the gun and whirled on Dan Parker, who was just behind him with a steel bar gripped in his hand as though it had grown there.

He drove his elbow into Parker's stomach and Parker doubled up in pain, the steel bar clattering to the deck. Then Eastman was gone at a dead run and Warren heard the bang of a door in the distance.

Metcalfe moved first. He ran to the side of the bridge and looked ashore and saw the ripple of movement as heads turned towards the departing ship. 'They heard that,' he said, and raised his voice. 'Johnny, come up here.' He turned to Tozier. 'The crew will have heard it, too. Can you hold the bridge while Johnny and I nail Eastman?'

'Carry on,' said Tozier. 'Nick, get Hellier up here, then look at our friend with the iron bar.' He turned to the officers. 'Who speaks English?' he asked conversationally.

'I speak English good,' said the skipper.

'Then we'll get along together. Get the loudhailer and tell the crew to assemble on the forehatch there. But first, where's the radio shack?'

The skipper took a deep breath as though nerving himself

to defiance but stopped short as Tozier's gun jerked threat-eningly. He nodded his head to where Warren was helping Parker to his feet. 'Through there.'

'Watch him,' said Tozier to Hellier, and went off fast. When he returned he found the skipper bellowing into the loudhailer under the supervision of Hellier and already the crew was assembled. As he had thought, there were few of them; the ship was undermanned.

'I'd give a lot to know if that's all,' he said, looking down at them.

Warren came forward with Parker at his side. 'This is Dan Parker; he might be able to tell us.'

Tozier smiled. 'Glad to know you.'

'I'm even gladder to know you,' said Parker. He looked over the deck. 'That's all – but I don't see the engine-room staff. If they stop the engines we're dead mutton.'

'They couldn't have heard the shot,' said Tozier. 'But we can soon find out.' He rang for full speed on the telegraph and it clanged obediently. 'No one has told them yet.'

'If we get them out of there I can handle the engines,' said Parker. He looked around. 'Where's Mike?'

'I haven't seen him,' said Warren. 'Where was he?'

'In his cabin, I think.'

'We'll find him later,' said Tozier impatiently. 'What can we do with the crew? We have to secure the ship before anything else.'

'There's an empty hold,' said Parker. 'They'll be safe enough in there.'

'Nick, you and Hellier go along with Parker and see to it – and take this lot with you.' Tozier indicated the ship's officers. 'They won't give you any trouble; they look a pretty poor lot to me.' He pulled at his lower lip. 'I hope Tom is doing all right, though.'

# III

Warren helped secure the crew and herded them into the hold, and then the three of them took over the engine-room. He left Parker and Hellier down there, put the three engineers with the rest of the crew, and then looked up to the bridge. Tozier leaned over the rail. 'We've got a problem – come up here.'

'What about this lot?'

'I'll send Abbot down – we have found him. Leave him your gun.'

Abbot came down and gave Warren a cheery grin. 'A nice bit of fun and games,' he said. 'I was very glad to see the gang.'

Warren gave him the gun. 'What's the problem?'

'That's a beauty – I'll leave your pals up there to tell you.'

Warren went up to the bridge and found Follet on the wheel with Tozier close by. Tozier said quickly, 'We have Eastman bottled up, but it's a stand-off. Tom is keeping the cork in the bottle down there, but it leaves us with a problem. He's down where the torpedoes are, so we can't get rid of the heroin until we winkle him out.'

'He went to protect the loot,' said Follet. 'It's my guess he's expecting to be rescued. The crew can't do it, but Delorme has Fuad's yacht and she might chase us.'

Warren dismissed that eventuality. 'What arrangements have been made for firing the torpedoes?'

Tozier pointed. 'Those two buttons near the helm. Press those and you fire two torpedoes.'

Warren nodded. 'We can get rid of half the heroin.' He took a step forward.

Tozier grabbed him. 'Steady on. Your man, Parker, has

293

been working too hard. All the torpedoes are live. He found some explosives – each warhead is carrying a hundred and eighty pounds of TNT.'

'Short of a hydrogen bomb it'll be the most expensive bang in history,' said Follet.

Warren was perplexed. 'But what's the problem?'

Tozier stared at him. 'Christ, man; you can't shoot live torpedoes indiscriminately in the Mediterranean – especially these. They have an eighteen-mile range, so Abbot says.' He pointed towards the horizon. 'How the hell do we know what's over there? We can't see eighteen miles.'

Follet laughed humorously. 'Last I heard the US Sixth Fleet was in these parts. If we knock off one of Uncle Sam's aircraft carriers that's as good a way of starting World War Three as I know.'

Warren thought about it. 'Are there any uninhabited islands around here? Or rocks or shoals? Anything we can shoot at without killing anything else except fish?'

'A nice way to cause an international ruction,' said Tozier. 'You fire torpedoes at any rocks in the Arab world and the Israelis are going to be on the short end of the stick. Things are touchy enough now and a few bangs around here could really start something.'

'And we'd still have half the stuff left on our hands,' said Follet. 'Maybe all of it. If Eastman is smart enough he'll have ripped out the firing connections.'

'So we have to get him out of there,' said Warren. 'I think we'd better have Parker in on this – he knows the ship.'

'Just a minute,' said Follet. 'I'm still hanging on to this goddam steering-wheel, so would someone mind telling me where we're going?'

'Does it matter?' said Tozier impatiently.

'Metcalfe reckons it matters,' said Follet. 'He saw Jeanette Delorme on the quay when we left – and she saw

294

him. She'll reckon it's a hi-jacking and Tom says she'll come after us loaded for bear.'

'So?'

'So we can stick to the coast or we can head out to sea. She has the same choice. What do you want to do?'

'I'd sooner stick to the coast,' said Tozier. 'If she caught us at sea where it wouldn't matter how many guns she popped off I wouldn't give much for our chances, especially if that yacht is loaded to the gunwales with her cut-throats.'

'Haven't you thought that she'll think that you'll think that and automatically come along the coast and catch us anyway? I'll bet she can see us right now.'

'How the hell do I know what she'll think?' burst out Tozier. 'Or what any other woman will think?'

'There's a way around that,' said Follet. 'Here, take the wheel.' He stepped on one side and produced a pen and a note-book. 'Now, if we go along the coast and she searches out to sea our survival is one hundred per cent – right?'

'Until she catches on,' said Warren.

'We could get clear away,' argued Follet. 'And the same applies to the situation vice versa – we go to sea and she goes along the coast. Andy, what chance of survival would you give us if she caught us at sea?'

'Not much,' said Tozier. 'Say, twenty-five per cent.'

Follet noted it down. 'And if she caught us on the coast?'

'That's a bit better – she couldn't be as noisy. I think we'd have a good chance of coming out – say, seventy-five per cent.'

Follet started to scribble rapidly and Warren, looking over his shoulder, saw that he was apparently working out a mathematical formula. Follet finished his calculation, and said, 'What we do is this. We put four pieces of paper in a hat – one marked. If we pick the marked paper we go to sea; if not, we stick to the coast.'

'Are you crazy?' demanded Tozier. 'Would you leave something like this to chance?'

'I'm crazy like a fox,' said Follet. 'How much have I won from you at the coin-matching game?'

'Nearly a thousand quid – but what's that got to do with it?'

Follet pulled a handful of loose change from his pocket and thrust it under Tozier's nose. 'This. There are eight coins here – three of them dated 1960. When I matched coins with you I pulled one of these at random from my pocket; if it was dated 1960 I called heads – if not, I called tails. That was enough to give me my percentage – my edge; and there wasn't a damned thing you could do about it.'

He turned to Warren. 'It's from game theory – a mathematical way of figuring out the best chances in those tricky situations when it's a case of if I do that you'll know I'll do it but I do the other thing because I know the way you're thinking and so it goes on chasing its goddam tail. It even gives the overall chances – in this case a little over eighty-one per cent.'

Tozier looked at Warren with a baffled expression. 'What do you think, Nick?'

'You *did* lose money consistently,' said Warren. 'Maybe Johnny has a point.'

'You're goddam right I have.' Follet stooped and picked up a uniform cap from the deck into which he dropped four coins. 'Pick one, Nick. If it's dated 1960 we go to sea – if it's one of the others we stick to the coast.'

He held the cap out to Warren, who hesitated. 'Look at it this way,' said Follet earnestly. 'Right now, until you pick a coin, we don't know which way we're going – and if *we* don't know how in hell can Delorme figure it? And the mix of coins in the hat gives us the best chance no matter what she does.' He paused. 'There's just one thing; we do what the coin tells us – no second chances – that's the way this thing works.'

Warren put out his hand, took a coin, and held it on the

296

palm of his hand, date side up. Tozier inspected it. '1960,' he said with a sigh. 'It's out to sea, God help us.'

He spun the wheel and the bows of the *Orestes* swung towards the west.


## IV

Tozier left Warren and Follet on the bridge and went down to the engine-room to consult Parker. He found him with an oilcan strolling amid shining and plunging steel piston rods at a seeming risk to life. Hellier was standing by the engine-room telegraph.

He beckoned to Parker, who put down the oilcan and came over to him. 'Can you leave here for a while?' he asked.

'We're a bit short-handed,' said Parker. 'But it wouldn't do any harm for a short time. What do you want?'

'Your friend Eastman has barricaded himself in the torpedo compartment in the bows. We're trying to get him out.'

Parker frowned. 'That'll be a bit dicey. I had a watertight bulkhead put in there in case anythin' went wrong wi' the tubes. If he's behind that it'll be bloody impossible to get him out.'

'Haven't you any suggestions? He's locked himself in and we can't do a damn' thing about the heroin.'

'Let's go an' see,' said Parker briefly.

They found Metcalfe crouched at the end of a narrow steel corridor, at the other end of which was a solid steel door clamped tightly closed. 'He's behind that,' said Metcalfe. 'You can open it from this side if you care to try but you'll get a bullet in you. He can't miss.'

Tozier looked up the corridor. 'No, thanks; there's no cover.'

'The door's bulletproof too,' said Metcalfe. 'I tried a couple of shots and found it was more dangerous for me than for him the way things ricochet around here.'

'Have you tried to talk him out?'

Metcalfe nodded. 'He either can't hear me or he doesn't care to answer.'

'What about it, Parker?'

'There's only one way into that compartment,' said Parker. 'And it's through that door.'

'So it's a stand-off,' said Tozier.

Metcalfe gave a wry grimace. 'It's more than that. If he can keep us out of there until the ship is retaken then he's won.'

'You seem a bit worried about that. Delorme has to find us first and taking us won't be easy. What have you got on your mind?'

Metcalfe swung round. 'When I took that stuff to Fahrwaz there were a few things left behind – a couple of heavy machine-guns, for instance.'

'That's bad,' said Tozier softly.

'And that's not the worst of it. She tried to flog four 40-millimetre cannons to Fahrwaz, but he wasn't having them at any price. They swallowed ammo too quickly for his liking, so she got stuck with them. If she's had the gumption to stick one of those aboard that yacht, she'd have plenty of time to jack-leg a deck mounting. All she'd need is steel and a welding torch, and there's plenty of both back in that shipyard.'

'You think she might?'

'That little bitch never misses a trick,' said Metcalfe violently. 'You should have let me get her back in Beirut.'

'And we'd have lost the heroin. We've got to get rid of that dope. We can't let her have it.'

Metcalfe jerked his thumb up the corridor. 'Be my guest – open that door.'

'I've got an idea,' said Parker. 'Maybe we can flush him out.'

'You mean flood the compartment,' said Tozier. 'Can it be done?'

'Not water,' said Parker. He raised his head and looked upwards. 'On the foredeck just above us there's the anchor winch. It's run by steam taken from the boiler. I reckon I could take a tapping off the line an' run it down here.'

'And what would you do with it?'

'There's provision for fumigatin' the ship – gettin' rid o' rats. There's a gas line goin' into each compartment an' I'm pretty sure the one leadin' into there is open. I find the other end an' connect my line to it. A bit o' live steam will bring Jack Eastman out o' there like a scalded cat.'

'You've got nice ideas,' said Metcalfe. 'Humane, too. How long will it take?'

'Dunno; an hour – maybe two. It depends on what I find topside.'

'Get cracking,' said Metcalfe.


V


Jamil Hassan was a methodical man and it was unfortunate that the bureaucratic organization he worked for was unyielding in its procedures and tended to be compartmentalized. The news did not reach his office at all and it was only because he decided to have a mid-morning cup of coffee that he heard anything about it.

On his way out he passed the duty officer's desk and automatically asked, 'Anything happening?'

'Nothing much, sir; just the usual. There was one odd thing – a report of a shooting on board a ship leaving Elgamhûrîa Shipyard.'

A young policeman who was writing a report close by, pricked up his ears. Hassan said, 'What was odd about it?'

'By the time it was reported and we got a man down there the ship was outside territorial waters.' The duty officer shrugged. 'There was nothing we could do about it.'

The young policeman sprang to his feet. 'Sir!'

Hassan eyed him. 'Yes?'

'Last night a man called André Picot was brought in for questioning – on your instructions, sir.'

'Well?'

The young man fidgeted a little. 'It's . . . it's just that I saw Picot leaving El-gamhûrîa Shipyard three days ago. It may not be . . .'

Hassan waved him quiet, his brain assessing facts like a card-sorter. Heroin – a large quantity of heroin – had left Iran heading westward; Picot, a suspected smuggler, had been questioned – unsuccessfully; Picot had been seen at El-gamhûrîa Shipyard; a shot – or shots – had been fired on a ship in El-gamhûrîa Shipyard; the ship had promptly left Lebanese waters. It was not much, but it was enough.

He picked up the telephone, dialled a number, and said, 'Bring in André Picot for questioning, and get me a car.'

Thirty minutes later he was standing on the quay in the shipyard interrogating the officer who had made the investigation. 'And the ship left after the shot was fired?'

'Yes, sir.'

'What was its name?'

'The *Orestes*.'

Hassan surveyed the deserted quay. 'And it was the only ship here. That's strange.'

'No, sir; there was a yacht. She left only five minutes ago.' He pointed. 'There she is.'

Hassan shaded his eyes against the sun and looked out to sea. 'And you let her go? Was the owner here when the incident happened?'

'Yes, sir. He said he did not hear or see anything. Nor did his crew.'

Hassan peered at the yacht. 'Very convenient for him. Who is he?'

'His name is Fuad, sir. He said he is to cruise in the Caribbean.'

'By the Living God!' said Hassan. 'Did he? What is that at the stern?'

The officer strained his eyes. 'A pile of canvas?' he hazarded.

'A sheet of canvas covering something,' corrected Hassan. 'I want a telephone.'

Two minutes later he was embroiled in an argument with a particularly stupid staff officer of Naval Head-quarters, Beirut.


## VI


The *Orestes* plugged away on her new course and the loom of land astern had disappeared leaving only a cloudbank to indicate Mount Lebanon. Warren made himself useful by finding the galley and preparing a meal; corned beef from tins and flat loaves of Arab bread to be washed down with thin, acid wine.

As he worked he pondered on the relationship between Metcalfe and Tozier. They were both of the same stripe, both men of strong will, and they seemed to work in harmony, each instinctively knowing that the other would do the right thing when necessary. He wondered if it ever came to a conflict between them, who would come out on top.

He finally decided he would lay his money on Metcalfe. Tozier was the more conservative and preferred his employ-ment to have at least a veneer of legality. Metcalfe was more the amoral buccaneer, unscrupulous to a degree and adept in the department of dirty tricks. Warren thought that if it ever came to a showdown between them that Tozier might show a fatal flaw of hesitation where Metcalfe would not. He hoped his theory would never be put to the test.

He finished his preparations and took the food to the bridge. Metcalfe, because of his knowledge of ships and the sea, was now in command, while Tozier kept an eye on Eastman. Follet was in the engine-room, having released a couple of the engine-room staff who were tending the engines nervously under the threat of his gun. Parker and Abbot worked on the foredeck by the anchor winch, and Hellier stood guard over the hold.

Metcalfe called up Abbot to collect something to eat, and also brought Hellier up to the bridge. 'All quiet?' he asked.

'No trouble,' assured Hellier. 'They've settled down.'

Metcalfe offered him a sandwich. As Hellier bit into it, he said with a wide grin, 'You've now added piracy to your list of crimes, Sir Robert. That's still a hanging matter in England.'

Hellier choked over the dry bread and spluttered crumbs. Warren said, 'I don't think Delorme will press charges, not with the evidence we have aboard.' He cocked an eye at Metcalfe. 'I wonder what she's thinking now.'

'Evil thoughts – that's for sure,' said Metcalfe. 'But I'm more concerned about what she'll be doing. She certainly won't be sitting on her beautiful bottom. When Jeanette gets mad she becomes active.' He nodded towards the foredeck. 'How is Parker doing?'

'He says he'll need another hour,' said Abbot.

Warren said, 'I'll take him some grub and see if he needs any help.'

Metcalfe steadied the wheel with one hand and held a sandwich with the other. 'What a hooker this is. She might do nine knots if she could go downhill.' He looked up. 'What's that gadget up there on the derrick?'

Abbot said, 'It's one of Dan's tricks.' He explained about the light ashore and the man in the crow's nest.

'Ingenious,' commented Metcalfe. 'Climb up there and see what you can see.'

Abbot went up the derrick and steadied himself at the top by holding on to the sighting telescope which was rigidly fixed. At that height, fifty feet above the water, he felt the breeze which stirred his fair hair, and the slow roll of the *Orestes* was magnified. 'There are two more buttons up here,' he shouted. 'Eastman wanted two sets.'

'Leave them alone. What do you see?'

Abbot looked over the bows. 'There's a ship ahead of us. I can see the smoke.' He turned slowly, scanning the horizon. 'There's one behind us, too.'

Metcalfe clicked into alertness. 'Overtaking us?'

'It's hard to say,' shouted Abbot. He was silent for a while. 'I think she is – I can see a bow wave.'

Metcalfe left the wheel, saying to Hellier, 'Take it.' Without breaking his stride he scooped up a pair of binoculars and went up the derrick like a monkey up a palm tree. At the top he steadied himself against the roll of the ship and focused the binoculars astern. 'It's Fuad's yacht. She's coming like a bat out of hell.'

'How far?'

Metcalfe did a mental calculation. 'Maybe six miles. And she has radar – she'll have spotted us.' He handed the binoculars to Abbot. 'Stay here and keep an eye on her.'

He went down the derrick and back to the bridge where he picked up the bridge telephone and rang the engine-room. 'Johnny, prod your chaps a bit – we want more speed . . . I know that, but Jeanette is on our tail.'

As he slammed down the telephone Hellier gave him a sideways glance. 'How long have we got?'

'This rust bucket might do a little over eight knots if

she's pushed. That yacht might do thirteen or fourteen. Say an hour.' Metcalfe walked on to the wing of the bridge and looked astern. 'Can't see her from here; she's still below the horizon.' He turned and there was a grim smile on his face. 'I was in a lark like this once before – over in the Western Mediterranean. Me and a guy called Krupke in a Fairmile. But we were doing the chasing that time.'

'Who won?' asked Hellier.

Metcalfe's smile grew grimmer. 'I did!'

'What can she do if she catches up? She can't board us.'

'She can shoot hell out of us,' Metcalfe looked at his watch. 'This tub isn't going to be too healthy an hour from now.'

Hellier said, 'We have plenty of steel plate to hide behind.

There was something of contempt in Metcalfe's voice as he said in disgust, 'Steel plate!' He kicked against the side of the bridge and rust fell in large flakes. 'Nickel-jacketed bullets will rip through this stuff like cardboard. You were in the artillery, so you ought to know. Tell me what a 40-millimetre cannon will do to this bridge?'

He left Hellier with that disconcerting thought and went up to the foredeck where Parker and Warren were working on the winch. 'Put a jerk in it – we're being followed. How long, for God's sake?'

Parker did not pause in his steady movements as he screwed in a pipe. 'I said an hour.'

'An hour is all you've got,' said Metcalfe. 'After that keep your head down.'

Warren looked up. 'Dan's been telling me about what you think Delorme will do. Will she really shoot us up?'

That was enough to make Parker stop. 'The first time I laid eyes on that cow I knew she was bad,' he said. 'I dunno how Mike could stand her. She'll kill the lot of us an' then go back an' dance all night without a second thought.' He hauled on the pipe wrench again, and said, 'That does it up here. The rest we do below decks.'

'If there's anything I can do to speed up the job just shout,' said Metcalfe. 'I'm going below to tell Andy the score.' He checked with Tozier and with Follet in the engine-room, and when he arrived back in the open air he saw that the *Stella del Mare* was visible from the deck, low on the horizon. He went right to the stern and explored, then went up on to the bridge and said to Hellier, 'This is going to be the prime target – anybody standing where you are is going to get the chop.'

'Someone has to steer,' said Hellier quietly.

'Yes, but not from here. There's an emergency steering position aft.' Metcalfe looked up at the derrick. 'Mike, come down from there and take the wheel.'

He and Hellier went aft where they dragged the emergency steering-wheel from the locker and fixed it in place directly above the rudder. Metcalfe surveyed it. 'A bit exposed,' he commented. 'It needs some canvas round it. It won't stop bullets but they might not shoot at the stern if they don't see anyone here.'

They draped a canvas awning around the wheel. 'Stay here a while,' said Metcalfe. 'I'll take Abbot off the wheel on the bridge – I need him. You can con the ship from now on until I relieve you.'

He dashed forward again, thinking as he went that he was covering a fair mileage on his own flat feet. He took Abbot off the wheel and regarded the course of the *Orestes*. After a preliminary swerve she continued on her way, and the bridge wheel turned slowly and evenly back and forth as though controlled by an invisible man.

'Nip into the officers' quarters,' he said to Abbot. 'Bring some pillows, blankets, jackets, hats – I want to rig up some dummies.'

They draped coats over pillows and fastened the uniform caps on top with meat skewers from the galley. They made three dummies and suspended them from the top of the wheelhouse by ropes so that they looked unpleasantly like hanging men. But from a distance they would look real enough, and they swayed lightly to and fro most realistically giving an impression of natural movement.

Metcalfe went out on the wing of the bridge and looked aft. 'She's catching up fast. About a mile to go – say ten minutes. You'd better get the hell out of here, Mike. I'm going to see what Parker's doing.'

'There's a ship over there,' said Abbot, pointing to starboard. She was going the other way and was about two miles on the starboard beam. 'Do you think there's any chance of getting help?'

'Not unless you want to make this a real massacre,' said Metcalfe in a strained voice. 'If we went over to that ship we'd just be adding to the list of the dead.'

'You mean she'd kill the crew of that ship, too?'

'A hundred million dollars has a lot of killing power. The ports around here are stuffed with men who'll kill anyone you specify for five thousand dollars, and I'll bet she has that yacht full of them.' He shrugged irritably. 'Let's move.'

Parker and Warren were tired and grimy. 'Five minutes,' said Parker in answer to Metcalfe's urgent question. 'This is the last bit o' pipe.'

'Where do you turn on the steam?'

'There's a valve on deck near the winch,' said Parker. 'You can't miss it.'

'I'll be up there,' said Metcalfe. 'Give me a shout when you want it turned on. And someone had better go and tell Andy what's going on. He might need some backing up, too, but I doubt it.'

He climbed back on deck to find the *Stella del Mare* coming up on the port beam. She slackened speed to keep pace with the *Orestes* and took station about two hundred yards away. He crouched behind the winch and looked across at her. Abbot said, from behind him, 'Look at the stern. What's that?'

'Keep out of sight,' said Metcalfe sharply. He looked at the unmistakable angles barely disguised beneath the canvas covering, and felt a little sick. 'It's a cannon. That thing can squirt shells like a hosepipe squirts water.' He paused. 'I think there's a machine-gun mounted forrard up in the bows, and another amidships on top of the boatdeck. A floating packet of trouble.'

'What are they waiting for?' demanded Abbot almost petulantly.

'For that other ship to get clear. Jeanette doesn't want any witnesses. She'll wait until it's hull down before she tries anything.' He judged the distance to the valve which was in the open. 'I hope she does, anyway.'

He drummed his fingers against the metal of the winch and waited to be given the word and at last he heard Warren call, 'All right, Tom; Dan says give it a three-minute squirt – that should be enough.'

Metcalfe came from behind the winch, stood over the valve, and gave it a twist. He was very conscious that he was in full view of the *Stella del Mare* and felt an uncomfortable prickling between his shoulder-blades. Steam hissed with violence out of a badly connected joint.

Far below him Tozier waited, the sub-machine-gun ready in his hands. Behind him Parker leaned stolidly against the wall waiting for something to happen. That something would happen he was certain. No man would stay for long in a steel box into which live steam at boiler pressure was being fed. He merely nodded as Tozier whispered, 'The clamp is moving.'

Tozier might have given Eastman a chance out of pity, but Eastman slammed back the door amid a cloud of steam and came out shooting. Tozier squeezed the trigger and the sub-machine-gun roared noisily in the confined space but could not drown the ear-splitting high-pitched whistle of escaping steam. Eastman was cut down before he had gone two steps and was thrown back to lie across the open threshold of the torpedo room.

The shriek of steam stopped. Parker said, 'He stood it for two minutes, longer than I expected. Let's see if he did any damage.'

Tozier lowered the gun. 'Yes, let's get rid of the damned stuff.'

Parker halted abruptly. 'That be damned for a tale,' he said violently. 'Those are weapons we've got in there. We can use 'em.'

Tozier's jaw dropped. 'By God, you're right. I must be crazy not to have thought of it myself. Check the torpedoes, Dan; I must get this organized.' He ran off down the corridor and climbed the vertical ladders to the forecastle. He was just about to step on deck when someone held his arm.

'Take it easy,' said Metcalfe. 'Or you'll run into a bullet. Look out there.'

Tozier cautiously looked past the door frame and saw the *Stella del Mare* very close. He ducked back, and said, 'Hell's teeth! She's right alongside.'

'There's a ship not far away, but it's getting further away every minute. Jeanette's waiting for a clear horizon.'

'Parker's had a thought,' said Tozier. 'He wants to torpedo her.' He grinned at Metcalfe's expression. 'Of course, he was a sailor – the idea came naturally to him.'

'It should have come to me, too,' said Metcalfe. There was a wicked glint in his eye. 'I'd better relieve Hellier – this is going to take better ship handling than he's capable of. Does Parker want help?'

'He will. You'd better tell Hellier to go and help him. I'll give Johnny the word.'

Tozier went below to the engine-room and found Follet sitting by the telegraph, a gun in his hand and his eye on an engineer officer who was inspecting a dial. He had to raise his voice to be heard as he brought Follet up to date.

'Son of a bitch!' said Follet admiringly. 'You mean we're going to torpedo her?'

'We're going to try.'

Follet looked at the sweating plates close by. Beyond that thin steel shell lay the sea. 'If anything happens – any trouble – let me know,' he said. 'I'm a good swimmer, but I'd like a chance to prove it.'

A grim smile came to Tozier's lips. 'What odds are you offering now, Johnny?'

'All bets are off,' said Follet. 'But we did the right thing, I *know* that. It's just that even if you have the edge you can't win them all.'

Tozier punched him lightly on the arm. 'Keep this junk pile working. Tom will be wanting to manoeuvre.'

He went forward to the torpedo compartment, and before he entered he dragged the body of Eastman aside. 'Everything seems all right,' said Parker. 'Eastman didn't mess around in here.' He slapped the side of a torpedo. 'I'll need help wi' these. Two are already in the tubes, but I can't slide these in on me own.'

'Hellier's coming down,' said Tozier. 'He's the beefiest.' He turned. 'Here he is now. Dan, let me get this straight. We just punch the buttons – is that it?'

Parker nodded. 'There's one set on the bridge an' another in the crow's nest; you can use either. But you'd do better in the crow's nest – there's a sightin' telescope up there.'

'I'll get back up top,' said Tozier. 'The fun will be starting.'

He nodded to Hellier and went away. Hellier said, 'What do I do?'

'Nothin' yet,' said Parker stolidly. 'We just wait.' He looked up. 'If you're a religious man you could try a prayer.'

\* \* \*

Tozier found Abbot and Warren at the stern. Abbot was lying flat on the deck and peering cautiously around the corner of the deckhouse at the *Stella del Mare*. He drew back as Tozier touched him on the shoulder. 'They're doing something with that thing at the stern.'

Tozier took his place. Three or four men were busy on the after deck of the yacht, stripping away the canvas to reveal the elongated barrel of the cannon. One of them sat on a seat and turned a handle and the barrel rose and fell; another seated himself and traversed the gun, then applied his eye to the sight. Tozier would have given his soul for a good rifle; he could have knocked off all of them before they could get away.

Further forward others were preparing the machine-guns for action and he distinctly saw a drum of ammunition being put in place. He withdrew and looked astern. The ship they had passed was a mere blob on the horizon surmounted by a smear of smoke. He stood up and called penetratingly, 'Tom -- action stations!'

The reply from behind the canvas awning was muffled. 'Aye, aye, sir!'

Tozier drew Warren and Abbot away. 'The port side won't be too healthy from now on. It'll be best to lie flat on the deck on the starboard side somewhere behind the bridge. We're going to try to torpedo her and Tom's in command; he has to be because he must point the ship at whatever he's shooting at.'

'But the firing buttons are on the bridge,' said Warren.

'Yes,' said Tozier. 'That's where the fun comes in. Mike, you stay back here and keep in touch with Tom – you pass the word forward when he's ready to attack. Nick, you'll be with me. When the word comes you make for the bridge and try to get at the buttons.'

Warren nodded and wondered momentarily what part Tozier had picked for himself. He soon found out because Tozier nodded to the derrick. 'There's another set of buttons at the top of that. That's my job in case you can't make it to the bridge.'

Warren looked up at the horribly exposed crow's nest and moistened his lips. 'Suppose you can't make it up there?'

'I'll be past caring by then,' said Tozier easily. 'Someone else will have to have a go. Let's get set.'

He and Warren crouched in cover on the starboard side and waited. When it happened it came suddenly and shockingly.

From where he sheltered Warren could see the rear of the bridge and, to the accompaniment of a din of rapid explosions, it began to disintegrate. Bright points of light danced all over it as the cannon shells exploded with ferocious violence, and the wheelhouse was, in a moment, reduced to a shattered wreck.

There was a thump above his head and he looked up to see, incredibly, a piece of glass driven into the teak coaming. Flung from the wheelhouse it had spun murderously towards him and struck with its razor sharp edge to sink an inch deep into the hard wood. Had his head been lifted another few inches he would have been decapitated.

He dropped back into safety just in time as the cannon fire swept aft. Shells exploded on the deck and splinters of planking drove all about him, one cutting through the hem of his jacket and tearing a jagged hole. Above the deeper roar of the cannon came the light chatter of the machine-guns and bullets ripped through the deck-house as though the walls were of paper, and he grovelled on the deck as though to dig himself into it.

The firing was heard four miles to the west by the young skipper of the Lebanese patrol boat which carried Jamil Hassan. He turned to Hassan and said, 'Gunfire!'

Hassan made an abrupt gesture. 'Faster – go faster.'

Warren cautiously raised his head as the monstrous noise stopped and everything was as quiet as before, with just the steady beat of the engines and the lapping of the bow wave. He looked up at the bridge and was horrified at the mass of wreckage. He had a sudden vision of the puppets which Metcalfe had constructed, dancing like marionettes on their strings as the bullets and shells drove through and among them until the roof caved in.

The *Orestes* slowly began to swing to port as though a restraining hand had been removed from the helm. Metcalfe called, 'I'm swinging over to get her athwart my bows as though by chance. We might just get away with it. Tell Andy to get ready.'

Abbot ran forward at a crouch and passed on the message. Tozier looked up at the pulverized bridge and shook his head. 'Up you go, Nick; but take it easy. Wait until she's on target before pressing the tit. If you can't fire at all give me a shout.'

Warren found he was trembling. This was not the sort of work he was cut out for and he knew it. He ran for the bridge ladder and climbed it quickly, ducking his head as he came on to the bridge and sprawling flat. He raised his head and looked at the wheelhouse. The front of it had been blasted off and there was very little left behind it. There was no wheel, no binnacle, no engine telegraph – and no small box with two buttons mounted on it. The bridge had been swept clear.

He shouted, 'No good here, Andy,' and twisted around to go back, afraid of being caught by the next blast of gunfire. He did not bother to climb down the ladder but launched himself into space and fell heavily to the deck in the precious shelter of what remained of the bridge.

He saw Tozier run past him, along the deck and out into the open space of the waist of the ship, zig-zagging so as never to take more than three steps in the same direction. He disappeared behind the donkey-engine casing at the foot of the derrick and Warren looked upwards. It seemed impossible that any man should climb that after what had happened.

Metcalfe had one eye on the derrick and the other on the *Stella del Mare*. He saw Tozier scrambling up and then turned the wheel so as to straighten the *Orestes* on her course. Tozier reached the crow's nest and bent to put his eye to the sight, but the yacht was sheering off, although Metcalfe did his best to keep the bows in line with her.

The sudden change of course of both ships confused the gunners on the yacht. The forward machine-gun could not be brought to bear at all, while the one amidships fired but the aim was wild. However, the cannon was perfectly positioned and it traversed smoothly and opened fire. A hail of shells drove past Tozier and it seemed impossible that he should not be hit. Astern of the *Orestes* the sea erupted in fountains for a mile as the shells overshot the ship and exploded harmlessly.

Tozier stabbed at the buttons and two torpedoes, worth the combined sum of $50,000,000, were on their way.

Then he scrambled down the derrick as fast as he could. He got within ten feet of the bottom and fell the rest of the way. The cannon stopped firing and Warren heard someone cheering from the stern and wondered what Metcalfe had to be so glad about. One thing was certain – the torpedoes had missed. There was no explosion from the sea and a machine-gun still continued its staccato conversation.

Metcalfe had tried to emulate a tortoise as the cannon shells whipped overhead, hunching his neck into his shoulders as though that would save his head from getting knocked off. If the cannon had been depressed a fraction lower the stern of the *Orestes* would have been swept clear and Tom Metcalfe with it. When the cannon fire stopped he looked through a hole in the awning and began to cheer loudly.

Things had gone wrong on the *Stella del Mare*; there was confusion on her poop deck and the long barrel of the cannon was canted upwards at an unnatural angle. The improvised mounting had not been able to withstand the incessant hammering as the cannon had pumped out shells and it was now out of action. From the yacht came a thin and distant wail, sounding as though someone had been hurt.

So Metcalfe cheered.

Below, in the bows, Parker and Hellier heard the hiss of compressed air as the torpedoes left the tubes. Hellier was disposed to wait to hear if they struck, but Parker was already closing the outer doors of the tubes in preparation for re-loading. He swung open the inner doors and stepped aside as the water gushed out, and then pulled smartly on the handles of the clamps which held the racked torpedo on the port side. 'Come on,' he yelled. 'Get the bastard in!'

He and Hellier heaved on the torpedo which moved slowly on its rollers towards the open tube. It was very heavy and moved a fraction of an inch at a time, but it picked up speed as they pushed harder, and finally went in sweetly. Parker slammed the door home and spun the locking wheel. 'Now the other one,' he gasped.

'Do you think the first lot hit?' asked Hellier.

'Dunno,' said Parker, his hands busy. 'Shouldn't think so. Must have been point-blank range judgin' by the racket goin' on up there. Let's get this one in, for God's sake!'

Warren looked to see if he could see Tozier but there was no sign of him. He stuck his head around the side of the bridge and looked across at the *Stella del Mare*. She had turned as the *Orestes* had turned and was still on the port side keeping a parallel course. The midships machine-gun was still firing in short bursts, and now the one in the bows could be brought to bear again and it also opened up, but both seemed to be concentrating on the forward deck.

He saw why. Tozier was sheltering in the break of the forecastle, just sitting there with one leg trailing behind him and oddly bent in a place where there should have been no joint. Even at that distance Warren could tell that the leg was broken. He saw Dan Parker dash from the doorway of the forecastle in an attempt to get to Tozier. He had not gone two steps when he stopped a bullet which flung him round and sent him crashing to the deck where he lay feebly moving.

It was too much for Warren. He broke from cover and ran up the deck, careless of whether he was in danger or not. Simultaneously there was a stentorian bellow from the stern. 'She's coming around to strafe us on the starboard side. She'll be crossing our bows – get ready to shoot.'

Warren heard the words but they made no sense to him; he was intent on getting to Parker and Tozier. But he was thankfully aware that the machine-gunning had stopped as the *Stella del Mare* began to swing ahead of the *Orestes* and firing became unprofitable. Thus he was able to reach Parker without a scratch.

He bent down and took Parker under the arms and dragged him into the forecastle. He was ruthless about it because he had no time to waste, but mercifully Parker was unconscious. Then he went back for Tozier who looked up and gave a weak grin. 'Busted leg,' he said.

'You can stand on the other,' said Warren, and helped him up.

'For Christ's sake!' yelled Metcalfe. 'Someone get up that bloody derrick.'

Warren looked back and hesitated as he felt Tozier's weight lean on him. He saw Abbot make a run for it, disappearing behind the donkey engine as Tozier had done to reappear halfway up the derrick, climbing as though the devil were at his heels.

Metcalfe, on the poop, had a grandstand view. The *Stella del Mare* crossed his bows three hundred yards ahead. At the sight of Abbot on the derrick the machine-guns opened up again, hosing the *Orestes* unmercifully. Abbot did not bother to use the sight. He slammed his hand on the

315

buttons just as a burst of machine-gun fire stitched bloody holes across his chest. He spread his arms as he was flung backwards to crash thirty feet to the deck below.

But then the yacht shivered and checked her stride as the torpedoes hit her, and she erupted as over three hundred and fifty pounds of TNT exploded in her guts. She was no warship built to take punishment, and the explosions tore her apart. Her mid-section was ripped and destroyed utterly, thus cutting her in half; her bows floated for a few seconds only, leaving the stern filling with water fast.

Several small figures jumped from the stern just before it went under in a boil of swirling water, and Metcalfe's teeth bared in a humourless smile. The *Orestes* ploughed on towards the bits of wreckage floating on the surface, and he saw a white face under long blonde hair and an arm waving desperately.

Slowly, and with intense care, he turned the wheel so that the stern of the *Orestes* slid sideways towards Jeanette Delorme and she was drawn into the maelstrom of the churning screw. With equal precision he straightened the *Orestes* on her course and did not look back at what might appear in the wake.


## VII

Metcalfe leaned on the rail and looked into the gaping muzzle of the second quick-firing gun he had seen that day. It was trained on the *Orestes* from the Lebanese patrol boat which ticked over quietly a hundred yards to port in exactly the same position the *Stella del Mare* had held. Everything was the same except that the engines of the *Orestes* were stopped, the companion was lowered and a small motor boat containing two ratings and a junior officer of the Lebanese Navy lay close at hand.

316

'Give me a hand, Tom,' called Warren.

Metcalfe turned and went over to where Warren was bandaging Parker's shoulder. He bent down and held the dressing so that Warren could tie it off. 'How are you feeling?' he asked.

'Not bad,' said Parker. 'It could have been worse – mustn't grumble.'

Metcalfe squatted and said to Warren, 'That civilian who came aboard didn't look like a Navy man to me.'

'I didn't even know the Lebanon had a navy,' said Warren.

'It doesn't; just a few coastal defence vessels.' Metcalfe nodded to the patrol boat. 'I've given those boys the slip many a time.' He frowned. 'What do you suppose Hellier's nattering about all this time? Those two must have been talking for an hour.'

'I wouldn't know,' said Warren shortly. He was thinking about Mike Abbot and Ben Bryan – two dead of the original team of five. Forty per cent casualties was a high price to pay, and that did not count the wounded – another forty per cent.

Tozier lay close by, his leg in splints, while Follet talked to him. 'Goddam it!' said Follet. 'I'll explain it again.' He jingled the coins in his hands.

'Oh, I believe you,' said Tozier. 'I have to, don't I? After all, you took the money from me. It's a neat trick.' He looked across the deck at the canvas-shrouded body which lay at the head of the companionway. 'It's a pity the idea didn't work later.'

'I know what you mean, but it was the best thing to do,' said Follet stubbornly. 'As I said – you can't win 'em all.' He looked up. 'Here comes Hellier now.'

Hellier walked across the deck towards them. Metcalfe stood up and asked, 'Is that a Navy man?' He nodded to Hassan who waited by the rail.

'No,' said Hellier. 'He's a policeman.'

'What did you tell him?'

'Everything,' said Hellier. 'The whole story.'

Metcalfe blew out his cheeks. 'That puts us right in the middle,' he said. 'We'll be lucky if we're not in the nick for another twenty years. Have you ever been in a Middle East jail, Sir Robert?'

Hellier smiled. 'I was a bit vague about your gun-running activities. He wasn't interested in that, anyway. He wants to talk to us.'

He turned to Hassan, who walked over to them, his hands in his pockets. He surveyed them with tight lips and said abruptly, 'My name is Jamil Hassan; I am a police officer. You gentlemen appear to have been conducting a private war, part of which was on Lebanese territory. As a police officer I find that most irregular.'

Some of the sternness softened from his face. 'However, as a police officer I find myself helpless since the high seas outside Lebanese territorial waters do not come within my jurisdiction – so what am I to do?'

Metcalfe grinned. 'You tell us, chum.'

Hassan ignored the interjection. 'Of course, as well as being a police officer I am also a private citizen of the Lebanon. In that capacity let me offer you my thanks for what you have done. But I would advise you, in future, to leave such pursuits in the hands of the proper and competent authorities.' His lips quirked in a smile. 'Which in this case were not very competent. But that still leaves unanswered the question – what am I to do with you?'

'We have wounded men,' said Warren. 'They need attention – a hospital. You could take them back to Beirut in that boat of yours.'

'Not mine,' corrected Hassan. 'You, I take it, are Dr Warren?' At Warren's answering nod, he continued, 'Any of you going back to Beirut in that boat would inevitably end in jail. Our small Navy does not have your English tradition of turning a blind eye. No, you will stay here and

I will go back to Beirut. I will send someone to pick you up and you will be landed quietly and discreetly. You understand that I am arranging this purely in my capacity of a private citizen and not that of a police officer.'

Metcalfe let out his breath in a long sigh. Hassan looked at him sardonically, and said, 'Our Arab nations work together very closely and extradition is easily arranged. There have been reports of a gang of international thugs roaming the Middle East, killing indiscriminately, using military weapons and – ' he fixed Metcalfe firmly with a gimlet eye – 'indulging in other activities against the state, particularly in Iraq. Owing to these circumstances you will leave the Lebanon at the earliest opportunity. Air tickets will be delivered to your hotel and you will use them. I hope you understand.'

Tozier said, 'What about the crew of this ship? They're still battened down in the hold.'

'You will release the crew just before you leave this ship.' Hassan smiled thinly. 'They will have some awkward questions to answer if the ship ever puts into port. In the circumstances I don't think we will see the ship again.'

'Thank you,' said Hellier. 'We appreciate your understanding of our position.'

Hassan nodded curtly and turned away. He was halfway to the companionway when he paused and turned. 'How much heroin was there?'

'One thousand kilos exactly,' said Parker. 'A metric ton.'

Hassan nodded. 'Thank you, gentlemen.' Unexpectedly, he smiled. 'I thought I knew all about smuggling – but torpedoes!' He shook his head and his face turned grave as he saw the shrouded body of Abbot. 'I suggest you bury the body of this brave man at sea,' he said, and went over the side to his waiting boat.

Tozier said, 'Well, Nick; it's over. It was nip and tuck towards the last, but we made it.'

Warren leaned against the hatch coaming. He suddenly

felt very tired. 'Yes, we made it. Some of us made it, anyway.'

But Ben Bryan would never be Lord of the Manor, although Warren intended to see that Hellier came through with his promise of a community centre for the treatment of addicts; and Mike Abbot would never again be found waiting on his doorstep for the latest dirt on the drug scene.

He looked up at Hellier – the man who had wanted blood – and hoped he was satisfied. Had the deaths been worth it? There would be an unknown number of people, most of them in the United States, who would live longer and presumably happier lives, quite unaware that their extra years had been purchased by death – and next year, or the year after, another Eastman or another Delorme would arise, and the whole damned, filthy business would start again.

Warren closed his eyes against the sun. But let somebody else stop it, he thought; the pace is too hot for a simple doctor.